# PEACE, LOVE & BROKEN HEARTS

## Growing Up on Long Island in the 1960's & '70s

MARIANNE MOROZ MASOPUST

# In Memory of Frank Costa

With Love to David

# Contents

"And while the future's there for any one to change

Still you know it seems

It would be easier sometimes to change the past"

Jackson Browne, "Fountain of Sorrow", Asylum Records, 1974

# The Introduction

Seconds of time are like pennies, easily and thoughtlessly thrown away. But when added together they become months, years, lifetimes. Every decision we make has an effect; some profound, some barely noticeable. Each day we are faced with thousands of simple choices. Should we go right or left? Do we stop at the drugstore first or on the way home? Shall I drive today or walk? The number of possibilities is endless.

Most of the time we never think about the consequences of these infinite selections because everything goes along smoothly. Until it doesn't. Then we can't stop replaying our options over and over again. What would have happened if Princess Diana had left the restaurant a few seconds later? Or if John Lennon hadn't gone out that night? What if it had rained in Dallas on November 22, 1963? What might have happened if the helicopter with Kobe and guests never took off that day? You could make yourself crazy thinking about alternative endings.

My first recognition of the power of decisions happened when I was four years old. It was my cousin Gigi's eighth birthday. She was the daughter of my mom's baby sister, Theresa. Aunt Theresa always made a fuss over everyone's birthdays. She believed it should be the best day of their year because, unlike holidays, it belonged just to them. She worked at a bakery and always made the cakes for our family occasions. They were delicious and beautifully crafted. This particular year she made a Cinderella cake for Gigi. It was in the shape of the Disney princess, her hands outstretched, holding a bird. Aunt Theresa wanted blue candles for the cake to match the dress but she had forgotten to pick them up.

Aunt Theresa had an older son, "from a previous marriage," as the family would say. She was the only one in our family who got a divorce. At the time the church "excommunicated" her. In our family it was a very big deal. But those who knew her first husband said the divorce was the best thing she did. They had a son together, Mickey, who was already seventeen years old on Gigi's eighth birthday.

Aunt Theresa asked Mickey if he could run to the store to pick up blue candles for the cake. She told him she was trying to get dinner on the table before the family came over to celebrate. He gave her a hard time, as was his way, protesting that he wanted to watch the end of *Bugs Bunny* on television. There was always conflict in the family involving Mickey, whether it was detention for pulling the fire alarm at school, his refusal to go to family gatherings or police involvement due to him stealing something. This was no exception. They argued about it for a few minutes. Finally Aunt Theresa grabbed her coat, got in the car and hurried off to get the candles.

Because I was so young I have no recollection of this day or the days that followed. The story handed down to me says Aunt Theresa was coming home from a Finest grocery store when a drunk driver ran a stop sign and plowed right into her car. Aunt Theresa was gone instantly at thirty-four years old, leaving two children, a husband and a family totally devastated.

Mickey would spend the rest of his life reliving that three-second decision not to go and get the candles. It tortured and haunted him until the drugs and alcohol could no longer numb the pain. He had nightmares and would wake up in a cold sweat. He told my uncle about a recurring dream where he was the drunk driver who killed his mom. In his mind he might as well have been. Finally, when the agony of his decision was too much to bear, he took his stepfather's police revolver, went into the basement and shot himself. Gigi found him. A family—families—destroyed and heartbroken over a single, simple decision.

For the next fifteen years this was the tragedy against which all others in my family were measured. It forever changed the dynamics, thoughts and actions of everyone involved. It was the tragedy my mom would go to whenever she needed a dramatic flair. "It should have been me…" It would take me years to realize how profound this loss and its consequences were. I was too young at the time to understand that it was the end of innocence for my family.

In this narrative I am recounting things as I remember them happening. Things were done and thought of differently then, so I have not edited for political correctness or to spare anyone's feelings. The '60s and '70s had their own story line that has brought us to today. I don't believe in amending history. If we do we will never learn from it.

When recalling the past it is easy to unconsciously incorporate our present perspective. Was I really a bold feminist at sixteen? I'd like to think so, but probably not. Was I truly so confrontational if I saw an injustice? Maybe in my mind, but I'm not so sure about my actions. It is tricky not to write the past the way you want it to be, but that is often the way we remember it. This story is about another single, life-changing decision that happened years after the death of Aunt Theresa. It is also about all that took place in between. This is the story of Rudy and me, at least as I remember it.

## CHAPTER 1

# The Families

Vincenzo (Vinnie) was born in January 1954, and Rudolph (Rudy) followed in April. I joined them in February 1955. We had different mothers, different birth dates and different ages, but nonetheless still "triplets," Long before Randall, Kevin and Kate, *This Was Us*.

My parents, Luciana (Lucy) and Paul, met on a blind date on New Year's Eve 1941. I always teased them about not being able to get their own dates on New Year's Eve. My dad, who rarely drank, got very drunk that night. He was so drunk in fact that, after he took my mom home, he slept in his car. He said he was very nervous that night. My mother could do that to you.

Both my mom's parents were born in Italy. Lucy was the oldest of four girls. On that infamous first date, my dad said to her, "If I take you out again, am I going to have to take your sisters too? I know how you Italians are, always bringing your whole family along."

My mom, highly insulted by this, thought she would make him fall in love with her and then dump him. Fast-forward to the second date. My dad took my mom and her three younger sisters ice skating after buying my mom new skates. She dropped her original plan. He won her heart quickly.

Lucy, as I often referred to her, especially when she was driving me crazy, and her sisters, Angelina (Angie), Mary and Theresa, in that order, were beautiful women. I mean turn-your-head beautiful. My mom was always dressed to the nines even if she was just going grocery shopping. They were like that even in their nineties. I would take my ninety-six-year-old mom out and people would stop us in the mall, the doctor's office or a restaurant to say how beautiful she was.

None of the sisters were highly educated and they frequently judged others on the basis of their appearance. My mom used to tell me this great story that happened during World War Two. My dad was overseas and she went to the Westbury movie theater with her sisters. They were doing a fundraiser for the troops—a special live show followed by a movie. The girls got a front-row seat. Young men, representing all the branches of the armed forces, came on stage, carrying the appropriate flags. The audience started to sing the "Star-Spangled Banner." My mom noticed all the men on stage were looking at them. She thought they must have looked especially pretty that night. Then she turned her head to see the entire theater was standing except for my mom and her sisters. She always considered that one of her most embarrassing moments.

My mom was what I call a reluctant feminist. She didn't believe in "all that stuff." If we passed roadwork and a woman was working on the crew she would say how terrible it was that this woman was taking a job away from a man. Yet she was one of my biggest role models. She worked when very few women did. She had her own business in her home. That may be something we take for granted today, but, in the 1960s, that was quite an accomplishment.

Like many during that time she felt boys and girls should be raised differently in order to grow up into their appropriate roles. When I was about six years old our Good Humor man was selling toy Good Humor trucks along with ice cream. The toy truck was a perfect replica with a working bell and doors that opened. Vinnie and Rudy both got one but my mom, who usually bought me everything I wanted, said, "No, it's a boy's toy." I was devastated. The boys let me play with theirs but it wasn't the same. Of the thousands of things my parents bought me over their lifetime, the one thing they didn't buy me is the thing I remember the most.

Every Saturday I had to go to catechism, first to study for my communion and then for my confirmation. I hated Saturday catechism for two reasons. First, I had to get up early to go. Second, I missed all the Saturday morning cartoons. No one should have to go to God school on a Saturday AND church on a Sunday. It wasn't fair. I recall bouncing home from Catechism one day and announcing to my mom that God had a vagina. She freaked out. I thought her eyes were going to pop out of her skull. She yelled, "NO, he does not! Who told you that?"

"The nuns," I said, quite sure I was right.

"The nuns are wrong. God is a man and does not have that!"

"But the nuns said I was made in God's image and I have a vagina."

"Stop saying God and vagina in the same sentence," she said. "God is a man. The nuns meant you were made a human, in God's image. A human, not a girl."

There were so many hidden inferences in that last sentence.

"Well," I said, not yet having learned when to end a conversation with her, "why can't God be a girl?"

"Because he is a man and I don't want to hear another word about it."

So much for my feminist mom. I will refer to God as "she" until I find out otherwise.

My dad's parents immigrated from Ukraine shortly after they got married. My dad grew up on a potato farm in Hicksville, Long Island. A McDonald's now stands on the site where he was born. He served proudly in World War Two as a sergeant stationed primarily in Italy. He rarely spoke about it and I never pushed. He did share two stories that always broke my heart.

On one march through a small town they had to check the contents of a freight car. My father said he and his buddy Joe pushed open the door on one of the cars. He said they could smell the dozens and dozens of decaying, naked bodies before they saw them: women, children and men of all ages piled high and discarded without thought. He always cried when he relayed that story, saying, "There are people out there who say the Holocaust never happened. Well, I saw it, damn it! It did happen and they should be ashamed of themselves."

It was one of the few times I ever saw my dad get angry.

On another occasion his unit was in Italy searching a bombed-out village for survivors. A man in his unit had ten children. My dad always tried to keep him in the back to protect him from any unexpected gunfire. On this particular day he was, as usual, near the end of the line. Suddenly a bombed-out building toppled over directly on this man. He died instantly. My father always cried when he told me that story too.

Although he was Ukrainian my dad looked Italian with his dark hair, eyes and mustache. My mom, on the other hand, was a blue-eyed, blond-haired Italian. I got my coloring from my dad, including the mustache. Dad wasn't wise in all things Italian, but he got a crash course from my mom and her family. He said he asked my mom once why they had pasta so often and my mom looked at him like he was from a different planet. He called the red stuff you put on macaroni sauce, not gravy. Gravy to him was brown and went on meat. He had so much to learn.

After the war my dad decided to go to college to become a teacher. He felt that since he had just been part of history maybe he should study and teach it. He became a social studies teacher after majoring in American history. He was a walking encyclopedia and would always take me, Vinnie and Rudy on vacations that had some historic significance.

My mom's dad was a tailor. He was adorable and had the cutest Italian accent. He had a small shop next to the movie theater in Westbury Village. He was very good and therefore always busy. Besides tailoring he would make custom suits and shirts. He had some high-end customers who were very generous to him and his family. My mom used to help out after school and eventually worked alongside him. She became even more skilled than him. When my grandfather got older and his arthritic fingers failed to let him do everything he needed them to, my mom ran the shop. When I was born my parents put in a basement entrance to our house and she moved the shop there. She was just as busy, even with Aunt Angie helping out.

Aunt Angie and my mom were always the closest siblings. All the sisters were two years apart, but the two of them seemed particularly paired. When my dad came home from the war he kept telling my mom about this gentleman Joe he had served with. Dad introduced Joe to Aunt Angie and it was a perfect match. They got married and ended up buying a house across the street and two houses down from my parents. It was great growing up, as you often didn't know or care where one house ended and the other began. We were always running back and forth between them. And every time someone came into our house they would yell, "Lucy, I'm home." It never got old.

Aunt Angie and Uncle Joe had two children, my cousin Catherine and, six years later, my cousin Vinnie. (Long before the movie, thank you.) Aunt Angie was about three inches taller than Uncle Joe, six when she wore heels. And she always wore heels. They may have looked out of proportion but they were a great match. They had the same sarcastic wit and would always one-up each other. It was like watching a comedy show. I loved them.

Uncle Joe owned a used car dealership, although he would give you a hard time if you called it that. He liked to say they were "gently appreciated." He dealt in high-end and specialty cars. My father loved cars and would hang out there so often that Uncle Joe gave him a part-time weekend job. All the kids worked there at some point, washing cars, filing or just doing whatever job Uncle Joe would overpay us for.

A few blocks from us lived Uncle Joe's sister, Roseann, her husband, Giuseppe, Rudy and his younger brother, Carmine. Roseann was my babysitter often and I ended up calling her Mama Rose. Everyone called Giuseppe G. I called him Papa G. He was a mechanical engineer and worked for the airlines. The family was able to fly all over the world paying only the tax on each flight.

So, Vinnie was my and Rudy's first cousin but Rudy and I weren't related. It really is a simple equation but for some reason people always had trouble with it. They couldn't understand why Rudy and I weren't cousins too. I would sometimes have to draw a chart.

My mom's other sister, Mary, and her husband, Phil, had two girls, Laura and Katie, both younger than me. They lived in Huntington and although it was only a half hour away, it might as well have been another country, not county. We didn't see them as often so my mom would always try to arrange sleepovers at our house. The trouble was, they never stayed. One would wake up crying she wanted to go home and then the other one would start crying. EVERY TIME! Regardless of the hour—and it was usually two in the morning—my dad would put them in the car and take them home. We tried it again and again and the same thing happened. Eventually we realized it would be better if I slept over there. I liked that because we would always go to dinner at a special restaurant called Hamburger Choo-Choo. They had a large, round counter with a train track running around it. Your meal would be delivered on a small choo-choo train that stopped right in front of you. It was so cool.

After Mickey died, Aunt Theresa's husband, Jimmy, and my cousin Gigi moved to Florida to be near his family. We didn't see them much. Sometimes she would visit or we would go there. When we were old enough Gigi and I became pen pals exchanging weekly letters for almost five years. In the summer of 1973 we all met at this new amusement park called Disney World, modeled after Disneyland in California. We continue to meet there every ten years for a reunion. Those reunions are some of my favorite memories.

We weren't very close with my dad's sister Ivanna and family. We saw them only a few times a year even though they lived only two towns away. Aunt Eva, as I called her, was married to Uncle Patrick, a real Irish bloke. For some reason he wasn't fond of Italians. He used to say the most horrible things about Italians in front of me and my mom, often using derogatory slang. But then he wasn't fond of anyone who wasn't Irish so I guess we were in good company. I rarely saw or interacted with my five cousins, all boys. I always wished we were closer.

People always asked me if I liked being an only child. I wasn't. At least I never felt like one. When I was little I thought Vinnie and Rudy were my brothers who lived at other houses. We were always playing something together, whether it was Cooties, Candyland or house. Yes, I made them play house with me. Vinnie was usually the dad; I was the mom and Rudy was the baby. They really loved me.

Vinnie, Rudy and I were so close in age we were rarely apart. We did everything together. We would nap in the same playpen, take baths together after going to the beach, go on vacations and sleep over at each other's houses. We were a very tight-knit family. It was not unusual for one family to go somewhere and take the other kids with them. Many of the places we frequented were well known while others were local secrets.

One place that everyone knew was the Westbury Music Fair, which in the beginning was just a huge tent in the parking lot. If Aunt Angie was taking Catherine and Vinnie to see a show there she would get tickets for Rudy and me as well. We would usually go to one of Long Island's diners or The Wheatley Hills Tavern for dinner. The boys and I would always have the open turkey sandwich. It was the best, like having Thanksgiving in March. The name of the Westbury Music Fair has changed, but it is still there hosting performers in the round. And we all still call it by its original name.

My dad would take all of us to Cantiague Park, an indoor ice-skating rink and sit in the freezing arena while we skated. The boys skated with speed and purpose but I had grace and form. We would also go to Old Westbury Pond, which was a beautiful place to skate when it froze over and the trees were covered with snow. Rudy and Vinnie would play ice hockey there when they got older.

We all had our own roller skates. They fit over our sneakers and were adjusted with our roller-skate keys. We would wear the keys around our necks on a chain or a rope as if they were the entry to some magical kingdom. We didn't know every key was the same and fit every roller skate ever made.

Aunt Angie and Uncle Joe also loved to roller skate and would take us to the Levittown Skating Rink. There you could rent real skates that you didn't have to attach to your shoes. We felt like professionals. I loved it because it was the one thing I could do better than Vinnie and Rudy. They would fall down A LOT and we would laugh so hard we would all end up on the ground. For some reason Rudy, this amazing athlete, could never stop when he was skating. He would put his toe down and topple over in slow motion. Or he would just skate into one of us to stop, usually knocking both of us down.

The best part of going to the skating rink was going to Jahn's afterward. There were several around the area but this one was right next door to the rink. I think Jahn's served food but we always went there for the ice cream. Jahn's was famous for its "Kitchen Sink." Uncle Joe always loved ordering it for all of us. Jahn's had twelve ice cream flavors and the "Kitchen Sink" had two scoops of each. As if that wasn't enough, on top was piled fudge, caramel sauce, bananas, pineapples, nuts, a ton of whipped cream, sprinkles and cherries. Jahn's wouldn't serve it to fewer than eight people, although I had heard stories that a party of five once finished the entire kitchen sink. It was gluttony at its finest.

About a mile or so from Jahn's was a small amusement park, my favorite place on earth when I was a kid. Its official name was Smiley's Happy Land, but everyone called it Jolly Rogers, the name of the restaurant/snack bar attached to it. My parents used to tell me that when I was little they couldn't go past it without stopping because I would cry and cry. Did I mention I was spoiled? My dad would sometimes have to go ten minutes out of his way to avoid driving past it. And, to my parents' chagrin, it was heated and had indoor rides too, which meant it was open all year.

My parents took me and the boys there often. They had "kiddie" rides, like boats in the water that went around in a circle. We would pretend we were pirates. I remember one time Rudy decided he wanted to go in the water and climbed out of the boat. I never saw my dad move so fast in his life.

My favorite ride there was the carousel. It had beautifully carved horses and elaborate carriage seats. Some of the horses went up and down and some were stationary. There were gold rings that poked out of a small box and when riders passed the box on their horses they could try and grab the ring. After the ride you could trade the ring in for prizes. I fell off my horse once trying to get a ring. I slipped right through the seat belt on the horse. The boys felt bad for me and gave me all their gold rings that day— after they stopped laughing.

Jolly Roger's had a game room with hundreds of arcades including pinball machines, a fortune-teller, basketball and small coin-operated rides. We would win tickets there to exchange for prizes as well. Rudy had his eye on this pocketknife for a while, but it was two hundred and fifty tickets. He saved for months. Vinnie and I gave him some of our tickets to make the last twenty-four he needed. But Mama Rose squashed his dream when she told him he was too young and couldn't get it. He got so mad he threw his tickets on the ground and spent the rest of the day in the car. When Rudy turned sixteen I bought him a Swiss Army knife with the engraving "Old enough now." He carried it with him everywhere.

The three of us went to another amusement park called Freedom Land. It was in the Bronx, so visiting it was a full day's outing. It was a theme park based on American history and my dad and Rudy would have lived there if they could. It operated from 1960 to 1964 and I would often get it confused in my memory with the World's Fair.

The families loved to go to the Westbury Drive-In as often as the weather permitted. We would pile in cars and as soon as we got there, we'd go to the playground, in our pajamas! That was a treat. Advertisements appeared on the screen of marching soda cups or a popcorn box with a face, legs and arms, reminding you to visit the snack bar. When we were little we thought that *was* the movie. The adults would always put us children together in the same car because we would fall asleep, usually after the cartoon movie about the popcorn box. When we got older we would go with our boyfriends or girlfriends and make out. I don't think I ever saw a movie there in its entirety, although I must have gone there to see the movie *M*A*S*H* a dozen times. We would hide in the trunk of the cars or under blankets in the back seat and only pay for the two people visible in the car. We thought we were so smart.

Papa G. had a friend, Mike, who worked at the Nassau County Jail. He was in charge of public relations and would have to preview movies for the inmates. For some reason I always remember them being religious themed movies like *Samson and Delilah* or *King of Kings*. During the summer, after Mike would show the movies at the jail but before he returned them, he would lend them to Papa G. They were on these big movie reels as there were no VCRs, tapes or DVDs then. We would put a white sheet on the side of our house and bring over lawn chairs. My aunts would cry at seeing Jesus' face on the side of the house, six feet tall. Neighbors would bring friends and we had our own little movie theater.

Every Friday night—and I mean *every*—we would go to the farmers' market in Bethpage. It was right across the street from Grumman's, the government's aerospace secret moon-landing place. The market was a local happening although people from as far away as Queens would shop there. It was a huge indoor flea market only open on the weekends. It had clothing, toys, mops, religious statues and all kinds of foods. You name it, it was there: anything you could ever need and items you didn't even know you wanted. I got my go-go boots there after searching all over Long Island for my size.

What I remember most about it is the little movie room where parents would drop their kids off while they went shopping. It wasn't even a room, just a tiny curtained-off area with a small screen and a projector that always seemed to be playing *The Little Rascals*. Our parents would just leave us there. Weren't they afraid someone would steal us? Maybe that was the point. Often the three of us would take off and walk around the market by ourselves, always making sure we were back before we got caught. There were only so many times we could watch Alfalfa sing "Figaro." There was sawdust on the floor and a distinct smell that I can't describe but remains in my nose to this day. You never knew what treasure you would find from week to week. It was a Nassau County landmark and I was sad to see it torn down years ago for yet another Long Island strip mall.

We also hung out a lot on our block. Our neighbors were our extended family then. Everyone knew and watched out for each other. There were very distinct boundaries for YOUR block. It consisted of the houses on one side of the street and the homes on the other, maybe twelve houses all together. If you crossed the street at the corner you were going "down the block." So, technically, Rudy wasn't on my block. But since he was always at my house or Vinnie's he was an honorary member.

There was always some kind of activity happening. The moms would visit each other in the morning and afternoon for "coffee," sitting around the table chatting, gossiping and comparing notes. At least that's what it always seemed like they were talking about. Nothing really too heavy in 1962. My mom would host them when she wasn't working. Sometimes the ladies would hang out in our basement while she and Aunt Angie sewed. She kept an electric coffeepot and cups down there all the time.

One day in first grade I was feeling sick and went to the nurse. I was scared until I walked in and saw Rudy there. We both had a slight fever and sore throat. The moms picked us up and off to the doctor's we went. He said it wasn't strep but we should stay home another day.

The next day Aunt Angie brought Rudy over and we hung out together while she worked downstairs with my mom. Some of the neighborhood moms came over to visit with my mom and Aunt Angie. We felt a little better and were sitting on the floor in the living room with our TV trays, lunching on Campbell's chicken noodle soup and ginger ale. That was a staple when we were sick. We were watching *Romper Room*, my favorite kids' show at the time next to, of course, *The Mickey Mouse Club*, which was in reruns by then.

The host of the show in New York was Miss Joan. She would play games with kids on the show, say a prayer before cookies and milk and always start the show with the Pledge of Allegiance. She also had this cool magic mirror. She would say a little rhyme before she looked in it and would mention the names of kids she saw watching the TV.

On this particular day, Miss Joan took her magic mirror and said she saw Peter and Kristen and Marion and Lisa. And then she mentioned Rudy and me, saying, "I hope the two of you feel better soon." We looked at each other in disbelief. We jumped up and down, screaming, and ran downstairs to tell everyone. Of course all the neighbors got as excited as we did, even though they knew my mom had called the station earlier that morning and asked for us to be put in that segment of the show. We went back to school the next day and told everyone. We felt like celebrities and believed in the magic mirror for a long time.

The kids on my block were always playing something together. Stickball and kickball in the street were interrupted often by someone shouting, "Car!" We would bang strips of red caps on the curb with a rock. I was always afraid of the loud sound and smoke, so I had a little rocket I put them in and threw it up in the air. We cut holes in the tops of jars and collected lightening bugs at dusk. I always made my holes too big and they would fly out. They were let go at the end of the night anyway. We drank out of the water hose, built snow forts in the winter and stayed in our bathing suits all summer.

When we went to play outside, which is where we were most of the time the weather permitted, the moms would yell, "Stay on the block." We never wore a watch; we just played until someone's mom would yell their name out the front door to come home It was always a mom, never a dad. And the way she shouted gave a hint of what she wanted. When Aunt Angie called for Vincent Joseph, we knew he was in trouble. Sometimes an order was called out, like "Vinnie, I need milk." We didn't need cell phones. We had moms!

There were nineteen kids on my block not including Rudy. Granted, seven of them came from the same family, but it was still a lot of kids running around. Besides me and Vinnie there was Sam and Lola two houses from Vinnie. Sam was Catherine's age, a nice kid and very quiet. I didn't really know him well. They used to call Lola "La La Lola" because at fourteen she had the body of a Playboy bunny, an unfortunate reference used at the time. The family of seven lived between them and Vinnie. They came in all shapes and sizes, with two sets of twins. Because of their vast differences in ages, I don't think all of them ever lived in the house at the same time. They wouldn't fit if they did.

On the other side of Vinnie lived the O'Hara's. They had two boys, one three years older than me and one a year younger. Together they had more freckles than I had ever seen in my life. They had freckles everywhere, even on their ears. When I was about seven, I heard fire trucks and ambulances come down our block. They stopped at the O'Hara house. There was no fire or smoke anywhere. I stood with my mom on our front lawn, waiting to see what the emergency was. A little while later Mr. O'Hara was brought out on a stretcher. His hands were folded over his chest. He had a massive heart attack in his living room and died instantly. I had never seen a dead body before and that image of him leaving his house for the last time stays with me still.

Mrs. O'Hara struggled for years with the loss of her husband. She was a very religious woman but lost her faith for a long time. She was thirty-two years old when he died and never remarried. Then, on September 11, 2001, she lost her youngest son when the South Tower collapsed. She gave up on God completely. I used to send her cards every September 11 after that just to let her know I was thinking of her. She told me the story of how, a few days after 9/11, they brought her son's car home from the train station. When her grandson got off the school bus that day he saw the car and ran toward it, screaming, "Daddy's home." She said that story illustrated clearly why she was angry with God. I hope she was able to reconcile her faith and come to peace with it before she passed.

Two houses up from me were the Alberts, a family of two girls and two boys. The Alberts went to Catholic school so we didn't see them much except during the summers. I got my first kiss from Tommy Albert. He was six and I was five and it happened under the slide in my backyard. I must have washed my mouth ten times after that. What did I know?

One of my favorite neighborhood families lived a few houses down from me: Cletus and Bob, and their two children, Virgina and Robert. They were animal lovers. You would probably call them rescuers today. They were always nurturing some animal back to health. The kids had bad allergies so they couldn't have the traditional dog and cat as pets. They had lizards and snakes. They rescued two box turtles that roamed the house like a dog would, only it would take them much longer to get from one side of the living room to the other. Cletus saved them from some boys who had drilled holes in their shells and were swinging them around on a rope. Those turtles had a happy home for many years.

They also had a bird named Oscar that would greet us with "hello" when we walked in the door. He also said many other things, some too naughty to reveal. Vinnie and Rudy loved that bird. I am not sure they weren't the ones who taught it the curse words. Cletus always laughed about it. Cletus and her clan gave me the best gifts ever—a love of animals, an appreciation for all living things and a compassion to help them. You can't buy that. You can't wrap it. Talk about a gift that keeps on giving. To this day I am active in wildlife and animal rescue. I thank my neighbors for laying the foundation for that important part of my life.

Vinnie and Rudy both had dogs. That was a big no for Lucy. Dogs were too messy and they tied you down. The only pets I had were the turtles from Woolworths or Newbury's, those little green ones that came in a plastic pool with a plastic palm tree sticking up—salmonella in my living room. They would often crawl out, never to be found again. I would be afraid I was going to come across their shell with their shriveled body in it somewhere in my bedroom. It was almost as bad as the fish we could win at the Italian feast by landing a ping-pong ball in the bowl. The poor things must have been frightened to death; I never had one live longer than a day.

Mama Rose had two dachshunds, Midge and Kippie. Rudy would get a kick out of having Kippie stand in a "beg" position while he held a treat out for him. The poor thing would start to shake, he got so excited (the dog, not Rudy). I would tell Rudy that was mean. How would he like it if I held out a meatball on a fork and made him beg for it?

I look back now and realize how very simple my childhood was: naïve, innocent, ingenuous. It was a welcomed innocence after war and nuclear threats, although both were once again present in my life. Still we all felt safe as long as we stayed on our block.

One summer afternoon in my eighth year, a bunch of kids on the block were playing in my backyard. Eddie, a kid from "around the block" was there with his sister Nancy. Eddie was explaining how there was a word that his parents told him he could never say. Me, being spoiled me, bragged that my parents would let me say any word I wanted. So I asked him what it was, and he spelt out the word "EFF-YOU-SEE-KAY. Rhymes with duck." I just gave him a grin and then in my loudest voice started shouting the word repeatedly about eight or nine times.

Out from the back door ran my mom, her hair going in a thousand different directions and looking like a cartoon character who had just put their finger in an electrical socket. She grabbed me, put her hand over my mouth and proceeded to scream at me to stop. It was obvious she was upset. She dragged me in the house, but not before I turned around to look at Eddie, who had an "I told you so" look on his face. Later that evening I got a lecture from my parents, although they didn't tell me at the time what the word meant. I didn't use it for a long time. However, over the years it has become my favorite curse word, if for no other reason than to see the shocked look I get from people when it comes out of my mouth.

Sometime around 1963 my parents got a pool. It was a twenty-four-foot round above ground pool, the largest available at the time. We were the only ones in the family and on our block who had one and someone was always in it. My father kept that pool immaculate. It was his full-time summer job. He loved when we had a house full of people over for a swim. Almost every weekend was devoted to some kind of family gathering. Everyone would bring a friend or two.

Now a normal family would throw some burgers and hot dogs on the grill and call it a day. Not my family. In 98-degree heat my aunts would be standing in the kitchen over a pot of boiling water. If it was Sunday we were having macaroni. I remember one Sunday I counted thirty-five people. How many pounds of macaroni did it take to feed that crowd?

Vinnie, Rudy and I were in the pool daily. My cousins Katie and Laura would come over and we would have underwater tea parties. My grandfather would throw in coins and we would dive for them. We would have races and, yes, play "Marco Polo." You would think after all those days spent in that pool I would have learned to swim, but no. I am fine if my feet can touch the bottom but not if the water is over my head. And don't get me started on swimming in the ocean. Rudy or Vinnie always had to go in with me.

The pool was a great way to have my family and friends come together. All my friends knew my family and vice versa. I loved having everyone in my backyard. My family and my "block family" helped define and shape much of my early life. It may seem archaic now, with no technology, but it really was a great time to be a kid. I think that was true because of the people I grew up with. But it was especially true because I had Vinnie and Rudy there with me every step of the way.

## CHAPTER 2

# The Friends

How do you choose a friend? Out of the thousands of individuals you meet in a lifetime, only a handful or so truly remain in your heart. Why? What makes them so special? Why are you drawn to them? Obviously it is easier to be friends with someone who lives close to you, with whom you have daily contact, who shares your likes and dislikes. But that still leaves a lot of people. And do you get to choose or are these people predestined to be in your life? Would you still find them if your circumstances were different? Rudy and Vinnie were my friends by family and that is always a unique bond. An old saying says, "Your friends are your chosen family." It is a nice surprise when they are both.

My earliest girlfriend was Lola (LaLaLola), who lived across the street from me and two houses away from Vinnie. She was the boys' age but she really didn't hang out with the three of us. I usually played with her by myself. I could only ask the boys to play dolls with me so many times. We did a lot of things around the block together. We didn't hang out in school. She was a "neighborhood" friend. We played dress-up and Barbie, had a lemonade stand and always played board games. One year we had a muscular dystrophy carnival for Jerry's Kids and raised $61.45. She was my partner in crime around the neighborhood. We drifted apart around junior high when playdates at other kids' houses started up. But she holds some of my best childhood secrets and memories and will always have a special place in my heart even though I haven't seen or spoken to her in decades.

Marie was another childhood friend. She lived next to Rudy so I like to say she was a friend by proxy. When we would go to Mama Rose's I would go next door and play with her, or she would come over and play with me and the boys. The four of us got into a lot of mischief together. Sometimes, when Vinnie and I were supposed to sleep at Rudy's house, I would end up at Marie's. She was in the same grade as me but not the same class. In elementary school we would see each other at lunch and on the playground. Sometimes I would do the unthinkable and go sit with her at her lunch table. The teachers would always tell me to go back and sit with my class until they finally gave up and let me sit there.

Marie had a best friend in school named Maria. They looked nothing alike. Marie was tiny with thick, curly brown hair, often worn short, and an olive, Italian complexion. She had the biggest smile and was funny with an infectious laugh that could be heard blocks away. Maria, by contrast, was tall and thin with long, straight black hair. Like my mom, she was an Italian with very fair skin. She must have had a smile but rarely used it. There was no mixing them up yet people constantly switched their names. It drove them crazy and they were always quick to correct you if you mislabeled them. They would get so frustrated and flustered. I think people mixed them up on purpose just to see their reaction. Kids can be mean.

Jackie was my best friend. We went from kindergarten through sixth grade in the same class. We did everything together, sitting next to each other every chance we got, including air raid drills when we sat on the floor and put our heads in our laps. Yeah, that was going to save us from a nuclear attack. All it did was give everyone childhood anxiety.

Jackie was and remains kind, funny, loving and giving—quite a package for a blond-haired, brown-eyed athletic powerhouse. She was talented at every sport she tried and excelled at softball in high school. I could barely catch a ball yet we became friends. She would always tell me I could dance. Then she would joke that, for a dancer, I was uncoordinated at anything else. She was right.

In fourth grade we had to choose between taking an instrument or chorus. I don't know why, but we decided we were going to learn the clarinet. That lasted for two weeks until we realized we couldn't play the clarinet and talk at the same time. We ended up singing. Besides, neither of us could keep that damn reed wet!

Jackie had a working mom. Not a lot of moms worked outside the home in those days. I never knew what she did but it must have been important because she wore a suit every day. Her dad did something with vending machines. We would go over there and in the back room there would be bags of pennies and nickels next to boxes of gumballs, charms and jawbreakers. We would sneak back there and take handfuls of each. We thought we were so secretive, but I am sure he knew what we did.

Jackie had an older brother, Matt, who was an amazing baseball player along with lettering in other sports. I think it was genetic. He would often be our cover when we were planning some shenanigan, like the time we all wanted to spend the night out over at our friend Richard's house. He was having a party and we thought we would all stay there and help clean up the next day—nothing naughty. We all told our moms we were sleeping over at Jackie's house. Of course my mom had to call. Matt pretended to be Jackie's dad and assured my mom he and his wife would be home all night to supervise us. We were tricky little bastards.

I am glad he did because that was some party! The entire football team and then some were there. Richard, a very dear friend to all, was one of the sweetest guys I ever knew. He was very mature looking, even at fifteen, with tight blond curls, blue eyes, an athletic build and the hairiest blond legs I ever saw. He played a number of sports but football and lacrosse were his standout games. Once during a lacrosse game he made a great interception that surprised even him. He got so excited he started to run toward the wrong goal. We were all screaming his name while he cradled the ball, smiling and running IN THE WRONG DIRECTION. He was teased about it forever and would laugh along with everyone else.

During this party, his parents weren't home. Well, I am not sure if he had a mom. I never saw her and he never talked about her. Let's just say there was no adult supervision. There was a lot of alcohol and pot that night. Someone had brought LSD and Richard decided to take it for the first time. I never took LSD but my girlfriend Gina did once. We were hanging out on the football field in the middle of summer. She told me she wanted to go home to get her winter coat because she thought it was snowing and she was freezing. That incident made me stay away from it forever.

On this night Richard had his first and only hit of acid. I had no idea he was doing it. There was too much going on around me to keep track of who was doing what. I was in the back room, facing the backyard, which was covered with teens. All of a sudden I saw Richard fall from the sky. There was a towel wrapped around his shoulders. I turned to Jackie and asked her if she had just seen what I had. She hadn't but the commotion outside made me think others had seen it too. We ran to the backyard.

Richard, in his "heightened state," thought he might try flying that evening. He tied a towel around his neck and with his cape jumped off the roof. Thank God it wasn't a high roof. Thank God he didn't get hurt. You can do stupid, crazy, idiotic things when you think you are immortal—or tripping. I can't tell you how many capes people made for him after that. He had a collection and was a good sport about it. Super Richard!

Jackie's brother, Matt, also took me, Jackie and our friends Gina and Janie to our first keg party. We were in ninth grade and Matt was a senior.

Normally we would never go to a senior's party but Matt vouched for us. Plus, the host, Matt's friend Roger, liked me. We paid $2.00 to get in and got a small paper cup and all the beer we could drink. Let me repeat that last part: all the beer we could drink. It didn't seem like I was drinking a lot, a couple of gulps a cup. Who knew you could drink so much from such small cups? I certainly didn't and it was the first time I got drunk, REALLY drunk. And then I had to go to the bathroom.

Roger escorted me to the bathroom, where I had the most difficult time. I had peed a million times before but for some reason this was a challenge. Everything from pulling my pants down to getting toilet paper took me what seemed like forever. It felt like I was doing all this for the first time and in slow motion. Then I had to walk back out, but not before Roger wanted to introduce me to his mother, who was in the living room.

We walked into this spotless room and I met a lovely woman all in black with short blond hair. She was holding a little white dog and had two more at her feet. We chatted for a few minutes, about what who the hell knows. Then, the story goes, the mom said to me that these two dogs at her feet were the parents of the dog she was holding. I guess I must have needed clarification; I was told I said to her, "Oh," pointing to the two dogs at her feet. "These two dogs fucked?"

Apparently all hell broke loose in that living room. The mom was screaming and Roger was pulling me out of the room by my shirt collar. I have no recollection of anything after I said hello, but it was big news at the party.

The next morning, before church, Jackie called me to tell me what I did as she knew I wouldn't remember. I was beyond mortified, trying to release any memory of this through my first hangover. After church I got on my bicycle to see if I could find Roger's house. I had no problem as I remembered a big statue of the Virgin Mary out front. *Oh great, his mom is religious.* I knocked on the door and Roger answered, looking more hung over than me. He was not happy to see me. I asked him if I could speak to his mom.

"Why? Didn't you say enough to her last night?" he said.

"Please. I want to apologize."

He let me in. His mom was sitting at the kitchen table and wasn't happy to see me either. And to think that less than twelve hours before we were all smiling. I apologized profusely, explaining I had no memory of what I said and it was the first time I had ever drank that much. I told her I was embarrassed and ashamed. I was hoping she would laugh and say she now had a great story to tell her friends. She didn't. She just kind of smirked a sour smile and shook her head. I never saw her or Roger again.

Jackie and I shared a locker and much more all through high school. We even joined our school's kick line together. That was a natural for me as a dancer. Jackie was a little shorter than me and had to really reach to get her leg high. One day during rehearsal the superintendent stopped by the auditorium and our coach asked him if he would like to see the presentation we were working on for *Newsday*'s Hofstra University band competition. We started our routine, and all of a sudden Jackie swung her leg so high it knocked the stuffing out of her. She fell down hard in front of the superintendent. She was really embarrassed, but I told her I had her beat with the dog story. She did admit I won.

I met Gina through Jackie in junior high even though we were all in the same elementary building together. Jackie was going out with Gina's older brother. How they met is a mystery to me as they lived several blocks away. I don't really remember Gina in the lower grades, but she must have been adorable because she was a natural beauty in high school with her blond hair, blue eyes, freckles and great figure. She would walk out of the ocean after a swim and look like she was in a James Bond movie (sorry, another bad, sexist reference). She was another one of my athletic friends. She held the record in field hockey goals all through high school.

Gina lost her mom to cancer when she was fifteen years old. In 1970 there weren't a lot of treatment options and cancer was only spoken about in hushed whispers behind closed doors. I never knew anyone my age who lost a parent, except my cousin Gigi. It was very sad as her mom had been sick for a while. Gina was the middle child of five siblings and even before her mom passed she was the designated caretaker of the family. She was fourteen years old going grocery shopping, preparing meals, doing laundry and taking care of her younger sisters. I watched her over the years in awe. She was incredibly responsible and brave. She never complained. She always made sure she had her Friday and Saturday nights free, though, to hang out and party. I was glad she at least did that for herself.

My friends and I were big sun worshippers. It was the times. Some kids would go away for spring break and come back tan. A tan meant you were affluent or at least had leisure time to soak up some rays. Plus everyone would comment on how good you looked. We thought we looked healthy, the darker the better. We even had tanning contests. We all knew the drill—baby oil stained with iodine, no sunscreen and a homemade reflector made out of a double album cover and tin foil. My personal favorite was the White Album by the Beatles. We baked. I am paying for it now with trips to the dermatologist every six months to have some precancerous thing removed. My legs are scarred from the sun I bathed in fifty years ago. If I could go back and change one thing it would be to wear sunscreen. Gina was very fair, Irish fair. She would usually burn badly before she tanned.

Jackie and I decided we wanted to give Gina a little surprise party for her sixteenth birthday. All our friends were helping out. It was going to be at my house and our moms would cook. Her birthday was on a Friday. We decided to have the surprise party that Saturday, thinking if we celebrated Friday night she wouldn't suspect anything on Saturday.

I didn't see Gina come down the hallway Friday morning, but I heard some mumbling as I opened my locker. I looked across the hall and saw Gina's long blond hair even lighter from the Sun-In she had been pumping in. Everyone's eyes were on her. How did they know it was her birthday? I yelled over to her, "Happy Birthday, Gina."

Everyone was looking at her. She didn't turn around. I thought she didn't hear me, so I yelled, "Hey, Birthday Girlfriend!" as I walked toward her locker. She still didn't turn around. I gently tapped her shoulder and she slowly turned her head to the left to look at me. I almost fainted and couldn't refrain from gasping out loud.

Gina had wanted "a little color" for her birthday and had fallen asleep under her sunlamp. My beautiful, gorgeous friend looked like a monster on her sixteenth birthday. Her face was unrecognizable and I knew it pretty well. It was swollen and she could barely see out of the slits of her eyes. There were many colors on her face—red, brown, blue, black, yellow—and she had pus coming out of some of the cracks. She was trying not to cry; I could tell it hurt her to do so. She told me what had happened and I asked why she came to school. She said her dad made her. Her father was a nice man who loved his kids, but he was having difficulty dealing with the loss of his wife. He had told Gina time and time again to stay away from the sunlamp and that she should throw it out. He was in an "I told you so" mood that morning.

Today it might be a call to Child Protective Services, but in 1971 it wasn't. I stared at her in disbelief, grabbed her and headed to the nurse's office. The bell for first period hadn't rung yet and as we walked through the hallway Gina tried unsuccessfully to hide her face with her notebooks. The nurse's reaction was the same as mine. I explained it was Gina's sixteenth birthday and her dad had made her come to school. The nurse said if Gina's dad saw her this morning and told her she had to come to school there was nothing she could do. *BULLSHIT!* I thought to myself. I really wanted to say it out loud. I told the nurse, "Look at her face. It is going to get infected. It needs to be treated now or she will have scars forever."

There I was, sixteen years old and someone who does not do "boo-boos," telling the nurse what to do. The nurse rinsed Gina's face gently and put some cream on it. After reexamining it, she said, "I think you need to see a doctor."

Now we were talking. She called Gina's father but he was on his way to work and unreachable. Meanwhile a large crowd had gathered outside, hoping to get a glimpse of the beautiful girl who was no more. Just then Dr. Willard, our principal, walked in to see what was going on. He was able to hide his reaction and was very sympathetic to Gina. He agreed I could call my mom and she could pick Gina up. I called and explained in my crazy, quick manner what had happened. My mom called Aunt Angie and they came to school.

My mom loved all my friends but held a special place in her heart for Gina. I think it was because her mom died so young. She started to cry when she saw Gina. Dr. Willard let my mom take Gina to the emergency room. Again, it was a different time. I went too. My aunt was finally able to reach Gina's dad, who said he felt he made the wrong decision that morning in insisting she had to go to school. He met us at the emergency room and cried when he saw her. We all did. The nurses and doctors were very sweet to her, especially after realizing it was her sixteenth birthday. Someone went down to the gift shop and got her some balloons and a stuffed animal. We all cried again.

We ended up having to tell Gina about her surprise party. Obviously she wasn't going to go, so we froze what we could and celebrated a few weeks later. Gina didn't return to school for a week. When she did she was the same beautiful girl we all knew and loved. She threw away her sunlamp.

And then there was my friend Janie. Where do I begin? Janie was and is the craziest, most loving—did I mention craziest? —person I know. Crazy in a risk-taking way. I will love her until one of us stops breathing and beyond. I know she will find me in eternity just to bug the hell out of me. She's THAT friend.

I first saw Janie when I was in elementary school. She went to Catholic school and her bus stop was at the corner of my block. Their school started late but also ended late. The bus didn't drop them off until around 3:45 p.m. By then my friends and I were an hour into play. One day we were near the bus stop and I saw this little bit of a thing get off the bus. She had long, thick, unruly black hair she had tried to put in a ponytail, only the left side was now hanging down in her face. The white shirt from her uniform, which I don't think ever stayed crisp and ironed for too long, was half out of her skirt, buttoned wrong. Oh, her skirt. That piece of plaid material was rolled up and hanging unevenly above legs almost as skinny as mine. She had on socks, one up and one down, with saddle shoes, both untied. Simply put, she was a mess. She was followed by a mini, neat version of herself. I found out later that was her younger sister. The thing was, every time I saw her get off the bus she looked like that. I wondered what went on at that school. It was like she was dropped from a tornado every afternoon. If you would have told tidy little me that this girl would become like a sister to me when I got older, I would have said you were nuts. No way. But she did and is.

I officially met Janie through Jackie as well. Janie lived on the next block up from Gina and knew her. When Jackie started dating Gina's brother she met Janie and so did I. We would have met in high school anyway as Janie didn't attend a Catholic high school. We always said the kids who came to our high school after Catholic elementary school were the wildest and Janie was their poster girl. She wasn't wild in a destructive way, but she was like no one I had ever met. She would try anything once as long as it didn't hurt her or anyone else. Whenever I got in trouble it was guaranteed that Janie was somehow attached to it. She was very good at convincing me to do things like chewing her Bazooka gum first to get the sugar out and then giving it back to her. People would always yell "ugh" when we did that. Thinking back, yeah, ugh.

When we were in tenth grade we decided to go get ashes for Ash Wednesday. The school let students leave for a religious reason if they had a parental note. We both did. We were going to miss lunch and one period as the church was distributing ashes at noon. We started to walk to church and when we got to Old Country Road, instead of making a left toward St. Brigid's Church, we made a right. We went to Friendly's for lunch and ice cream. We took the ashes from my cigarette and blessed each other on the forehead with them.

The second I walked in my house my mom knew they weren't ashes from church. What was she, the ashes police? Of course I cracked right away and told her what Janie and I did. I couldn't go out for the next two weekends. And my mother never backed down on a punishment. Janie? She told her mom the ashes got "sweated off" during practice; that's why they looked like that. I made Janie spend the next two Saturday nights at home with me.

One Saturday Janie, Jackie, Gina and I decided to walk to the newly created 5:00 p.m. mass at church. We could now go on Saturday and it counted for Sunday. We loved that as we could sleep in on Sunday after a rough Saturday night. It was maybe a two-mile walk along busy Old Country Road, but it went fast and usually someone we knew stopped to pick us up or take us home. This time Janie wanted to take a shortcut through the cemetery, which is connected to the church. By the time we got to the other side the gates were closed as it was a few minutes past five. Those athletic girls decided to climb the fence. This fence was iron with spikes on top of each pole that went along the length of the fence. Why I have no idea. Were they keeping people out or the dead in? Either way it was a tough climb.

Jackie and Gina went over first like it was an Olympic event while Janie stayed on the other side to help me. I had on a culotte skirt. Janie was pushing me up while Jackie and Gina were trying to grab me to pull me over. Of course I got stuck. One of the spikes at the top of the fence went under the left leg of my shorts. I was now balancing on top of the fence unable to move up or down. At first we couldn't stop laughing. Janie was yelling at me to pull my shorts leg up to release it from the spike, but I didn't have enough room or material to do so. Someone was pulling, someone was pushing, someone was laughing. And there I was turning into the first living gargoyle our cemetery had ever seen. People who were late for church were watching this with both amusement and horror. Janie thought she'd find a worker who was still in the cemetery to open the gate, but she couldn't leave me. Her hands were holding me up and I don't know what would have happened if she had let go.

Finally I knew what I had to do. On top of that fence I unzipped my culottes and Jackie and Gina caught me as I tumbled down. Now I was standing on the sidewalk next to the church in my underwear and platform sandals while passing drivers were slowing down to have a look. Janie went over the fence, but not before grabbing my skirt that was hanging up there like the flag of some weird country. I put the culottes on as fast as I could and in my hurry I put them on backward. *The show is not over, folks.* I had to take them off and turn them around. We walked into church a little late, but not before I turned to Janie and said, "You just HAD to go through the cemetery, didn't you?"

Janie was very rebellious. Not in an "I'm going to march for equality" way, although she would. She was rebellious in more of a "Fuck you, you can't tell me what to do" way. I loved that about her because I had so little of that in me. Janie was unbelievably gifted in sports. She played everything and she played well. She could try something once and be better than someone who had been practicing for years. She was really special. She played field hockey, volleyball, softball and lacrosse. She was the best at basketball even though she was only about five foot three. She was also a fearless swimmer, surfer and tennis player and she even excelled at bowling. I was the anti-Janie although, like Jackie, she told me I was the dancer. I always felt like a consolation prize.

Our high school had an annual activity called PEP Night. I don't know what PEP stood for, maybe Physical Education Program. It was a chance for nonathletes like me to participate and show off our creative side. It was a competition between the Red Team and the Grey Team, even though our school colors were the horrific combination of maroon and grey. The high school girls participated in team events like basketball and volleyball but there was also dance, calisthenics and artwork, along with a theme for each team. That was the extent of my participation in high school sports. (I was on the lacrosse team one season but I think it was a pity placement. I played a total of twenty minutes that year.)

Janie was also a cheerleader. In those days being a cheerleader brought some prestige. It gave girls a certain kind of status among their peers. She tried to help me try out, but I couldn't even do a cartwheel. She would joke that, for a dancer, I had no rhythm. One afternoon I wanted to go out to the smoking section for a cigarette. Yes, in 1971 our school had a smoking section right outside the cafeteria and gym. It was a chilly day so I asked Janie if I could borrow her cheerleading coat. Someone saw me smoking in the coat and thought I was Janie. We looked alike except for our height. They went back and told the coach and Janie got suspended from the squad for two weeks. We tried to explain to the coach that it was me, not Janie. Janie didn't smoke. Her coach said it didn't matter. Someone in a cheerleading coat was seen smoking and that was not the leadership image the squad should be projecting. I wanted to tell her she should think about the image on a Friday night when cheerleading coats are roaming the streets drunk and stoned, but I said nothing.

Sometimes Janie's stubbornness and ideas would lead to conflicts with her parents. When we were juniors she wanted to go camping with her boyfriend. Her parents said no but Janie went anyway. When she came home some of her clothes and things were in a box on the front lawn. Her mom threw her out. Again, that might be a CPS call today but not then.

She ended up sleeping in my basement for about four nights. She would sneak in through the basement door after my mom closed up shop, get up early the next morning, shower at school and go through her day. Then she would repeat it the next day. I would sneak food and snacks down to her, but it really wasn't sneaking. Both our moms knew she was there. After the fifth day her parents came and took her home. I don't think she was ever punished for that. AND she got to go camping with her boyfriend. Me? I'd be dead. Or at least headless.

Janie, Jackie and Gina were my girls. We had a lot of other friends along the periphery but the four of us were the core, the ones we shared everything with, who kept each other's secrets, helped each other without being asked, loved each other unconditionally and would defend each other to the death. I would not be who I am today without them. I love them still.

## CHAPTER 3

# The Beatles and More in '64

February 9, 1964. Six days before my ninth birthday. It was a Sunday and like most of them, we were over at my grandparents' house for a late lunch, early dinner. Aunt Angie and her crew were with Rudy's family this particular afternoon as they often switched between grandparents.

As usual my nanny made my favorite macaroni with her famous meatballs and special salad dressing. I always sat at the right hand of my grandfather. It sounds like a religious thing, but he just got a kick out of me. I made him laugh. Aunt Mary and her family were there so I hung out with my cousins not doing anything specific. We spent a lot of time on the porch talking about a band that was going to be on Ed Sullivan's show that night. It seems everyone was talking about this group.

On Sunday nights we often got together with Vinnie and Rudy's families to watch TV. I am not sure how that evolved, but the parents would get together in the kitchen and leave us kids to watch television. On this particular night we watched *Lassie* and *My Favorite Martian*. Then we all crowded around the TV to watch *The Ed Sullivan Show*.

There was something special about watching this show with a group of people, everyone critiquing the acts. It was similar to an early *America's Got Talent*, only the acts were all good. We all had our favorites. I loved Topo Gigio, the little mouse puppet that would end all his routines saying,

"Eddie, kiss me goodnight." And he did. I even had a puppet of him (the mouse, not the host).

The boys would hoot and holler when this gentleman would try to keep five glass bowls and eight plates spinning on top of long poles. Rudy would get so excited he would stand up and start swaying the same way as the poles. He was a skinny little string bean who moved like rubber, a show in itself. My mom and aunts loved the Broadway musical numbers, always hoping Robert Goulet would be on. Everyone loved the female stand-up comics. "Such a novelty," they'd all say. Little did we realize that Joan Rivers, Phyllis Diller and Tottie Fields were breaking the glass ceiling and paving the way for all the funny ladies who came after them. My dad just loved being entertained. He would say it was good, clean, cheap fun.

We usually watched at my house. Being the youngest I had to go to bed right after the show while the adults and sometimes the boys stayed up to watch *Bonanza*. On these nights everyone was crammed on my mom's large white sectional. Like most couches I knew at that time, it was sheltered in clear plastic slipcovers that stuck to you in the summer and winter. On this particular night Rudy, Vinnie and I were sitting on the chaise lounge part of the couch with Catherine. Because she was six years older, we really didn't see her that much. But tonight she walked across the street to watch this band she had heard on the radio. I didn't know it at the time but 74 million other people were also sitting on couches across America, waiting for this moment, not knowing what to expect.

I don't remember the order of things, but I do remember all these girls screaming before they even came on. Then Ed Sullivan said five words that changed my life: "Ladies and gentlemen, the Beatles." The roar from the studio audience was deafening even in our living room. And then it happened. On screen, without warning. Him. My future husband. This dewy-eyed, smiling guy, his head bobbing back and forth, his long hair

34

following. Underneath that smiling face flashed one word: Paul. Just like my dad. There was no turning back now.

I jumped off the couch and sat on the floor as close to the TV as I could, secretly hoping it would suck me onto that stage to get a better look. Everyone, especially the boys, yelled at me to move back because I was blocking their view. I reluctantly got back on the couch, never taking my eyes off the screen. When Rudy and I were toddlers we would tell everyone we were going to get married. Now? Rudy who? THIS was that guy. At almost nine years old I had my first real crush that, technically, has never really ended. To this day, when people ask me if I have any regrets in life, I have a few. One is when you Google Mrs. Paul McCartney, it's not me.

It might be hard to imagine how seeing one band on a TV show can change everything. The timing was perfect. It was a revolution, a transformation in culture that had a date, place and time: February 9, 1964, my parents' living room. Every generation has one. It was my Frank Sinatra, my Elvis Presley, my Kurt Cobain, my LL Cool J. It was a television event right up there with watching Neil Armstrong walk on the moon and the last episode of M*A*S*H. And of course my two best friends were there to witness it with me.

The three of us became obsessed with everything Beatles. And believe me, EVERYTHING was Beatles. Their pictures, logos and signatures were on all kinds of items, from jewelry, schoolbooks and lunch boxes to sweatshirts, dolls and headbands. I had to have everything and I wish I had kept it all. Down from my bedroom walls came the pictures of Paul Petersen (*The Donna Reed Show*) and Annette Funicello and up went pictures of my new "boys." Rudy, Vinnie and I became consumed with collecting Beatles trading cards. At first we would buy them for five cents a pack. It came with the same thin, pink, delicious gum that was in the baseball cards. There were all different series and they eventually came out in color. One of the earlier sets had a puzzle on the back. If you collected all the cards in the set and turned it over, it formed a huge picture of the Beatles. The three of us put all our cards together but no matter how hard we tried we never got the card that was George's left eye. We would put our duplicate cards on the spokes of our banana bicycles with clothespins. The boys used to do that with their baseball cards but this seemed much cooler. The cards would make this great whirring noise and it made me smile knowing a picture of Paul's head was doing that.

We bought all their 45 singles with the orange and yellow label and every album. They were the only band whose albums I bought before hearing them. You knew they were going to be great. And then, in August of that year, came the movie. *A Hard Day's Night*, aside from being a Beatles movie, is really quite brilliant in its design, cinematography and execution. I loved it as a nine-year-old and during each of the twenty-five or so times I have seen it since, I have found something new. But we almost didn't get to see it the first time.

The movie was playing at the Levittown movie theater every two hours, starting at 10:00 a.m. and running through 10:00 p.m. All day, every two hours. It wasn't a long movie, but I guess they needed time to clean up and get all the screaming girls—and boys—out. Vinnie, Rudy, Marie, Jackie and I decided to go to the Saturday noon showing. My dad was going to take us and pick us up. When we got there around 11:30 a.m. a line was already wrapped completely around the building. We didn't know it at the time, but it went around twice.

We bought our tickets and got in line, knowing we would never get into the noon showing. My dad, God bless him, came back at 1:30 p.m. and we were still in line, not really any closer. It was looking like we wouldn't get in the 2:00 p.m. show either. But we refused to leave that line, which now looked like it went around the building three times. There was a gas station across the street and, as one of us stayed in line, my dad took the rest of us there to use the bathroom. He gave the guy at the station a few bucks to let us do that. We each used it twice.

The theater was a big brick building that stood alone in a parking lot. We could hear kids screaming inside along with some muffled dialogue and music, but that was all. When the movie was over the kids poured out of the exits and emptied right into the middle of the line. Some kids in line tried to sneak in through those doors. Others hid in the bathroom and tried to stay for a second showing. Eventually they put security outside, which was really just some scared sixteen-year-old trying to keep us organized and calm.

When it was obvious the 4:00 show was also a no go, my dad showed up with sandwiches and drinks from my mom and aunt. That is how amazing my dad was. He knew I really wanted to see this movie. It was all I had talked about for weeks and he did whatever he could to make it happen. I always say he was my most favorite person on earth. This is just an example of why.

We finally got into the 6:00 p.m. showing after waiting in line for six and a half hours. Thank goodness it was a nice day. We wanted to stay for the 8:00 p.m. show but the moms said staying out alone until 7:30 p.m. was late enough. They couldn't believe we waited that long. It was worth every second.

It was like watching a Marx Brothers movie, which we all loved, only with cuter guys and music. I look back at it now and see how funny and clever it was. At the time it was all about how many close-ups of Paul I could see. Kids were screaming, crying and running up to the screen and we all got caught up in the crazy, wonderful madness of it all.

This was a time of innocence and discovery when a paper card on a bicycle spoke could bring happiness. For about sixty-five cents we could buy a 45 record and get two songs that we played until we knew every beat, every word, every pause. And all that mattered was saving another sixty-five cents before the next record came out.

I would go on to see the movie three more times before it originally left the theaters. My last viewing was at our local movie house, the Salisbury movie theater, situated at the end of a strip mall. Eventually this theater became a bank and is now a CVS, but not before it had one last run as an "adult" movie theater. One afternoon Rudy and I were leaving Mr. Wong's Chinese restaurant, a few doors away from the theater. An afternoon matinee was letting out as we walked towards the car. The man getting into his car next to us asked me if he had just seen me in there, pointing to the theater. It was all I could do to hold Rudy back from punching the guy. When we got in the car, Rudy asked me if he meant IN the theater or ON the screen? We laughed all the way home.

On my fourth viewing of the Beatles' movie at Salisbury I brought my little vinyl Paul doll with me. Why I don't know. Maybe I thought he would enjoy the show. A few months before my dad and I had driven all over Long Island looking for this doll. If we found a store that still had Beatle dolls, there were never any Paul dolls left. It never occurred to me to buy the other three. Two years ago, at an antique store, the complete set was going for $550. My dad had tried everywhere to find the Paul doll. We went to Coronets, the local toy store where I got all my Barbie dolls, the farmers' market—any place that might sell them. No Paul. My dad finally got one from a woman at work who overheard him telling his tale of woe in the faculty cafeteria. She had bought two and had an extra. Finally, my own Paul doll.

Even though I had seen *A Hard Day's Night* a number of times, I was still caught up in the excitement, so much so that I left the theater without little Paul. I realized it when I got in the car and I started crying. Vinnie,

Rudy, my dad and I went back to the movie theater, the doors of which were now locked. My dad pounded on the door and the manager finally opened it. My dad explained the situation to him as I cried like a baby. The manager finally let us all in to look.

Where was I sitting? I don't know. In back of the girl with the long blond braid. That didn't help. We all started looking on the floor, which was covered with popcorn, spilt soda, candy wrappers and chewed gum. Vinnie was thrilled because he found a dollar. Then I heard Rudy yell, "I got it."

Sure enough, covered in sticky soda, with a popcorn kernel stuck to his hair, there was my Paul doll. I ran over to Rudy to hug him and almost knocked him down in my excitement. My mom washed the doll and its hair and it was as good as new. It never went on another outing again. It holds an honored place in my toy cabinet now, along with my Popeye the Weatherman Colorforms, Mary Poppins rub-ons, That Girl paper dolls and Flintstones memorabilia.

We first listened to the Beatles on our tiny transistor radios, on station WABC 77, I believe. We eventually graduated to a bigger radio and FM. That's when the songs started changing and so did the Beatles. I was a little afraid of them for a while with all their drug references, changing appearance and songs I didn't understand, like "A Day in the Life." It took me years before I realized what "four thousand holes in Blackburn, Lancashire" meant. People began listening to their recordings backwards or in slow motion, looking for hidden meanings. It was cultlike. I was very naïve and missed my boys.

Then a few years later it all went terribly wrong. My favorite band in the world broke up. I was devastated. They were gone. But they never really left. I believe their music will be played and studied for hundreds of years like the music of Beethoven and Mozart. John Lennon may have sung, "The dream is over," but the music will never be. And neither will the feelings I get every time I hear it.

I feel lucky to have experienced Beatlemania firsthand with Rudy and Vinnie. It was the first time I had ever bonded with anyone over music and it opened up an entire new road to explore. I can't listen to a Beatles song without thinking about where the three of us were when we first heard it and what we experienced with each new record. Of all the ways we "came together", our love for the Beatles remains the most special and 1964 our special year.

This was also the year the World's Fair came to New York, Queens to be exact. During April–October 1964 and April–October 1965 it was a short ride to one of the most ambitious, spectacular events we had ever seen. Vinnie, Rudy and I went countless times with different groups of parents, aunts, uncles and cousins. Whatever the combination, the three of us always went together.

My mom had made plaid shorts for us and she had gotten World's Fair patches to put on them. The boys wore theirs with white polo shirts and I wore mine with a white ruffled T-shirt. I must say we looked adorable. People thought we were triplets. They would stop and take pictures of us. The boys had outgrown the shorts the second year so my mom and Aunt Angie made us T-shirts with our names and the words "World's Fair" on them. People kept asking us where in the park we had bought them. It made us feel special.

Admission in 1964 was $2.00 for adults and $1.00 for children. The next year the adult admission went up to $2.50. Kids were still a buck. My dad would say it was good, clean, cheap fun, just like *The Ed Sullivan Show*. And like *The Ed Sullivan Show*, everyone had their favorite attractions at the fair. Mine by far was "It's a Small World" with its beautifully crafted dolls from every country, singing and dancing. The World's Fair was its debut and no one had ever seen anything like it. My mom would cry every time she went through it and we would wait in that line at least twice during each visit. Some days it seemed as if all 50 million visitors were waiting in that line at the same time. I got the recording of the song and two replica dolls, a French one and a boy from Italy that rode in the gondola. I wish I had them now too.

Most kids, even today, go through a dinosaur phase. Rudy continued to be fascinated with them all his life. Naturally his favorite World's Fair attraction was the Sinclair exhibit. Guests rode in these new convertible cars on a trip through time. The first time we went on the ride, Rudy, Vinnie and I sat in the front of the car with Vinnie at the wheel. My parents, Aunt Angie and Uncle Joe were squeezed in the back seat. Mama Rose, Uncle Joe and Carmine were in the car behind us with Catherine and her boyfriend Johnny. We went through a dark tunnel and came out among the dinosaurs. A huge twenty-foot tyrannosaurus, jaws opening and closing, growling, greeted us. I screamed and hopped in that back seat so fast the boys didn't even realize I was gone. Nine different life-sized dinosaurs were on display. While I was hiding my face in my dad's shirt, it was all my father could do to keep Rudy in the car. He wanted to get out and walk among them. Over the course of the fair he must have gone on that ride ten times. I never went back, even when the boys told me I could sit in the driver's seat.

The best part of the ride was the end, but not because it was over. At the conclusion of the ride stood Moldarama machines that made realistic-looking plastic dinosaurs. The cool thing was we saw them being made. We watched the two sides of the hot mold being poured, pressed together and finally released to us forever. Rudy had about twenty of them. We just had to get one or two every time we went. And for twenty-five cents a pop you could take home a great souvenir. They smelt like crayons when they came out of the machine and we found out the hard way that they melted just as quickly. It took Papa G. weeks to get a melted dinosaur off the back seat after Rudy had left it in the car in the heat. The boys eventually drilled holes in them, stuck firecrackers in the holes and blew them up. Nice. I still have one of mine in my toy cabinet.

Vinnie loved everything but was particularly intrigued with the exhibits that looked into the future: the moving sidewalks, the house under water, the picture telephones, space travel. He couldn't get enough. Sometimes Rudy and I were a little bored but we never let on. He was always so patient with us that we just had to indulge him.

We all loved taking the gondola ride above the fair. You could see the entire layout of the park, the exhibits and the people. Plus it was a good way to get from one side of the park to the other. We felt like we were in a spaceship looking down on a new world. We never tired of it. We always wondered why they would leave all of this up for only two years. We wanted it to stay there forever.

My mom, my aunts and Mama Rose always had to go see Michelangelo's *Pietà*, which was on display all the way from Italy. Visitors stood on a conveyor belt so no one could stay in front of it for too long. As we got on the moving walkway the tissues would come out. Sometimes they would cry in anticipation before they even got there. Even at nine years old I could appreciate its magnificence.

A little gift boutique was attached to each attraction at the fair. I remember getting a small replica of the *Pietà*, which I bought again years later on eBay for my mom. We also bought rosary beads blessed by the Vatican as well as picture postcards of the *Pietà* and other Michelangelo works. My mom got my grandmother a small glass bowl and some holy water from the Holy Land. For some reason, of all the shops we went in, this one remains the most vivid to me.

And then there was Abraham Lincoln. At the State of Illinois Pavilion stood a life-sized audio-animatronic Abraham Lincoln that delivered a five-minute, fifteen-second speech, a culmination of various speeches Lincoln had given. In 1964 we had never seen anything like this. A talking robot that looked like President Lincoln. And when that robot stood up out of that chair I thought Rudy and my dad were going to cry. I swear I saw my dad's eyes tear a little. He must have gone to see that as many times as Rudy went to see the dinosaurs. He even went by himself a few times.

Before I leave the World's Fair—and I always hated to leave—I have to mention the food. It was obviously from all over the world. My dad was particularly fond of a European pavilion that served skinny steak sandwiches and international beer. We ALWAYS had to stop there to eat. The French pavilion had the most amazing fresh pastries I have ever tasted. I still remember the light, sweet crust and fresh whipped crème. I was never able to match that anywhere else. I loved everything British now that I knew my future husband Paul was from England. My mom and I always brought home tea and biscuits from that pavilion. It was a nice way of extending our visit.

By far the treat we always talked about the most was the Belgian waffles: oversized, warm waffles with strawberries, fresh whipped crème and powdered sugar. We could have other things on it but why would we? These were not new to us. Every year our families would go to Atlantic City for a few days during the summer and there was a man on the boardwalk selling them fresh and saying they were "Oh so good." But at the World's Fair they just seemed better. They also became a tradition for us. Yes, 1964 was a very memorable year.

## CHAPTER 4

# The Costumes

Halloween was always a big holiday on my block. It was not on the scale that it is today with houses decorated with themed lights, skeletons popping out of the ground and motion-detected monsters. It was big in the sheer volume of kids who went trick-or-treating. My mom would sometimes have to call me home and pilfer my candy because we had run out, even though she had bought a hundred pieces or more. It was always such fun. And we got to wear our costumes to school.

Ah, our costumes. Unlike today, there weren't pop-up costume shops or party stores that sold creative, inexpensive costumes. Most people made them. The most popular costume at the time was a bum: an oversized flannel shirt, jeans, burnt cork on the face and a stick with a sack. Think about how that would go over today. Some kids would buy flimsy costumes with plastic masks that pinched their ears and never stayed on their faces. And if they did stay put, wearers couldn't breathe through the pinhole at the nose and mouth. Anyone wearing one of those costumes had better stay away from an open flame.

Being a seamstress, my mom made the costumes for Rudy, Vinnie and me every year. We always went as a trio. Our first Halloween together I was eight months old and still in a stroller. I was Piglet, Rudy was Pooh and Vinnie was Eeyore. The detail in our costumes would have made Disney proud. At every house we stopped people wanted to take pictures. It was like that every year. My mom and Aunt Angie would start thinking about next year's costumes on November 1.

Our second Halloween together we were Mickey, Minnie and Goofy. Rudy was an awesome Goofy with oversized shoes and long ears on a hat that kept falling down over his eyes. He couldn't walk or see. The moms said it was hysterical. Somehow I don't think that's how Rudy remembers it.

I think the costume that defined us forever was when the boys were four years old. My mother and Aunt Angie took velvet, lace and crayon and transformed us into the Three Musketeers. These were gorgeous costumes in unbelievable detail. We had sword accessories, big hats with feathers and painted-on mustaches, beards and eyebrows. We played with those costumes afterward until they were rags.

When the boys were seven we went as the Marx Brothers. Rudy was Chico and I swear he looked exactly like him. Vinnie was Groucho and I was Harpo. (Years later we would go to the Uniondale Mini Cinema for Marx Brothers marathons, with pillows, blankets and pot. But for now, we were happy watching commercially cut up versions of their movies on television.) The boys made a bet with me that I couldn't be silent like my character while we were trick-or-treating. They said if I was I could have my pick of ten candies from each of their bags. So I made a sign that said "Trick or Treat" and I would honk my horn and hold up the sign at each house. Everyone loved it. Afterward I took the ten best treats from both of their bags. A man lived around the corner who worked for Wise Potato Chips and he always gave out big five-cent bags of chips. I took them from the boys too. They were not happy, but a bet is a bet.

The next year it was the Three Stooges. I think the boys loved this the most because they kept hitting each other and grabbing one another by the nose. One time during a particularly lively slap fest they got yelled at and Vinnie said, "Hey, we're in character here." They never smacked or grabbed my nose and came home with lots of candy and a couple of bruises that year.

When Rudy and Vinnie were nine we went as action heroes: Superman, Batman and Wonder Woman. It didn't matter who we were as much as what I got in my trick-or-treat bag that year. We were two blocks from my house and really on a roll. We went to a house in the middle of the block and the boy who answered, still dressed in his Catholic school uniform, dropped a small Halloween bag in each of our bags. These were little paper bags with a Halloween design on them, usually folded over or tied. They were always exciting to get, as you never knew what special treats were in there. We couldn't wait until we got home and always looked inside them before we made it off the stoop. Sometimes there was a small toy like a yo-yo; other times there was some candy and maybe a dime. It was always fun to compare what you got.

As we walked away Rudy opened his first and it had a Chunky, a wax bottle filled with some kind of sweet liquid and a wrapped fireball. Score for him. Vinnie was next and he got a Zotz Orange, a Now and Later taffy in the hard-to-find watermelon flavor and a piece of Bazooka gum. Double score. As they got closer to me, Rudy yelled, "Who farted?" No one claimed it and we told him whoever smelt it dealt it. We were so sophisticated for our age. I took my bag out and we realized the smell was coming from inside it. Charlie Brown may have gotten a rock, but I don't think he ever got a bag of dog poop. I started crying immediately. Vinnie was ready to go back and confront the kid. Better heads prevailed as Rudy suggested we take it home to show my dad. Vinnie carried it home, holding it as far away from himself as he could.

I was still crying when Rudy and Vinnie told my parents what had happened. My dad was the most peaceful, calm, nonconfrontational man I ever met—unless you did something to his daughter. He told us to hop in the car and show him where the house was. Rudy asked him if he was going to hit the kid. The boys loved the idea of a good fight.

When we got to the house, we all got out of the car. My dad banged on the front door. I was next to him and my two superheroes were behind us, at the ready. The boy answered the door and my dad asked him if his parents were home. Within seconds his father appeared. My father held out my entire trick-or-trick bag, with three hours' worth of candy collecting in it, as well as the poop bag. He had already told me I couldn't eat any of the candy in my bag because the poop bag had contaminated it. He explained to the father what had happened. The man said they didn't have a dog.

"OH, MY GOD!" my father yelled.

I didn't understand what was going on and looked at Rudy, confused.

"They don't have a dog," he said.

"Then where did he get the poop from?"

Rudy slapped the palm of his hand on his forehead and said, "Marrone. It's not dog poop!"

"Then whose poop is…OH!" I felt sick and thought I was going to throw up. "That's disgusting."

"No shit," Vinnie said.

"Yes shit," Rudy laughed back.

The boy had disappeared, but he came back with his trick-or-treat bag from school, full of candy. The dad exchanged his son's bag for mine. He was angry and very apologetic to me and my dad. He said he would deal with his son appropriately and made him apologize. Then he took out his wallet and gave me $10.00 "to buy any candy you didn't get today." Ten dollars! As we walked away, the door slammed and we heard screaming from the other side. Rudy and Vinnie threw out their bags from the kid even though they had good stuff in them. I turned around and noticed a beautiful German Shepard in the yard next door. To this day I still believe it was dog poop. No one can be that devious.

About a week after Halloween, when the trick-or-treat candy was running low, we took our bikes up to Ha-Cha's. This was a very popular little store that sold cards, magazines, cigarettes, candy and gift knickknacks. It was one of the first strip malls I remember, located on Old Country Road, nestled between a Finest grocery store, a kosher deli, Birchwood Pharmacy, Mr. Wong's and the Salisbury movie theater. I would go there all the time to buy my *Tiger Beat* and *16* magazines. The man who worked there was small and sat behind a big, high counter. It was a long time before I could reach it to pay. He would always come around the front to take my money and give me my change, a real sweetie.

So here we were with $10.00 to spend on candy. It was Christmas in November. We immediately went to the magazine section. Vinnie grabbed a *Superman* comic, as he was obsessed. Rudy went for *Ritchie Rich*, the poor-little-rich-boy comic. I wanted to see what adventures Archie and Jughead were getting into. (Actually, I was more interested in Betty and Veronica.) Then it was on to the candy. Rudy picked out another Chunky, a box of Lemonheads and a box of Red Hots. Vinnie went for Sweet Tarts, a box of small jawbreakers and a Hershey bar. They both got the gold nugget gum, which looked like its name and came in a beige sack with a gold pull tie. I loaded up on anything chocolate. And we all got the big jawbreakers.

Turns out $10.00 was a lot of money, as we thought. I was also able to buy my mom a tiny blue bottle of perfume, "Evening in Paris," I think. I got my dad a pack of Newport cigarettes. Eight-year-old kids could buy their parents' cigarettes then. Sometimes kids needed a note, but the owner knew us. And we had money left over to make another small trip there. I thought that was a pretty good exchange for a bag of poop, whoever's poop it was.

The next year, Rudy's younger brother, Carmine, wanted to join us. The boys were resistant at first, but I told them another Musketeer would just make us stronger. They finally gave in. They always did where I was concerned. Since there were now four of us we went as the Beatles. My mom made Nehru jackets modeled after a picture of them and we wore white shirts with skinny black ties. She embroidered the names of each Beatle on our jackets. I went as my Paul. Rudy had the perfect face for John. Because Vinnie was learning the drums, he was Ringo, with a plastic ring on each finger. Carmine went as George, hanging a toy guitar around his neck. Aunt Angie got some realistic-looking Beatle wigs that she must have paid a fortune for. They made us look authentic. We decided to talk with English accents for the entire trick-or-treat walk. Our accents were so bad we were bent over with laughter most of the time.

We skipped the "poop house," as it was now called, but heard there was controversy there again. Apparently this year the kid hid candy in a bucket of sand. He asked kids to put their hand in the sand and pull out a treat. I wondered, *why is this kid at home and not out with his friends?* It was going well all afternoon until he went into the house to refill the bucket. The next kid who put his hand in pulled out a dead mouse, or so the story goes. True or not, the police were involved this time around. It was now the "dead mouse poop house."

Four years later, which was the last time we trick-or-treated together, we were the Beatles again, from the cover of Sgt. Pepper's Lonely Hearts Club Band. We were all our original Beatles from the last go-round. Vinnie gave us a hard time because he insisted Ringo was in red, not pink, on the album cover. We said George was in red and Ringo was in pink. He refused to wear pink so my mom got a lighter shade of red for him to wear. *Hey, dude, it's a costume.* We all had mustaches and those costumes could pass for originals in a museum, except for Ringo's color.

The boys were fourteen years old now and, to tell you the truth, I was surprised they had gone along with our act this long. The following year they went out with their friends dressed as bums. My mom made Raggedy Ann and Andy costumes for Jackie and me that year, which were incredible again. I think that was the last year we all got dressed up. The ladies had started getting orders for costumes a few years earlier based on what people saw us wearing. Halloween turned into a big season for them, which meant Christmas was extra special for us. I swear if the ladies had been more ambitious and business savvy they could have designed and sewed for movies and theater. But as much as they kept making costumes for others, I think they were sad we had outgrown ours.

Before I leave this chapter I think it is only fair to share my own "poop" story of something that happened with my always partner in crime, Janie, maybe eight or nine years after the original incident. We were hanging out at a group of stores near the Carmen Avenue pool. That is where everyone usually met when we weren't sure what we were doing that night. Janie and a bunch of my girlfriends got someone to buy us Boone's Farm Apple Wine. Ninety-nine cents a bottle would guarantee you got drunk and threw up. Janie and I did both that night.

We were walking home and suddenly both of us had to go to the bathroom really bad, and not number one. The more Janie said she had to go, the stronger my urge was. So we did what any two drunk teenage girls would do when they had to go. We went ON SOMEONE'S FRONT LAWN! This is without a doubt the most disgusting thing I have ever done in my life and the first time I am admitting it to anyone.

I was a wreck that night, not able to sleep, thinking I was going to be arrested or worse. I got up at 5:00 a.m. and left my parents a note that I had lost my wallet on the walk home last night and was going to look for it. I even took my wallet with me so I could show them I "found it." I also took some paper towels and plastic bags and a pair of old gardening gloves. I walked the four blocks to the house and there it was on the front lawn, right where we left it. Just as I was about to bend down to pick it up, the front door opened and a man in his pajamas stepped out to get his Sunday paper.

"May I help you?" he said, a little confused.

*Oh my God! Busted! How do I explain this?* I couldn't believe my brain that morning. I was proud of it for thinking so fast.

"Oh, good morning. I was walking my dog last night and she left a present on your lawn. I didn't have anything to clean it up with, so I came back this morning."

Well, you would think I had handed him a million dollars. He was very surprised and kept repeating how thoughtful it was of me to not leave it there. Then he asked what kind of dog I had.

*Oh, geez!* "A small one," I stammered. *Great, where is my brain now?*

"Oh, what breed?"

*Isn't a small one a breed? Why the questions? Can't I just take my poop and leave?*

"A mutt," I replied. *Thanks again, brain.*

As I was getting ready to leave he said, "Oh, no, don't carry that home. I'll put it in my garbage can for you."

He came forward and took the bag of my and Janie's poop and threw it in his garbage can. I was mortified not only by the act but also lying about it. As I walked home I thought, *if that man only knew. If anyone knew.* Now you all do. The most shameful moment of my life. And Janie? She didn't remember any of it. The boys would be very disappointed I never shared this story with them. They loved a good poop story. And just as our costumes were changing each year, so were we, not only physically, but emotionally too, in ways no one could have predicted.

## CHAPTER 5

# The Pliés and Chaines Turns

I started taking dance lessons probably around the same time I started to walk. I don't ever remember not dancing. First it was cute little girls with their hands over their heads, turning to the right, then to the left, stepping out of line, or just sitting down and resting in the middle of a routine. The audience loved the babies and they always got the biggest applause, not to mention some tears from moms and grandmothers - a flap here, a pointed toe there and the place went wild.

Some kids like me continued when they got into elementary school, taking multiple classes in tap, ballet, jazz and modern dance. I was constantly running to classes almost every day, not because my mom wanted me to go, but because I loved it. Something happens to me when I am dancing that I don't experience at any other time: a confidence, a grace, a feeling of freedom that is both calming and exhilarating.

I loved the classes and the discipline I needed for them, especially ballet. Over the years my teachers told me I had "perfect turnout." It was the effortless way my skinny legs could contort, because nothing in ballet ever felt natural to me. Arms up, shoulders down, abs in, butt lifted: there were always so many things to remember, even before taking a step. I eventually went on point, which to me is the most unnatural and brutal thing to do to your feet.

Most of the girls—and there were all girls in my classes—were obsessed with dance. That's all they did. There wasn't any time to do sports (not my strong suit anyway), join clubs, hang out with friends. I was always at the dance studio. That was expected if we wanted to be a ballerina. It was your life. At some point I felt like I was missing too much and made the painful decision I was not going to pursue this professionally. My instructors were disappointed but understanding. I continued my classes, but I took a few ballet classes a week and stopped performing in recitals altogether. I always hated them anyway. We spent so much time learning and perfecting the routines that we only studied the craft half a year.

What I did love about the recitals was that Rudy and Vinnie had to go. And they hated them too. I would always locate them in the audience when I was on stage; they would be slumped in their seats, the most distressed and annoyed looks on their faces. But they never let on that they were bored, always greeting me afterward with flowers and hugs and "good job" high fives, like I would do after one of their games. They started to perk up when they got a little older and were checking out the seasoned dancers with the long legs and tight buns—the ones on their heads too.

My obsession with dancing was almost as competitive as my gift-giving. The boys and I were always trying to outdo each other when it came to gifts. We would try to think of something unique or silly the others didn't even know they couldn't live without. One Christmas, on a whim, I gave Rudy and Vinnie six ballet lessons each. They were in high school and looked at me like I was crazy.

I told them I had read that some famous football players took ballet classes to help them on the field with balance, pivots and such. I think I told them it was Joe Namath and Emerson Boozer. I made that up. They reluctantly agreed to go, but refused to wear tights. My ballet teacher at the time, Sheila, said they could attend the adult beginner classes and I went with them because, well, I wasn't going to miss this.

Talk about a fish out of water. The six women who were regulars in this class thought the boys were hysterical. They were. Every move was like twisting a pretzel. They would literally fall over their own feet. The three of us would scream with laughter. It got to the point where Sheila said we were too disruptive to the other students, so she gave us our own class. Eventually she came on board and we would do more laughing than dancing.

When their coach found out what the boys were doing, he thought it was a great idea and contacted Sheila about teaching a class for some of his athletes. Next thing you know I was assisting in a class full of football and baseball players. Some even wore tights! I SO wanted them to be in the recital. Sadly they said they would only go so far.

Every year the dancers would have pictures taken in their costumes both as a group and individually. This was a big moneymaker for the photographers and the dance studio. Along with the costumes, the photo sessions were big expenses, especially for those of us who danced in multiple numbers. One year, when I was about eleven and at what I thought was my most awkward, the photographer took extra pictures of me in different poses. He brought them to a friend of his who had a dance costume company. Long story short, I was hired to be a catalogue model for dance costumes. Skinny, ugly me. I guess that perfect turnout was good for something. I did this for at least four years. Several times a year I would be called to a studio in Lake Ronkonkoma, where I would spend two to three days shooting. The money was good, the work was easy and I got to say I was a model, if only for tutus and tap shoes.

When I was around fifteen years old I finally started to put on some weight. My body was changing. Those long, skinny ballet legs were now taking shape with definition and muscle. My arms seemed to be at a normal length rather than down to my knees, and, most surprising, I was getting boobs. Big ones. The kind ballerinas sometimes have to tape flat. My modeling "career" moved from dance catalogues to bathing suit ads, but not because I was some beautiful Christy Brinkley model. No one was going to put me on the cover of *Seventeen* or *Vogue*. But I was tall and thin, with a fit physique from dance and I had boobs.

It wasn't professional. The photos appeared mostly in newspaper and circular ads for stores out west and down south. It paid well so I didn't have to work at the local supermarket or my Uncle Joe's car dealership. My parents would give me a little bit of money to spend, but the rest went in the bank. It paid for college, a car and then some. And I owed it all to my love of dance and my many years of lessons.

It wasn't only the formal dance classes that I loved. Any music would get me up on the floor. Even as a toddler I was dragging Rudy and Vinnie up to dance with me. As a result they turned out to be pretty good dancers who eventually didn't have to be dragged on the dance floor. I think anyone they ever danced with at a dance, prom or wedding owes me a debt of thanks.

And we had some great music to dance to. My favorite was and always will be the Motown community of recordings. I had every blue-labeled 45 ever released and would play them over and over again, singing and making up dance routines to them. I loved doing classical ballet moves to Motown tunes. It was always unexpected and well received. Me, Smokey and a pair of toe shoes. I even convinced Sheila to let me put together a ballet routine to "Track of My Tears" for one of the recitals. It was a big hit.

But my all-time favorite song to dance to was also my favorite Beatles' song, "In My Life." Actually, it is probably my favorite song ever. I devised a little dance routine for Vinnie and Rudy, which they hated when they were younger because it was slow dancing. They eventually came around as they got older. The three of us must have done this dance over a hundred times. Anytime we heard that song and we were together, no matter where we were, we would all get up to dance. We could be at the beach, a party, a restaurant. We even stopped the car once, got out and danced on the side of the road as it played on the radio. It didn't matter. We always got up to dance. That is probably why it is so near and dear to my heart. Plus it is just a beautiful song.

In the fall of 1971 Vinnie's class decided to have a talent show as a fundraiser for a classmate who had been dealing with cancer for the past eight months. Vinnie asked me if I would choreograph a song we could dance to. I was really surprised he wanted to do this and told him absolutely. We chose "This Old Heart of Mine" by the Isley Brothers. I had so much fun teaching him the routine and rehearsing. He was really serious and focused during practices. I actually had to tell him to loosen up and have fun. We performed to a standing ovation and came in second.

My family loved music and we always had a little family band. Trust me, we weren't the Partridge Family or The Cowsills. We called ourselves The Westbury Whiners. Vinnie played drums and Uncle Joe played a mean saxophone. Uncle Phil was our piano/organ player and everyone else plucked guitars at some point. Since almost every Motown song had a sax solo, we usually stuck to that playlist. In addition, my aunts loved to sing the Andrew Sisters and Papa G. was hilarious as Elvis. He had the twitch, the twists and the hair. He would do this thing with his legs where they would shake like jelly, only in slow motion, like Rudy's did when he would "assist" the plate spinner on *The Ed Sullivan Show*. It was a perfect impression. Mama Rose, who was the biggest Barbara Streisand fan I ever met, would always have to sing something from *Funny Girl*. She had her movements down perfectly but not so much her voice. We loved it every time and laughed until we couldn't breathe.

I loved Gladys Knight and her Pips so I would always sing one of their recordings. And I had my own Pips. We would play at family barbeques or gatherings. Sometimes friends would come over and join us. We weren't good, but we had fun. Rudy would pick up the guitar occasionally but mostly I would just dance with him if I wasn't singing. He was a Pip once in a while too. My father would do the worst impression of Ed Sullivan on the planet—we never told him—and introduced all of us. One day some friends from football were over and my dad introduced me and my Pips. Our friend Erick, God love him, yelled out, in front of my parents and family, "Tits? She is going to show us her tits?" And he wasn't even drinking.

We sound like the Walton family, singing and dancing our way through life. We weren't, although I remember thinking we were pretty close. The boys did get into a lot of mischief and usually I wasn't far behind. One summer day—they must have been going into eleventh grade—I overheard Rudy and Vinnie talking to some friends about going to the Carmen Avenue pool around midnight and skinny-dipping. Why? I have no idea. The boys loved a dare. So I told my mom I was sleeping over at Jackie's (I really was this time) and we went there with Janie and waited for them. A little after midnight they showed up, climbed through the hole in the fence, stripped down and started swimming and jumping off the diving board.

We carefully sneaked through the hole in the fence and grabbed their clothes, everything. They were having such a good time they didn't even notice we were there. We folded the clothes nicely and put them on top of Vinnie's car, which was down the hill in the parking lot, across from Carvel, under a streetlamp. Vinnie always parked near a light so he could see if someone was near his pride and joy. He didn't see us that night. He was having too much fun frolicking naked in the community pool. Then we went on the other side of the pool, unseen in the dark, and waited. Our friend Gerry got out of the pool first and started yelling, in a whisper, "Where's our clothes?"

It took a minute or two for the others to catch on and they were furious, yelling that whoever took the clothes better come forward right now. Of course we didn't. They waited for a few minutes and then they saw their clothing on Vinnie's car. We couldn't see them as they were standing in the shadows.

All of a sudden, into the light, they went running down the hill, totally naked and soaking wet, hands trying to hide their privates and keep their balance. We could have stayed quiet, but instead we just started hooting and hollering and ran away. I am sure they knew it was us. I spent the rest of the summer on edge, dreading the payback. But they were smart. They never did anything to get us back. They just made us wait in terror, always looking around the corner, over our shoulder, under the bed sheets, for their revenge. I now realize that keeping us in that heightened state *was* their payback. Tricky little bastards. But, oh, how they could dance.

CHAPTER 6

# The Fashionista

The moms were always going shopping and dragging us kids along. Malls were fairly new and the two big ones in our area were Mid Island Plaza and Roosevelt Field. The latter was the bigger, more expensive mall. It was built on the site of an old airfield that hosted Amelia Earhart. Charles Lindbergh's solo transatlantic flight left from there in 1927. It was named for Teddy Roosevelt's son Quentin, who died in World War One. My father would get upset at thinking such a historic site was now home to Alexanders and Gimbels.

The entrance to Roosevelt Field had lighted globes, each one a letter that spelt out the name of the mall. I remember a lot of fountains there as well. One time we were all walking through the mall and noticed Rudy wasn't with us. He must have been six years old. We turned around and there he was, wading in the water under one of the fountains. Mama Rose got him, took off his clothing and wiped him down. She put him under her arm and walked to the car with little naked Rudy wrapped in her big blue sweater. There was something about that kid and water.

I have a very vague memory of Roosevelt Field and Senator John F. Kennedy. I wish my parents were around to ask. I was about five and a half and remember going with my dad to the Old Country Road entrance of Roosevelt Field. He had me on his shoulders to watch as a black limousine drove past us with the future president inside. According to history, on

October 12, 1960, Senator Kennedy gave one of his last campaign speeches before becoming president at Roosevelt Raceway, which was adjacent to the mall. My father being a history buff, I am sure that memory is a real one. At least I like to think it is.

It was always an adventure going to the mall because there were so many stores to choose from. When we got to a certain age, the moms would let us wander free, without supervision, as long as we reported back to them at designated places and times. It was our first real sense of independence. I think our moms didn't want us around while they tried on dresses and bras.

We all had our favorite stores. Whenever we went there I would have to go to Teepee Town. It was a store that sold Native American jewelry, clothing and novelties. I would hang out trying on jewelry and moccasins while the boys would check out the bow and arrow replicas. I realize now that most of the items there were probably not made by Native Americans but by someone in China. Still it gave me my love for Native American design and I have been fortunate enough to travel out west and purchase items directly from the artists who made them.

I also loved all the clothing stores. I got my love for fashion at an early age. I guess with a seamstress as a mom, I was born into it. Design, fabric and structure were topics discussed in my house on a daily basis. I was aware of how things fit, how a hem was stitched and why there was a huge difference in price point between two pairs of black pants (think material and cut). This made me a very discerning shopper. I also happened to be born at the most exciting time for fashion of the past century.

Before World War Two teenagers and adults basically dressed alike. They acted alike too, for the most part. Fashion started to take a bit of a turn in the 1950s but did an all-out spin in the 1960s and 1970s. Clothing is as much a cultural statement as a fashion statement, influenced in large part by music, movies, necessity and technology. Think about the bobbysoxers of the Frank Sinatra age, Marlon Brandon and the black leather jacket in *The Wild One* and the psychedelic clothing of *Laugh In*.

Many of the styles I owned and adored growing up have made a resurgence and are now called vintage. I love that tie-dye, paisley and batik fabrics are back, along with granny dresses and skirts, peasant blouses and wide-legged bell-bottoms. Several times a year I attend the Manhattan Vintage Clothing Show in NYC and spend a small fortune buying similar pieces to those I once owned.

When I was younger my fashion style was influenced by many different people, including my mom, Twiggy, Goldie Hawn and Cher. The Beatles were a huge influence too and what their girlfriends or wives wore also sent me shopping. This was the "Mod" era (short for "modernist") coming out of London. The British Invasion sent a style over here that, in my opinion, has never been matched. "The Swinging Sixties" consisted of flowing materials, oranges, yellows and pinks, flower power, bell bottoms and, of course, my favorite, the introduction of the miniskirt.

English designer Mary Quant is credited with popularizing the miniskirt in the 1960s. It was truly a fashion revolution. Some saw the miniskirt, along with the Beatles' long hair, as the end of civilization as we knew it. Surprise, that didn't happen. But it was probably the single most important piece of clothing to come out of this time. And with it came the arrival of tights and pantyhose.

The introduction of pantyhose and spandex in the early 1960s was probably not coincidental. Prior to pantyhose women had to wear a god-awful garter belt with stockings. With my long legs, the stockings never stretched to the top of the hooks on the garter belt. It might look sexy in a Victoria Secret catalogue but, trust me, it was extremely uncomfortable. Plus the hose would always run where the stocking and garter met.

At first pantyhose were expensive and not widely marketed. The miniskirt increased the demand and a change in manufacturing made them more affordable. But in my early days of wearing stockings, I started out with the garter belt and spandex-free hose. I was allowed to wear stockings when I was twelve, but my mom wouldn't let me shave my legs until I was fourteen.

One day, after church, I heard my dad and mom discussing something in the bedroom. They were talking about my legs. Apparently my little hairy limbs looked like "a monkey in stockings" according to my dad. The hose just magnified my already bushy legs. My mother felt I was too young to shave them. Aunt Angie came to the rescue. She told my mom about Nair, a cream hair removal that smelt like the devil farted.

Aunt Angie had picked some up at the store for me and my mom and I went over to try it out. Uncle Joe thought it was a scam and said this would never remove the "mountain of hair" on my legs. Thanks Uncle Joe. He was so sure of it he put a big patch on his leg. Twenty minutes later he had a nice, smooth hairless spot in the middle of his leg. That was enough convincing for me. I used Nair for the next two years. To this day even the thought of the smell makes me sick.

As with the age restriction on shaving my legs, my mom arbitrarily decided I couldn't wear makeup until I was fifteen. But in junior high I got around that. I would put it on at school and take it off before I got home. Heavy, dark eyes with long bangs were the look then, with several layers of false eyelashes. I was partial to Maybelline's blue mascara. I would cake that on so thick it would sometimes take me ten minutes to take it off.

One day I forgot an important report at home and did something out of character for me. I called my mom and asked her to bring it to school for me, totally forgetting I was made up for a burlesque show. My mom pulled up outside the main entrance as she was not made up and didn't want to come in the building. As soon as she saw me she noticed the makeup and went ballistic. I had to give her all my makeup when I got home. And wouldn't you know it, two weeks later SHE was wearing my blue mascara. I stopped putting all that eye makeup on at school, just a little mascara, or sometimes Vaseline, on my eyelashes. Rudy and Vinnie said they thought I looked better without all that "goop" on my eyes, as Vinnie called it.

I still wore my white lipstick. I wasn't giving that up. I loved anything Yardley, a company out of England. They made this great lipstick called Slicker. My favorite color was Frosted. It was white with a shine to it. That was the style. I even had a necklace with a Slicker lipstick/whistle on it. It was $3.50, a lot for a lipstick then. Years later I replaced it with one from eBay and paid $165.00 for it. The lesson here is to never throw anything you once loved away, because you will love it again.

Even the comics and dolls influenced us. Betty and Veronica and Brenda Starr were always fashion plates and Barbie's outfits reflected the times. Barbie's hairstyles changed as the clothing changed and so did mine. I never went the short route like Twiggy or Mia Farrow. In a family where the way you looked was very important, long hair was a must, at least down to your shoulders. Aunt Angie's signature style was a headband and flip, sometimes with bangs, sometimes without. Aunt Mary wore hers long in a braid or ponytail. She didn't like it on her face. My mom had the same bouffant until she was in her nineties; a teased top and curled bottom, resting on her shoulders.

When I was very young my mom would put me in banana curls, à la Shirley Temple. She would put either rollers in my hair or "spoolies" that you wrapped the hair around and laid flat to your head. I liked them better as they were easier to sleep in. I swear at five years old I was the only kid who went to bed with their hair "set." And don't forget the Dippity-Do and Aquanet hairspray to hold everything in place.

For most of my teen years I wore my hair in the popular style of long and parted in the middle. Think Cher in her early years. It was easy to manage and could be put up in a ponytail or beehive, my mom's favorite "dress look" for me. I would often take a bandana, fold it in a triangle and wrap it around my head, tying it in the back. My dad called it my babushka. People would even put these half-wig things called falls in their hair to give them more height or to enhance a hairdo. Of course I had one of those too.

Even Rudy and Vinnie got a bit caught up with the hair fashion. For a while they had the "mop top" style of the Beatles, although Rudy pulled it off better than Vinnie. Rudy's hair was thick, dark and had a great wave to it. Vinnie's hair was blond and very curly. His hair was more suited to the Beach Boys' style and he wore board shorts and Hawaiian shirts well. Rudy wore them too, but I always thought he looked best in jeans and a leather jacket. Something about that look complemented his athletic frame and gave him a bad boy edge. It was also the introduction of long, narrow collars on men's shirts and suits—very seventies. And don't forget the mut-tonchops and goatees (not sure why they referenced meat).

Rudy was always more formal in his dress than Vinnie. He rarely wore T-shirts outside of athletics. He usually wore a collared shirt even hanging around. I think some of this was influenced by his coaches. He felt athletes should present themselves in a "neat and respectful" manner. Around this time casual dress for males and females was becoming more unisex. Vinnie, Rudy and I even bought the same pair of shoes, Earth Shoes, although God only knows why. Supposedly they had this secret sole and negative heel that was not only good for your feet but for your back and posture as well. My dance teacher had a pair and highly recommended them. They were called Earth Shoes, so we thought, you know, peace, love, the earth. The boys decided to get the deep brown color and couldn't con-vince me NOT to get the baby food puke orange color. They had a round toe with a long front. Mine looked like I was wearing a duck bill. I thought

I was so cool walking around with these shoes. They did nothing for my feet or back. Give me a nice pair of white go-go boots. I was also a big fan of platform shoes and it is a miracle I never broke my ankle. I was always falling off them, which brought Rudy and Vinnie to uncontrollable laughter. They would ask if I was okay once they stopped.

My all-time favorite shoe, which did nothing to help my poor, abused feet, were Buffalo sandals. I don't know how they got that name. Maybe their creators wanted us to think they were made out of buffalo hide (ugh!), or maybe they wanted us to equate them with things out west. Either way I lived in them. They were flat and had absolutely no support. I think I liked them because it was like being barefoot, something I still love today. Any time I could get away without wearing shoes I did. I even went barefoot in the supermarket. My mother was always telling me to wash my feet.

The Buffalo sandal was a very simple design with the big toe going through a toe ring, which was attached to a strip of leather that went down the foot and attached to a band. When we got a new pair, which I did often because I would always break them at the toe ring, we were supposed to wet them. We'd put them on and soak our feet and sandals in the bathtub so they conformed to our feet. I don't know if they really did or if it was just a marketing tool. I do remember me, Jackie and Gina sitting on the edge of my tub, soaking our sandaled feet in my bathtub. My mom brought us ice cream. It was the first and only time I ever ate in the bathroom: good times in the name of fashion.

The other popular sandal at the time was Dr. Scholl's exercise sandals. They were a "therapeutic" flip-flop with a wooden sole and heel, billed as "better than barefoot." They were close. It became the hip summer shoe for years and I had many pairs in all colors. Known as toe huggers, they were supposed to tone the wearer's calves by just walking. I heard they are making a comeback. I wonder what my feet would think about them now.

For all the fringes and Pooka beads, peace signs and pop art, ponchos and crocheted vests ("Ribticklers") I wore, my favorite thing was what I didn't wear. Women started to go braless. That was in part connected to the women's movement and going braless signified the freedom and equality of the crusade. Some women even burned their bras as a symbol of this. For me, it was just relief. I hated wearing them. I still do. This became a bit of a battle between my mom and me.

When I would leave the house she would always feel my back to make sure I had a bra on. She would do the same thing when I came home. In between it came off. I would sometimes take it off on my walk to Janie's in the morning or wait until I got to her house. Then I would put it back on before going home, after taking my eye makeup off. My mother would tell me my boobs were going to sag when I got older if I went without a bra. I like to think it is gravity and age that got them there.

I love that a part of my closet today has some very familiar and similar items in it that reflect my youth and this great fashion time. I also love that I was there on the first go-round. It's fun trying to find things that I had or things that are close to them. I get a kick out of the fact that I was once "mod" but now I'm "vintage." Now if I can only find that paper paisley dress ...

## CHAPTER 7

# The Junior High Experience

Rudy, Vinnie and I had been in the same school since I started kindergarten; however, when I got to sixth grade, they moved on to junior high. We now had different schedules so we didn't go to school together and didn't get out of school at the same time. I didn't like them moving on without me, but I don't think they minded. They started to act like big shots, changing classes, having lockers, playing sports and talking about girls. We weren't drifting apart, just in different directions. I secretly felt they were outgrowing me.

I would see them at our many family functions and they would fill me in on the wonderful world of junior high. I think Mama Rose or Aunt Angie must have told them I was feeling left out. Around November they started to try to include me in things, even though I was only in elementary school. I would go to their games all the time. They both joined football and were on track. Vinnie played lacrosse while Rudy continued to be outstanding at baseball. They really made an effort, but we were at different developmental stages and in different buildings.

Once the summer came around again, everything went back to normal. Only now the boys were experts on junior high and shared all their year's learned wisdom with me. They told me what teachers I should get (like I had a choice), where the best place to have a locker was, what bathroom to avoid, all the essential survival skills needed for junior high. They didn't tell me how to deal with bullies, what it felt like being the youngest in the school again or how to juggle all the different assignments. Those things I had to figure out on my own.

Our seventh and eighth grade classes were in the same building as our high school, although they tried to keep us separate. When I got to junior high it was great to see Rudy and Vinnie in the halls again. They immediately resumed their roles as my older brothers and protectors. We didn't have much contact during the day, but we were back to going to school together and coming home at the same time.

In seventh grade I had to take home economics. All the girls did. The boys' mandatory class was shop and we wouldn't dare ask to switch. Girls learned to cook and sew. Boys worked on small engines and made things out of wood. That was it. My seventh-grade home economics teacher was very strict. I called her Miss Cranky, behind her back of course. She was kind of stuck in the 1950s, even in her look and was very rigid in enforcing school rules. Girls were not allowed to wear pants to our public school. What was THAT about?

One day it was really cold and, for some reason, Vinnie, Rudy and I didn't have a ride to school. I put a pair of pants under my skirt and off we walked. It was a Monday, which was always the coldest day of the school week. They usually shut the heat off in the building for the weekend if nothing was going on. It was chilly so I left my pants on in school. It was not the best fashion statement, but I was warm.

When I got to home economics my teacher reminded me of the rule about girls and pants. She sent me down to the nurse. Why the nurse I don't know. I was mortified. I had never been sent to any office for a discipline issue, let alone for what I was wearing. The nurse called my mother. My mom always sided with the teacher: no sticking up for me. If the teacher said I was wrong, I was. But this time my mom surprised me and insisted

I leave the pants on. She even called the principal, which was a huge deal for her.

I went back to class with my pants still on and Miss Cranky had a fit, questioning if I even went to the nurse's office at all. I told her I did and that my mom spoke to the nurse and the principal. She was livid and after class marched into the principal's office to see why I wasn't ordered to take my pants off (that sounds so wrong!) or given detention.

Dr. Lou, as everyone called the junior high principal, explained I had to walk to school, it was cold out and it wasn't a big deal. Apparently it was a big deal for Miss Cranky, who started yelling we shouldn't have rules if we are not going to follow through, how are students going to learn right from wrong, etc. Next thing I knew I was in the office with Miss Cranky and Dr. Lou and she was screaming that at least she should be allowed to give me detention. I think Dr. Lou just wanted to shut her up, so I was given detention after school the following day. I saw Vinnie in the hall and explained the whole story. He was as angry as Miss Cranky was. He said I shouldn't have to serve detention and that my mom should protest. Some of the other teachers had now heard about it and it became the topic of conversation in the faculty cafeteria, or so I was told.

I went home and told my mom the rest of the story and she said not to go to detention. Of course my dad, being a teacher, did see the other side. He told me I should use this as an opportunity to address the issue and make a change. He was ever the social studies teacher, God bless him. They did agree detention was ridiculous, but my dad said I should serve it. I said I would play it by ear.

When I walked into school the next day almost half the girls in junior high had pants under their skirts and dresses, some with just pants and a top. I stopped counting at 137. Even my math teacher wore pants under her skirt. Apparently Vinnie, Rudy and Jackie took it upon themselves to start this campaign. They spoke to and called everyone they knew and asked them to call everyone they knew. They briefly shared my story and encouraged them to wear pants to school the next day. They thought everyone couldn't be sent down to the nurse. My detention was cancelled. I eventually worked with the student government to address this issue with the Board of Education. Before the year was out the Board voted to allow girls to wear pants to school. I ran on that platform and was elected as vice president of our student government in eighth grade. The best part was I didn't have to worry about the hair on my legs. No, really, the best part was it gave me my first success at policy change. I got the bug.

I do have to give Miss C., as we really called her, credit for some things. No one can iron like I can. She taught me how to press a shirt like it's nobody's business, a skill I still use today. The trick is to iron the collar first and last. She also taught me how to set a table and, to this day, I still know where to place the cutlery. Unfortunately, I never learned how to fix small engines or make things out of wood.

Everything seemed different in junior high. In elementary school we went the entire six years with the same class, the same group of kids. Now we were in classes with different students. I just went with the flow; I was open and friendly to everyone. I liked people. I still do. I find them interesting. But some old friends didn't understand our new ones. And puberty and hormones were added to the mix.

In seventh grade we blended with the students from our other elementary school. It was a time when friendships built in the lower grades were tested by new people and ideas. Groups started to split up and new ones formed. People who had been your best friends for six years were now not a part of your life anymore. Different cliques emerged. It was strange and often scary. I met a lot of new girlfriends but still hung out with Jackie the most. She was starting her journey to becoming a very accomplished athlete, playing both intramural and team sports and making new friends as well.

Entering junior high was the first time I started to notice being bullied: maybe it was because some of the kids didn't know me, maybe because some thought they were older and felt powerful, I don't know. I was super skinny and tall, awkward in my own body when I wasn't dancing. I had acne issues, a nose too large for my face and, to make matters worse, I got braces. Coming from a family where looks mattered, I thought mine were awful. I never really shared the bullying with Vinnie and Rudy because I thought they would start a fight with whoever was doing it. It did depress me for a while, though I had a strong support system of friends and family to help guide me through puberty hell.

It was hard figuring out where I belonged in this place called junior high. Jackie, our friend Anna from our elementary class, and I found a "home" in our seventh-grade social studies teacher's classroom. Mr. Howard knew my dad and watched out for me in seventh grade. He was a really nice man. A bunch of us would hang out in his classroom after school. He had a small TV and we started watching this afternoon soap opera called *Dark Shadows*. Sometimes we would go home and change and bring snacks back. Mr. Howard was one of those teachers who always seemed to be at school. After a while Rudy, Vinnie and some other guys joined us after practice. Rudy and Anna started dating. She would be the first to break his heart. At one point we had about fifteen kids around this small black-and-white TV set, hanging on to every word Barnabas, the vampire in *Dark Shadows*, said. The boys thought it was alright to watch this soap opera because it had a vampire. Who were they kidding? I bet they knew all the characters on *General Hospital* too.

Mr. Howard and his classroom provided a comfortable and safe place for me to hang out after school. No one bullied me there and Mr. Howard insisted everyone be treated equally and with respect. I don't think he ever knew what that refuge meant to an insecure, skinny kid just trying to find herself and fit in. It was my glass slipper. I gained a lot of confidence in that room. Thanks Mr. Howard.

Developmentally junior high is its own little world. I believe any traumas a child experiences in life are either marginalized or magnified depending on two things—their coping skills and their age. Many students I went to school with had to deal with some very heavy concerns: an alcoholic or abusive parent, divorce, moving to another district or state, a death, suicide and even murder. It always seems to me that if any of these experiences occur during early adolescence, the challenges to successfully overcome them are more difficult. In elementary school it was often disguised. Today a divorce group becomes Banana Splits. A board game is played to negotiate a home with an alcoholic parent. A buddy or mentoring program is initiated for new students and those being bullied.

By the time a child is in high school they have developed some strong coping mechanisms. Some work and some don't. Some are healthy and some are not. But they do have a "bag of tools," as I like to call it, to choose from and, hopefully, adults who can guide them. But in junior high nobody knows who the hell they are. It's that in-between stage and children are dealing with all the new things that come along with not being a kid but not yet being considered a teenager. I believe the word today is "tween." When I was growing up it was called chaos. Our bodies were changing, our friends were changing, opportunities were becoming available on all sorts of levels, our sexuality was awakening (unless your mom tried to squash any feelings you were having), academics started to count and alcohol and drugs were introduced on a wider scale. I don't know anyone who has ever said junior high was easy, a breeze. And if they did I think they are glamorizing their memory.

Now throw in a divorce or a move and everything magnifies. Yes, there may be kids who came through tragedies in junior high unscathed. I just don't know any. Eventually it all catches up with you. If your district is smart enough, social workers are placed in schools to help students at every level. When I was in junior high a social worker only came to school to remove you from your home, or so we thought. There weren't a lot of support services for someone struggling emotionally. You had your family, but they might have been the issue. You had your friends—also often the issue—or maybe a sympathetic teacher. Otherwise you were on your own. I remember very distinctly a situation that clearly illustrates this.

In mid-September of my seventh-grade a new student showed up at our school. Her name was Maggie and she was from Upstate New York. That is really all any of the students knew about her. The staff, however, knew much more. She was different from us. She dressed differently, didn't have our Long Island accent and always appeared disheveled. Her long, dark hair wasn't in any kind of a style and always seemed in need of a wash. She was beyond shy. If she had a shell she could have crawled into she would have. Yet she had a wicked wit and would say the most insane things under her breath, which always got me laughing. She was in my homeroom and I liked her right away.

We had the same lunch period and I never liked to see anyone sitting alone, so I invited Maggie to our table. I swear the first few weeks she barely said a word. She did tell us she was living with her aunt and uncle. When we asked her about her parents she said she was here because the schools were better. I don't know why but I felt a profound sadness about her, like my old Pitiful Pearl doll. She broke my heart. My friends and I would invite her places but she rarely went. We did manage to get her to hang out at Mr. Howard's classroom after school and she came every day. She got hooked on *Dark Shadows* and I think she developed a crush on Vinnie. He was always nice to her and paid her the attention I don't think she got from boys or anyone else. Vinnie would get her to laugh all the time. I just love that boy.

One day Maggie asked me if I wanted to sleep over. I said sure and my mom and her aunt made the arrangements. My mom would never let me sleep over at a house where she didn't know the friend or mom. Turns out she knew Maggie's aunt from, of all places, Bingo. Maggie's Aunt Debbie and Uncle Rob were really nice people. They had two girls, both older than Maggie. One was in college and one was in eleventh grade. Maggie had her own room but I got the sense that she never felt at home there. She was always cautious about where she sat and what she said. She just never seemed relaxed. That night we had take-out pizza for dinner and ice cream for dessert. I was in heaven.

After dinner we hung out in Maggie's room. We listened to music, talked and laughed. She was different away from school, more open with her humor and a chatterbox of sorts. She asked how I was related to Rudy and Vinnie and I explained the whole equation to her. She was very smart. She got it right away. She said she thought Vinnie was very cute and really nice. She had been stung by the "Vincenzo Bee" as I called him. She had a crush. I told her she should let him know, but she said she wasn't the girl-friend type. I shouted back, "Me, either."

She then went into all her reasons why boys didn't like her and I went through my own checklist with her. We were so hard on ourselves. You should never define yourself by whether someone likes you or not, but we were in seventh grade and hadn't received that memo yet. Never really having the most appropriate filters I told Maggie I thought she needed to do something with her hair. Heck, that's what friends are supposed to do, right? I asked her how often she washed it and she said once or twice a week.

"A week? I sometimes do that in a day." Again, no filter.

I suggested we go to the salon and get her hair shaped and pick up some shampoo for oily hair. I then told her she really had to wash it at least every other day. Like I was the beauty police or something. The next day we went with her aunt to the beauty parlor. The new cut and product gave her hair fullness, bounce and a real shine. She looked great and it boosted her confidence. Her aunt bought her a few current pairs of pants, some sweaters and a great pair of boots. She came in Monday morning with a jump in her step. Vinnie was smitten. Maggie started doing more things with us and before I knew it she and Vinnie were officially dating. He was a really sweet boyfriend, very attentive and kind, like Rudy. Jackie convinced her to try out for basketball and she was a natural. It seemed like she had found a home.

One day, about a week before Christmas break, Maggie came to school very down and not herself. Vinnie, Jackie and I noticed and asked her what was wrong. She said she was just tired and we left it at that. I sensed it was something more. She didn't want to go to Mr. Howard's room after school so Vinnie and I walked her home. She asked us both to come in. She needed to talk to us about something.

No one was home as Vinnie sat next to her on the couch and I sat across from them. She started to cry. Being the Italian I am, I said the first thing that came into my mind. "Is someone sick?"

"No," she said through her tears.

"Did somebody die?"

Wrong question to ask. She immediately became hysterical, unable to speak for a good five minutes. Vinnie got her a glass of water and started gently rubbing her back to calm her down. He told her to take deep breaths in and breathe out slowly. He was so good. She finally was able to calm down enough to quietly tell us her saga, but not before we swore not to tell anyone, including our parents. We swore.

Maggie grew up in Minetto, New York, a small town in Oswego County along the Oswego River. It was the company town of the Columbia Mills Textile Factory, which closed in 1977. It was declared a Superfund site some years later, designated a health risk due to contamination. Maggie's dad was a company man at the factory and held an important supervisory position. At least Maggie thought it was important; she said they had a big house and a lot of things her other friends didn't. Her dad was always working. Her mom was a nurse and worked two days a week at the local hospital, twelve-hour shifts each day.

Maggie had a brother, Dennis, five years older than her. She explained Dennis was very outgoing and popular at school while she was the opposite. As long as she could remember she was always shy and preferred playing at home by herself to going on playdates with classmates. Her parents tried everything to get her to be more social but she was never comfortable in all their attempts. They even took her to see a doctor, who said she would eventually outgrow it. She loved to read and did really well in school, something her brother envied.

She described her parents as loving and her family as normal, whatever that means. When she was about nine years old she started to notice a change in her dad. She said it was subtle and quiet at first. He was always a little moody but this was different. He would have bouts of being very happy and then being what Maggie described as sad. She said during these times she would sometimes see him sitting in his chair in the living room, just staring at the floor. She and her brother would try everything to make him smile. She thought maybe it was something she was doing that made her dad sad but her mom assured her it was nothing she had done. Her mom would say he had a bad day at work.

Eventually his happy moods were less and less and he just seemed sad or angry, with real unpredictable fits of temper. Maggie said he would be mean to her mom and would say awful things to and about her. Her mom asked him many times to see a doctor but he refused, saying there was nothing wrong with him. Maggie said she sometimes wished he would move out of the house. Vinnie and I were listening quietly, hanging on her every word, not knowing where this was going. We never could have imagined it would go where it did.

Maggie started crying again, taking those deep breaths Vinnie had shown her. She said one morning last summer her brother had gone to his girlfriend's house and she had gone for a bike ride. When she was heading home she turned down her block and saw flashing lights and fire trucks. As she got closer she noticed police cars too. They were near her house. She started riding faster and realized they were in front of her house, where a crowd of people had gathered. She didn't see or smell any fire and thought it was probably a false alarm. And then she saw Dennis. He glanced at her riding down the street, broke loose from a neighbor who was hugging him and came running toward her. She thought he was going to tell her everything was fine, that it was a false alarm. But as he got closer she saw his face and knew everything would never be fine again.

Maggie said she was overcome with a fear she had never experienced. She jumped off the bike before she could stop it and ran into Dennis's arms, not knowing what was going on. Dennis would later say he should have thought before he spoke to Maggie, but all he could say was, "Mommy and Daddy are dead."

Maggie then stopped telling her story and started to cry again. Vinnie and I just looked at each other, helpless, trying the best we could to comfort her.

"Oh my God, Maggie," Vinnie said, sincerely. "I am so sorry. I had no idea."

"Me too, Maggie," I said. "You don't have to tell us anymore of the story."

"Oh, no," she said through her tears. "I have to tell someone."

She took a deep breath and started to give the details as best she could. She said Dennis and his girlfriend Nicole went to his house to have lunch. He noticed their dad's car was there, which wasn't unusual because he sometimes came home for lunch. When they went into the house Dennis commented to Nicole how silent it was. He yelled for his parents but they didn't answer. Nicole joked that maybe they were having a little "afternoon delight."

"Ugh," Dennis said. "That is disgusting." Dennis then started up the stairs, calling his parents' names as he climbed to the top, getting no response.

Maggie stopped again, taking some deep breaths and then she closed her eyes and said, "In the bedroom, he found our parents, shot to death."

You could see the body language change in Vinnie and me. We both jumped out of our seats a little as that was not what we were expecting to hear. Maggie then opened her eyes. "We thought it was a robbery gone bad. It wasn't until a few days later that we found out my dad …" She paused for a long time. "Shot my mom and then himself."

I instinctively let out a scream while Vinnie quietly said, "Oh my God."

We sat there for what seemed like eternity, not saying a word. There were no words to say. The unthinkable was her reality. After a while she explained that her brother, who was a senior in high school, had stayed up in Minetto to finish school. He was living with the family of his best friend. Maggie came to Long Island to stay with her aunt and uncle.

There was no rhyme or reason to this horrific act. No loss of finances. No infidelity. No illegal activities. Just a man quietly sitting in his living room chair, slipping away while his young daughter looked on, wondering how she could bring him back. You can label it depression, bipolar disorder or mental illness, but it doesn't change the outcome. And now Maggie was sharing it with us.

Vinnie and I started crying. I moved over to the couch and we gave her one of our famous threesome hugs, except instead of Rudy, we were hugging Maggie. Maggie, who had to spend the rest of her life as the victim of a murder-suicide. We sat in that hug for a long time. I kept wondering if anyone ever comes back from a tragedy like this.

When we finally let go of each other, Maggie explained a lawyer was figuring out all their financial and legal options. Dennis wanted to become Maggie's legal guardian when he turned eighteen in January and move back into the house. Maggie never wanted to see that house again. They weren't sure what they were going to do but, for now, they were just trying to get through it one day at a time. She told us the upcoming holidays, which were always spent joyously in her home, made her feel extra sad. She was getting counseling twice a week and her therapist said the holidays were a trigger. She wanted us to know because, she said, "You two are my best friends."

When I finally was able to speak I told her we would be there in any way she needed us. Vinnie and I kept saying how sorry we were and how we would not share this with anyone. We kept asking her what we could do and she said listening to her helped. "This has been a really tough time," she said slowly. "But the two of you have been so kind and welcoming and that has helped a lot."

Vinnie said, "We will always be here for you. Always."

I left before Vinnie, giving them some alone time. As I walked home I couldn't digest what I had just heard. It seemed like a true crime novel. How does someone move on from that? Are they sad? Angry? Confused? I understood Maggie much better after that and thought she was one of the bravest girls I knew. She deserved a medal for just getting out of bed in the morning. And here I was telling her she had to wash her hair more often. I felt like a jerk.

Maggie and her aunt, uncle and cousins were going to Pennsylvania to spend Christmas with her mom's other sister and family. Dennis was meeting them there. They all thought it would be best to be in a totally different environment this holiday with no memories attached to it. Vinnie had a nice Christmas celebration with her before she left. At the last minute he got her an extra gift, a round gold disc necklace with her birthstone on it. On the back he had inscribed the word "Strong."

I never saw Maggie again. She ended up staying in Pennsylvania with her other aunt and family. I think it was a better fit for her. Vinnie went up to see her once or twice and they spoke on the phone a lot in the beginning. Eventually they lost contact. She and I spoke a few times and wrote letters to each other on and off for years. I sent her birthday and Christmas cards until I lost track of where she was.

I wish I could say Maggie lived happily ever after. Maybe she did, but that is not the part of the story I know. She "got in with the wrong crowd," as my mother would say and by the time she was in eleventh grade she was cutting class, had terminated two pregnancies and was taking some heavy-duty drugs. She ended up in juvenile detention for stealing a car. I am not even sure she graduated high school. She did a lot of odd jobs until she turned twenty-one, when she inherited her part of her parents' sizable estate. Then she disappeared.

When I was about thirty, a letter addressed to me arrived at my parent's house. It was from some penitentiary in California and it was from Maggie. I don't know why she was there. She never said and I never asked. She just wanted to thank me for helping her through a very difficult time in her life. She said she would always remember the kindness and love that Vinnie and I showed her. She told me it helped her get through some tough times. We corresponded for a while during her incarceration but I lost track of her again when she got out. I like to think she is living a happy, peaceful life somewhere surrounded by people who love her.

I always wondered what would have happened if Maggie had stayed on Long Island. Would she have had a different life? Did that decision to stay in Pennsylvania seal her fate? Would she have fared better if her tragedy had happened earlier in her life? Later? It was so long ago yet those questions still plague me. I will always hold a place in my heart for that seventh-grade girl with the dirty hair and wicked wit. That's how I like to remember her.

I missed Maggie for a long time as junior high continued. It was only two years then so the boys quickly moved on to ninth grade and high school. I was stuck in eighth grade once again without them. It was the time of gum wrapper chains, Clearasil, the introduction of Kotex and period cramps. Thank God eighth grade flew by.

In the summer of 1969, when I was between eighth and ninth grade, a music event was happening in upstate New York. A friend from school, Debra, told me her parents were taking her. Debra and I were in a lot of classes together, but we really didn't see each other outside of school. She would meet me in the bathroom every morning and we would paint our eyes with eye shadow and blue mascara. I was a little surprised when she asked if I wanted to go camping upstate with her family for a weekend in August.

I slept out a lot at friends and family's houses but I never went far away or with a family I didn't know. I never thought my mom would let me go so I said sure, but I would have to ask my parents. My mom was in touch with her mom twice while she talked it over with my dad. I was shocked they were leaning toward my going. My mom said it sounded nice. Unfortunately, or maybe fortunately, at the last minute her dad had to work and we couldn't go. I was secretly relieved. And that is the story of how I almost went to Woodstock when I was fourteen years old. We all know what the concert became and how important it was to the culture of that and future generations. Then there was that musical lineup and unforgettable concert moments. And the rain and mud and the drugs and lack of food. The concert got a lot of coverage on TV. I remember my mom standing in front of the television, looking at the footage, saying, "Thank God I didn't send you. We would be driving up there now to get you."

I have to admit I probably would have needed therapy for years from the experience. I was so naïve at fourteen. Vinnie and Rudy thought it was cool that I almost went, so that is how I spun the story. Truth is, I would have been scared shitless, probably crying for my mommy and daddy. But better things awaited me in August, 1969. I was just weeks away from entering high school. I thought things were going to change. And I was right. Just not in the way I expected.

## CHAPTER 8

# The Sammy Davis Jr. Encounters

I grew up listening to "The Rat Pack"—Frank Sinatra, Dean Martin and Sammy Davis Jr. One of them was always playing on our Victrola and every family member had his or her favorite. Frank Sinatra was a big deal for my mom and Aunt Mary, but for Aunt Angie, he was "it." She would have given up her children, husband, family, home and planet for him. She absolutely adored him. My mom enjoyed him as well but was more partial to Dean Martin. She liked his looks, voice and sense of humor.

My favorite was Sammy Davis Jr. He could sing, act, dance and tell jokes. He was in the movies, on TV and on Broadway. My dad called him the consummate performer and I have to agree. He was also active in social causes, marching for equality with Dr. Martin Luther King Jr. When I was twelve years old I bought myself a copy of his book *Yes I Can*, the story of his struggle from childhood to stardom and beyond. I couldn't put it down.

My youth was very sheltered. I was ingenuous, living in my all-white community. I had no idea what racism was. No one in my family had any black friends. I don't think I even knew a black person. I was in my own little white princess bubble. My mom grew up in a time of "colored people," a term she used not because she was racist but because that was all she knew. One day I was with her on a doctor's visit when a beautiful, young black woman entered the waiting room. My mom was hard of hearing and thought everyone else was too; she would often speak loudly when she should have been whispering. This was one of those times. My mom leaned over to me in this small office and said, "What a beautiful *colored* woman."

The woman looked at us and I just smiled sheepishly.

"She is ninety-four years old," I said, "and means no disrespect."

"Well," the woman replied abruptly, "at ninety-four she should know better."

As we got into the car after her appointment my mom asked what the woman had said to me. I didn't have the heart to tell her the truth. I told her she said my mom was pretty too. That's not to say I didn't try to improve my mom's political correctness. Whenever my mom would say "colored" I would ask her, "What color, Mom?"

"Black," she would reply.

"Then that is the word you should use," I would tell her. "Although you needn't specify color."

She would also use the word "queer" and I would correct her all the time. She would get frustrated, saying there were so many new things she had to remember. She was from a different era—no excuse, just another time.

In his book, Mr. Davis talked about dancing as a child with his father and uncle in the Will Mastin Trio. He shared the details of the horrible car accident that cost him his left eye. He bravely described the love he had for his second wife, May Britt and the pain and degradation they experienced because she was white. He told stories about performing in front of thousands of people but not being able to stay at the hotels at which he performed. He revealed how some restaurants wouldn't serve him and how others wouldn't even allow him to enter. As I read, I turned each page in tears.

Where had I been? At twelve years old I didn't have the slightest idea this other America existed. I had learned about slavery, well, at least the schoolbook version, whose lesson usually ended with the Emancipation Proclamation. My history books made it seem like everything was all right after that. I hadn't yet been taught it wasn't. But once I did I became outraged. Land of the free? Home of the brave? For whom? If we were brave we wouldn't permit this to happen. I had long discussions with my dad about this. I began to watch the news. I learned about the civil rights movement. (I guess they hadn't gotten up to that part in school yet.) I started following Robert Kennedy Jr. because I liked what he was saying about freedom and equality. I learned about segregation, a new concept for me. I read about the work of Dr. Martin Luther King Jr. Tragically, within months in 1968, both Senator Kennedy and Dr. King would be assassinated. This was a lot for a blossoming teenager.

I was already aware women were fighting for equality. I now realized there was much more of a struggle happening. I wondered what it must be like to be a *black* woman and became enraged. I told Vinnie and Rudy about everything I read. This new awareness eventually led me to a life of activism. I'd like to think I would have gotten there eventually but reading *Yes I Can* at such a young age provided a life-changing moment for me. Thank you, Mr. Davis. If my story about Sammy Davis Jr. stopped here I would be forever grateful to him. But there's more.

Mr. Davis lent his amazing talents to many diverse television shows. When we would get our weekly TV guide I would look to see if he was appearing in any programs that week. I would arrange my schedule so I was available to see his guest performance that night as VCRs and DVDs weren't even dreamt of yet. Aside from the typical variety shows like *Hollywood Palace*, he also appeared on *The Patty Duke Show*, *Ben Casey*, *Batman*, *I Dream of Jeannie*, *77 Sunset Strip* and *The Rifleman*, to name just a few. He gave that famous surprise kiss to Archie Bunker on *All in the*

*Family*. And his tag line, "Here comes the judge," on the television show *Laugh In* became a cultural classic. My parents always watched with me. They got a kick out of how excited I would get to see him.

My appreciation of Mr. Davis's life struggles and amazing talents grew. And then one day I got the opportunity to see him in person. I was fifteen years old and my parents were going to take me to see him in concert at the Copacabana in New York City. I wanted to get him a present with the hopes that I might be able to give it to him. Vinnie and I went to World Imports, a great gift store in Roosevelt Field. We picked out a brown, leather braided bracelet. Vinnie tried it on my wrist and said if it fit me, it would fit him because he was thin too. I wrapped it and included a letter about how his book had impacted me and my friends.

October 25, 1970. I can't remember what I wore but I am sure it was fabulous because I was going into Manhattan to see Sammy Davis Jr. My father hated the city, rarely going there, so this was a big deal for all of us. I don't know what I was expecting but I was a little disappointed when we got there. The club was in the middle of the block with an awning and entrance that had its name on it. That was it. There were no big lights or fuss out front. We were brought to a table near the stage. It wasn't a raised stage like at the movies. It was at the same level we were. There was a microphone, stool, water and a few towels and napkins. It was very close to where we were sitting. I was surprised how intimate the Copacabana was. No matter where you sat you had a great view. It was hard for me to imagine that in a few minutes Sammy Davis Jr. was going to be standing there.

First to perform that evening was a young singer named Debra. I can't remember her last name. Ironically, almost fifty years later I would work with her at Harborfields Elementary School in Suffolk County on Long Island. Talk about a small world. Then a comedian performed. Then it was Sammy Davis Jr.'s time. Our table was positioned so he had to walk right past us to get to the stage. The first thing I noticed about him was how petite he was. I thought what a huge talent in such a tiny frame.

Sammy Davis Jr. was phenomenal. He performed for over two and a half hours, smoking at least a pack of cigarettes during that time. He was often lighting a new one with the one he was still smoking. Most of the time they were left burning in the ashtray, but I remember he smoked a lot. He sang, danced, told jokes, did impressions and shared stories, some funny and some heartwarming. It was and remains one of my ten best nights ever!

After his third encore he walked by our table again. I tried to give him my gift but failed to get his attention. A kind security guard saw my disappointment and with my dad's permission, took me by the hand and led me through the kitchen to a small freight elevator. He grabbed the doors just as they were closing. When they opened there stood Sammy Davis Jr., drenched in sweat from his performance. I entered the elevator and gave Mr. Davis the gift. Crying, I told him how amazing he was. He took the gift, thanked me and leaned over and kissed me on the cheek. As I was led off the elevator and the doors closed he gave me a cute little wave and held up my gift. Then the security guard, my nameless hero, took me back to my parents. I sat down and cried even more, trying to tell them and the crowd gathered around us what happened. I went over to where he had just performed and took the napkin he was using to wipe his brow. I have no idea why. Maybe I thought one day I could clone him from his sweat. The weird thing is, I still have it.

About two or three days after the show Mr. Davis was appearing on *The Merv Griffin Show*. As usual I was ready and waiting. Merv performed his opening monologue then the program went to a commercial. My dad got up to go to the bathroom and my mom went in their bedroom for something or other. As Mr. Davis was introduced I yelled to my parents that it was on; there were no pause buttons then. Suddenly I let out a scream that had my parents running into the living room, visibly shaken. On Mr. Davis's right wrist was the bracelet I gave him. I couldn't believe it. I started jumping up and down in front of the television as my parents laughed with excitement. I ran to the phone and called Vinnie to tell him to turn on channel five and check out Sammy's wrist. I then abruptly hung up. I don't remember anything that was said or sung on the show. I was too focused on that bracelet. Vinnie came to the house after the show and was excited he had helped me pick out the gift.

A few days later I received a beautiful letter from Mr. Davis, dated October 27, 1970:

> Thank you ever so much for the lovely gift. I'll wear it with the wish of luck you gave me. Best wishes to you in all your endeavors in life.

Peace,

Sammy Davis Jr.

It was signed by him with a black marker, not a stamp of his signature. I still have that letter too and the envelope with the six-cent stamp. Now, if my story about Sammy Davis Jr. ended here, I would be ecstatic. But wait, there is STILL more.

A few years later, Vinnie surprised Rudy and me with tickets to see Sammy Davis Jr. at the Westbury Music Fair. He had gotten up early one day to be at the box office at nine o'clock when the tickets went on sale in order to make sure he got good seats. This time I remember exactly what I wore: a pink suede miniskirt with fringe at the hem and a matching embroidered vest. I wore a purple turtleneck underneath. The sides of my hair were tied up in a purple bow. And I wore lots of purple eye shadow. And for some unknown reason I had on white tights, the one and only time

I ever wore them. Ugh! How do I remember exactly what I was wearing? Well, I have this little picture ...

The Westbury Music Fair is a theater in the round so every seat is great. An accomplished performer like Sammy Davis Jr. knew exactly how to work the stage so you weren't spending the entire night looking at the back of his head. Sometimes he would walk around the stage and sometimes the stage would spin around very slowly. I always wondered if the stage ever malfunctioned, sped up and threw some unsuspecting performer out to row R.

Sammy (as I now referred to him because we had history) was a "people's performer." He would chat with members of the audience and let them take pictures with him. In those days there were no announcements saying, "flash photography is not allowed." I was clicking away all night with my Kodak Instamatic. This particular camera had a four-bulb square cube on the top that didn't always go off. Vinnie and Rudy kept nudging me to get up and take a close-up picture. All of a sudden I only had two pictures left in the camera. Finally Rudy got up, took my hand and walked me to the stage just as Sammy was coming around. He was talking at the time and stopped when he saw us. He said to me, "Come on down. Come on stage."

Rudy took the camera from me. As I walked on stage Sammy put his arm around me and we both smiled. Rudy took the picture. I thanked Sammy and gave him a kiss on the cheek. Rudy had to hold me up while I walked back to my seat. I was shaking so much I thought my knees were going to give out. Now for all of Rudy's wonderful qualities, photography was not one of his best. He was notorious for cutting people's heads off in pictures. We had one shot and I worried it would be of our knees and shoes. The next day we took it to our local pharmacy to be developed. There was no one-hour turnover. The store had to send it out to be developed. I waited three agonizing days. Finally there it was—the most beautiful picture of me and Sammy Davis Jr., with our heads. That is how I remember exactly what I was wearing. I have a picture of it, me in my pink suede outfit and Sammy in his hot pants and knee-high boots. (He made it work.) I was saddened but not shocked to learn years later that Sammy died of lung cancer at the early age of sixty-four. I felt privileged to have witnessed his brilliance and kindness not once but twice. And my boys, as always, were a special part of it.

Now, when I watch performances of the Rat Pack, I cringe at the racist jokes they made at Sammy's expense. Was it just the times? Those men should have known better. They had a moment and a platform, but they went for the joke instead. Yes, they might have thought and acted differently in their private lives. Shame on them. Shame on all of us.

In the sixties and seventies, as now, resolution of such problems required awareness, understanding and mutual respect. Change begins with the individual. We have had a black president and a black vice president. Commercials, movie and television present interracial couples with children of all shades. Many people don't notice or care. I hope Sammy Davis Jr. is watching and smiling.

## CHAPTER 9

# The Realization

One late summer afternoon before sophomore year Marie and I were hanging out at my house when we decided we would take a walk to Friendly's for ice cream. Instead of going the shorter distance along the busy main street of Old Country Road, we decided to walk the quieter neighborhood of Birchwood. This neighborhood was built after ours. The houses were twice the size and cost of our neighborhood homes. The girls that lived there shopped in Macy's and Orbach's, not Mays and Korvettes. They went away to summer camp and had their nails done. These were the kids we met in junior high.

As Marie and I headed toward the back route to Birchwood we passed Aunt Angie's house. Vinnie and Rudy were in the driveway playing basketball. Basketball was one of the few sports Rudy and Vinnie didn't play in school, which allowed all of us to actually go to a sporting event together. The boys were a little sweaty and had their shirts off. I noticed for the first time that Rudy was not a skinny little Italian boy anymore. He had grown into a lean, muscular athlete. I was surprised at how that made me feel. We called over and told them we were going to Friendly's. Never thinking they would stop playing, we asked them if they wanted to join us. To our surprise they said yes and started to wipe themselves down with towels. Rudy looked great, I thought, as he walked toward us, pulling his shirt down over his abs. He was all muscle without an ounce of fat to pinch anywhere. I got that same surprising feeling again.

Both Rudy and Vinnie were growing into handsome young men. I use to call them Ying and Yang because their coloring was so different. Rudy had a darker complexion with thick, wavy brown hair, sparkling brown eyes and a smile that could melt an iceberg. He had this perfectly classic Roman nose that defined his face and made him look very Italian and extremely handsome. He was about five eight. He always told us he would have a growth spurt in his twenties. He didn't. Vinnie, on the other hand, was already six feet tall with a very fair complexion and curly, blond ringlets. He had the most amazing blue eyes. They were the same color as my mom's and they use to tease her that Vinnie was really her son. Yet as different as the boys appeared, if they stood next to each other you could tell they were related. They had the same mannerisms, voice and personalities. They also shared the exact same sense of humor, which often drove me crazy. They were both athletically gifted. Rudy was a runner, with track giving him a sculpted physique. One of his teammates, Brad, used to call him Gladiator because he had big, muscular "gladiator" thighs. Soon everyone on the team called him that. Rudy said he hated that nickname, but I think he secretly enjoyed it. Football and lacrosse gave Vinnie a great body too but he was my cousin. It would be icky to actually acknowledge that.

The four of us walked to Friendly's in record time. I think the boys were still hyped from their basketball game. Marie and I kept falling behind and I kept looking at Rudy's behind. What is going on here? We sat down in the exact same booth we were in when the Great Chocolate Fribble Incident happened. This would be a story carried down through time. We were there to witness it in person.

It was after a Friday night basketball game. These events were always well attended. Afterward, if we had rides, we would go to an Italian restaurant, Borelli's, for pizza. It is still there and the pizza is just as delicious. We were usually on foot, though, and would take the short walk from the high school to Friendly's. After a game the entire restaurant was wall to wall teens with a few families and elderly couples sprinkled among the booths and counter. It was THE place to be.

One night this guy Jack, who was in the same grade as Rudy and Vinnie, walked in with his "freshmen de jour," as I liked to call them; young, unsuspecting, innocent girls who fell for his fake charm and good looks. It was typical of him to try and sleep with them and then move on. I always wanted to tell them to stay away, as if they would listen to me. If it sounds like I didn't like Jack, it is because I didn't. He was arrogant and self-centered and could be outright mean. He would insult someone or make fun of them for a laugh and I don't think he ever showed empathy toward anyone. He was handsome in a way others often swooned over, but he wasn't my type on so many levels. One night we were all hanging out at the Carmen Avenue pool when he came up to me and in a loud voice said, "How come you are so skinny but your tits are so big?"

I was shocked and embarrassed as everyone stopped and turned toward us. I looked at him and said, "You'll never know." That got a lot of oohs and aahs from the crowd as Jack stared at my chest and crawled away. How can you like someone like that?

This particular night Jack came strolling into Friendly's with this adorable, petite ninth grade girl on his arm. She was floating on air to be with this handsome upper classmate. They sat at a booth near us and quickly ordered. I paid him as little attention as possible. I wasn't going to feed his ego.

A little while later I started to hear some commotion coming from their direction. I turned around just as Jack picked up his chocolate Fribble and poured it over this little girl's head. She started crying immediately as the place got silent. I ran out of our booth and escorted her to the bathroom. Low chatter began to fill the restaurant. Marie followed me in and we tried to clean her up as the waiter tried to clean the mess Jack had made at his seat. When it was obvious a few paper towels were not going to help this little girl, we slipped out the back door. I went around to the front window and motioned Rudy to come out. I told him we were going to walk to my house so she could wash up and then take her home. He and Vinnie left with us and the manager was nice enough not to charge us for our half-eaten food. I heard he asked Jack to leave.

Now here the four of us were in the same booth. We started talking about that crazy night. Of course I had to add, as I always did, what an ass Jack was. Then, for some reason I still don't understand, I started to tell them the Alka-Seltzer story (see the next chapter). I had never shared this with anyone and don't know what prompted me to do so then. As I told this story I watched the compassion and sadness grow on Rudy's face. It was like I was seeing him for the first time and he was very handsome. When I was finished he got up and hugged me. We had hugged a gazillion times over the years, but this one startled me. I sat back down a little rattled, wondering what was going on.

As I was attacking my vanilla chocolate chip sundae, I kept looking at Rudy and blinking my eyes shut, as if when I opened them again the old Rudy would be sitting in front of me. Nope. It was still this handsome new one. Rudy noticed my blinking and asked me if I was alright. "Yeah," I said. "Something in my eye."

He got out of his seat, came over to me and said, "Let me see."

He bent over and our faces were about an inch apart as he pulled on my lower lid to take a better look. "I don't see anything," he said as he got back into his seat. "Try not to rub it."

Again I thought, *what the heck is going on?* This was Rudy, my brother, best friend and confidant. How could I be having feelings even remotely related to what was happening? But it was right in front of me. The kindest, funniest, most generous little boy I ever knew had grown into this incredibly handsome young man. All of a sudden there was no one else in the world. Not even Paul McCartney. On that day, in Friendly's, in that booth, I began my long crush on Rudy.

The whole thing was weird. I thought as time went on the feelings would go away. But, to my surprise, they got stronger. I told no one, not even Janie. It took me a long time to even fully admit it to myself. I tried my best to act normal around him and I think I was pretty successful. No one suspected a thing, least of all him. I watched as he dated one of the prettiest girls in school, holding her hand and kissing her at a party. I sat next to him on a chaise lounge as he held hands with a bikini-clad girlfriend sitting on the other side of him. And I listened as he talked about asking the new girl at school to the movies. I just went about my business, knowing these girls would never have the relationship I had with Rudy. It dated back to before I was born and would last forever. Still it was hard sometimes and very confusing.

Most of my girlfriends were dating now, some seriously, some casually. I wasn't, but I must admit I never put myself out there. I would watch Gina or Janie flirt with a guy and think, *I could never do that.* I never felt comfortable enough in my own adolescent skin. I saw myself as too tall, too thin, gangly and awkward, with a large nose, bad skin and braces—I could go on and on. I was my own worst enemy. The only time I felt graceful and beautiful was when I was dancing. I would hide under different tutus and leotards and dance a pretend life, one where I was a beautiful swan. I laugh now when people say they remember me as very confident in high school. I had no self-confidence. Not a drop.

One Friday after school, when no one was in a particular hurry to get home, a bunch of us were hanging out near the gym area. No one was bothering to chase us home yet. It was some of the guys from football, including Rudy and his current girlfriend, our friends Erick and Gerry, Vinnie, me and, ugh, Jack. I don't know how we got on the subject, but I started talking about a behavioral analysis survey I was working on for my math class, which I would later expand and adapt for my intro to psychology class.

My hypothesis was that if you asked a high school teenager to name three characteristics they look for in choosing a boyfriend or girlfriend, attraction/looks would always be at the top of the list, as opposed to smart or intelligent, which I felt was all I had to offer. Gerry spoke first.

"We're teenagers. How smart can we be?"

We all laughed.

"Okay," I said. "What are your top three things?"

He thought for a moment.

"Good hygiene, fine manners and a job."

Again we laughed. Erick spoke up next.

"I like big boobies. What? I'm being honest. I'm in high school. I have plenty of time to talk quantum physics later."

Erick never had a filter but he was always kind and funny, not nasty like Jack. We were all shocked he had even heard of quantum physics. (This is the same Erick who bet kids at a party that he could crazy glue his nostrils closed. He left the party with $57.00 and a bloody nose.)

"That's right, Erick," I agreed. "When I walk down the street I don't hear guys yell out, 'Hey, check out those brains.'"

"That's because you have big boobies. Nice ones."

"I don't know if I should take that as a compliment or slap you."

He turned and lifted his butt to me and laughed, "Oh, definitely slap me."

He was too adorable and sweet to ever get mad at.

Gerry then turned to Rudy, who looked at his new girlfriend, and he asked, "What about you, Rudy?"

"Well, you do have to have things to talk about, things in common."

*We do*, I thought.

"And you do have to be attracted to that person."

*I can be cute*, I thought.

"But to me the biggest thing is a sense of humor. You have to be able to laugh together."

Trifecta!! The voice inside my head kept screaming, *"Look, I'm right in front of you!"*

Then Gerry turned to me.

"Well," I said, "a sense of humor is a must for me too. And intelligent with a social conscience. And kind. You know, in a world where you can be anything, you should be kind."

"Sounds like a greeting card," Vinnie said.

"I think I saw it on one," I shot back.

"So," Gerry said. "Have you found this funny, kind, smart guy?"

I must have turned bright red because they all started howling and teasing me.

"Who is it?" they all asked, almost at once.

I wouldn't say anything for a while and then Gerry said, "Spill it."

"Well, I have had a crush on someone for a long time now ..."

"Who? Who?"

Erick piped up. "Is it me? Oh, please let it be me!"

We all laughed.

"It better not be me," Jack snarled.

"Not for all the money in the world."

I looked at Rudy and he was smiling at me with a question mark all over his face.

Again Gerry said, "Who?"

"I am not going to tell you. He doesn't even know."

"Wait," Gerry said. "You've liked someone for a while and you haven't told them? Why not?"

"Because if he wanted to ask me out, he has had plenty of opportunities."

"Oh no," Gerry said. "We have to tell him."

"We? Can *we* please be done with this conversation?" I said, trying to get off the subject.

Gerry looked at Rudy and Vinnie and asked them, "You know?"

Vinnie shook his head as Rudy said, "News to me."

I got up and couldn't get away from them fast enough. "You're like a bunch of little old ladies."

I saw Rudy and Vinnie later that weekend and they asked me who this mystery person was. I told them I'd rather not say and they left it at that. They never asked me again. Meanwhile Gerry couldn't let go of it. Every time I saw him he would mention a different name. This went on forever. It became a joke between us. And my survey? Turns out I was wrong. Attraction/looks was only number one in 18 percent of the kids I asked and was in the top three only 28 percent of the time. Smart/brains/bright came up 23 percent as number one and in 53 percent of the top three answers. At the time I didn't look at male versus female responses. I wish I still had the data to do so. And the number one characteristic across the board? Yup, sense of humor!

CHAPTER 10

# The Alka-Seltzer Story

I was in eighth grade. I believe it was late fall, maybe early spring. The time of the year doesn't matter. The incident would stay with me forever. It was between classes, third going into fourth period. I would always take the long route to my Spanish class so I could walk past Kevin, my latest crush.

Kevin was our newsboy. Every Saturday he would knock on our door and yell, "Collect." I would give him the envelope with the fifty-cent tip and weather and time permitting, we would sit outside my house and talk, sometimes for an hour or so. I had grown up with Kevin. We weren't in the same elementary school classes but I knew him from lunch, the playground and around the neighborhood. He was smart and athletic and could be really sweet. COULD be. Every once in a while I would be on the receiving end of his mean side, the bully. If I passed him in the hall he might say, "Nose," referring to the nose too large for my skinny face. Sometimes he would pretend to cough or sneeze and say "Bones" or "Metal Face," referencing my weight or braces. He even called me "Pimple Face." He should cough, I mean talk. We all were going through puberty. We all had pimples. (Except Rudy. That boy never had a pimple.) But in spite of how mean Kevin could be, I was still crushing on him.

On this fall or spring or even winter day, I was passing Kevin in the hallway. He was with our friend Gary. Kevin was always nice to me when we were alone, but I could never guarantee what he would do or say when he had an audience. Would I get a hello today or a sneeze? I got a note. Kevin passed me, smiled and handed me a note. It was folded in the popular triangle, easy for passing, especially in class, and easy to hide. This one was particularly thick and a little crunchy.

I was over the moon. What could it say? Maybe he wanted to hang out after school or go for a bike ride on Saturday. Maybe he was asking me on a real date, like to the movies. I went into my Spanish class and asked Mrs. Smith if I could go to the bathroom, carefully concealing the note in my hand lest she discover the real reason for my wanting to go. Mrs. Smith was one of my all-time favorite teachers, right up there with my science teacher, Mr. Crowley and my future psychology teacher, Mr. Conn. She was the only teacher of color in the entire district of two high schools and four elementary schools. She was funny, open-minded and very patient. I didn't know it at the time, but I had a learning disability in language. In those days there was no testing or labeling of special needs, no accommodations and certainly no individual education plans. Students were placed in honors, Regents—where I was—and regular classes, which earned a non-Regents diploma. Kids also went to special classes where they took courses like cosmetology or small engine repair. They were always all-female or all-male classes and on the other side of the building. Then there were the students who were labeled "mentally retarded," an absolutely horrific title that was common at the time. They were always bussed to a "special" school that no one ever saw.

Mrs. Smith realized everyone learns differently. I had difficulty with Spanish no matter how hard I tried. And I tried. Mrs. Smith appreciated my efforts and always changed my 68s to a 70. Spanish was the only class I ever got below an 86 in. It kept me from the high honor roll every time. After six years of taking it, I can only speak and understand a few words.

Mrs. Smith said I could go to the girl's room and I literally skipped down the hall into the bathroom. I couldn't open that note fast enough. No time to go into a stall. I was leaning against the green-and-black tiled wall, trying frantically to figure out how to open this triangle. I finally got it open and out fell a tinfoil packet of Alka-Seltzer. I didn't get it. Did Kevin think I was sick? Then I read the note.

Every once in a while, if you are lucky or paying attention, you will have a moment or two (or three) in your life when everything changes. I'm not talking about those obvious moments like a marriage, birth or death. I'm referring to a moment that might start out quietly, like with a package of Alka-Seltzer and morph into a moment you carry with you the rest of your life, the moment a new vision, a philosophy of life, if you will, emerges. Here was one of my moments, scrawled across this paper in five simple words, put together in such a hateful and hurtful way. In big letters across my note, Kevin had written, "*YOUR FACE MAKES ME SICK.*"

I had to reread it twice to make sure I was seeing it correctly. I felt my knees buckle while my skinny back slid painfully against the raised green and black tiles, registering every bump where one tile ended and a new one began. I was sitting on the floor now. I was sitting in disbelief on a dirty bathroom floor with an Alka-Seltzer in one hand and this note in the other. I started to cry and cry.

I don't recall which girls came in and out of that bathroom while I was sitting there, crying, on the floor. I do remember some faceless friends asking if I was alright. I said I was. I'm not sure how long I was sitting there, but it must have been a while. Mrs. Smith sent a classmate to the bathroom to check on me. The poor thing walked in while I was having a particularly intense crying fit. She saw me sitting on the floor, wailing in appropriate dramatic fashion and ran out of that bathroom as fast as she could. The look on her face was pure fear.

A few minutes later Mrs. Smith walked in. In those days a teacher would think nothing about leaving their classroom unsupervised for a few minutes. I guess teachers felt they didn't have to worry about kids jumping out the window, going through a teacher's grade book or dancing on chairs. We were all too scared to even think about those things. Well, most of us were. She saw me on the floor, didn't think twice and joined me. In a beautiful navy dress, she sat on that dirty floor with me.

By this time I couldn't even speak. I just showed her the Alka-Seltzer and note, both still clutched in my hands. She looked at them, then looked at me and her eyes filled up with tears. She put her arm around me and said, "You are beautiful, inside and out. You are caring, kind, funny and smart. You have loyal friends. I have met your parents and they are wonderful people. Teachers and staff adore you. You are very loved."

And then she said five words that still resonate with me today, as if to erase Kevin's five words. "Don't let this define you." I didn't understand the significance of her wisdom at that time, but I now comprehend the weight of those words. She told me I could go to the cafeteria or library if I wanted to. I didn't have to go back to class. Then she hugged me and went back to her students. I stayed on that bathroom floor for a long time, thinking. She was right. Even at thirteen years old, I sensed the importance of what she meant. I could make this the worst moment of my life or I could take charge of it and turn it around. Making the negative a positive eventually became a new way of looking at things. For me, this was so my dad. He was a glass half-full guy. Hell, he was just happy to have a glass. Not so much my mom. She not only wanted a glass but she wanted it filled to the top with an extra pitcher on the side. The glass half-filled philosophy remains with me to this day.

Did Kevin's note hurt? Absolutely! But I decided in that bathroom, on that floor, I would never let anyone hurt me like that again. My nanny used to say, "People will only do to you what you let them." I was not going to let a selfish, nasty, eighth grade boy define who I was. I couldn't change him and his insensitive, cruel ways, but I could change the way I reacted. And yet, after all these years, that fourth period so long ago remains one of the most significant forty minutes of my life.

I never mentioned that letter to anyone except Mrs. Smith, until I told the story in Friendly's the afternoon I fell in love with Rudy. Why then, I don't know. I never acknowledged that note to Kevin and we remained good friends right through high school and graduation. I also never threw that note or the Alka-Seltzer away. I brought them to my tenth high school reunion. No Kevin. He was at the twentieth reunion and I managed to get him alone for a few minutes. He had moved away and was very successful in his field. The ladies still loved him.

I pulled out the note and crumbled packet of Alka-Seltzer that was now all powder, if any was left in there at all. He saw both and, like Mrs. Smith so many years ago on that bathroom floor, his eyes filled up with tears. He said, "That is my handwriting, but I don't remember this. Obviously it was important to you if you kept it all these years." He then paused to catch his breath. "I am so sorry. I don't remember myself being this mean. I am so very sorry."

I shrugged my shoulders and grinned a smile that said, "Well, you were." As he went to hand them back to me I pushed his hands back toward him. "That has been rattling around in my sock drawer for twenty-four years. You keep it now." He put them in his pocket, leaned forward and hugged me. The next day he sent me flowers.

## CHAPTER 11

# The Kiss

The fall of 1972 was Rudy and Vinnie's last football season together. I had been going to their games since their shoulder pads were bigger than they were. They were seniors now and a certain amount of melancholy was attached to the excitement.

It was a tradition that the Friday night before a Saturday home game someone from the football team would host a dinner, usually pasta. All the team members, some parents, coaches and teachers would attend. When Rudy and Vinnie hosted them, I always slipped in under the disguise of family and cook.

From an early age I loved to cook. By the time I was in high school I had mastered some special dishes. My best was lasagna, my grandmother's recipe. Rudy liked it but Vinnie LOVED it. The previous two years I had been making it for his football dinners and everyone came to expect it. It was a lot of work. There were a lot of hungry boys at these dinners. I would take off from school the Wednesday before and cook all day. It always tasted better when it was a day or two old and had time to settle.

Vinnie was having his last pasta dinner the final Friday in September and asked me to make my lasagna. I would have been insulted if he hadn't. We went shopping together and this year he took off on Wednesday to help me. It was a joy, just the two of us in the kitchen, music blasting.

We would break out into an occasional dance every now and then. I don't think I've ever had so much fun cooking before or since. And the lasagna was delicious.

It was a packed house that Friday night. I think every football player showed up plus my parents, Rudy's parents, the coaches and a few teachers. Catherine and her boyfriend, Johnny, also came. Johnny had been a great football player in high school and the coaches were thrilled to see him again. Motown was blasting as usual and there was dancing in the street, literally. Everyone clapped when I came out with my lasagna. I did have to give Vinnie credit that year as well. It was a wonderful evening filled with nostalgia for the seniors and wonder for the freshmen. Endings and beginnings often come with such emotions. Passing the torch is not always easy.

My mom had baked some of her famous Italian cookies and my favorite chocolate cake. She asked Rudy and me to go to the house to pick them up. We didn't mind, thinking we could both grab a cookie on the way back. They always were the first to go. Rudy and I walked out of Aunt Angie's driveway, among the trees that were beginning to pop with deep yellows and bright oranges, toward my house. While we were crossing the street he casually said to me, "Donna and I broke up."

I stopped and turned to him and said, "I'm sorry. Are you alright?"

I continued across the street, hearing him respond behind me with a simple "Yeah."

We got to my house and as I went to get the desserts from the dining room table I heard Rudy yell, "How come you never ask me what happened?" I wasn't sure what he meant. As I walked out of the dining room, balancing trays of cookies and a cake, I gave him a quizzical glance. He was looking back at me the same way.

"When I break up with someone how come you never ask me why?"

"It's none of my business," I retorted. "I figure if you want to tell me you will." I looked at his face and laughed, "Do you want to tell me?"

"Yes, I do. *She* broke up with *me*. She said she really liked me, but didn't want to be second."

"Second to what? Football? Friends?" I didn't get it.

"No. Second to you."

"ME?" I was totally shocked. Sure, I remembered having accompanied Rudy and Donna on several dates over the past couple of weeks. But Rudy had insisted each time that I come along. I hadn't thought about how my presence might upset Donna. Now I felt guilty. And nervous, which is why I began to talk a mile a minute.

"Yes, you," he said. "She told me that I liked you."

"Well, of course you like me. We've known each other since we were babies. We love each other. We're family."

"No, she meant in another way. Like 'LIKE' you." He moved his hand back and forth between us.

"Oh my God, that is so silly. Rudy, I'm like your sister. You wouldn't date your sister."

He quickly snapped back, "I might if she looked like you."

I began wondering if maybe I was becoming a little too obvious. Maybe my secret crush wasn't as secret as I thought. I started to panic.

"So?" I asked, trying to sound as normal as possible. "What did you say to her?"

"Nothing."

"Nothing? You said nothing? You didn't deny it? Tell her she was crazy? Fight for her a little?"

Rudy shrugged. "I didn't know what to say. It was so weird, especially after what Gerry said to me the other morning."

*Oh God*, I thought. "Now I am really confused. What did he say to you?"

"He told me he was sure I was your secret crush."

"What? Oh, please, Rudy. He has guessed it was everyone in the school. He is obsessed with getting a name from me. You were probably the last one left."

"Which makes me wonder if it is me."

My whole body felt like it was on fire and my head started pounding the most unpleasant rhythm. I wanted to say, "YES! YES! It has always been you." But for some reason the words were stuck in my gut. Instead I said, "So let me get this straight. Donna tells you that you like me and Gerry tells you that I like you?"

"Yeah. That's it, pretty much. Weird, right?"

"Very," I said, too quickly.

"I mean, neither of those are true, right?" he said, sounding like he was trying to convince himself.

I started to sense an awkwardness rising up between us. I knew this was going to haunt us if we didn't resolve it right now. So out of my mouth, before I could stop it, spilled the words "Kiss me." Rudy looked at me surprised, but not disgusted, which was good. I continued. "Yeah, kiss me. It is going to be creepy and then we can move on."

"What if it's not?" he whispered.

"Then everything changes," I said, praying he didn't hear how hopeful I was. I mean, this was it. The moment I had waited and dreamt about for so long. I thought he might be repulsed by the idea of kissing me, but instead he said sure, almost anxiously. He came toward me and I instinctively stepped back. He turned his head to the side, shaking it like he couldn't believe he was going to do this. For a second I thought he was going to change his mind. Then we both laughed at the absurdity of what we were about to do. When he turned back toward me his face was different. Serious. His eyes looked at me like I had always hoped they would.

He took his hands and cupped my face, pulling it toward him. And then, in an instant, I was kissing Rudy. It wasn't just a quick smooch. It was a deliberate, deep kiss. His lips were soft, warm, gentle, moist. It was an experienced kiss but it felt fresh, new and wonderful to me. Not having ever been kissed like this before, I didn't know how long was appropriate. *Do I pull back? Will he? Oh, shut up*, I thought, *and just enjoy it*. My heart was racing and my breathing labored. From one kiss. Finally our lips separated and we both looked down, just our foreheads and arms touching. I noticed Rudy was also breathing heavily and I thought maybe this was where the term "heavy petting" came from. I was thinking way too much by now.

We didn't say anything for about fifteen seconds, which seemed like an eternity. I was enjoying the way that kiss made me feel when he whispered, "Not creepy. No, not creepy at all."

Although we were still locked at the foreheads, I managed to quietly breathe out, "No, not at all."

Then we looked at each other, both managing a sly grin, while I raised my eyebrows as if to say, "What now?" Rudy looked at me, read my mind and said, "We better make sure."

He moved forward toward me again, only this time I didn't move backward. He leaned in and kissed me. It was harder, longer, more passionate, with a little tongue, which at first made me giggle. When we broke apart I grabbed the cake and handed it to him, took the cookies and headed for the door. I didn't want to hear that the first kiss was a mistake and this was really creepy. He stopped me in my mad dash out the door and kissed me again! Then he smiled and said, "I could kiss you all night."

I responded, "I could let you!" and we both laughed.

He then did something he would do over and over again, which I loved. He kissed me on the top of my head as I asked, "Now what?"

He replied, "Everything changes!"

And indeed it did from that moment forward. I walked out my front door into what looked and felt like a brand-new neighborhood. As we walked back to Aunt Angie's I suggested maybe we should keep this a secret for now. He shot back sarcastically that he was going to have a sky-writer draw a heart with our initials.

"Too much?" he smirked.

I gave him a shot in the arm, to which he responded, "Girlfriend abuse!"

Girlfriend. I was Rudy's girlfriend? I liked the sound of that. As we started to walk across the street I stopped and looked at him, muttering out of the corner of my mouth, "It was you."

"What?" he said, seeming genuinely puzzled.

"My crush. It was you. It was always you." I started walking up Aunt Angie's driveway. I turned back to look at him standing in the middle of the street holding the Tupperware cake plate. He was shaking his head and grinning a shit-ass grin.

## CHAPTER 12

# The Reveal

When we walked in the backyard everything looked the same, but everything had changed for Rudy and me. He waltzed in with his usual swagger and put the desserts he was carrying on the table. I walked in thinking everybody knew. They were all looking at us. *They MUST know.* Plus I had this huge smile on my face. Gerry said to me, "What the hell are you grinning about?"

Always such a doll!

"Not you!" I said, laughing.

I put the cookies and cake down and then didn't know where to go. *What do I do? If I go over to Rudy will he perceive me as insecure? If I don't go will he think I am being distant?* Were there new boundaries now? I started to panic and ran inside. If everything had really changed, then my interaction with Rudy would have to change, be adjusted. I didn't want the friendship part of it to change. I just wanted to add kissing.

I was really freaking out. After all these years, I didn't know how to behave around Rudy. I didn't like that at all. Although I enjoyed the kissing and the idea of being his girlfriend, I would give all that up for the comfort we always had together. I never second-guessed anything I did with Rudy. It was all so natural. Now I wondered if it was ever going to feel like that again. I sat in my aunt's den, pondering this over and over, listening to the music and laughter outside, wondering where I belonged. Vinnie walked by on his way to the bathroom and saw me sitting there.

"Are you okay?" he asked, always concerned about me.

"Yeah. I'm just thinking."

"Oh, I thought so. I saw the smoke."

I shot him a sarcastic grin. He was now in the den with me.

"Anything I can help you with?" he said sincerely.

"You just did," I said as I got up to give him a hug. And he really did. I decided I would interact with Rudy the way I always had. If I wasn't sure I would ask myself what I would do if we weren't dating. It was as simple as that. We would find our new rhythm, but in the meantime I would dance to the old song. I went outside and sat down next to my dad. We split a huge piece of my mom's chocolate cake and ice cream.

Around 9:00 p.m. the coach told the team it was time to clean up. He always made the football players help out at the house that hosted the dinner. Of course my mom, Aunt Angie and Mama Rose already had the kitchen spotless so the boys started breaking down the tables and chairs, gathering the garbage and tidying up.

It was a big game the next day and Coach Axman wanted to make sure the boys were rested for it. Highly unlikely. He knew most of them would be headed to one of the two local bars, Gatsby's or the Mai Tai. But he felt he at least had to make the effort. I packed up some of my lasagna for Gerry, who was over the moon, telling me he was going to have it for breakfast.

The boys slowly started to leave, thanking the adults for everything. Most even came over to me and thanked me for my lasagna. They were always very kind to me, probably because of my relationship with Rudy and Vinnie. I always felt like an honorary football member. They even ordered me a football jersey with my name and the number 00 on it. My mom altered it in just the right places so I could wear it as a mini dress. Vinnie always said I looked hot in it. I would remind him I was his cousin. Before I left I went over to Rudy and told him I was going to leave my pocketbook there and he should bring it over to my house. I don't know why I even had my pocketbook, but it now served as an excuse to see Rudy alone and maybe get in some more smooch time.

My parents and I finally walked home, talking about what a great night it was and how sad we were it was the last one Aunt Angie would host. I said good night and went upstairs. My mom started putting the leftovers away while my dad turned on the TV. About ten minutes later I heard a knock on the door and Rudy walked in. He rarely knocked so I was surprised. My dad said I was upstairs and I heard Rudy taking the stairs two at a time.

"Oh, thank you for bringing me my pocketbook, Rudy," I said in a loud enough voice for my dad to hear—the worst acting ever.

"You're welcome. I thought you would need it," Rudy replied the same way.

Then he grabbed me and we started kissing. Our first real make-out session. You would think we were ten years old the way we were giggling and carrying on. He asked me if I would wait for him after the game tomorrow.

"Don't I always wait for you and Vinnie?"

"Yeah, but I wanted to be sure."

He stayed for about forty-five minutes. I knew he gave up going drinking with the guys to come over.

"Are you going to go home or to the bar?" I asked.

"Home. I'm tired. It has been a very eventful night." He smiled. "This is going to be good. Really good. I'm excited."

"Me too," I said as we walked down the stairs toward the door.

"Good luck tomorrow, Rudy," my dad yelled as he was leaving.

"Are you going to be there?" Rudy said.

"Wouldn't miss it."

I walked—no, floated—upstairs, knowing this *was* going to be good. I was excited too. *It's about time*, I thought to myself as I replayed this magical night in my mind, finally falling asleep.

My dad loved to go to see Rudy and Vinnie play and he would try to make a Saturday game whenever he could. This was a big game and he was right when he told Rudy he wouldn't miss it. Even though Aunt Angie would bring enough food to feed the entire bleachers, my dad and I stopped at the deli for egg-and-cheese sandwiches with potatoes on a roll. It was a tradition for us. We even got one for Janie, who was cheerleading.

We found Aunt Angie and Uncle Joe in the stands with Mama Rose and Papa G. They were already dipping into Aunt Angie's cooler, which was full of leftover surprises from last night. We sat down and soon Jackie, Gina and Marie joined us. The stands were packed and there was a huge cheer when our team took the field.

I don't know what got into Rudy that day, but he played the game of his life. He made three interceptions. The crowd was going nuts. I like to think it was my kissing that gave him this superpower. The game was filmed that day and that film would become an essential tool in Rudy's college admission package.

We won, in part because of the extraordinary day Rudy had. Whenever I would go see the boys play, I would always wear a bright color so they could find me in the crowd. That day I had on an orange shirt and both Rudy and Vinnie spotted me right away. After each interception Rudy looked up directly at me. I was glowing.

My dad was excited and wanted to stay to see Vinnie and especially Rudy when they came out of the locker room. A lot of people hung around that afternoon, including our principal and Rudy and Vinnie's junior high coach, Mr. Rogin. As the boys came out they were each met with applause and cheers. I saw Vinnie and Rudy from a distance. They were walking through the gym, their hair wet and dripping in their eyes. Rudy looked gorgeous. Vinnie, God bless him, stayed back a few feet when they walked out of the gym so Rudy could get all the glory. I just love my Vinnie.

Rudy turned the corner and everyone went wild, screaming and clapping. Dr. Willard, our principal and Mr. Rogin were the first to greet him and Rudy was truly humbled by their kind words. Meanwhile my dad was jumping out of his skin. While Rudy was talking to Mr. Rogin he saw my dad, excused himself and went over to hug him. I thought my dad was going to cry. He loved Rudy like a son and Rudy always gave him back the same emotion. Then he saw me.

There was a brief second of moving toward and then away from each other. *What are we supposed to do?* Then I moved forward and hugged him a little longer and tighter than usual. Rudy whispered in my ear, "Can I kiss you?"

"Not now," I said, rather disappointed.

We were there for over a half hour, everyone congratulating Rudy on his incredible game. My dad ended up going home. I told him I was going to catch a ride with either Rudy or Vinnie. Finally everyone started to leave. Rudy asked if I wanted to go for pizza. We asked Vinnie and I secretly was happy when he said no. Rudy and I got in the car and went on our first official date. We favored this pizzeria in Westbury Village, so we headed in that direction. Halfway there Rudy pulled over, put the car in park and leaned over to kiss me.

"Is it okay if I kiss you here?" he joked.

"Oh, if you must."

We had been to this pizza place a thousand times before and knew Louie, the best pizza maker in New York, very well. We walked in and he greeted us with a big hello.

"Where's the third one?" he joked.

We ordered our slices and sodas and went to a table. We were talking about the game and when Rudy got up to get the pizzas, he leaned over and kissed me. Louie saw it and gave Rudy a huge smile. "It's about time, man," he said.

We sat at the table and laughed and laughed. It felt very relaxing and I was beginning to feel like I always did with Rudy. When we got up to leave, Louie said to Rudy, "You better be good to her." Then he looked at me and said, "You tell me if he's not."

We both smiled. Rudy grabbed my hand and we strolled out.

He dropped me off at home. Erick was having the party that night and I knew Rudy really wanted to go and talk about the game with his teammates. We had decided that, in order to keep this from crazy Lucy, we would probably have to keep it from everyone else. We would go to the party together like we always did. He said he would pick me up around eight. Vinnie would meet us there. I decided I would wear my football jersey "dress" as it was a perfect night for it. Rudy grinned when he picked me up.

"I love you in that."

*Oh, he just said he loves me! I think it was a mistake.*

"But then again, you look great in anything."

*Yeah, but you love me in this*, I thought. *I may never take it off.*

The party was really going when we got there. Erick had a lot of parties at his house and they were always fun. He had a Levitt home with a huge extension off the back. There was a wall of windows that looked out to the backyard, where the party always spilled over to. We walked into the kitchen and all the guys in there started yelling when they saw Rudy. I snuck in behind him as they whisked him deeper into the kitchen, slapping him on the back and cheering.

I walked past them, through the dining room and living room, looking for my girlfriends. I saw them through the window outside and Janie gave me a huge wave to come join them. Jackie told me she loved my outfit and I looked adorable. I didn't tell her Rudy loved me in it too. We started talking and Maria told me she heard Joanne liked Rudy. Joanne was probably the most beautiful girl I ever saw in person, the prettiest in our class, in our school, maybe the world, and she liked my Rudy. I suddenly had a sick feeling in my stomach.

About a half hour later I saw Rudy trying to make his way toward the backyard. It was almost impossible. Everyone was stopping to congratulate him and talk about the game. On the other side of the fireplace, in the dining room, I saw Joanne leaning up against the brick wall. She looked beautiful as usual. She stopped Rudy, hugged him and started talking to him. For the first time ever I felt jealous, a feeling I never wanted to have toward Rudy. They talked for about five minutes and then Rudy saw me looking at him through the window. He excused himself and walked toward me, taking another ten minutes to walk a few feet. Outside the same thing happened again. It took Rudy another fifteen minutes to get over to me. By the time he was at my side we were both laughing.

"Sign any autographs?" I asked.

"No way," he joked. "I'm charging for them."

Suddenly I lost control of my mouth. It was no longer connected to my brain. I blurted out to him, "I just found out Joanne likes you. If you want to go for it I will totally understand."

I saw his face turn to anger and he said to me, "Are you crazy? Are you not serious about this?"

"Yes, I am, but you know, it's Joanne. She is gorgeous."

"And so are you. More so. And besides, she has no personality. I never see her smile or laugh."

Then he grabbed me and started kissing me.

"Let's let them all know," he whispered.

And they did. I swear time stopped. It seemed like everyone was looking at us in slow motion. All of a sudden, from our left, we heard someone say, "Ugh, they're cousins. That's disgusting!"

We stopped kissing and said in unison, "We're not cousins." And then we continued.

Time rejoined us and I could hear people talking. I looked over at Janie and she had the biggest smile on her face. Jackie stood there with her mouth open and Maria and Gina were high-fiving each other. Through the window I could see Gerry smiling and Joanne shrugging her shoulders. Don't feel too bad for Joanne. She went on to marry an NFL football player and has had a very happy life.

All of a sudden Vinnie came running outside and started jumping on top of us. We were really concerned about what Vinnie would think. We knew this would change the dynamics of the Three Musketeers and it was important to us that he was on board with it. He was more than on board with it. "It's about fucking time!" he kept shouting over and over again. We were now in a deep threesome hug with him and none of us wanted to let go. He kept kissing both of us, which of course started me crying. I never realized it, but I cry a lot.

"This is fucking great! Does the family know?"

"No," we said, in unison again. "We are not telling them yet."

"Okay," he said. "This is great. This is amazing. How long has this been going on?"

I looked at my watch and told him about twenty-six hours. He laughed and told us it had to start sometime. "Everyone knew it but you two," he said, finally releasing us from his bear hug. Janie came over and punched me in the arm, mad I hadn't told her. Everyone that night kept repeating the same words over and over to us: "IT'S ABOUT TIME." I guess they all realized it before us.

Gerry finally came over to me and said, "So, is it Rudy?"

"Bingo!" I said to him and he hugged me.

"I love you two together," he said.

Of course word spread fast by the same method it does today: the phone. Only then it was the actual telephone, people dialing a number and talking to each other, one at a time. We were the topic of conversation and gossip for a day or two.

I had always liked Donna, Rudy's previous girlfriend who had helped put this in motion. They had been dating about two months when all this happened. I didn't want to feel awkward around her, even though her friends were sending me daggers with their eyes. I waited about a week and then one day I found her in the library. I went over to her and said hello. I told her Rudy had shared with me the reason they broke up and that it was the beginning of Rudy and me getting together.

She was graceful and kind, explaining she always thought there was something between us. She said she would watch the way we looked at each other and told me Rudy never looked at her like that. She ended the conversation by saying, "Things are the way they are supposed to be." I was so overwhelmed I hugged her, thanked her and yes, cried. It seemed like the whole world knew now, except our families. I was afraid someone would go home and mention it to their mother and it would trickle down to our moms. I didn't want them to find out that way, so we decided to tell them at Sunday dinner. I asked Rudy if he thought we should wait a few weeks or months until we saw where this was going.

"It's not going anywhere. I mean, it's going everywhere. I mean, oh, this is it."

He was right. We knew everything about each other. Every memory we had involved the other. And most important, we really liked each other. We were friends forever. We always loved each other. It had just moved to another level. It made total sense. We made total sense.

Sunday rolled around and Rudy's family and my family got together for macaroni and meatballs, our Sunday staple. I can't remember where Aunt Angie's family was. Out of nowhere, Mama Rose asked, "Rudy, how is Donna? I haven't seen her around."

"We broke up."

"Oh. I liked her. She was a nice girl."

I thought it was a perfect opportunity to share our news.

"Rudy has a new girlfriend," I said, not even looking up from my plate.

"Who?" Mama Rose asked.

"Me," I said.

Everyone around the table laughed and Mama Rose asked, "No, really, who?"

"Me," I said again. And again they laughed.

I got up from the table and walked around to Rudy, who was sitting across from me and motioned him to stand up. Then I kissed him.

"Me," I said for the third time. A wave of cheers erupted. Mama Rose and Papa G. stood up, shouting and clapping. I thought my dad was going to faint. They all came over to us and hugged us, congratulating us like we just got engaged or something. Carmine repeated that famous line, "It's about time." They were all very excited and happy. Well, almost all.

During all this frivolity I looked over at my mom to see her sitting there, lips pursed, with a half-scowl on her face. "Isn't that great?" my father said to her, trying to get some positive reaction as he noticed me looking at her.

"Puppy love," she finally responded.

"Puppy love was when we were six, Mom," I said.

"We'll see," was all she said.

Everyone started asking questions and wanted to know how it happened, when it happened and why it took so long. My mother sat there ominously eating her macaroni. The next evening, as I was looking for a snack to take upstairs, my mother said to me, "I am not happy about this."

"Not happy about what?" I replied, playing dumb.

"You and Rudy. I am not happy about this."

I saw my father getting physically agitated. I kissed my mom on the cheek and, grabbing a banana from the fruit bowl on the table, said, "That's O.K. It's not about you."

I then kissed my dad and as I went upstairs, I heard her yelling at him. The poor man. It was going to be the silent treatment for who knew how long. Surprisingly, it didn't last long. The next day, after school, she proceeded to tell me how Rudy was not allowed in the house with me when no one was home and how he definitely couldn't go upstairs by himself anymore. I just smiled and said, "Of course." And so it began.

## CHAPTER 13

# The First Time

Of our Three Musketeers, Rudy was the one who always dated. Vinnie and I had crushes, but Rudy ALWAYS had a girlfriend. When we were young he and I would say we were girlfriend and boyfriend and he would announce that we would get married someday, "when we are bigger." And he always assured me if I didn't have a prom date he would go with me. What made him think, when I was five, that I wouldn't have a prom date I don't know. All the moms thought it was cute. Then one day Rudy realized I wasn't the only little girl in town and all that changed.

In kindergarten he was partnered with Arlene, a little blond girl with big blue eyes. They would walk in line to the lunchroom or recess, holding hands. So cute, everyone said. In fourth grade he told us he met the love of his life. Her name was Diane and she had long ginger curls cascading down her back. He even got her a Valentine's present. It was a little white stuffed dog with a small box of chocolates taped to it. Dating in elementary school meant you would walk together to lunch and sometimes sit together, but not usually. You would say hi at recess and maybe sit near each other on the bus. If you were at a school dance there was the obligatory slow dance. You might call one night but disguise the conversation as homework help. And, if you were really serious, your parents would chaperone a trip to the movies or mall. It was fourth grade.

Then we got into junior high and things got more serious. Kissing, exploring and wearing an ID bracelet with your boyfriend's name on it were big deals. Your initials in a heart on the *outside* of your notebook where everyone could see it was major. Some couples started things up early. We had these books going around called slam books. Simply put, it was a notebook with students' names on the top of each page. It was passed around and people wrote things about you. Mine always said "nice" or "too skinny" and, occasionally, "cute." Some girls had the word "slut" written on their page. Talk about a label that will follow you forever. I noticed the word was never on the boys' pages. So just who were these girls being sluts with? This was one of my earliest realizations of the double standard between the sexes.

Actually, my friend up the block, Jill, first brought this to my attention when we were about seven or eight years old. She was walking with her cousin Steven to Elmer and Pike, the grocery store up the street. It was hot and they both had shorts on and no shirts. I asked Jill why she didn't have a shirt on and she said, "Boys don't have to wear shirts. Why should I?" Ah, the beginnings of a feminist!

Jill was also the person I learned about sex with. No, it didn't happen the way that sounds. Truth be told, I didn't know a thing about how the baby got in the belly. Maybe I thought parents wished it in there. One day my mom thought it was time. Jill was over and my mom called her mom. The next thing I knew Jill and I were in my parents' bedroom, reading this book she gave us. WITH ILLUSTRATIONS! Basically it was a book explaining to children how to make a baby. I think that might have been the title. It was about ten pages with large type. Did I mention it had pictures? We started reading it together, quietly but out loud. When we got to THAT part we threw the book in the air and started screaming. "You mean they put that there? OMG! That is gross! How could anyone do that?"

Then Jill had the most horrible thought. "My parents have three kids. THEY DID IT THREE TIMES!"

"My mom had three miscarriages. My parents did it four times!"

Seriously, we were eleven years old and didn't know a thing. Then we looked down at my parents' bed we were sitting on, leaped up shrieking, and started brushing ourselves off as if we had cooties. Jill and I walked out of the bedroom dazed and shaking. My mom was in the kitchen, cooking like nothing had ever happened. Oh, but we knew. We knew her dirty little secret. It took me a long time before I could look at her and my dad normally again. When I found this out I wanted to tell everyone I knew. So of course I went to Rudy and Vinnie first. I asked them if they knew how to make babies and they both said sure. "Why didn't you ever tell me?"

"My mom said you don't talk about this with anyone, especially girls," Vinnie said.

I started looking at both of them differently too. And then I got my period and everything changed. Well, at least everything changed for my mother. She would always drop little lines about good girls waiting until they got married, how having sex before marriage was a sin. She emphasized the shame it brought to a family if someone got pregnant before they were married. It was heavy stuff for a twelve-year-old going to her first boygirl birthday party. It got worse as I got older. Then I got my period and it meant I could actually get pregnant. When I was thirteen she started saying to me, as I was leaving the house to go out, "Don't come home pregnant." What? I was thirteen! And then the threats began.

"If you come home pregnant, I'll disown you."

"If you come home pregnant, I'll kill you."

"If you come home pregnant, I'll kill myself."

So much for introducing me to the beautiful concept of making love. She scared the sex right out of me. She became obsessed with this. It was odd. None of my other friends said their moms talked like this. Finally one day I went to Aunt Angie, whom I could go to for anything, and asked her what was going on with my mom. She said she would tell me where she thought it was coming from but I couldn't tell anyone.

Aunt Theresa had become pregnant with Mickey before she was married. None of our generation knew this because she added an extra year to her wedding anniversary. Aunt Angie said my grandparents were mortified and saw it as a disgrace to the family. So did my mom, who, seeing how embarrassed and defeated my grandparents were from this, spoke out quite forcefully and repeatedly against my aunt, offering her little support. Aunt Angie said if I got pregnant before marriage it would cause the same feelings in my mom and she would appear to be a hypocrite. My mom carried this humiliation around with her constantly. To Lucy, this was a sin bigger than all the commandments. It was a sin against God and herself.

I also found out my mom, at twenty-four, was a virgin when she got married—talk about too much information—and expected me to wait until marriage also. Her thought was she had waited because of her mother and I should wait because of her. She didn't win that one. This was the same woman who once told me you should love your mom more than your husband because you know her longer and she took care of you as a child. My poor dad. On both counts.

So, me dating, not good. Rudy dating, adorable. Rudy would always make sure Vinnie and I were never excluded. If he was going to ride his bike with his eighth-grade girlfriend he would tell her we were stopping by my house to see if I wanted to go. I would hang out in the pool with him and his girlfriend, go to the playground or take a walk to get ice cream. If a girl liked Rudy I knew it before he did because she would start talking to me. She would want to hang out with me to get to him. Sometimes Vinnie and I would both go along on a date and the girlfriend would think she was on a double date. In high school this pattern continued. I never really gave it much thought. But apparently Donna did.

The boys and I never talked about sex, except that one time about where babies came from. But something happened when Rudy was almost fifteen. He and Vinnie would make these little off-color jokes and references I didn't understand. I found out later that was around the first time Rudy had sex, with a sixteen-year-old girl.

Rudy and I were having these wonderful make-out sessions that started to become a little more and more intense. I would become breathless after them, feel things in parts of my body I had never felt before and get a little wet in my panties. Finally one day I brought up the elephant in the room, telling him I knew he was sexually active but I was still a virgin. He handled it in typical Rudy fashion, pulling me closer, kissing the top of my head and telling me he knew. He said there was no pressure; he would wait as long as I wanted to. "I am not going anywhere. And I am not here because of that." He didn't have to wait too long. I decided to go to Planned Parenthood to start birth control pills, just in case.

I had been on the pill two months and as fate would have it, both our parents were going away for the weekend at the same time. My parents were going with my godmother Betty and Uncle Dom to Atlantic City Friday through Sunday night. Rudy's parents were spending the weekend in Pennsylvania for a work-related wedding. And they say there is no such thing as a coincidence. This would be the first night we would spend together since we started dating.

My mom was stressing out about leaving me alone, not because she was concerned I would have a party or something would happen to me.

She was worried Rudy would happen. So instead of leaving me at home with some of my girlfriends, she said I had to stay at Aunt Angie's house and Rudy wasn't allowed in our house while they were gone. Really? Rudy was raised in our house. I just said of course and left it at that.

Aunt Angie knew my mom was being ridiculous, bordering on psychotic, about my spending any unsupervised time with Rudy now that we were dating. She even tried to talk to my mom a few times but got nowhere. My aunt was much more reasonable and trusting of my decisions. After my parents left I went over to her house to tell her the plan Rudy and I had devised. I don't think she really wanted to know but I felt I needed to be accountable to her.

Rudy paid Carmine $20.00 to stay over at a friend's house for the weekend so we could have the house to ourselves. I would go over to Aunt Angie's Friday, be seen by Uncle Joe and then go to Rudy's house, where I would stay over. I told Aunt Angie if Uncle Joe asked or my mom called she should say I was with my friends or sleeping. She didn't want to lie for me but she did. I am sure she told Uncle Joe what was going on, or he guessed. I would be seen Saturday around her house and repeat the same thing Saturday night.

Before I embarked on this elaborate scheme she sat me down in a way my mother never did. She talked to me honestly and openly about having sex, what it represents to different people and how beautiful and healthy it can be in a loving relationship. She also said not to do anything I was uncomfortable doing and she knew Rudy would be respectful of whatever I decided. I couldn't believe an adult was having this conversation with me and discussing intimacy in a way it had never been presented to me before. I started crying and told her I wasn't planning on going all the way that night. I said I was grateful to be spoken to in such a warm, mature way and I was sorry I had put her in the middle of this. She hugged me and told me she loved us both. I love her still!

I took three showers Friday just to be sure. I clipped and shaved everything on my body I could find and put on my lace bra and matching panties that Janie and I had stolen from Gertz a few weeks before (a story for another day). Rudy came over to Aunt Angie's for dinner, which I am sure was awkward for him, knowing she was aware of the evening's plans. After dinner Vinnie dropped us both off at Rudy's before going over to Erick's to play some basketball. If he knew about the events we were planning that evening he never let on. He very casually told us to have a good night.

It was weird being in the house with no one expected home. We were both a little uncomfortable and ill at ease, which was never like us. He asked me if I wanted a beer or wine and I said no, just some water, which he got me with a lot of ice, the way I liked it. He then ran upstairs, put on some records and came back downstairs. We started to dance. He knew that would relax me and it did. We were dancing and laughing and having a great time at our own little party. Then Al Green's "Let's Stay Together" came on. I believe this is the greatest foreplay song ever recorded. If you don't believe me, dance to it and see. By the end of the song we were upstairs in his bedroom.

It was obvious Rudy had spent a great deal of time cleaning his room. It was spotless. He had lit candles, pulled down the bed cover and even put tiny mints on the pillows.

"We can go back downstairs if you want."

"No, I'm okay."

We sat on the bed and he gently kissed me then pulled away and said, "Are you alright?" He was so worried about me that night. Before I knew it, we were lying next to each other on his bed, me in my stolen pantie-and-bra ensemble and he in his undies. He took my hand and gently guided it down his underwear. Hello? I had seen Rudy's penis many times when we were little. It had grown. A lot. And apparently was still growing. He showed me where to touch it and softly told me how to move my hand up and down, press harder or softer, go faster or slow down. Looking back, I didn't know what the hell I was doing but, whatever it was, Rudy was enjoying it. His groans turned to moans and as he arched his back up he let out the most euphoric sigh I had ever heard. My hand was covered with wet, sticky stuff as his whole body relaxed back down into the bed and he let out a huge breath. We quietly lay next to each other for a little bit. Then I sat up and said, "Now do me."

He got hysterical laughing and started to kiss me, passing his hand down my lace panties. I had never been touched like that and it was obvious he knew what he was doing. With every stroke of his fingers I felt better and better. He knew where to touch me, how long to be there before he moved on, when to be gentle and when not to be. He would move his hand and ask me if it felt good. Everything he was doing felt good. I was aware of myself getting warm and moist. Several times I thought I was "there," but he kept whispering to me, "Not yet. You'll know."

As my hips gently rose in the air, I knew. WHEW! My first orgasm. It was a whole different ball game now. To think my mom was trying to keep me away from the most rapturous feeling on earth. We were relaxing and snuggling when suddenly I sat up and started to talk nonstop. "So does everyone feel like that? Why would people even go out if they can stay home and do that? How many times a day can you do it? How long do you have to wait in between?"

"Oh my God," Rudy laughed. "I have created a monster."

Yes, he had.

The rest of the weekend was relaxing and filled with A LOT more investigative ways for both of us to "reach completion," as Rudy called it. It was loving, tender and fun. I had never related fun to sex before and I understood the love part even more deeply. We had always loved one another, but we were now in love with each other.

I stopped by Aunt Angie's several times during the weekend to be seen. Rudy stayed at home. When I went to bed Sunday evening I was still a virgin but newly in love with my vagina. And, of course, with Rudy.

A little while later, unplanned, we finally went all the way. Rudy was as tender and caring as always and that is all I am going to say about it. It was beautiful, special and ours. The dancer and athlete in us knew practice makes perfect, so we practiced. A lot. And it was perfect.

Because of my mother's issues with my having sex, it was always difficult for us to steal time together. But we were determined and creative. My dad probably knew but was much more relaxed about it. My dad, Uncle Joe and Papa G. used to take us upstate camping all the time. If time permitted we would go to Vermont and Maine, usually in the summer months. Sometimes the moms would join us, but not often. It definitely wasn't my mom's thing. I could see Aunt Angie going, even Mama Rose, but Lucy wouldn't have any of it. It was always a special time to be with our dads. The boys and I would stay in one tent and the dads in the other. I loved it. We would hike, swim, ride our bikes, cook, have campfires. And the dads were much more laid back without the moms there.

We continued this right into our teens. You can guess how crazy my mom was about this once Rudy and I started dating. Late that fall the dads had planned an extended weekend camping trip to the Adirondacks. At first Lucy wasn't going to let me go, but my dad and I put up a real fight. I think Aunt Angie was the one who convinced her. My mom told my father Rudy and I must be chaperoned at all times and never left alone. And I had to either have my own tent or my dad had to sleep in my tent with me. She was adamant.

So we were setting up our tents and my dad asked us how we wanted to do this. Vinnie looked at him and said, "Like we always do. Us in one tent, you dads in the other."

My dad made a frown and Vinnie said, "What? They're not going to do anything. I'll be their chaperone."

He looked at Uncle Joe and Papa G., who shrugged and agreed. So Rudy and I zipped our sleeping bags together and crawled inside while Vinnie put himself right next to me like he always did. Vinnie kept teasing us, telling us he wanted to see our hands at all times. We would never do anything with Vinnie there or with the dads in the next tent. That would be disrespectful. But it was nice to snuggle and sleep together. My dad told us not to tell my mom. He said that a lot to me.

My dad rarely if ever got mad at me, except for the time he caught me hitching. In the early 1970s kids would hitchhike all over. You would always see them on the side of roads with their thumbs out. My girlfriends and I hitched a lot. It was a way of transportation for us. It's not that our parents wouldn't take us wherever we wanted to go. This was just easier and made us feel a little independent. Yes, there were murderers, rapists and kidnappers at that time but we never thought about that. It was all peace and love. We never got in a car if someone looked suspicious or we had to sit in the back seat of a two-door car with no escape. I guess we were think-ing about the danger but never took it seriously.

We had a strict rule of never hitching alone. And none of us did. We always went with at least three of us, although I know Janie and Gina would sometimes hitch together. We would always put Gina out front on the road because she was so stunning. If there were three or more of us we would hide in the bushes or behind a building. When they stopped to pick up Gina we would run out. Sometimes they drove away; sometimes they took all of us.

We usually hitched to Mid Island Plaza, Roosevelt Field or Jones Beach and we never hitched after dark. That was a definite no for all of us. We would go as far as the driver was going then get out and start hitchhiking again. Sometimes people would take us all the way to our destination, even if they weren't going there.

One time the four of us were hitching to Jones Beach when two young guys picked us up with all our beach gear and we stuffed ourselves in the back seat of the car, a four-door. The driver said he had to stop at home in Massapequa and then he would take us to field four. We got to his house and it was hot in that back seat. We got out of the car and he invited us to come into his backyard. His dad was mowing the front lawn so we figured we were okay.

We went around back to a beautiful yard with a built-in swimming pool and deck. We sat down on expensive outdoor chairs as if we were family or old friends. His mother came out with a tray of ice-cold lemonade and cookies. She had no idea who we were but figured we knew her son. So we sat there in this vacation setting, eating chocolate chip cookies and sipping lemonade at a house full of people we didn't know. We then got back in the car and he drove us to the beach. End of story.

But not all stories ended that nicely. One day we were hitching home from Mid Island Plaza. A young guy in his early thirties stopped to pick all four of us up. Janie got in the front and Jackie, Gina and I sat in the back. We were on Old Country Road, approaching the Howard Johnson's Restaurant, right before the Wantagh Parkway Bridge. We were about two miles or so from home when Janie said to him, "This is good. You can drop us here."

We all started protesting in the back seat that we weren't home yet. Janie turned around and widened her eyes as if to tell us to shut up. She then said, even louder, "THIS IS GOOD. YOU CAN DROP US HERE."

He stopped and we tumbled out. As he pulled away we were all yelling at Janie that we weren't home yet. She then proceeded to tell us this guy had cards on his dashboard and he was turning them over to show her as he was driving. They were naked people, some having sex. We walked the rest of the way home.

You would think that would have stopped us from hitching, but no. One Saturday afternoon we were hitching home from Roosevelt Field when a car stopped for us. We ran to the car to look in and it was my father behind the wheel. He was test-driving one of Uncle Joe's cars, which is why we didn't recognize it. He pointed for me to get in to the front seat and the girls got in the back. No one said a word the entire ride. It was the longest ten minutes of my life. He dropped us off two blocks from home and Janie, Jackie and Gina ran out of the back seat. I looked at him, not scared, because he wasn't a screamer. I was sad because I knew he was disappointed. He said to me, "You are NEVER to do this again. And let's not tell Mommy." I never hitched again.

My dad and I kept secrets from my mom for our own survival. I am pretty sure he knew Rudy and I were sexually active, although he never came right out and asked. He never treated Rudy any differently if he knew. One day, out of nowhere, he said to me, "Are you and Rudy being careful?"

I assumed he was talking about contraception and said yes.

"Good," he replied. "Because I couldn't deal with your mother if you weren't."

Neither one of us ever told my mom.

## CHAPTER 14

# The Vietnam War

I am ashamed to say I don't recall the Vietnam War having a huge direct impact on my life when I was growing up, although it had a tremendous influence on the time I grew up in. The war officially started eight months after I was born, on November 1, 1955, but I didn't pay it much attention until 1967 or 1968. That is when the protests started to show up in the newspapers and on the evening news.

When I was ten years old, a small group of peace activists objected to the war as the United States began bombing North Vietnam. In the next three years the protests became more visible and abundant. I first heard the phrase "conscientious objector" in April, 1967, when Muhammad Ali refused to be drafted and was banned from boxing for three years. I remember hearing discussions among my dad and uncles, all World War Two veterans and all disagreeing with Mr. Ali, although my dad was more sympathetic than the others. By 1968, with no end to the war in sight and over $25 billion a year being spent to keep it going, it seemed like the country had exploded into two different factions: those in support of the war and those against it. Guess which one I fell into?

I was a budding hippie, although I didn't know it at the time and I was definitely a "make love, not war" thirteen-year-old. War seemed like a stupid way to resolve conflict, with too many people dying at the whim of someone with more power, who, by the way, never had to risk his own life. For a long time I could never understand how men and women went so willingly to fight during World War Two. They volunteered. I grew up during the Vietnam War. I had friends who got low numbers in the draft pool and were freaking out. As a teenager, I saw these young men, bloodied and screaming, on the evening news. Why would anyone want to go and do that? I could never understand the concept of war. Whoever kills the most wins? So barbaric. Someone once told me war can be good for the economy. How can you measure someone's life in dollars and cents? But I do understand and totally appreciate the sacrifices soldiers made and continue to make for all of us. I always said the Pledge of Allegiance when I worked in schools. I would tell the kids, especially the ones who didn't say it, that it was for my dad, a World War Two vet. Usually the next day, they would stand up and say it, "for your dad." I always will thank vets if I see them out and about and will pay for their dining tab if I see them in a restaurant. I know I have the life I do because of them and I am forever grateful. I just wish there was another way to go about it other than sacrificing the lives of twenty-year-old men and women.

I do acknowledge the two wars were very different. One night my dad and I were comparing the songs from World War Two and the Vietnam War, which made the differences very clear. Think about the Andrews Sisters' "Boogie Woogie Bugle Boy" (1941) versus John Lennon's "Give Peace a Chance" (1969). We really got into it and my dad was so inspired he made it an assignment. He got together with the general music teacher and an English teacher and they did a cooperative learning exercise. The students had to compare the songs of the two wars and explain how they mirrored the times. Dad would bring the papers home and I would love reading the songs the students chose and their interpretations.

It is often said that the Vietnam War was different because it was in our homes, on the news every night while we were eating dinner or doing our homework. You could tune in or out, your choice. I think I tuned it out more than not. I was more interested in *The Monkees* than what was happening half a world away. Then, in 1970, Marie's older brother, Anthony, got drafted and everything changed. Because Marie and Anthony lived next door to Rudy we were all very close growing up. Now I knew someone who was there fighting. The war became personal. It became real.

Anthony was a good-looking, all-American kid. Think of Richie Cunningham from *Happy Days*, only with dark hair and a mustache at fourteen years old. Rudy and Vinnie idolized him. Rudy had trouble pronouncing his name when he was little and called him Ant-Knee. The name stuck. Anthony always took the time to play ball in the street with the boys or take them for pizza and ice cream. He was like an older brother to them and when he got drafted, they both cried. We all did. His mom's first reaction was that he should go to Canada. She wasn't antiwar or anti-American; she just didn't want her son to "go over there" and risk his life. By the war's end over forty thousand draftees had fled to Canada. Anthony would not be one of them.

A lot of reasons could keep men from going to Vietnam. Conscientious objector status usually revolved around religion such as being a Jehovah's Witness, Mennonite, Quaker or Amish. Anthony was a practicing Catholic, whatever that meant. Those in the clergy or who were missionaries could also claim conscientious objector status. Anthony had no chance of that happening either.

A health condition could also keep men from going. Anthony was "healthy as an ox," as his mom used to say. Some kids—and, let's face it, they were kids—would try to make up a health condition, often taking drugs and staying awake all night. If they couldn't get a physical discharge, some went for a mental health one. Many young men pretended to be homosexual as that also disqualified them at the time.

Of the dozen or so reasons to be excused, the one most often used was a college deferment. Anthony was not in college; he had been working as an electrician's intern and was trying to get into one of the unions. It was too late for him to apply to college. He also didn't have an essential civilian job, wasn't married with kids and didn't have $5,000 to buy forged National Guard or Reserve papers. So, on a beautiful Sunday in March, we all said goodbye and sent him off with our prayers and love.

Rudy, Vinnie and I began sending him letters and packages almost immediately. Along with Marie and our other friends, we would ask people to donate food, books, self-care items, anything we could send to him and the men in his unit. We would get back letters from him and the others thanking us and sharing stories of what the packages meant to them. It was a mission we kept up for the two years Anthony was in Vietnam and beyond. It gave us a purpose and made us feel we were helping out "our boys," if only one bottle of shampoo or toothbrush at a time.

Eventually we formed a school club to collect and distribute letters and packages to other units in Vietnam. Vinnie, Rudy, Marie and I were recognized by the Board of Education for our efforts. I remember the president of the Board saying we were "other directed." I liked that term. It was a good description of us and I think that experience steered me toward a career in the helping professions.

Some of the letters I got back from Anthony were short and to the point. Others were several pages long. Between the lines were dread, reflection and often a sense of hopelessness. One time I sent him a letter casually asking him how the weather was, a very benign question. I got back a heart-wrenching response that, in part, said,

> We are in the middle of our summer here. It is hotter than hell, if you pardon the phrase. This is actually what I would expect hell to be like, on so many levels. We are moving constantly, not settling

*in any one place too long, so carrying around all our gear adds to the intensity of the heat. And the humidity is a whole different story. Along with the frequent fear and anxiety we feel, it's often impossible to breathe. Yesterday my buddy passed out right next to me. Went down like a rock. I panicked, because I thought he had been shot. How I long for a nice glass of ice water, or five minutes in air conditioning. And what I wouldn't give for a cold beer.*

That is a pretty heavy letter for a fifteen-year-old to receive. In reality, Anthony wasn't too much older than I was. I always wondered if he put that letter in the wrong envelope by mistake or if he was just being honest. I still have that letter and all the other correspondences with him.

People looked for other ways to connect with the soldiers in Vietnam and in 1970 Carol Bates developed a way to honor those missing in action and prisoners of war. Ms. Bates was a member of Voices in Vital America and wanted people to remember the MIAs and POWs. The organization developed nickel-plated and copper bracelets that had the name of a soldier, their rank and their loss date. They sold for $2.50 to $3.00 and over 5 million were manufactured. Although they came out in 1970, some of the soldiers named on the bracelets had been missing since the 1960s.

I had one but I could never wear it because my wrists were so damn skinny it would fly off. I feel bad that I can't remember the name of the person on my bracelet. I do remember he had been missing since 1968. I don't know what happened to that bracelet. I would never have thrown it away on purpose. We were supposed to leave them on until the named soldiers or their remains returned home. I had a friend from college who wore his until the 1990s. Eventually it didn't fit him anymore. He still has it and continues to search for his soldier.

Anthony had been in Vietnam for a little over two years when he was shot in his left hand and lost his pinky and ring-finger; a permanent reminder of his time served. Because of his injury, he was sent home. There was a huge party when he came back. He would joke he could never get married because he didn't have a ring finger and that he should get a discount on a manicure. The jokes didn't last too long.

After the relief of Anthony's return wore off the reality of his new life hit him hard. With two of his fingers gone, he did not feel that he could progress on the path to becoming a master electrician. He drifted from job to job. Rudy was the first to notice a change, saying Anthony rarely smiled or joked anymore and wasn't fun to be around. He spent a lot of time drinking and staying in his room. I can't imagine the pain he was feeling, negotiating this new world without instructions or support.

About six months after he returned home Anthony got a visit from his high school girlfriend, with whom he had lost touch. She was attending Alcoholics Anonymous meetings and invited him to one. He reluctantly went and would later say it changed his life. Not only did he meet other alcoholics but he also met other veterans who were struggling in the same way he was. He networked with them and ended up going to occupational therapy to learn how to negotiate a ten-fingered world with only eight. He went with a friend to employment counseling and enrolled in Nassau Community College. He attended group counseling and therapy. And very slowly, painfully, he found a door where he felt comfortable to reenter.

Please don't think I am sugar-coating or condensing this story into a happily-ever-after ending. I am not. Anthony will tell you he continues to struggle to this day, every day. It just doesn't take up all of his day. He eventually became a counselor and has been instrumental in helping those who returned from the wars that followed and those who still struggle with what went before. He is married with two children and three grandchildren. He has moved forward, like all of us, with the day-to-day distractions of life. But every once in a while I can see in his eyes, if even for a moment, that he is back there. His posture and face change. Then he takes a deep breath and is back with us. Vinnie still calls Anthony his superhero without a cape.

Janie's older brother was also in Vietnam. The first time I went to her house, right next to the front door, was a makeshift altar her mom had set up with statues, candles, holy water and crucifixes. My first thought on seeing that was, *Is this legal? Can you set up an altar in your home?* It was there for years, until her brother came home. His struggle was different from Anthony's, but a struggle nonetheless. He moved to California after he returned and dealt with his depression and anxiety through nonstop physical activities, sports and eventually counseling. Over seventy years old now, he still smokes pot, which he credits with getting him through his worst days in Vietnam. He always says, "Whatever works." He is another superhero, barefoot, in swim trunks and a T-shirt.

By the time the war officially ended on April 30, 1975, approximately 58,000 men and women were killed and over 1,500,000 had been wounded. Less than a third of those who served are still alive. Several years ago I visited Mount Rushmore. In the evening I attended a ceremony honoring the veterans of war. Only two men from World War Two were there and it dawned on me how fast they are leaving us. But what struck me even more were the men and women who acknowledged being Vietnam vets. I still think of them as young kids. Instead they were the age of our World War Two vets I remembered. "The circle of life," Aunt Angie would say. Everything moves on, but there always seems to be another war somewhere.

It seems almost every generation since our country's inception has been influenced by a war. Vinnie, Rudy and I and our generation were no different. Maybe it was because it was OUR war, but the Vietnam War seems to have had a huge cultural sway on our nation's development and direction at the time and since. You can read about it in books, but you had to be there to understand its daily impact and the cumulative effect it had on everyone. I will not pretend I can fathom what it was like being a nineteen or twenty-year-old kid in the rice fields and jungles of Vietnam, never truly able to let your guard down. Watching your friends succumb to horrendous, painful deaths just a foot away from you. Thinking of that split-second decision—if you had gone right instead of left, been in front of him instead of behind, it would be your mom they were calling—and dreaming, always dreaming, of coming home, whole.

There were no parades waiting for those who made it home, no confetti or balloons. For the most part, those who served in Vietnam weren't embraced by a grateful nation. Yes, people congratulated them for their service and sacrifice, but others labeled Vietnam veterans "baby killers," "warmongers" "commie sons." At that time a hat indicating you had served in the Vietnam War should have been a badge of honor but often, instead, it gave people a license to badger. One Vietnam vet told me he was spit on at a movie theater and called "a crazy drug addict."

Many vets also brought a "souvenir" home with them: post-traumatic stress disorder, a simple phrase bantered about then as now to describe the difficulty many veterans have with reacclimating to their previous life. Only that is an impractical task. Veterans are not the same, they never will be and because of that their previous life doesn't exist anymore. I first heard the term "PTSD" in the seventies. Prior to that it was called soldier's heart, shell shock, war neurosis or combat fatigue. In 1980 it officially appeared in the DSM III, the *Diagnostic and Statistical Manual of Mental Disorders*. It is now used to describe reactions to many different types of traumas. It was officially recognized from the term that grew out of the Vietnam War.

We should not forget women also volunteered to serve, 90 percent of them as nurses. Our high school nurse's daughter was one of them. In all, five female nurses died during the conflict and eight women are listed on the Vietnam Veterans Memorial, which, by the way, was designed by a twenty-one-year-old female college student named Maya Lin.

It is not my intention to debate the pros and cons of the Vietnam War. Plenty of books already do that. But I lived those chapters and I can tell you we were a divided nation. The war played a major role in changing the tone and structure of the culture. You can't write about growing up during this time without recognizing the enormous way it shaped all of our lives, even if covertly. It influenced several generations and its effects continue to ripple out and beyond. But, most important, it changed forever the lives of the 2.6 million men and women who served and those of their friends and families. Anthony's story was a close-up look for all of us who loved him. So was the story of Janie's brother. There are millions of stories like that. Every day I say a silent thank you to all those who served and who continue to serve, and to their families. I pray for all the souls who didn't make it home. I hope everyone, regardless of political affiliation, does the same.

## CHAPTER 15

# The Choice

Rudy and I started dating in the fall of his senior year. By then he had already started to send out his college applications. He knew he wanted to go away and was hoping to play football or baseball at college, preferably on a scholarship. His coaches, more than his guidance counselor, helped him with the applications.

When Rudy was around eight his family went on a trip to the Grand Canyon and, two years later, they went out to Utah's national parks. Rudy fell in love with it all. He loved the weather, the history, the dinosaurs. Ever since his first trip out there his dream was to go to college in Arizona. Among the eight schools he applied to, Arizona State University at Tempe was his top choice. The school had an amazing baseball team. We never talked much about his going away to school. We were too busy having fun and enjoying this new romantic level of our relationship. Besides, September 1972 seemed a long way off. So many things could happen before that.

Vinnie was also applying to schools. He was looking at State University of New York schools with the prospect of playing football or lacrosse. I just couldn't think about the two of them leaving at the same time, so I didn't.

The year was going by quickly. After a successful senior football season that included the county playoffs, Christmas break was almost here. I always bought my own, separate gifts for Rudy and Vinnie for Christmas, trying my best to be creative and unique. We all tried to top each other in different or unexpected ways, like I had with the ballet lessons I got them. This year was the first Christmas Rudy and I were a couple, so we bought our usual gifts for each other and Vinnie and then he and I exchanged our own, more personal ones.

That first year Rudy went overboard and bought me a lot of presents. He knew how much I loved getting them. The two I remember the most, which I still have today, are a locket and a T-shirt. The locket was gold with a little diamond in the middle. Rudy put in a picture of us as kids on one side and a picture from that Thanksgiving on the other. The back of the locket was engraved "IWALY." We used to pronounce it "eye-wally." It meant "I Will Always Love You." I cried when he gave it to me.

The other gift was wrapped in beautiful silver paper and had a big red bow on it. I opened the box to find a long-sleeved grey jersey T-shirt that was very soft and flowing. On the front, in big letters, it said "Proud Feminist." The word "feminist" was sewn in black sequins. I took it out of the box and went to hold it up against me when I noticed another grey-collared T-shirt underneath. On the pocket of this shirt, in much smaller letters, it said "Proud Boyfriend of a Feminist." Rudy had them made for us. I did what everyone expected me to do. I cried. We both wore the new shirts all day.

December turned into January and before we knew it we were celebrating our first Valentine's Day and my seventeenth birthday, with two separate celebrations and gifts. No combos were allowed. Rather than go to a crowded restaurant on our first Valentine's Day, Rudy made me dinner at his house while the rest of the family was over at Aunt Angie's. It was very romantic and delicious. He was an exceptional cook although my lasagna was still better than his. He bought me a beautiful pair of turquoise earrings that he made sure were crafted by a Native American. He also bought me a little white stuffed dog with a box of candy attached, like he did for his elementary girlfriend many years ago.

The next day, a school day, was my birthday. He greeted me with a birthday crown and an egg sandwich. Such a romantic. He sent flowers to the school for me, took me out to lunch and had the entire chorus sing "Happy Birthday" when I walked into class. He knew how much I loved my birthday. I still do. We celebrated with family that night and he gave me a beautiful pearl-and-diamond ring. Everyone teased me for weeks that it was an engagement ring.

February was also the junior prom, making it a very expensive month. I didn't think Rudy would want to go since he was a senior and it was not really a big deal to me. It was in the gym. Plus I had Rudy's senior prom in June. I told him I could go with Richard or Erick as friends but he insisted he wanted to go. We had to get permission from the class advisor and the principal because he was not in our grade. He was given the green light.

My mom made me a beautiful red halter gown, very fitted, with a slit on the right front that went up to my mid-thigh when I walked or danced. It was very simple, elegant and flattering. I wore the turquoise earrings Rudy gave me for Valentine's Day as a nice contrast to the red. Rudy loved it. He didn't look too shabby in his tuxedo either. It was a great night and a prequel to his Senior Prom. Or so I thought.

Around this time Rudy and Vinnie were starting to get letters from the colleges they had applied to. Vinnie was over the moon that his "reach college," Marist, had accepted him to play lacrosse and offered a nice scholarship. So far, Rudy had been accepted to every college he had applied to, but he was still waiting for scholarship news.

A few days after the junior prom Rudy was called down to the gym. Both his football and baseball coaches were waiting for him. They sat him down and said in very somber voices that they had heard from Arizona State University. They shook their heads sadly. Rudy told me later his heart sank. Then they both quickly looked up, smiling, and said, "They want you!"

If Rudy started crying he didn't tell me, but I bet he might have. They told him the university wanted him to play both football and baseball as a freshman and they would assess his skills at the end of the year. They were offering him a sizeable scholarship. The coaches told him he should get a letter that day or the next outlining all this.

Rudy immediately ran to my English class, interrupted the lesson and told my teacher he had to see me, that it was an emergency. Now my heart sank. We walked down the hall and he turned to me and told me he got into his dream school. I let out such a scream three teachers poked their heads out of their classrooms. He told me about playing sports and the massive scholarship. I started hugging and kissing him in the middle of the hallway. Anyone who saw us must have thought we were nuts.

"Do your parents know?" I said anxiously.

"No. I just found out and wanted to tell you first."

"Go to the office and call them. This is so exciting."

He grabbed my hand to go to the office with him, but I told him I had to use the bathroom. He went to the office to give his parents the greatest news of his life. I went to the bathroom to cry. I really was happy for him. This had been his dream for so long. I was sad, though, because he would be leaving to go away to college. And not 100 or 200 miles away, but 2,363.5 miles from me, thirty-five hours by car if you didn't stop. I had done my research.

I sat on the windowsill in the bathroom, composing myself and wondering what this meant for our relationship. I decided I would not mention the distance or its impact on us to him or anyone else. He would have to bring it up. I would NEVER tell him not to go to Arizona. It was not my place, no matter how much I wanted him to stay. It was odd that so many of my important decisions were reached in the school bathrooms.

News spread fast and by the end of the day he had gathered with all his buddies by the gym with Arizona the topic of conversation. When I walked over they all looked at me cautiously, not knowing what to expect. I told them what I would end up saying to everyone. "Isn't this great? What a wonderful opportunity for Rudy. I am so proud of him."

I would say that to teachers, friends, family, anyone who would ask me if I was going to miss Rudy or how I was going to deal with him being so far away. People loved to remind me how far it was. "It is all the way on the other side of the country," I would hear often. My response was always the same: "2,363.5 miles to be exact."

When I got home my parents already knew, but they didn't react until they could gauge how I was. I told them the same thing I told everyone else. Then I began to cry. "Please don't tell anyone I am sad about this decision. Not Aunt Angie, Mama Rose, or anyone. Please?"

They promised. They knew.

"Why does he have to go so far away from home and leave his family?" my mom asked over and over again. I told her it was to fulfill his dream, to take advantage of this incredible opportunity.

She didn't see it that way. She saw it as him leaving his mother. "How could he do that? A good, loving son wouldn't do that."

"How could he not?" I answered. "A good, loving mother wouldn't stop him."

Suddenly Rudy had a big, exciting adventure in front of him that didn't include me. For the first time in his and Vinnie's lives they were embarking on something new without me. They started focusing their energy and time on preparing for their new life. I walked around with a fake grin on my face all the time. *The tears of a clown*, I thought. Don't misunderstand me; the three of us were still enjoying their senior year and each other. But a huge clock was hanging over us and the enormity of it was weighing heavily on me.

A few days later Rudy and I decided to take a ride to the beach. It was a clear, sunny and warm enough day to sit on the boardwalk if we bundled up. We sat on a bench overlooking the water, silent except for the sounds of the waves crashing and a few seagulls chatting to each other. The sun felt warm on my face, the only part of my body exposed to it. It was very peaceful and a welcome calm from the excitement of the past few days.

Finally Rudy spoke. "I have to send my acceptance letter to Arizona by the twenty-fifth. You know I don't have to go."

"What are you talking about? You're going," I said without looking at him.

"I was also accepted to Hofstra and they have great football and baseball teams."

I stood up to face him, leaning against the railing.

"And why the hell would you do that?" I protested.

"To stay here with you."

I turned my back to him and faced the water, breathing deeply and searching for my next words. I turned to him again.

"No way. This has been your dream since we were little. Arizona is all you would talk about to me and Vinnie. This is an amazing opportunity and I am so proud of you. I love you and I can love you when you're in Arizona too. Besides, I am thinking of all the beautiful Native American jewelry and presents you can buy me."

"For real?"

"For real. I wouldn't pretend about something this big." *Liar,* I thought.

He stood up, grabbed me and started kissing me.

"I love you too," he said. "Nothing will change."

We both knew that wasn't true. This decision was going to change everything. At the time though, neither of us could have possibly imagined to what extent.

## CHAPTER 16

# The Prom, Part One

It was sometime toward the end of May. What a great time it was to be a senior. Rudy had a few more baseball games left before his high school athletic career was over. Then it was sports awards, yearbook, Regents, prom, graduation. And let's not forget the famous Senior Cut Day. There is something about a high school in May. If September smells like the beginning, May reeks of the end.

The weather was getting warmer, girls were wearing less and boys were noticing more. Students started to cut classes, rules were not always enforced and reports students once toiled so deliberately over were scattered on the floor. On this day a group of students had gathered outside the cafeteria and gym. The doors were open to the smoking section and a mix of warm spring air and the smell of cigarettes floated in. About twenty kids were milling around. Rudy was sitting in a desk chair and I was sitting on top of the desk. Everyone was involved in their own conversations.

A few feet away from us were Dana and two of her friends. I had met Dana when I was in ninth grade. I had a hole in my schedule because I took a Regents class in eighth grade. My guidance counselor filled it by giving me an art elective with tenth graders and Dana was one of them. In today's terms Dana would be diagnosed as on the spectrum, probably with high-functioning autism. People who saw her and didn't know better often mislabeled her as having Down syndrome. She was teased and bullied, often called retarded to her face. She was sweet and kind and very funny. She did very well in all her classes but excelled in art. I have never seen anyone so talented in all the media: paint, sculpture and especially sketching. Her pencil sketches were so detailed and beautiful people wanted to buy them. Her work was featured prominently around the building and she had been recognized on both the county and state levels.

I was almost as bad in art as I was in Spanish. I always believed it was a genetic gift like a singing voice. It couldn't be learned, at least not by me. Dana helped me all the time. We did projects together and became friends, eating lunch at the same table all year. We socialized outside of school a few times although her parents were very cautious about what she did and with whom. They were very protective of her. I would always stop and chat with her when I saw her in the hallway. I think she had a secret crush on Rudy. She would get all giggly when she saw him and he said hi.

Dana and all those around her were enjoying this beautiful day when, without warning, in through the doors crept Jack. Just seeing him made my skin crawl. I had hated him ever since the dog poop Halloween and Fribble incidents. Yes, that little boy who gave me the Halloween poop turned out to be Jack. His actions since then only deepened my distain. There was an arrogance in the way he moved, an apathy in his voice and God only knows what going on in his head. He expected everyone to take notice when he walked in and, when no one did, he made sure we looked up. He went over to Dana and in a very loud voice said, "Dana, would you like to go to the prom with me?"

Everyone stopped and turned their attention to Jack. He had gotten what he wanted. Then we all looked at Dana. She smiled, started to clap her hands and said, "Yes."

Jack shot back, "Well, too bad. I don't want to go with you."

I couldn't believe what I was hearing. I thought Rudy was going to jump out of his seat and punch him, but I got up first. Dana had started to cry and I went over to comfort her. I had to pass Jack to get to Dana and my mouth spoke before my brain thought.

"FUCK YOU! You are the most disgusting piece of shit I have ever met," I said. Or maybe I yelled it.

He gave me a "fuck you back" laugh and looked around. No one else was laughing so he slithered back under his rock and was gone. I hugged Dana, something she wasn't always comfortable doing but that she welcomed this time. I looked over her shoulder and saw Rudy's face. I knew what he was thinking and slowly shook my head up and down.

Rudy got up and walked over to Dana. I stood back a little. He took her hands, looked her right in the eyes and said, "Dana, would you do me the honor of going to the prom with me?"

She looked at him, shocked, and said, "For real?"

He said, "For real."

She then looked at me and said, "But you have a girlfriend."

Thinking on his feet, he said, "Yeah, but she is a junior. This is a senior prom. She can go next year."

Dana looked at me and said, "Is it all right?"

"I wouldn't have it any other way," I replied.

She looked at Rudy and said she would have to ask her parents but that she would love to go with him. He then leaned forward and hugged her while everyone around them clapped. I was never as proud of him as I was at that moment, or as much in love. The bell rang and we all scattered to our classes.

During eighth period one of the main office secretaries, Mrs. Kane, knocked on my classroom door, saying the principal wanted to see me. Of course everyone "oohed" and sang, "You are in trouble." I got up and Mrs. Kane said to bring my books.

Mrs. Kane was a very sweet and funny lady who protected Dr. Willard with her life. NOBODY got to see him unless they got past her first, not the superintendent and especially not an irate parent. She always had a piece of gum, bobby pins or a sanitary pad in her desk drawer should we need one. Just don't try to get past her to see the principal. Truth be told, she ran the school. Everyone, including Dr. Willard, knew that. But the secretaries always do. They are the unsung heroes of education.

As I walked to the office with Mrs. Kane I wondered what I was in trouble for. I couldn't think of anything except that Rudy and I were making out a little under the bleachers the other day. We didn't think anyone had seen us. When I got to the main office I saw Rudy sitting on "the bench." As I walked in he said, "What did we do?"

I explained about the bleacher incident and he shook his head. He was nervous he had done something that would prevent him from walking across the stage at graduation. He didn't want to disappoint his parents.

The large, heavy wooden door to Dr. Willard's office opened and he motioned us to come in and sit down. I actually think Rudy was sweating. Before we went in I told him to play dumb and admit to nothing. He didn't find that funny. Dr. Willard sat down across from his desk with the leather blotter and pencil cup on it and said to us, "So what happened today?"

*Whew*, I thought. It wasn't about the bleachers.

"Sir?" I asked.

He didn't seem angry or upset. He actually appeared amused, like he was playing a game with us.

"During lunch, outside the cafeteria?"

*Oh*, I thought. *Whew again.* I started to tell him about the horrible thing Jack had done to Dana and, as is usual when I am nervous, I was on speed talk with no stops. Rudy jumped in to try to get me to take a breath but I kept going. I even told Dr. Willard about Rudy asking Dana to the prom. He then asked me if I had forgotten something and I looked at Rudy puzzled, saying I didn't think so.

"Did you happen to say anything to Jack?" he said.

"Oh, yeah. Right. I might have said something to him. I don't remember," I replied in my best innocent voice. Truth is, I really didn't remember.

"Well, let me refresh your memory."

He took out a piece of paper and read from it.

"And I quote," he said. "Fuck you. You are the most disgusting piece of shit I have ever met."

Rudy and I were in total shock, first at hearing those curse words come from our principal's mouth, then at having him repeat what I had said verbatim. I looked at Rudy and he said to Dr. Willard, "Yeah, that sounds about right."

I then went into another of my rapid dialogues, explaining Jack WAS disgusting and that he had even given me a bag of dog poop one Halloween. He said, with a straight face, that he hadn't heard about the Halloween incident. He then said to me, "We are not here to debate Jack's moral character. Your feelings about him were made quite apparent today, as several teachers reported."

"I am sorry," I lied. I was not.

"I have a school to run, young lady and I would appreciate it if you would keep this type of behavior and language outside of here."

"I will, Sir. Do I have to apologize to Jack?"

"No." Then he turned to Rudy.

"What you did today was so heartwarming, especially after knowing what happened beforehand. I have collected many principal stories over the years but this will always be one of my favorites."

I thought he was going to cry. I know I almost did. He then said to me, "If you would like to go to the prom as a junior I will personally buy you a prom bid."

"Thank you for the offer, Dr. Willard, but I don't want to go and spoil it for Dana. This is her prom and Rudy is her date. I think she will have a better time if I am not there. No one wants your date's girlfriend lurking in the corner. I mean, really, who wouldn't want this date all for herself?" I motioned at Rudy and we all laughed. Dr. Willard stood up, letting us know the meeting was over. He shook Rudy's hand and hugged me.

"What do you see in this guy anyway?" he joked.

"Pity."

We all laughed again. As we were walking out his door Dr. Willard yelled to us, "And stop kissing under the bleachers."

We kept walking as I raised my arm above my head and gave him a thumbs up. I loved Dr. Willard. After school that day Rudy went directly to Dana's locker to walk her to her mom's car. I followed a little behind them. Her mom brought her to and from school every day. Dana had some bad bullying incidents on the bus when she was younger and her parents thought it was best she avoid it. (Did I mention that was also Jack's bus route? Coincidence? I think not). They approached the car and Mrs. Floyd looked a little confused seeing Rudy with Dana.

"Hi, Mom. I am going to the prom with Rudy," Dana said.

Rudy introduced himself and explained he had asked Dana to the prom that day. He apologized for not asking her parents first and said he hadn't thought about that. Rudy was VERY good with parents, always polite and respectful. They loved him. I could see he was charming Mrs. Floyd. She was a little flustered but appreciative of Rudy's thoughtfulness.

"I will discuss it with her dad. You know Dana has special needs?"

"Yes, she is very special," Rudy said, turning Mrs. Floyd's sentence around as he looked directly at Dana. "I would be more than happy to discuss this with you and Dana's dad."

Mrs. Floyd was thrilled at the offer and two nights later Rudy was over at the house talking to her parents. They said Dana sometimes had difficulty with loud noises so they might have to take a break from the music from time to time. But she loved to dance so he should expect to be on the dance floor all night. He joked I was a dancer and he was used to that. They didn't want her in a limo with other kids who were partying and they didn't want him drinking that night. Rudy said he wasn't going to even though, at eighteen, he was of legal drinking age. She could go to the prom but not any other activities that weekend. Rudy asked if she could go to Great Adventure in New Jersey with the other kids on Sunday. They said no but that they might take her there that day. There were a lot more rules. As I said, Dana's parents were very protective. Rudy was very patient listening to all the accommodations they expected. He never once complained to me or anyone else about them. He was kind beyond his years.

About a week later Dana stopped me in the hallway and asked me if I wanted to go shopping with her for her prom gown. I thought that was sweet but also a little strange. She said I knew Rudy's taste and she wanted to get a dress he liked. Again, strange but sweet. I said I'd go.

Mrs. Floyd picked me up that Saturday afternoon and we headed out to Buckner's, a very exclusive dress shop in Roosevelt Field I had been to several times with my mom. It was two floors full of wedding gowns, bridesmaid gowns, mother-of-the-bride gowns and gowns for any other occasion you could think of. It was really fancy and not my first choice for prom gowns, but there we were. Seeing how excited Dana was, I was glad I was there.

Mrs. Floyd and I sat down in red velvet chairs while Dana and the saleswoman took Dana's selections in the back. Dana came out and modeled each one for us. Dana was short and stocky and her gown choices were long and lanky. She was frustrated and disappointed in the first few she tried on. I attempted to make it fun and by the third gown we were laughing about too much boob showing or not enough. I walked around the store while she was trying on gown number four and found a pretty blue empire-waist gown with sheer sleeves and cuffs with pearl buttons. She tried it on and it looked beautiful on her although it was in desperate need of alterations. I told her Rudy loved the color blue and she told the saleswoman, "Sold." We capped off what was a surprisingly delightful day with a nice lunch.

Some kids gave Rudy a tough time about taking Dana to the prom, but he always said they weren't true friends. He made sure he stuck by everything the Floyds wanted. He got a separate limo, ordered Dana a corsage and got a tuxedo with a bowtie and cummerbund to match her dress. He kept asking me if I was alright with this and I kept telling him I was better than alright. Little did I know he had something else up his tuxedo sleeve.

Seniors never went to school the day of the prom—too much primping and preening to do. Janie was going with, of all people, Erick, while Jackie was going with Vinnie, as friends. Maria had said yes to a boy named John who was on Rudy's track team. The day of the prom Gina, Marie and I went to the beach with the girls, who had been working on their "prom tan" every chance they could get. (And yes, Gina lathered on the sunscreen.) Juniors didn't get detention for cuts that day either, as many eleventh-grade girls were going to the senior prom too. They just needed a note from their parents. To my amazement, my mom wrote one for me. I think she felt bad that I wasn't going.

For some reason it was very important to Janie that I go with her to get her nails and hair done. She wouldn't let me go home after the beach so I sat in the kitchen while she showered and her mom put the finishing touches on the beautiful, strapless green column gown Janie was wearing. I was now feeling a little sad that I wasn't going.

I went with Janie to the beauty parlor and she drove the poor hairdresser crazy with what she wanted her hair to look like. With Janie's wild, unruly, thick, coarse hair, no matter how hard the woman tried, it was NEVER going to look like the picture Janie brought. We all decided it would be better to curl it in banana curls. She looked adorable.

We got back to Janie's house and I told her I would see her later. She turned her whole body to say goodbye. She was not moving her head for anything lest a curl come loose. I got home and announced my entrance by saying, "I'm home."

I heard several voices say at once, "Out back." I walked out the back door into a transformed backyard. There was a huge canopy over the patio with lights and decorations. There were tables with beautiful flowered cloths covering them, balloons all around and a big sign across the back of the house that read "Welcome to the 1972 Motown Dance Party." My dad, mom, Aunt Angie, Mama Rose, Vinnie and Rudy were in the backyard.

"What is all this?" I asked.

Everyone yelled, "Surprise!"

"Surprise for what?"

My mom couldn't keep from being the one to tell me. "It was Rudy's idea. Since you weren't going to the prom he decided to have a little of the prom come to you."

I looked at Rudy as he shrugged his shoulders and grinned.

"We are having a little party tonight with all Motown music. It was Rudy's idea," my mom said again.

"Ah." I laughed. "That's why Janie kept me from coming home."

I walked over to Rudy and of course started crying. "You are too much."

"No, you are. I wouldn't be comfortable dancing at the prom knowing you weren't dancing. This is really to make me feel better," he laughed.

Then Aunt Angie explained Rudy, with Vinnie and Jackie's help, had been planning this for weeks. I didn't have a clue. Rudy gave out invitations to my friends who weren't going to the prom and to my family. He got the tent, ordered balloons and decorations and picked out all the music. They were expecting about twenty people. I kept shaking my head in disbelief.

Rudy and I went inside and I started kissing him all over his face. We were in the exact same spot where we first kissed and he said to me, "Now *this* is a little creepy," after I must have given him twenty smooches on his face. I looked in the living room and there were two beautiful bouquets of flowers on the coffee table. I walked over to read the cards. They were both for me.

"Yeah," Rudy said. "Dr. Willard stole my thunder."

One of the bouquets was from Rudy with a note that read, "In my life, I love you more. Love, Rudy," a line from the Beatles song. I gave him a real kiss and grabbed the other card. It was from Dr. Willard. His attached note said, "To one special junior. Have a great night. Dr. Willard." I started to cry again. Rudy and Vinnie left to get dressed while I went upstairs to shower. I couldn't believe what he had done. I was starting to get excited about this Motown dance party.

A senior named Bobby was having a pre-prom "cocktail" party over at his house. It was a place for everyone to take pictures and for those who were of age to have a drink. Rudy got the Floyds to agree to let Dana go. He wanted me to go with him to pick Dana up but I said absolutely not. This was HER night and he better not forget that.

"Aye, aye, captain," he said.

I would meet them over Bobby's with my "not going to the prom" group, which was now the "Motown Party" group featuring me, Marie and Gina. I wore a great mini dress my mom made for me, did my hair and put on a little extra makeup. I wanted to feel pretty too.

We got there and everyone looked gorgeous, like mini grownups playing dress-up. I went over to Vinnie and Jackie and told Vinnie he cleaned up nicely. Jackie looked very pretty. She always did, but she never wore makeup or fussed much about her appearance, so this was a big change. I was checking out everyone's gowns, telling them how beautiful they looked, when into the backyard walked Rudy and Dana. Oh my God! Rudy looked like a movie star, so handsome. I couldn't take my eyes off him and when he saw me he gave me the biggest smile he had. I felt my insides melt. Dana looked beautiful too. She looked like a princess and was very happy with all the attention. Rudy and I had agreed we would not show any affection in front of Dana. That night he was her date, not my boyfriend. It took all my strength not to go over and hug him. I walked calmly over with a smile on my face and said, "May I take a picture of the best-looking couple here?"

"You may," said Dana, grinning from ear to ear.

I took several and told her how beautiful she looked. She turned to Rudy and said, "She helped me pick out my gown."

"Well, you both picked out a winner" he said.

I didn't hang with them long. I was feeling a little down being there. I mingled. Every time I looked at Rudy he was looking at me. Before I knew it everyone was getting ready to go to the Huntington Town House, a huge catering hall in Huntington that had what I guessed was the largest chandelier ever built hanging in its window. I saw Rudy and Dana coming over to me.

"Dana wants to tell you something," Rudy said.

"Rudy and I are only going to the prom as friends," Dana said as if to reassure me. I nodded.

"Have a great time, you two," I replied.

When I went to hug her goodbye Dana whispered a soft "thank you" in my ear. As they walked away Rudy turned around and mouthed the words "I love you" to me. I felt better and went home to dance.

By the time I got home people were already dancing to Stevie Wonder. Rudy had invited all the football players from my grade plus some of my girlfriends and my cousins. I ran upstairs to change, as you really can't dance crazy in a mini dress and still be "ladylike," as my mom would say. I put on a great sleeveless, form-fitting jumpsuit with bell-bottoms my mom had made me. The material was orange and pink paisley and she had modeled it from something I saw Goldie Hawn wear on *Laugh In*. It had a little used thing called Lycra in the material and it moved with me when I danced. I put my hair up in a ponytail and I was ready

I think I danced nonstop for three hours with everyone. Rudy had gotten my dad and Uncle Joe to change the records. Cassette recorders were fairly new and they didn't have the sound quality for a dance party yet. Rudy had brought over his stereo and speakers, which were much better than mine and showed the dads how to operate it. He had dozens of those great blue Motown singles ready in a special order with a tall round disc in the center of the turntable. They would stack a bunch of 45s on and let it go. He also had albums with specific tracks outlined for play. He must have spent a fortune at Titus Oaks, a local record store in Westbury. All my favorites were there. I danced to "I Can't Help Myself," "Get Ready," "Reach Out and I'll Be There," "River Deep, Mountain High" and of course my Supremes. I was in Motown heaven.

Around eleven o'clock people started to leave. But a little after that other people came. I was dancing with Richard when who came in the backyard but Vinnie and Jackie. Vinnie had no jacket, tie or cummerbund on and his shirt was half out of his pants. Turns out he lost those parts of his tuxedo somewhere along the way and had to pay for them the next day when he returned the tuxedo, or what was left of it. He was also a little drunk. He came running on the dance floor, grabbed me away from Richard and started dancing, yelling, "This is my cousin and I love her." I looked at Jackie and she shrugged her shoulders, rolled her eyes and shook her head. I think she was glad the prom was over.

Following them into the backyard were Erick and Janie, both drunk and very happy. They were followed by Maria and John, probably the most mismatched couple at the prom. Several other couples showed up and I realized that instead of going to the Hamptons after the prom like most of the class, they were coming here. And if they were coming here that meant Rudy was too. Before I could even get excited about that, he walked in the backyard, tuxedo still intact. We gave each other a big grin as I pulled away from Vinnie, which wasn't an easy task. I ran up to Rudy to hug him but stopped short when I realized he had a crown on his head.

"Oh no," I laughed. "Were you and Dana prom king and queen?"

He took the crown off his head and put it on mine.

"She must have been so excited."

"She was," he said, pulling me close to him and giving me a kiss. "Did you have a good time tonight?"

"It was awesome. But even better now that you are here."

He went over to the stereo just as "Ain't too Proud to Beg" was finishing and pulled out a record that was hidden and separate from the rest. He put on Sam Cooke's "Unchained Melody." Now don't get me wrong. The Righteous Brothers did an amazing recording of this song. But our favorite version was Sam Cooke's. It is hauntingly beautiful and we always loved to dance to it. It was the perfect ending to an unexpectedly marvelous evening.

The girls decided they wanted to sleep over so we had a pajama party while I listened to all the exploits of the prom. It must have been 2:30 before we went to sleep. That evening was added to my ten best nights ever.

In the morning my dad went to Maria's Italian Bakery and brought home all kinds of goodies for breakfast. Rudy and Vinnie came over to clean up and Erick stopped by to help, although I think he wanted to see Janie.

Some of the class of '72 had rented several houses in the Hamptons for the weekend. Lucy would never let me go. I told Rudy to go as his grade wouldn't have too many more opportunities to get together and party. He said he would rather hang out locally and a bunch of us went to Lido Beach the next day and immediately fell asleep. Aunt Angie and my mom had pizza waiting when we got home and we again hung out at my house. It was really lovely being together with those who were the most special rather than a crowd of hundreds of drunk kids.

The next day we went to Great Adventure in New Jersey. It seemed like the entire amusement park was filled with kids from Rudy's class. Even a few teachers showed up. Dana and her parents were there. Dana was wearing her prom crown. Rudy and I took her on a bunch of rides. At one point Dana and Rudy went on some kind of "vomit comet" thing that was too much for me. While they were spinning upside down in reverse Mr. and Mrs. Floyd came over to me. They wanted to thank me and Rudy for making the weekend so special for Dana. I said it wasn't me but Rudy. Mrs. Floyd said this would not have been possible if I didn't make a few sacrifices. They handed me an envelope that contained a beautiful letter and money for me and Rudy to go out and have a post-prom celebration. They were a lovely family. We got home late Sunday and I was exhausted. Of course I had to get up early Monday to take the last Regents of the year. For someone who didn't go to the prom, I had the prom weekend of my life.

## CHAPTER 17

# The Summer Before

Graduations are exciting and bittersweet. New beginnings await you, but you are leaving behind old friends and traditions. I always equate it with getting a new pair of sneakers. The old ones are ripped and falling apart; their time is up. You get a new pair but are never sure if they are going to be as comfortable and reliable as the old ones. Even if they are the same brand they are not the same sneaker.

Rudy and Vinnie graduated. I was proud to watch them walk across the stage to get their hard-earned diplomas. Our little cheering section was probably the loudest. The boys didn't want big fancy parties at a restaurant and since their families overlapped, they had a barbeque at Rudy's with dancing, singing, laughing and tons of food. Some friends stopped by and everyone got a little drunk.

Over the next two weeks Rudy, Vinnie and I, along with our friends, went to a lot of graduation parties. By this time they resembled football parties with a hundred kids or more. I was a maniac about people drinking and driving because of what had happened to my Aunt Theresa. Students Against Drunk Driving wouldn't be established for another nine years, so if you weren't directly affected by a drunk-driving incident you probably didn't think much about driving while drunk or high on drugs. I was a mother hen, checking out who was driving and who'd been drinking. I never believed the person who is the least drunk drives. It had to be a sober person who didn't drink any alcohol at all. It sometimes was exhausting being me.

Around the same time as these parties, the graduating football players and some of the soon-to-be seniors decided to go into the city for one last get-together. They were going to have dinner then maybe go to a few bars or clubs. I jokingly told Rudy not to call me for bail money. Apparently they had a great time; they came home around four in the morning, with a few of them crashing at Vinnie's house.

About one o'clock the following afternoon I got a call from a very hungover Rudy. Usually a beer drinker, he had been drinking scotch last night and was paying for it today. He said he and Vinnie wanted me to come over. They had something to show me. I wondered why they couldn't come to my house but I guess the walk and sunlight would have been too much for them. I immediately asked if they had gotten me a present and Rudy said kind of, but not really. That piqued my curiosity.

I walked over and into the kitchen. For some reason no one ever used Aunt Angie's front door. We always went around back to the kitchen entrance. She was cleaning up what looked like breakfast for twenty. She just rolled her eyes at me and motioned to the den. "Good luck," she said with a laugh.

In the den were Rudy, Vinnie, Gerry, Erick and Richard. They were hung over. Bad. I had a smirk on my face. Gerry let out a tired "Shut up."

"I didn't say a thing," I said in almost a whisper, still smiling.

"Do you have to talk so loudly?" Erick joked.

I sat down, not even kissing Rudy hello, which I always did. I thought if he had to pucker his lips his head might cave in.

"So, how was last night?" I asked sarcastically.

"Who remembers?" Erick joked again.

I sat there, looking at them suffering so, and chuckled. "Anyone want to go swimming?" I said in a very upbeat voice. I got five groans back. "Okay, what is it that you want to show me?" I finally said, turning to Rudy.

They all looked at each other suspiciously and cautiously. Rudy then leaned forward and took his shirt off. I was really confused. Then I saw a bandage on his left shoulder/chest area and one on his right forearm.

"Oh my God! Did you get stabbed? What happened?" my voice was now loud and clear.

They all started removing or lifting up parts of clothing to reveal they all had bandages on them in different places. Vinnie's was on his calf, as was Erick's. The top of Gerry's arm and his back were bandaged. Richard had the top of his right arm covered. I had no idea what the hell was going on. Then Rudy slowly, painfully, removed the bandage from his chest. It was bloody and I couldn't make out what the black underneath was. A bruise? Stitches? Oh no. Nothing so dramatic. After a few beverages the boys had all decided to go to SoHo and get tattoos.

I sat there with my mouth open for what seemed like a long time. Not many things could make me speechless but this was one of them. I had heard Rudy and Vinnie talking about getting a tattoo every now and then. They used to say when they were eighteen years old they would go, but they never did.

"Thank God you didn't get them on your face," I joked. I didn't know if they woke up happy or regretful about their decision. Since it was already a done deal and they couldn't turn back, I played it as a happy thing. I turned to Rudy and said, "What'd ya get?"

Rudy and I had this "snuggling position" thing, as we came to call it. He would always lie to my right and put his left arm up. I would snuggle my head and face in his chest and upper shoulder while he wrapped me in a warm hug. I would tell him it was my favorite place on earth and no matter where we were, it always felt like home. He pointed to that now-bloodied area and said, "It says CASA. That is home in Italian."

I just stared at it for what seemed like forever and started to cry. "I can't believe you did that," I must have said five times. I reached over to him—carefully so as not to touch his tattoo—and gave him a tear-stained kiss. When I pulled away a tear or two dropped from his eyes. I don't think he was being sentimental. I think it was from the pain of removing the bandage. "You know that's forever?"

"So are we" was his response. Of course Gerry and Erick had to make some choking sounds like they were going to throw up.

"Jealous?" I said to them. "What's on your arm?" I said to Rudy.

Rudy started to take the bandage off to show me and I stopped him.

"You can just tell me."

"It says 'La Familia.' Italian for family. I had initials of my parents, Carmine and you put into the design with a rose for my mom and grandmother incorporated in it as well." He showed me a picture of it that had been drawn at the tattoo parlor and of the Casa tattoo. They were done in such a way that they looked like beautiful symbols. It wasn't just letters; it was art. If you didn't know what it said you might think it was a design. They were stunning.

I turned to Vinnie and said, "Next."

He had a ram on his calf. That was our high school mascot and it was copied perfectly from the school's design. It was a nice remembrance. Erick had a moon-and-sun combination on his calf I would have wanted to turn into a piece of jewelry. Gerry got a football helmet with the school's ram design on his back. He had a crown of thorns tattooed around his arm. Richard, who I just adored, had a Superman emblem put on his arm. Instead of an "S" it was an "R", to commemorate his LSD jump from the roof. I told them I thought they all chose beautiful and personal tattoos and I couldn't wait to see them when they healed. Of course I had to ask, "Did it hurt?"

In unison three said yes and two said no. We all laughed. The tattoos healed and they were exquisite. The people who tattooed them were real artists. I asked Rudy how they came upon that particular parlor. He said a guy in one of the bars had outrageous tattoo sleeves on both of his arms and they all started talking. The guy told them the name of the parlor he used and they decided to go. He even called ahead to announce they were coming and went with them. The owner kept his shop open late for them, brought out a bottle of scotch and the rest is history.

Rudy was very nervous that I would be upset that he got the tattoos. He kept apologizing for not discussing it with me first and I kept telling him it was his body and his decision. I told him I appreciated his concern for what I thought and I absolutely loved them. I was touched that he would even think of getting a tattoo related to us. It was a forever gesture I would always cherish.

"Just not on your face, okay?" I joked.

I wanted this summer to go slowly but, like every one before it and every one since, it flew by. The three of us spent a lot of time together, I think, in part, because we all knew this was the last time we probably would or could. Rudy and I were able to steal a lot of intimate time alone. We had to make up for the time he would be away.

The boys had saved all year so they wouldn't have to work this last summer before college. Plus they got a lot of money as graduation gifts. They would work maybe once a week at Uncle Joe's dealership and he would overpay them ridiculous amounts of money. We had the summer free and made the most of every second.

I was seventeen that summer and had fake proof so I could get into bars. I wasn't really a big drinker and never really liked the bar scene. I still don't. Not my thing sitting around watching people get drunk. Alcohol makes me tired. I was a pot smoker, though, big time, even though that made me tired AND paranoid. Rudy was an athlete. I am not saying he thought his body was a temple, but he was very aware of how what he ingested affected his performance. A few beers and occasionally a hit or two of pot was his normal partying routine. Maybe mushrooms or LSD if he didn't have a game or was doing something special. Almost everybody was doing something.

I also smoked cigarettes and that drove Rudy crazy. I always blamed Vinnie for that one. The first time I ever smoked, Vinnie and I stole cigarettes from Uncle Joe and went behind his garage. I was twelve and he was thirteen. I had a few puffs, coughed my head off and went home. Vinnie continued to smoke. Wouldn't you know it, Uncle Joe had to get something from behind the garage and caught him. I got away in the nick of time. Uncle Joe was furious with Vinnie. As a punishment he made Vinnie smoke the four other stolen cigarettes in a row. I heard Vinnie was turning green, he got so sick. CPS call today? Maybe. But Rudy never smoked another cigarette again.

I wasn't as lucky. I smoked on and off until I was thirty, then quit. Along with all the pot smoke I am sure I did permanent damage to my lungs. I tried never to smoke around Rudy and not to smoke before I saw him. I quit once or twice with his help. I smoked a lot my senior year, both cigarettes and pot, when he was away at school. My older self would now tell my younger self not to smoke but I doubt I would listen, even to me.

I have always said that summer vacation was like a weekend. July was Saturday and August was Sunday. As long as we were still in July, I was okay. We packed a lot into those July days. We did something every afternoon and every night. Rudy, Vinnie and some of his friends put together a soft-ball league so we spent a lot of time at Salisbury Park, I mean Eisenhower Park. The name changed in 1969 but we still called it by its old name. Janie and Jackie convinced the team to go co-ed and I was delighted they agreed. Of course the league complained, but they did it anyway. They even had a write-up about it in *Newsday*, the local Long Island paper.

One long weekend we went camping with our dads. Vinnie, Rudy and I slept in the same tent as always. We loved to hike and often went to Bailey's and Planting Fields Arboretums. We spent a lot of time at the beach, in the pool and anywhere else that would bring relief from those humid Long Island summer days. Yes, we had them even back then. A bunch of us took our bikes on the ferry to Shelter Island. I love the city so we would try to go to Manhattan as often as possible to see a show, go to a museum or just hang out. Rudy would even go in with me to go shopping, but Vinnie said, "the buck stops there."

A new village had opened in Bethpage a few years earlier. Actually, it was an old nineteenth-century village with the original houses moved to the site. It was over two hundred acres and I loved going there. I felt like I was in an old town. I especially loved the schoolhouse. I never tired of the place and I loved the history. We would go several times a year, during different seasons, but always in the summer. My dad and Papa G. loved going with us too.

One day Rudy had planned a special surprise for me in the city. We were going to go out to lunch and then he was going to take me someplace I had never been. I would have bet the house he was taking me to see the revival of *A Funny Thing Happened on the Way to the Forum*, starring Sgt. Bilko himself, Phil Silvers. I didn't know the city that well then but, after lunch, when we got in the cab, I knew we weren't heading toward Times Square. Eventually we stopped. We were in SoHo, outside a tattoo parlor.

"Are you getting another tattoo?" I asked.

"No. We are."

I walked out of the cab protesting and confused. We walked into the parlor and Rudy was greeted like an old friend by the owner, Evan. "So you finally convinced her to come in for that tattoo?"

"No," Rudy said. "She just found out about five seconds ago."

"Hello?" I whispered. "I am right here. Can someone tell me what this is all about?"

"We are getting matching tattoos," Rudy boasted.

"We are?" I said, very surprised.

"Yeah, we are," he said, kissing me on the top of my head.

It was very unlike Rudy to make a decision affecting me without discussing it with me first, especially one that involved a tattoo. But he seemed so sure in his determination to do this. I asked what he had in mind. He pulled out a piece of paper and on it he had drawn a ring, a band with the letters IWALY spaced around the front of it, along with a heart on one side and a peace sign on the other. It was beautiful and incredibly romantic.

"I thought we would have these done on our left-hand ring fingers. Kind of like commitment tattoos," he said, proud of himself for thinking of it. For the second time that summer I was speechless. This was even more thoughtful than the Casa tattoo. There was no way I was going to say no to this even though I was petrified of needles. I whispered to Rudy that he should tell Evan I don't do boo-boos well. He laughed and told me it would be fine. Evan decided to tattoo Rudy first in case I wanted to change something on mine. I watched as these needles went all the way around Rudy's finger. He didn't flinch although I think he wanted to.

It turned out beautiful and I wished I had gone first so it would be over. Evan was very sweet and first let me know what it felt like without the ink. I will not lie—it hurt. It wasn't horrific pain, but it was enough to bring tears to my eyes. Evan told me I could take as many breaks as I needed, sharing with us that it once took him three hours to do a quarter-sized heart tattoo on his friend Rick.

Rudy held my right hand, squeezing it often, while Evan worked his magic. I didn't take any breaks as I wanted it done as quickly as possible. It wasn't too long before he announced he was finished. I LOVED it. It was exactly like Rudy's. Once again I told Rudy this was permanent and once again he said we were too. I hugged Evan for this beautiful gift I would have with me always. He wrapped both of us up in bandages and Rudy hailed a cab.

In the cab I snuggled next to Rudy while we both held out our left hands, admiring our matching boo-boos. The cab drove right past our parking garage and I looked at Rudy, wondering where we were going now. You guessed it. It stopped right in front of the marquee that said *A Funny Thing Happened on the Way to the Forum*, starring Phil Silvers. We were going to the theater.

Rudy wasn't a theater person. It was hard for him to sit still that long. Plus it really wasn't his cup of tea. I've loved the theater as long as I could remember. My parents would take me to see musical shows at the Jones Beach Marine Theater. After the shows we would go to the Schaefer Beer Tent and listen to Guy Lombardo. When I was eight, Mr. Lombardo and I did a little jig together. Somewhere there is a picture of that. But Rudy never got that bug. He told me he loved watching *me* watch the shows. He said I would sit on the edge of my seat and my face would light up. He joked I didn't stop smiling the entire time and that was always the best part of going. Well worth the $3.50 ticket, he would joke.

On the way home I told Rudy I couldn't wait to show Vinnie. Then I said, "Oh my God, Lucy!"

"What about her?"

"She is going to have a fit that I got a tattoo."

Rudy smirked and said, "Tell her you have a cut on your finger and, when it heals, put a ring over it."

"You really have thought of everything," I said smiling.

"Yes, I have," he proudly responded.

July was setting and August was rising on the horizon. Rudy and I still hadn't discussed the distance or separation we were about to experience or its effect on our relationship. I said I wasn't going to bring it up and I didn't, although I sometimes had to put my hand over my mouth not to say anything.

We spent some of August getting Rudy ready to leave. I went with him and Mama Rose to buy sheets, towels, a bedspread, all the essentials he would need. He wanted to fly out there, not drive, so all of his things were shipped to the university. I could tell he was getting really excited about leaving and I had to remind myself he wasn't excited about leaving me but about going to Arizona. It was hard not to take it personally.

Rudy's parents had a little family going-away party for him and Vinnie, with a few friends invited as well, almost like the graduation party. Everyone would say the same thing to me: "You're going to miss Rudy." I would smile and give my standard answer of "This is a wonderful opportunity for Rudy. I am so proud of him." What I really wanted to say was, well, you get it.

I got Rudy and Vinnie puka shell necklaces because it was 1972 and everyone was wearing them. I also got Rudy a really nice pair of binoculars for hiking that he went wild over. I sent Vinnie away with a small turntable and a collection of Motown tunes.

"I can't dance to these without you," he said.

"Oh, I am sure you will find a suitable replacement," I told him.

They were both leaving in less than a week. Couldn't they spread it out? They had to leave on the same day? Vinnie told us he wanted to go to the beach one last time before he went away so we decided to go Tuesday as the weather looked perfect. Rudy and I were not aware of the real reason Vinnie asked us to go.

I too had to prepare to go back to school. It was my senior year and as sad as I was that Rudy was leaving, I was excited about being a high school senior. And no matter where Rudy went, he wouldn't be back at the high school. I had been doing a little shopping, but the girls and I were going to go to the Roosevelt Field mall on Saturday and make a full day of it. We were taking the bus and my dad would pick us up. We had learned our lesson.

Tuesday came quickly and Rudy, Vinnie and I stopped at Tony's Hero Shop, which was on Old Country Road around the corner from Rudy's. Next to our family recipe, they had the best meatball heroes around. Of course we could never tell the moms we went there for meatballs. They would be highly insulted.

We decided we would go to Robert Moses Beach. It was a little farther but we hadn't been there in a long time and this was a special day. We went past TOBAY and almost stopped there but decided to go with our original plan.

We went to field three. Vinnie wanted to sit away from the lifeguards and the crowd so we parked ourselves in an almost empty part of the beach. We devoured our lunch and Rudy said he was going to walk down to the swimming part of the beach in about half an hour. We all laid down on the blanket like we did when we were little and started telling beach stories.

Suddenly Vinnie sat up and got very serious. "I want to tell you guys something confidentially."

Rudy and I were concerned about his tone and we both sat up too. Then Vinnie said to us, "I'm gay."

"Gay, like happy?" was my stupid reply. It was the first thing out of my mouth.

"No," Vinnie said. "Gay like homosexual."

Then another stupid thing came out of my mouth. "Are you sure?"

"Yes," he smiled, replying softly. "I am sure."

"But you are a football player." I just couldn't get my mouth to shut up.

Vinnie laughed. "You could be gay and play football. It's not against the rules."

*Rules? What rules? Are there football rules about being gay? Gay rules about playing football?* I realized he was kidding and this was another Sammy Davis Jr. moment all over again. I couldn't believe how naïve I was about this too. I looked at Rudy, who looked at me. I had never had anyone tell me they were gay and I am sure in 1972 Hallmark didn't have a card for that. "Congratulations?" I said, hoping for a laugh, which I got. "No, really, Vinnie, thank you so much for sharing this with us."

"Yeah," Rudy said.

"Nothing changes between us, right?" Vinnie said.

"Not for us," I said, pointing to Rudy and myself and trying to get another laugh. "Are you seeing anyone?"

"No."

"Does the family know?" I just had to ask.

"My mom and Catherine know. I just haven't had the right time to tell my dad. Maybe when I come home for Thanksgiving."

Again trying for levity, I said to Vinnie, "You are my first gay."

He smiled and said, "Oh, no, I'm not. You would be surprised who else is in this secret gay society." I knew he was kidding about the secret gay society. I think.

There was a moment of awkward silence. Vinnie then told us he had known ever since he was a kid but tried to hide it. He tried to fight it. He had dated a few girls but realized that wasn't for him. He told us how growing up he felt alone and isolated, like he was the only one in the world who felt like this. We both told him we wished he would have told us sooner, but he said he was too scared. He was afraid we wouldn't love him anymore. I started to cry and told him we would always love him, that we loved him even more now for taking us into his confidence.

"Vinnie," Rudy said. "I wish for you what I always wish. That you find a partner as crazy, loving, kind and beautiful as mine."

Vinnie and I both made the choking throw-up noise and we all laughed. We then decided to go for a swim, but not after we had one of our enormous group bear hugs, in which we all cried. On the way to the water Rudy shot Vinnie an adorable grin.

"What?" Vinnie shot back.

"All those times we were watching *Bewitched* and fighting over who was going to marry Elizabeth Montgomery ..."

"I was really watching for Darrin."

"Which one?"

"The second one, of course."

We all started laughing and the next thing I knew the boys were chasing each other in the water. Nope, nothing changed. I don't have to go through what it was like for gay, lesbian, bisexual, transgender and questioning youth in 1972. Put simply, it was a nightmare, as it remains for many today. They had nowhere to go, no role models, no support groups, fear of being outed and bullied or worse. As a heterosexual adult who spent my career working in high schools, I would like to think gay adolescents are more mainstream now, for lack of a better word. But I know that isn't the case. I know LBGTQ youth still face abuse by ignorant and malicious people every day. And for those of us who know them, love them and care about equality for LBGTQ people, it remains heartbreaking. A while later, when my mom found out, she was surprisingly supportive, saying the heart wants what the heart wants and you can't control who you love. *Way to go, Lucy.*

Vinnie told Aunt Angie we knew and the first time we were alone, she brought it up. She said her only concern was for Vinnie's safety. "People can be so cruel to gays." I understood what she was saying. I explained Vinnie had the love and support of many, especially his mom. We both cried because we loved him so much and wanted him to be happy.

The countdown to Rudy and Vinnie leaving was now in hours, not months, weeks or days. I remained a smiling wreck and think I should have been nominated for an Oscar that year for my performance. We all went over Aunt Angie's for breakfast to say goodbye to Vinnie, who was driving to school with Aunt Angie and Uncle Joe. Rudy really wanted me to go to the airport with his parents and Carmine even though I didn't want to have to say goodbye there. I went, but not before he came over to say goodbye to my parents. I was surprised they both cried, although I shouldn't have been. He was like a son to them. My mom had made him some of her famous Italian cookies for the plane ride, just like she made for Vinnie. He was touched and also got a little teary.

When I got in the back seat of the car with Rudy and Carmine I told Papa G. I was only going to the airport because Rudy said we could make out on the way there.

"Go for it," he said.

"Ugh, no way," Carmine groaned.

We were all chatting in the car as Rudy held on to my hand so tightly I thought my fingers would go numb. He kept rubbing his fingers over my tattoo ring. I just smiled at him. We never did talk about his going away and what that would mean for us. We would just take it one day at a time.

We got to the airport, to his gate and it was time to say goodbye. Carmine and Papa G. hugged and kissed him. Then Mama Rose hugged him and cried. They all walked a few feet away while Rudy and I said our goodbyes. I wasn't going to cry, but he did, so I did too.

"This is just temporary," he said. "It's not a tattoo or anything."

"No," I said.

He then gave me a kiss I still remember today. I told him I needed oxygen afterward. He said he would call me when he got settled. I told him to wait until the next day because he would be busy and I would be sleeping. He gave me a kiss on my head, whispered he would always love me and disappeared into the airplane to begin this new chapter of his life. And, for the first time in his life, it would be without me.

## CHAPTER 18

# The Senior

Rudy called me every day from Arizona. I told him he didn't have to as he was going to get a huge phone bill. He said he didn't care; he wanted to talk to me. I didn't want to tell him I was afraid I would get used to the daily phone calls and when they stopped, I would be upset. So we talked every night. It was nice to hear his voice.

He would tell me about practice, his classes, his roommate, friends he met and how many times he had to explain his commitment tattoo to people. Sometimes our talks got a little naughty. The more we talked the more I thought this separation might be good for us, until of course I got off the phone and missed him more. It certainly was an adjustment.

The night before my first day as a senior I didn't sleep much. Does anyone sleep before the first day of school? Twelve years and it was always the same anticipation, dread and excitement. The next morning, while I was getting dressed, my phone rang. Who was calling me that early? It had to be Janie saying she wanted to borrow a dress or something. It was Rudy wishing me good luck on my first day as a senior. He told me it was four o'clock in the morning there and that he had to set two alarm clocks to make sure he got up. It started my day off perfectly.

I walked to Janie's, which was odd because we had gotten used to Rudy driving us to school. Gina joined us and these three badass seniors walked into the building to start their last year of high school. The school always had a senior breakfast where the twelfth graders would be served by the eleventh graders. Then the seniors would stay for a brief assembly by the administrators on the dos and don'ts of senior year.

I always hated the first day of school, even when I worked in one. Everyone hugged and screamed when they saw me. "How was your summer?" If they really cared, they would have called me. Ugh, I just hated it. I walked in with people greeting me like they hadn't seen me in years. Everyone wanted to know how my summer was and how Rudy was, which was nice of them to ask. From across the room I saw Dr. Willard, who came trotting to greet me. He gave me a big hug and whispered in my ear that we were going to have a great senior year. Then he looked at me and asked, "How's our boy? Did he get to Arizona alright?"

"Yup," I said.

He then repeated it was going to be a great senior year. And I believed him. I was going to make sure it was great. I had a perfect schedule with some Regents classes and some electives I was really excited about. It was odd at first walking around the building and not seeing any of last year's seniors, especially Rudy. But we all adjusted rather quickly. I had two psychology classes with Mr. Conn, who I had had the previous year for Intro to Psychology. I adored that man and he really liked me. We got along great, maybe in part because I did A+ work in his class. I loved psychology and ended up making it a career. Mr. Conn was the teacher who taught me to love it.

In September the school always had a lot of assemblies for many different reasons. Around the third week of school there was a double-period assembly about something or other. A group of friends and I decided to cut the assembly and go to our friend Danny's house to hang out. He lived a few blocks from the school and we were going to make breakfast.

When we got there Danny's brother Jeff was home. He was going to CW Post College but didn't have classes that day until the afternoon. When we walked in the house Jeff was in the living room with his friend Jimmy and the biggest, most beautiful water pipe I had ever seen. Truth be told, it was the only water pipe I had ever seen except in pictures. They were just about to fire it up and asked if we wanted to join them.

I had smoked through a bong that you fill with water to cool the pot going down your throat and into your lungs, but never anything this fancy. It reminded me of the Beatles on their visit to the Maharishi. So a few friends and I figured, what the heck. I must have taken three or four hits, which was a lot for me. I didn't feel like I was smoking anything. I felt fine for a while. We never did make breakfast as we got too stoned. We ate Trix and Cheerios dry from the box. Then it was time to walk back to school.

It was a beautiful day and the two-block walk back to school started out fine. But as the school got closer I got more and more stoned, a different kind of high than I had ever felt. I could smell the colors, taste the flowers, that sort of thing. Something more than pot was in that water pipe. Danny and the others seemed to be dealing with the high, but my paranoia kicked in big time and my heart started racing. I didn't like this at all and wished I had gone to the assembly instead. There was nothing I could do now except to go to my sociology class and say as little as possible.

Mr. Conn was waiting to greet his students at the door as usual. He said hi to me but gave me a strange look. No, I was just being my paranoid, stoned self. I sat in my seat and it felt like an hour before the late bell rang. He walked to his desk, took attendance and then addressed me personally, asking me to come up to his desk to get something or other. I felt every eyeball in that room on me as I carefully, slowly, lifted myself out of my seat. I was three rows from Mr. Conn's desk. A ten-second walk took what felt like the entire period. Then I had to walk back.

One of the major side effects of marijuana is the change in perception of time. Everything slows down—really slows down. A drunk driver will usually speed on the highway, but a stoned driver will probably drive very slowly. I was driving, I mean walking, up to that desk at a snail's crawl. But I made it back to my seat without an incident. I was quiet the rest of the class.

I knew I couldn't go through the rest of the afternoon like this so I went to the nurse and told her I threw up. I think my color was off and my heart was racing. Even though I didn't have a fever she asked me if I wanted to go home. I told her no, but could I lie down? She obliged and I slept until the end of the school day. She had to wake me up. I was still stoned. I went home, told my mom I didn't feel well and fell asleep until Rudy called me at 8:00 p.m. I didn't tell him what had happened, just that I wasn't feeling well.

I NEVER, EVER again went to school stoned or smoked during school or at any school-sponsored events. That was the first and only time. (Except for the Edgar Winter concert in the auditorium, which was the first time I ever smoked pot.) It was hard to function and concentrate. And I thought it was disrespectful to Dr. Willard, whom I really liked and who had always been so kind to Rudy and me. Students shouldn't come to school drunk so why should marijuana be any different? But a lot of kids smoked joints in between classes in the smoking section. I never did. I always thought that, if you needed to get high in school, if you couldn't wait six or seven hours to get stoned, then you had a real problem.

The next school day was going along well as I headed to Mr. Conn's class. I gave him a big smile and hello at the door. He asked if he could speak to me. I was sure it was about the brilliant essay I had just written about nature versus nurture. The essay was brilliant, he would tell me later, but that was not what he wanted to speak to me about. We moved a few feet down the hallway away from his door. I looked at him and he wasn't smiling.

"Don't you ever come to my class like that again," he said in a stern voice that had never been directed at me before.

I wasn't expecting that, thinking I had gotten away free and clear. I felt sick to my stomach, not because I got caught, but because Mr. Conn caught me. I could tell I had really disappointed him and by now you know how important it was for everyone to like me.

"I am so very sorry. It will never happen again, I promise."

"Well, it better not, in my class or any other. Do you realize you could be suspended for the rest of the year?"

I thought he was exaggerating for dramatic effect, but it scared me like it was supposed to. I never gave a thought to what the consequences would be if I got caught stoned in school. I was angry at myself for not doing so.

"No," I said, starting to cry.

"I know you are a better person and student than that so I will keep this between the two of us. But never again, right?"

"Never." I was almost sobbing now.

"Go to the bathroom and wash your face. It's alright. Let it go."

In any other situation this could have been the end of a great student-teacher relationship, but we both made sure it wasn't. I went after school that day to apologize and we had a great talk, which lasted all year. He became a sounding board for me; others would say counselor/mentor. Wherever you are, Mr. Conn, thank you for being such a special teacher.

Senior year, for me anyway, was a mixture of fun and agony. Even though I only had a few Regents classes to take, I had to pass them to graduate. Although all states today have some sort of annual statewide exams,

New York is the only state that still has Regents. And then, even more than now, they were a big deal.

In my entire school career I only cheated twice in my life. They were both on Regents exams in my senior year. As detailed earlier, I had a learning disability in language, undiagnosed and untreated. Although I was a solid B+ student it took a lot of effort on my part to maintain that. Some people could open a notebook, review a lesson and get an A on a test. I had to start studying at least a week before, sometimes two.

I am a visual learner. If I don't see it written down it doesn't stay in my brain. Because of that I was a ferocious note taker. The worst thing for me was to be absent and rely on someone else's notes for that day's lesson. If I were in school today my individual education plan would call for a copy of the teacher's notes.

The subjects that suffered the most because of my disability were, naturally, Spanish and English. I rarely read a book for pleasure, I had a limited vocabulary and I couldn't spell for shit. (Nothing has really changed since then.) And no matter how hard I tried, and I really tried, I just couldn't grasp a foreign language. Rudy was amazing with languages, speaking English and Italian at home and mastering Spanish in school. He would try to help me but I would get frustrated, even though he had the patience of a saint. To get a Regents diploma I had to pass the Spanish, Math and English Regents. Math was a breeze for me. That side of my brain was exceptional. It was the other side I had to worry about.

Marie, like Rudy, spoke Italian at home and was fluent in Spanish. I was freaking out about the oral part of our Spanish Regents, where the teacher read the question and answers in Spanish and we wrote down a, b, c or d. One afternoon, a few days before the Regents, Marie was over my house helping me study when I broke down crying. I told her I was okay with the written part but the oral section, worth ten points, was starting me off with a disadvantage.

I swear this next idea came from Marie, not me. The proctor would read the oral question twice. The first time we had to listen and the second time we could write our answer. Marie said she would put her head down and write the answer as soon as it was read the second time so I would know what letter it was. This was unthinkable to me because it was cheating on the Regents. But it was only cheating for the first ten points, so I agreed.

We were all taking the exam in the same room. Marie made sure I had a clear view of her. It didn't take long for most of the class to realize what she was doing as she wasn't very subtle. (Think Jimmy Fallon writing thank-you notes). Turns out almost everyone who was in that room scored ten points on the oral part. I ended up getting a 68 on the Regents. If it wasn't for Marie, I don't know what my graduation would have looked like. I was remorseful about passing that way but I have long since gotten over it.

The English Regents was a total fluke. The first part of that Regents was vocabulary and spelling—my two worst topics—along with oral comprehension. We were read a story and then answered questions about it. We couldn't take notes during the reading. That was a tough one for me too. The rest of the Regents was usually writing essays and I was surprisingly good at that even though my language was simplistic and limited, in case you haven't noticed.

The day of the English Regents I was waiting outside the gym with a bunch of friends when I heard someone call me over. A group of kids was surrounding our friend Chuck. He somehow had gotten a copy of the spelling and vocabulary part of the Regents. No one ever figured out how he got it. It was locked in a safe somewhere. There were no computers or

Internet to "hack". And it was only that part of it. He never shared with us how he happened to come in possession of it but I was glad he did.

He read the question and someone in the crowd would give the right answer. Truth be told, of the twenty questions, I would have gotten six wrong. After we went through the questions Chuck went outside to the smoking section and burned the paper before going to the gym to take the test. We all could have gotten in huge trouble. Again, I gave no thought to the penalties had I gotten caught. I was risking my diploma and reputation, two things I had worked very hard for the prior four years. We were stupid kids taking stupid risks. I ended up getting an 87. I would have passed with or without those points, which made me feel a little better about it. So there it is, the great cheating scandal of '73.

Aside from the pressure of the schoolwork, which I usually put on myself, senior year was also a lot of fun. A core group of kids in my class were very close. Things we might not normally do, like cutting an assembly and smoking from a water pipe, we did because, hell, we were seniors. We thought we were untouchable.

Among all the frivolity of being a senior, twelfth grade was also the year I applied to college. A lot of my friends were going directly to work but I always knew I was going to continue my education. I never even gave it a second thought. Many students had already done school visits over the summer. I didn't think I wanted to go away to school but Rudy had other ideas. He really wanted me to apply to his school in Arizona. He kept telling me how great it would be for us to go to school together. I wasn't sure I wanted to be that far away from home, even with Rudy. It never occurred to me the importance of this decision and how life altering it could be and in fact was.

I had the obligatory college conference with my guidance counselor in mid-September. We talked briefly about my ambitions. I told her I was interested in doing something in the helping professions like counseling or teaching. I will never forget her response. She said to me, "Oh, you are pretty enough. You'll get married."

"*Pretty enough? Not just pretty?*" I laughed, in my head. It was one of the most insulting things anyone has ever said to me, like the way I looked had anything to do with my college or career choice. And only "pretty enough" girls got married? THIS was the woman the school chose to counsel and guide me past high school?

I thanked her like she was giving me a compliment or something. It took years before guidance counselors regained my respect. I told her I wanted to stay home at least for the first year or two. And Lucy offered an irresistible bribe; if I stayed home my parents would buy me a new car. I intended to apply to the State University of Arizona at Tempe just to see if I could get in. My guidance counselor gave me all the packets, financial information and a guide to writing my college essay. I had already decided I was going to write mine about my Alka-Seltzer incident with Kevin, but the guidelines helped. My English teacher would supervise the essay.

Besides Arizona, we agreed I would apply to Nassau Community College (a sure thing), Hofstra and CW Post Universities, SUNY Old Westbury and Stony Brook. I also threw in Adelphi University for good luck. The next few weeks of my senior year were filled with homework, studying and college applications. Most schools were offering me an academic scholarship. But the fee for Arizona, as an out-of-state student, was very expensive. I wasn't going on an athletic scholarship like Rudy. I had the money saved for college from my "modeling," so I wasn't tied to Lucy financially. But there was that emotional guilt she dished out so generously. If I decided to go, most likely without her blessing, she would have made life absolutely miserable for my father. I couldn't do that to the kindest man in the world. As much as I missed Rudy, and I missed him terribly, there was also a part of me that wanted to try this on my own. In retrospect I should have gone to Arizona but Rudy and I were managing to see each other quite often.

The only school to which I didn't get accepted was SUNY Old Westbury. The letter said something about affirmative action. I wasn't upset because Hofstra was offering me a sizeable scholarship. The administration agreed to my double major of psychology and women's studies, the only school that did. They also approved a minor in dance. It was a no-brainer.

I was accepted into Hofstra's New College. It was a smaller subdivision of the university that offered an individualized and interdisciplinary curriculum, a flexible format and varied modes of learning. I couldn't see myself in a lecture hall with two hundred other students. That was not the best way for me to learn. Here the classes were maybe twenty students, with a smaller, diverse and, may I add, excellent faculty and close-knit student body. I saw it more as an intellectual extension of high school which was a perfect fit for me.

Even though I was staying home I decided I wanted to experience dorm life and live on campus. Hofstra was fifteen minutes from my house, ten if I made all the lights. Still I would be out of the house, making my own decisions, yet close enough for Lucy's apron strings to reach. We agreed on some ground rules like no popping in to see me uninvited, limited phone calls and no expectations of my visiting on weekends. We would see how it worked.

I had money saved so I offered to pay for the dorm expenses. Because Hofstra was offering me such a large scholarship, my parents took some of the money they had saved for my tuition and helped pay for my living expenditures. I am forever grateful for that.

Rudy was excited about what Hofstra was offering me but a little disappointed I wasn't going to Arizona. We talked about my going out there my junior year, but that was way off. We were both committed to our relationship and were not as concerned about the distance as we had been in the beginning. It would have been nice to be in the same state but we would survive. We agreed this was the time for us to explore and pursue our dreams. Rudy used to kid me that we had the rest of our lives for him to annoy me. That would have been a great time to have a crystal ball.

Once the pressure of choosing a future was over I felt more relaxed and enjoyed the rest of my high school experience. I was looking forward to living on my own, so to speak. It would be a nice transition for me, living in the dorms and still being close to friends and family. It would also make sneaking off to Arizona or Rudy sneaking into New York much easier. But for now I would concentrate on graduation, my senior prom and passing the Spanish Regents.

## CHAPTER 19

# The Shower

It started out as another ordinary, beautiful October Saturday in my senior year. I had bought a new sweater to wear to the football game that day but swapped it out for a T-shirt. It was only supposed to get up to 69 degrees but the bright sun and slight humidity made it feel warmer.

My day began with an early-morning call from Rudy. Again, early for him because of the time difference. He had a football game that morning too and was certain he was going to get some play time. The coach had told him the day before to be ready. It seems those interceptions he made the previous year were no fluke. He was good at them. He was very excited. His voice also sounded a little nervous as he told me how much he wished I was there. I really wanted to witness his first appearance on a college field but I told him I'd be there in spirit. He said he would call me later. I kept my fingers crossed all day, hoping he would play.

Our game was late in the morning. Jackie and Gina came to pick me up and of course we had to stop at the deli. Eggs, potatoes and cheese on rolls for us and a snack for Janie, who was already there with the cheering squad. She was co-captain of the team now and felt she had to be there early.

We weren't there late. The game hadn't started but the bleachers were packed. We were playing a neighboring rival school and between that and the weather, it seemed like the entire school community came out for the game. Our team was on the field, practicing maneuvers, while the other team was getting off the bus. The marching band was playing some loud "Rah Rah" music.

As I looked over the immaculate green playing field I couldn't believe that just a year ago I was sitting in those very bleachers watching Rudy play. So much had changed in that year. Now he was on a different playing field thousands of miles away, with a crowd of strangers cheering him on, hoping to get some playing time. It was a strange mix of sadness and exhilaration.

It was a very close and exciting game, with each team owning the lead and volleying it back and forth. In the end we won by a three-point field goal and the stadium went wild. I could feel the vibrations of hundreds of people stomping their feet on the bleachers. There was high-fiving, butt slapping and jumps of joy (I never got the butt slapping). It was a well-earned victory. I usually didn't stay after the games now that Rudy and Vinnie weren't there. I took a pleasant stroll home, imagining Rudy had experienced the same triumphant ending to his game.

My parents were out doing their Saturday errands when I got home. The house sounded tranquil compared to the rowdy football crowd. I took off my shoes and bra, the first two things that always came off when I was wearing them and made myself a PBJ and glass of chocolate milk. I sat at the kitchen table to read Liz Smith's column and the comics in the *Daily News*.

The big news was still Vice President Spiro Agnew's resignation a few days earlier due to income tax evasion and of course the Mets making it into the World Series, which they eventually lost to the Oakland Athletics. It was exciting thinking a New York team might win. With the names Koosman, Seaver and of course Manager Yogi being bantered around, it was a great time to be a Mets fan.

I cleaned up lunch, went to my room, opened all the windows and put the fan on. I faintly heard "I Got You Babe" by Sonny and Cher playing on someone's radio. I had been a fan of Cher's since I was ten years old. I loved *The Sonny and Cher Show* and had always wanted one of her Bob Mackie outfits. I started humming the song, building my voice to a real crescendo by the end. I could do that when no one else was home. I sat down on the floor, got my English research paper out and waited for Rudy to call.

I had an exceptional English teacher, Mr. Jackman, my senior year. He was petite and always meticulously dressed. Kids used to say he was a "fag," as that was the word people used in the politically incorrect 1970s. I didn't care who he slept with. He was a nice man and a good teacher. And besides, my Vinnie was gay. When kids, mostly boys, would call him a fag I would ask, "How do you know? Did you sleep with him?" That usually shut them up. Sometimes I would flat out ask them, "Why do you care?" I never understood how people can judge others on a perception or stereotype. But in 1972 many people did. And, I am sorry to say, many still do. I guess we didn't change the world as much as we thought we would.

One Friday night a group of seniors, some from the football team, found out where Mr. Jackman lived. They went over to his house in the middle of the night and overturned his orange VW bug. These were some of the same idiots who had robbed a house when they were in eighth grade and taken pictures of each other carrying out stereos, TVs and whatever else they wanted. Did I mention they forgot the camera? They left it behind for the police. They were still on probation in twelfth grade and Mr. Jackman knew it.

Mr. Jackman came in on Monday and told our class about the incident with humor and forgiveness. I know he knew some of the kids who had vandalized his car were sitting across from him as he told his tale. But he never let his smile down. He never pressed charges. He never even called the police. He went into a hysterical routine about how he and his neighbors tried to turn the car right side up. My heart broke for him having to pretend like that about so many things.

Mr. Jackman was exceptional at guiding our class through the steps needed to write a perfect research paper. I had chosen to write my "compare and contrast" senior thesis on Christopher Marlowe's *Doctor Faustus* and Oscar Wilde's *The Picture of Dorian Grey*. That's right. I, who still secretly read *Tiger Beat* magazine and wanted Cher's clothing, was going to take a big literary dip into the classics. Me, the one with the learning disability in language. I used the multilevel techniques he taught me to write undergraduate, graduate and postgraduate papers. I never got below an A, beginning with my first one in that class. Thank you, Mr. Jackman. You helped me write this book.

I was trying to put my notes in some sort of order when the phone rang. I leaped on it and heard Rudy's voice on the other end.

"Well? Well?" I said, unable to control my excitement. "Did you play?"

I heard him laugh. "Well, let me first say that we lost."

"Oh," I moaned.

"But not because I didn't make the greatest interception of my life," he said. I could hear the smile in his voice. I started squealing with excitement in the most annoying voice I never knew I had. I jumped on my bed and asked him to tell me all about it. He did for over an hour. No research paper today.

Five minutes after I hung up with Rudy the phone rang again. I thought he had forgotten to tell me something, but it was Janie letting me know our friend Chris was having the party that night. We spent about twenty minutes mapping out the arrangements for the evening: how we were getting there, who was getting the beer, what we were wearing. Oh, the plans of kings and high school seniors; it was like our lives depended on it.

Chris was a junior and a good football player. He was a nice kid who had a thing for Janie. Any time he spoke with her he would get all tongue-tied. He would turn bright red and start to sweat and his voice would go up three octaves. I thought it was adorable but I am sure Chris was humiliated by the whole transition. Chris had hosted a party the previous year. He had a beautiful home, provided tons of food and drew a big crowd. I was expecting the same tonight.

I took my second shower of the day and decided to wear my new sweater as we would probably be outside. Chris's basement was built into a hill, with sliding glass doors that went out to a patio. There was a deck on the main floor that we had to walk under to get to the patio. It was a perfect party house. No one had to go on the main or second floor. There was a bathroom in the basement and a small kitchen, so the party was self-contained.

By the time we got to the party, a little after eight, it was packed. A bunch of kids had started drinking right after the game so they were very drunk and obnoxious. A couple of football players asked me how Rudy was doing and I gave them a truncated version of his big day.

Chris' parents weren't home. Most houses where there were parties had absentee parents for the night or weekend. His parents knew he was having a few kids over. A few kids turned out to be about 150. It was a fun party with kids laughing, dancing, eating and drinking. And drinking. And drinking. As a result a couple of kids threw up. "Amateurs," Gina always called them. I took a few hits of a joint but that was it for me.

At some point Janie and I had to use the bathroom but there was a line, so Chris said we could use the one upstairs. Of course he got all red and a little sweaty when he told us. Janie had worked her spell on him yet

196

again. He took us upstairs. Normally I would go into the bathroom with Janie to pee. She was the only friend I ever did that with and still do that with. Janie closed the door on me so I figured nature was calling her in a different direction. Chris motioned upstairs and said to use the bathroom to the right of the stairs. As I walked through the house I realized how large and meticulously maintained it was. No wonder there was a sign on the front door telling us to go around back. He certainly didn't want any drunken teens in here.

When I got upstairs I saw doors that led into spacious bedrooms and a small desk and seat that got lost on the large landing overlooking the living room. The door to the right of the stairs was closed. *Ugh, don't tell me someone is in there too. The poor plumbing.* As I got closer to the door I heard water running and people laughing. It was uncomfortable laughter. I don't know what possessed me to try the door, but it was unlocked. I opened it but had trouble going in. It was partially blocked by someone. I pushed and pushed until I was able to get the door open. I shoved my way in and couldn't believe what I was seeing.

Yes, that was water running. The shower. A senior, CeeCee, was in the shower drunk and totally out of it. She was wearing just her underwear. She could barely stand were it not for the three sets of soapy hands holding her up. Some boys I barely knew, Barry, Craig and Ralph, were giving her a shower. And off to the side was Jack, home from school for a wedding, shirtless and in the middle of taking his pants off.

I stood silent for a moment in utter shock, unable to speak or move. They didn't even know I was there until I screamed, "WHAT THE FUCK ARE YOU DOING?" They all turned around at once and Barry tried to push me out the door, but I stood firm. (Thank you ballet legs.) I started screaming at the top of my lungs, "Help! Help! Janie! Chris!" Chris ran up the stairs with Janie behind him. He poked his head in and looked away, apparently embarrassed, not wanting to see CeeCee almost naked.

By this time I was punching and scratching them to get them off her. Chris was yelling and I asked Janie to go downstairs and get Marie, who was a closer friend to CeeCee than I was. It was utter chaos: water everywhere, CeeCee slipping down inside the bathtub, me screaming, "Animals!" Barry, Craig and Ralph finally ran out and down the stairs, leaving Jack on the landing, tripping over himself trying to get his pants on. Chris ran screaming after them out the front door.

Marie, Maria and Janie were now upstairs with me. Janie had filled them in quickly on the run between the basement and second floor. I had turned the shower off and was now in the bathtub with CeeCee, trying to hold her head up, my new sweater soaking wet and feeling like cement. Chris came upstairs and asked through the door, "What can I do?"

"Towels," I replied. "Lots of towels."

"In the bathroom closet."

Marie had the closest relationship with CeeCee and knew her family. I asked her to call CeeCee's parents. "Use the phone on that desk," I said in a panic. I told her to give them Chris' address and let them know CeeCee was okay, but to also tell them they needed to get here as soon as possible.

"What if they ask why?" she said.

"Then tell them she was sexually assaulted, but only if they ask."

While Marie went to execute her orders, Janie, Maria and I, with much struggling, got CeeCee out of the bathtub and put her on a towel on the toilet seat. It was obvious she was very intoxicated, drifting in and out despite our pleas to stay with us. (I found out later she had been drinking since before the game and continued all day and into the evening.) We started to dry her off and looked for her clothing, which had been carelessly thrown in a pile in the corner. Marie came back a while later, telling us CeeCee's dad was giving her the third degree but he was coming.

While the others were drying CeeCee off and trying to dress her I stepped outside the bathroom and told Chris her parents were coming. I suggested he ask everyone to leave as the police might also be involved. Oh, naïve me! With Chris going down the stairs and the girls attending to CeeCee, I found myself alone on the landing. Shaking, I dropped to my knees and started crying. I couldn't get past the image of those assholes putting their hands all over CeeCee. And what was Jack getting ready to do? Rape her? It was the vilest violation of a person I had ever seen or could imagine. I got up and rummaged through the desk for a paper and pen. I then sat down and wrote everything I had seen before I forgot any details, not that I ever could. I thought the police would want a specific description. Again, little, naïve me.

CeeCee was finally dressed. Maria brushed her hair and tied it back out of her face. Chris had made some instant coffee and brought it up for her. It wouldn't sober her up, but she would be a more alert drunk and, we hoped, she wouldn't pass out. That was our thinking anyway. I thought the only thing good about this was that she was so drunk she probably wouldn't remember any of it.

I went downstairs and heard the cars of kids pulling away. I listened to soft and loud conversations fade as kids started walking home or to another party. A couple of kids stayed to clean the basement and backyard. Chris and I waited for CeeCee's parents in the living room. It was my guess that everyone at the party knew before they left the house what was happening on the second floor. If they didn't they probably would soon.

Chris and I waited. And waited. And waited. CeeCee lived about six minutes away but it had already been a half hour since Marie called. I looked at the clock and realized if I stayed any longer I was going to miss curfew. My curfew as a senior was eleven o'clock. Freshmen had later curfews than me. And if I was even five minutes late I couldn't go out the next weekend. My mother's thought was five minutes this week, ten minutes the next. I would have friends speeding to my house just to get me there in time. But if I called to say I would be late I wouldn't get in trouble. I called every time I was out to extend my time. When I turned eighteen my curfew was finally extended to midnight. My mom was also flexible about it when I was with Rudy, but not by much.

I got up from the plush couch and called home. I told my parents there had been a serious incident at the party and that I was okay but I was waiting for the parents of a friend. I said I would be home as soon as the parents came and I would explain it all when I got there. My mom sounded concerned, but just said, "Be careful."

I sat down on the couch and still we waited. I called up to Marie to ask if she used the word "emergency" on the phone with CeeCee's parents. She said she used the words "sexual assault," a phrase you didn't hear a lot at that time. Finally, after about forty-five minutes from the initial phone call, came a knock on the door. I jumped up before Chris and ran to the door like it was my house. Chris followed. I opened the door and before me stood two men dressed in expensive but casual clothing. I looked at one of them and said, "Mr. Carter?" motioning them in the house. The other man quickly shot back, "That is DOCTOR Carter. I am Claire's father."

Right away I didn't like this man. It was how he held himself in such an "I am superior" way. As they walked past me I asked the other man, "And who are you?" DOCTOR Carter shut me up quickly by asking where his daughter was. I pointed and as we started walking up the stairs DOCTOR Carter turned around and said to me and Chris, "That will be all." Did I hear right? Was CeeCee's father dismissing us? Chris backed down but I kept right on walking. We got to the bathroom and CeeCee's father ushered Janie, Marie and Maria out. As I peeked in CeeCee showed no sign of recognizing her dad. He then closed the door.

We were now all standing outside the bathroom like crumbs whisked off a table. I turned to the other man and said, "So, really, who are you?" He replied he was the family lawyer. I didn't even know there was such a thing. Nobody I knew had a family lawyer. I never went to anyone's home where they introduced me to their family lawyer. I got the paper with my recollection of the incident from the hall desk and gave it to the family lawyer, telling him he might want to share this with the police. I also told him I would be available to talk to the police if need be. He didn't even look at it and thoughtlessly stuffed it in his pocket.

I started thinking. *Let me get this straight. DOCTOR Carter gets a call that his daughter is at a party; she is okay but has been sexually assaulted. He then waits for his family lawyer to come to his house and forty-five minutes later he shows up to check on his daughter.* I don't know about anyone else's dad, but mine would have been there before Marie had even hung up the phone. And where was her mom? I would want my mom at a time like this. At that moment I felt sorry for CeeCee that this was her dad.

When the DOCTOR opened the bathroom door he motioned for the family lawyer to help and they got CeeCee down the stairs and out the door. We all followed outside. They put her in the back seat of her dad's big Cadillac and both came toward Chris.

"Is this your house? Your party?" the dad said.

"Yes," Chris replied.

"Where are your parents?"

"Not home."

Doctor Carter took a card from the family lawyer and said, "They should expect a call from my lawyer here, Mr. Hamilton."

We all looked at each other, confused but not really surprised. They both got into the car and I watched CeeCee in the back seat as they were pulling away. Her head was down, but at the last minute she looked up at me and I swear her eyes were screaming, "Help."

Chris started freaking out that he was going to get in trouble. I assured him he had nothing to do with the incident and we would say so if we had to. I also said his parents had nothing to do with it and that DOCTOR Carter was an asshole and a bully.

"Did you notice he didn't even ask us about who the boys were or what happened? I am glad I had all that written down and gave it to the lawyer."

"The FAMILY lawyer," Maria said in her best pompous-ass voice.

"I wasn't expecting a thank you," I continued, "but it would have been nice if he acknowledged us. I hope he treats his patients better."

We all hung out for a little while longer, trying to assure Chris he wasn't in any trouble, except for maybe having such a large party. The basement, backyard and upstairs bathroom had been cleaned by kind and helpful partygoers. They even took the garbage and bags of empty beer bottles. It looked like no one was ever there. I suggested Chris tell his parents what happened in case they got a phone call from the family lawyer.

When I got home my parents were waiting up for me and greeted me at the door. I expected them to be anxious and nervous considering my phone call. I gave them the Cliff Notes version of the evening and my mom immediately started in.

"I don't know why you have to go to these parties with all this drinking and carousing. (Yes, she used the word carousing.) And why are these girls so drunk? They are asking for it with their breasts hanging out ..."

I felt my blood boiling as my mom started to blame the victim. That was usually the way it was then. Who am I kidding? It is like that now too. But, in 1972, most police departments didn't even have a sexual crime unit and there were few female officers to walk a female victim through the reporting process. And, as with so many abuse cases, the victim would be blamed. What was she wearing? Was she drinking? Well, she DID go to his car with him.

I couldn't do this with my mom at that moment so I said I was tired and started to walk upstairs. We could talk about it the next day. As I turned away I realized CeeCee's father never talked about or called the police. He never would. Those boys walked out of that bathroom without any accountability for what they did. Some even bragged about it to others. "Oh, yeah, that was me," like it was some medal to wear with honor on their chest. CeeCee became the villain in her own story. I got ready for bed but knew I couldn't sleep. I looked at the clock. Still early enough in Arizona. Would Rudy be out yet celebrating or could I still catch him? I started crying, so confused by everything.

## CHAPTER 20

# The Surprise

I started to dial Rudy's number. If he wasn't there I had nothing to lose. After two rings a girl's voice answered in a singsong hello.

"Oh," I said. "I must have dialed wrong."

"Wait. Who are you looking for?"

"Rudy."

"No, you dialed right. Hold on."

I heard her call Rudy and say, "It's for you."

He laughed, "Well of course it is. It *is* my room."

She laughed back. Instead of my heart singing when I heard Rudy's voice it sank. I started to shake even more. I wanted to hang up but couldn't.

"Hello? Who's this?"

"Hi, Rudy. It's me." My voice was trembling.

"Hi. What a surprise."

*Yeah, right*, I thought.

"Are you okay? What's wrong?" he said.

"Oh, you sound busy. I'll talk to you tomorrow."

"No, no," he said. Then I heard him cover the phone and say, "I have to take this. I'll see you later."

He sounded concerned when he asked again what was wrong. I broke down in tears. Between the shower and the girl answering the phone in Rudy's room, it was more emotion than I could control. I proceeded to tell him what happened at Chris'. Rudy sounded truly disgusted by it all. He said I did the right thing. He told me how lucky CeeCee was that I was the one who opened the bathroom door.

"Someone else might have just walked away."

"I don't know how anyone could do that."

"Do you think everyone is caring and concerned like you?"

"Yes."

"Well, you are wrong. You have a very special way with people."

I heard him talking, but all I could think about was the girl who answered the phone. I knew girls would be in his room. He was in college. I just never actually came across one when I called. And he was laughing. Not with me, but with this mystery phone-answering person, who I already decided was gorgeous. I tried to push down any jealousy I was feeling, but it was hard. She was there with Rudy and I was here. That thought alone made me jealous.

I blurted out, "It's hard sometimes with you being so far away."

I swore I would never mention the distance. I never wanted him to know how sad I was that he was living his dream so far away from me. Then I asked about the elephant in the room. (First she was gorgeous, now she was an elephant.)

Very softly I said, "Rudy, who answered your phone?"

He let out a long "OOHH" and laughed a little. The last thing I needed right now was to be laughed at. Especially by him.

"That was Alicia, Bernie's girlfriend."

Bernie was the first friend Rudy made at school. They met at football practice. He was from Wantagh, Long Island, and the two of them had much in common besides their home base. Rudy mentioned him a lot and that he had a girlfriend, also from Long Island, who went to the university.

He continued, "The three of us just got back from dinner and we are getting ready to go to a party."

"Oh, don't let me keep you."

"I would much rather talk to you."

"Yeah, right."

He then explained how the three of them had become their own Three Musketeers, only this time he was Vinnie. I laughed, trying not to let on how upset I was.

"Listen," I said, "I don't want to be one of those possessive girlfriends."

"I would be upset if I called you and a guy answered."

"Well, we know that is not going to happen. Not with Lucy."

"I'd like to think it wouldn't happen because you don't want it to, not because of your mom."

We talked for a few minutes longer. I knew his friends were probably waiting for him. We said goodnight and he said he would call me in the morning. HIS morning. I was feeling like everything was on his terms. But that was what I had signed up for. We hung up and I didn't feel any better than before I called him. As a matter of fact, I felt worse.

I thought I would never fall asleep. I was out after about five minutes. Surprisingly, I had the best night's sleep since Rudy left. And I slept in. No church, dance lessons or family dinners to get up for. I woke up to whispered chatter downstairs and the smell of my mom's pancakes. If anything could get me out of bed, her pancakes could. The talking stopped and I heard her coming up the stairs. I turned to get my robe and when I turned back, it wasn't my mom standing in the doorway. It was Rudy, arms crossed, leaning against the door opening, looking freaking adorable.

"Am I dreaming?"

He opened his arms and responded with a soft "Surprise."

He then started walking toward me. I was so stunned I couldn't even move to meet him halfway. He put his arms around me and enveloped me in the most warm and comforting hug. I started crying. He kissed the top of my head. I poked my head up from his arms.

"I am so confused. How are you here? Why are you here?"

He leaned down and kissed me.

"Sorry, morning breath," I said.

"Plane breath," he said.

He then explained that, after he got off the phone with me, he had asked Bernie and Alicia to take him to the airport. Bernie was one of the few freshmen on campus who had a car. He said he knew there was a 10:00 p.m. flight that zigzagged its way to New York. He hoped there was a family standby seat for him. There was. And now here he was.

"Rudy, that is crazy. You were flying all night. You must be exhausted."

"I slept on the plane. Lucked out and got first-class. Never had to change planes, so I slept the whole way."

"Why?"

"Why? Because you needed me. And I needed to see you. I needed to see you really bad."

Just then my mom called, telling us the pancakes were ready. I was still confused when we sat down to eat. It was an awkward foursome at first. My mom asked Rudy if Mama Rose knew he was here.

"No, it was a spur-of-the-moment thing."

This was the first time I had seen Rudy since he left. In the weeks he was gone he had developed a deep tan and looked even more handsome than I remembered. I kept trying to hold back tears. I knew he wasn't staying. He told us he was leaving Monday, early evening if he could get a seat. We laughed when he said the round-trip first-class ticket cost him $18.00. My mom *had* to remind me I had school on Monday. I said I had two tests in the morning. I raised my eyebrows at Rudy, hoping my parents didn't see. That was our secret sex sign. Not so secret really. I found out that was EVERYBODY'S secret sex sign. I hoped it wasn't my parents'.

After we finished eating Rudy said he was going to go home and see his parents, take a shower and come back to my house. My dad offered him a ride home but he said he wanted to walk after so many hours sitting on a plane. I told him I wanted to stop by CeeCee's house to see how she was doing. He said he would take me over and then we could get sandwiches and go to the beach. Rudy missed Long Island's delis and oceans. Sounded like a good plan. He left. I showered and of course shaved my legs. It was going to be a shaved leg kind of weekend, I hoped.

I got our sleeping bags and a few other things ready for the beach. It was October so my summer equipment wasn't readily available. Rudy picked me up and we headed to Prochell's, our local flower store. It was across from the cemetery, which I thought was awfully convenient. I picked out a nice bouquet of flowers and we headed to CeeCee's. Although she lived within minutes of us, it could have been a different planet. Huge house. Big yard. They even had a landscaper. Rudy pulled up to this mini mansion and said he would wait in the car. I got out with my flowers and walked up to the front door, which was twice the size of mine. I rang the bell, hoping DOCTOR Carter wouldn't answer. He did.

"Hi, DOCTOR Carter," I said, in my most pleasant voice. "Is CeeCee around?" He looked at me like he didn't know me, then it registered.

"No, she is not available."

"Oh. Well, can you tell her I stopped by?" I gave him the flowers.

He abruptly shut the door, again not thanking me. They had a large picture window in the front of the house and as I walked back to Rudy's car, I turned around and peeked in. I saw DOCTOR Carter take the bouquet and throw it in the kitchen garbage. I was outraged and wanted to walk back up to the door and start banging. But I changed my mind. I wasn't up for that confrontation. And besides, that would be time taken away from Rudy and me. I got in the car and told Rudy what had happened. We both decided he was a jerk and felt sorry for CeeCee.

The ride to the beach was beautiful and we talked and laughed all the way there. Rudy wanted me to sit next to him, not over in the front passenger seat. He put my hand on the shifter and put his over it so we were changing gears together. It was so easy being with him. It felt like I just saw him yesterday. We went to Jones Beach, although I can't remember which field. I know it wasn't four because that was always the busiest, even in October.

We had stopped at our favorite deli and got sandwiches and drinks. It was cooler and windy at the beach, so we set up behind one of the dunes. I opened our sleeping bags and zipped them together. We crawled in and closed it all around us. We were like two kids again camping, about to tell secret stories. Only this time we didn't talk. We kissed and kissed. I had forgotten how wonderful it felt to kiss Rudy. One thing led to another and then to another. And then to completion. We then settled into our snuggling position and fell sound asleep.

We woke up after about an hour, had our lunch and got back into our sleeping bag to repeat our earlier performance. I could have stayed there forever. We then got out of the sleeping bag and laid on top of it to get some sun, not that Rudy needed any more. We made images in the clouds, listened to the waves crash and just enjoyed the silence. We eventually got up and went for a walk on the beach, came back to our spot, packed up and headed home. It was a perfect surprise day.

Rudy dropped me off so I could study a little for my Spanish and Math tests. He went home to visit with his parents and then came back later and we went for pizza. Louie was surprised to see Rudy and greeted him with a big hug, getting him full of flour. Rudy really missed his New York pizza. He used to tease me and say of all the things he missed about home I was tied at number two with pizza. He never told me what was number one. We came back and surprisingly my mom didn't have an issue with us watching TV upstairs, in my room, alone. We had the TV on—*Columbo*, I think—but we weren't paying much attention. We talked a lot.

We made plans for the next day. I had tests third and fourth periods. Rudy was going to pick me up after fourth period and I would take the consequences for cutting the rest of the day. Rudy was not happy about that but I insisted. He was worried my mom would blame him. No one wanted to get on the bad side of Lucy. We weren't sure what we were going to do, but I told him to put the sleeping bags in his trunk just in case.

We talked about a great new show we both were watching, *M*A*S*H*, based on the movie we had seen so many times. We were both crazy about a Led Zeppelin song called "Stairway to Heaven," even though neither of us could figure out what it was about, just that it was very long. During a commercial a newsman reported Henry Kissinger, who was at the Paris peace talks, had reached an agreement to end the Vietnam War. We both jumped up and down, screaming, and ran downstairs to tell my parents.

"It's about fucking time," my dad said. That was the first and only time I ever heard him use that word. We talked a lot about the end of the war and what that would mean. I loved that Rudy was so socially conscious.

He cared what was happening, noticed what needed to be changed and thought of ways to make a difference. We were a lot alike in that way.

He left about 11:00 after a brief make-out session. It was great knowing I was going to see him the next day. I hadn't seen him for two days in a row in a long time. I was happy he came but I knew I was going to miss him even more this time when he left. I laid out my clothes for the next day. Forget the new sweater. It still wasn't dry from the shower. I didn't know if it ever would be. It was on top of the dryer in the basement, shrinking. I picked out a pair of khakis that I looked particularly cute in, if I must say so myself and an orange-colored top, one of my best colors. I wanted to look extra nice so Rudy would see what he was missing.

I walked over to Janie's in the morning. She knew Rudy had surprised me and wanted to know how my Sunday went. It was all giddy girl talk on the way to school. But when we got there the conversation was anything but light. Everyone was talking about CeeCee and Saturday night. They were talking about how drunk she was, the shower, how her father had to come and get her. No one was talking about the boys who molested her. But I did, loud and clear. I had two periods that day to spread the news to students and staff if they would listen. I made sure everyone knew who the boys were and that CeeCee was sexually assaulted. I used that term, which made most people uncomfortable. I also stressed how I felt the police should have been called and the boys arrested. Many students and some adults felt like my mom did and blamed the victim. I wish I had had more time that day to stand on my soapbox.

CeeCee wasn't in and of the boys involved, only Barry showed up to school on Monday. Thank God I didn't see him. I don't know how I would have reacted. Third period came around very quickly. I hadn't even looked at my notes that morning. I needed to do well on these tests, if for no other reason than to show my mom seeing Rudy this weekend was the right decision.

Between third and fourth period Janie came over to me holding up a key. I didn't understand.

"Nobody is home at my house. Vic is on a field trip, my dad didn't go in to work until ten, my sister is in school and my mom is at a conference in the city. It's perfect for you and Rudy to hang out over there."

"No, that wouldn't be right."

"Why not? Where else are you going to go? You can hang out in my room. Or just hang out. It's chilly today. You don't want to go to the beach."

"I am uncomfortable with that."

"Take the key and if you want to use it you have it. Either way, leave it under the back door mat."

I took the key and put it in my pants pocket. That felt like a naughty thing to do. But it did make sense. We would have to walk there from school. Just one block. I wouldn't want Rudy's car to be seen out front. It was such a distinct one. I couldn't believe I was plotting all this on the way to my next test. I had to drop it for now and concentrate. Everyone got quiet when I walked into my fourth-period class. They knew I had the key and what my afternoon plans were. I just knew it.

I sat down and a student I didn't know well asked me if it was true that I had walked in on the shower Saturday night. I stepped up on my emotional podium and said yes. My Spanish teacher seemed as interested as everyone else. She was careful to guide the discussion in the right direction, for facts, not rumors and she knew when it was time for it to end. The test wasn't too bad, but it was long and took the entire period.

I couldn't get out of my seat fast enough when the bell rang. I ran down to the cafeteria. Rudy was going to park near the bleachers and I would meet him outside the smoking section. I carried my stuff with me all morning so I wouldn't have to stop at my locker. I was trying to get every second I could with him. When I got to the cafeteria a crowd was outside the gym and I realized Rudy was in the center of it. They were as surprised as I was to see him: friends from football, baseball, track, the neighborhood. I didn't realize Rudy was so well known.

"Hey," I said, breaking through the crowd. "Is that Paul McCartney?"

Rudy looked relieved to see me and gave me a quick smooch. We probably could have stayed there all period but the clock was ticking. We excused ourselves and as we walked to the car, I pulled out Janie's key and told him my plan. To my surprise he liked it, so we walked to Janie's, careful not to be seen. The school didn't have cameras and there were no camera doorbells then. I felt like we were spies trying to get to our rendezvous, our very own *Mission Impossible* (the TV show, not the movies).

Without getting into much detail, we ended up in Janie's room for a couple of hours. It felt a little dirty, but in an exciting, sneaky way. I put a fresh sheet over her bed and we, well, you get the picture. Again twice, to completion. I was going to have to take a cool bath that night. I was a busy girl the last two days. It is not that we were sex obsessed. We didn't do it this much under normal circumstances. We just missed each other, missed the closeness. It was always more than just sex for both of us. I hate the term "making love." It sounds so cliché. But when Rudy and I were intimate, it really went to another level. And each time it just got better. The sex got better. The feelings got stronger. I had never had sex with anyone else, but I couldn't imagine it ever being any better than what we had. And to paraphrase a Journey song that wouldn't come out until over ten years later, I got "the joy of rediscovering" him again every time we came back together.

We decided to go get something to eat. Rudy wanted deli again. I crumbled up the sheet and took it home to wash. We left Janie a cryptic note, put the key under the mat out back and snuck back to the car in the school parking lot. We got our lunch and went to Salisbury Park. We sat at a picnic table, ate and talked for a long time.

During our conversation I got up enough nerve to ask Rudy how he thought our "distancing," as we called it, was going. He said it was hard but he imagined it was harder for me. He was distracted by the newness of school and Arizona and I was left with the gap it left in my life. He was absolutely right. I was scheduled to go see him in two weeks for parents' weekend with his parents and he said he had been looking forward to that. He couldn't wait to introduce me to his new friends.

He then pulled out a piece of paper with a schedule on it. SO Rudy. He said he had figured out a way for us to see each other every few weeks, or at least once a month. Flying standby was inexpensive with the family discount. And he didn't have classes on Mondays so he could do a Friday flight and stay until Monday when he didn't have a game. I told him that was great but he had responsibilities at school and I thought he would want to hang out with friends. He was honest and said yes but that he could fly to New York one or two weekends a month.

He showed me this paper with every month planned out around events and my period. I was on the pill so he knew when it was my time of month. He said he didn't plan it that way because of sex. Rather he saw how sick I would get every month. The pill helped a little but not a lot. He didn't want me to feel bad that he was here and I was home sick, throwing up, with cramps and diarrhea.

"Bullshit," I laughed. "You planned it around sex."

He then started to show me this elaborate chart he had come up with. I just looked at him, my mind filling up with all these dates. I told him I thought that was a great idea but he was missing the point of being away, especially in beautiful Arizona.

"Why would you want to fly back to New York for a weekend when you can drive through the desert or hike the Grand Canyon?"

"To see you."

"Rudy, I was so happy to see you this weekend. I had such a great time. But do you think we really should have to work this hard to stay together? You flying back and forth? Missing key events at school?"

I couldn't believe what came out of my mouth next. It wasn't something I had planned or even thought about. It just hit me as an obvious choice we had never discussed.

"Listen, I would totally understand if you wanted to take a break and see what happens when you come home. This is your time and it will only happen once."

In all the seventeen years I had known Rudy, he only got mad at me once and it was a minor thing, something about eating all his M&Ms. Well, here came number two. He got up from the bench, his face red, his voice so loud it scared me.

"Is that what you want? Is that all this relationship means to you? Is that all I mean to you?"

There weren't many people around, but they were looking at us. I asked him to quiet down.

"Quiet down. Really? You just asked me if I wanted to end this."

"That's not what I said." I tried to explain again.

He finally quieted down and asked me if that's what I wanted. I told him no but I felt he deserved that option. It wasn't about him seeing other girls. He didn't have to go to Arizona to do that if that was his intention and I really did trust him. It was about him being connected to this new place he called home, not being pulled back to New York by me physically or emotionally every time I got needy or jealous. He needed to immerse himself in his college experience. I needed to remember and understand that doing so took nothing away from our relationship.

I also told him I thought it was crazy for him to fly two time zones so often to come and visit. Who ever heard of that? He had thought about that. He quickly said to me, "People fly all over the country every week for business. I'm flying for pleasure!"

Smart-ass.

We had a very long and exhausting talk after that, both letting out our thoughts. Yes, it was challenging to be apart and then come back together only to separate again. I think that is what we were both feeling that day, the euphoria of being back together only to have to part again. We were both very emotional talking about our feelings for each other and how they had been nurtured over seventeen years. We knew it was special. We agreed Rudy would fly standby once in a while but I didn't want to hold him to a schedule. This was the talk we should have had when he first left but we had both been too scared to start it. I felt much happier, more secure and more relaxed with him going back this time. I think, during all that happened that weekend, I had grown a little more confident in myself, in Rudy and in our relationship. He could go and enjoy being a college freshman and I could have fun my senior year. It wouldn't change how we felt for each other. Both of us growing, even in different ways, could enhance the relationship, not necessarily end it. But I still cried when he left.

The next morning I didn't even get to my seat in homeroom before I was handed the dreaded yellow slip. If you got one of those you immediately went to the assistant principal's office to work out your detention time. I knew it was for cutting the day before, but I got it so fast. And my yellow slip had written across it in red pen, "See Dr. Willard." *Oh, boy.*

Dr. Willard and Mrs. Kane were having a lively discussion about a movie, *Jeremiah Johnson*, they both had seen over the weekend when I walked into the office. Mr. Willard's tone changed when he saw me and, in a booming voice, he said, "My office, young lady."

I thought, *Oh, shit. He's going to throw the book at me and definitely call my parents.* We sat down and he said, "Explain. SLOWLY."

So I did. I told him about the party, the shower, DOCTOR Carter, Rudy and the girl in his room and Rudy coming home. I don't think Dr. Willard expected that much information but he sat and listened. He finally said, "I am very disappointed in you and Rudy."

"Sorry," I said, looking at my shoes.

"He was here and he didn't stop in to see me?"

Oh, THAT is what he was disappointed in.

"Well, it was kind of rushed and obviously not well planned if I am sitting here. Are you going to call my parents?"

"Well, I should. You cut half a day. But I won't. THIS TIME."

"Thank you. And I promise this will be the only time."

"You will have detention, though."

"Okay."

"Now, let's talk about what happened Saturday night." And we did.

No one ever saw CeeCee again. She never came back to school. The image of her scared face pulling away from the curb that night is the last thing I remember. Her parents wouldn't let anyone visit her or speak to her on the phone. Rumor has it she was sent away to rehab and then finished school somewhere in New England. Nothing ever happened to any of the boys involved in her sexual assault.

## CHAPTER 21

# The Prom, Part Two

Everyone always made a big deal about the prom. Even Barbie had one. I guess it is the final goodbye to high school, playing dress-up and driving around in limousines. When I was a senior only couples went to the prom. I don't remember a boy or girl going alone or dateless in a group. There was such pressure to be asked and not in the elaborate way kids ask each other today. Skywriting? Having a famous athlete ask for you? Writing it on the side of a building? Having a waiter put a note in your date's mashed potatoes? Having the priest ask at mass? Really? Really. I was in church when that last one happened.

Sometimes someone would find out a person was going to ask you and let you know in advance. That way you could practice your acceptance or rejection speech. But, a lot of the time, it caught you off guard. It usually started with "Are you going to the prom with anyone?" If that was followed by a no, the next question was "Do you want to go with me?" Of course there was the spur-of-the-moment proposals like Rudy and Dana, still my favorite.

It was a game of sorts. If you liked Glenn but Gary asked you, do you say no to Gary and hope Glenn asks you? And, if Glenn doesn't, do you end up not going? It was a math equation worse than those two trains traveling the same speed in opposite directions. I never liked that the girls had to wait to be asked. Several girls did ask boys to go, often as friends.

But some girls were never asked and didn't go because they didn't have a date. Sometimes they would take a cousin or family friend. To me the asking process was another ugly way to objectify women and keep them in passive roles.

Easy for me to say. I didn't have to worry. I was asked a few times if I was going with Rudy. I was. He was excited to go with me since we didn't get to go to his senior prom together. I would have been happy having the Second Annual Motown Dance Party at my house, even if it was just Rudy and me.

It was a very expensive venture. The bid was $35.00 a couple, we had to get a limo (usually shared with friends), buy a gown, rent a tux, order a corsage and boutonniere, get our hair and nails done—a lot of money. And then came the after-prom weekend activities. Some groups rented houses in the Hamptons. Mine didn't. We usually went out after the prom to a club, crashed on the beach the next day and went out that night, usually to the city. The final day of the weekend was spent at Great Adventure. That was a tradition every year and the park would make announcements and have special deals throughout the day for the class. Teachers, parents and administrators showed up there as well. All told, you could spend close to three hundred dollars in one weekend. Today that is the cost of hair and makeup but, in 1973, that was a fortune, especially for a teenager making the minimum wage of $1.60 an hour.

I told Rudy it was my prom so I would treat, but of course he wouldn't hear of it. He had a little bit of that macho Italian man in him and I was determined to purge him of it. Even though he agreed to split it with me, he ended up paying eighty percent.

As he was at my junior prom, Rudy was friendly with many of the guys who were going. I felt better about that but I knew he would have gone with me even if he didn't know a soul. Our friend Dorothy, who had the most amazing organizational skills, coordinated who was going in which limousine, who was sitting at what table, where the tables would be—it was exhausting just watching her. She always carried around a notebook overflowing with papers and she always had a pen behind her ear. She did an incredible and memorable job. She does our reunions now.

Janie had such a great time the year before at Erick's prom that she asked him to hers. Jackie went with this guy Mark she had been seeing for a while, who was on the football team. Gina went with her steady, Bob. Marie was asked by several guys but I think they all had romance on their minds and she wasn't interested in any of them in that way. She just wanted to go with a friend and have a good time. At my suggestion she ended up asking Vinnie, so Rudy was thrilled. We were all going to be together again, at a prom no less. Maria went with Sean, one of the funniest people I have ever met, but she still had a miserable time.

The day before and the day of the prom, my girlfriends and I hit the beach to work on our tans. My cousin Catherine's friend Susie was a hairdresser (now we call them stylists) and she came to my house and did all our hair. I wore mine down with a little curl. My mom, Aunt Angie and Mama Rose were in charge of doing our nails, toes and make-up. Aunt Mary and the girls stopped by with treats and opinions. Plus they wanted to stay and see us all dressed up. My mom made me the most beautiful gown that had red and pink roses all over it. The material was very expensive at $10.95 a yard. She outdid herself.

The pre-prom gathering was held at Bob's house. Mama Rose went home to get Rudy and I melted when I saw him. He really cleaned up gorgeous. When I walked out into the living room to greet him he just said "Wow" and got a little teary eyed. Such a mush. Everyone in our limo met at my house so the moms and now the dads got to see us all dressed up and take pictures. All the neighbors came over to see us too. It was very special.

I was eighteen by now and legally able to drink but I wanted to pace myself and not get drunk at my prom. Bob's parents had the backyard decorated for the event and provided "snick snacks," as my mom would say, so we weren't drinking on an empty stomach. They were proofing everyone who wanted an alcoholic beverage but I think in the end they were letting everyone drink. It was fun and very different from the year before, maybe because I was excited to be attending this year. After about an hour my group got in our limo and off we went. Someone had bought beers so the drinking continued on the ride.

By the time we got to the prom a lot of the kids were drunk or on their way. I have a picture of our table from that night with beer bottles and mixed drinks on it. It seems very strange from today's perspective, but most of us were of drinking age or had fake proof. Even weirder is that the chaperones, our teachers, administrators and parents, were also drinking. I would have gotten fired if I drank while chaperoning anything when I worked at a school, but again, it was a different time.

Dr. Willard was so excited to see Rudy and Vinnie that they spent about twenty minutes in a corner talking and laughing. I even got Dr. Willard to dance with me to a Motown tune. He was really good. I don't remember the food or who wore what, but I do remember dancing all night. It was a wonderful way for Rudy and me to reconnect after spending most of the school year apart. We picked up from where we left off. We were good at that.

We had the limousine until four in the morning and after the prom, we all went to some club I can't remember and drank and danced even more. Before we left the prom Rudy made sure he went over to the staff and thanked them for allowing him to attend. I told you he was a charmer. But he was also sincere. We both made sure we said good night to Dr. Willard.

When I leaned in to give him a kiss on the cheek he whispered in my ear, "I hope to be invited to the wedding."

I blushed and whispered back, "You'll be in it." We both laughed and he told us to be safe and enjoy the rest of the weekend.

I was exhausted when the limousine dropped us off at 3:30 a.m. I went inside to rest and then changed for the beach. Vinnie and Rudy crawled their way across the street to Aunt Angie's. I slept a little and then showered. Before I knew it, everyone was at my house again for the beach. My mom and Aunt Angie had filled up some coolers with breakfast and lunch foods, snacks, ice and, hidden under the ice, some beer. We were surprised. It really was the last thing anyone except Erick and Janie wanted. "The hair of the dog," they said.

I believe we went to field four at Jones Beach, not that it mattered which beach we went to. Most of us fell asleep as soon as we hit the sand. We were lucky in having three beautiful days that weekend. We left the beach midafternoon to go home and rest, shower and go out again. That night we were going to the Riverboat, a club on the street level of the Empire State Building. I have no idea where I got the stamina to do all this. Just writing about it makes me tired. Ah, youth. I guess it's true what they say: it is wasted on the young.

That night I wore a funky pantsuit, not usually my style. It was white with a small black pattern on it. The top was a halter, midriff with a low neck and ruffles around it. My very tan abdominals showed. The pants were palazzo style, very form-fitting around the bum. The nice thing about having a seamstress mom was that, if she didn't make the outfit, she would fix what I bought to fit me perfectly. Of course I had my black platform shoes on, the ones I could dance in, which came off before I even hit the dance floor. Rudy loved the look. He knew I loved fashion and would always give me an honest answer when I asked his opinion.

We divided up into three cars. Rudy had offered to drive but his Charger had limited seating. Besides, I thought he was entitled to have a few beers. We went in Sean's car. Sean was naturally funny and very quick-witted. I always ached from laughing after hanging out with him. He was also known to party just a little too much at times.

We had a huge table and the people at the Riverboat treated us graciously, not like we were a bunch of teenagers getting drunk in the city, which we were. When we got there I told Sean to give me his car keys as I would drive home if he had too much to drink. He gave them up without an argument. I think he thought that gave him permission to drink even more.

We had a great time that night, sort of like a second prom, only with just the kids we truly loved. Some of last year's seniors who were home from college, like Gerry, joined us. It was a great mini reunion. I danced with everyone that night, including the maître d'. My face hurt from smiling and laughing so much. Rudy got a little drunk. He kept kissing me all over my face and all I could do was laugh. We had one of our waiters take a group shot of us, which is framed and hanging in my office still. I loved those kids. I loved that night. Well, most of it.

We left the club sometime after two in the morning. Unbeknownst to us, John, who was driving one of the other cars, had left early with his date and the kids who had come to the club in his car were stranded without a ride. At the same time Sean asked for his keys back. He was obviously drunk and stupid me gave them to him. I was a fairly new driver and I had little experience on the highway, let alone a bridge or tunnel. I was glad to give up the keys. Stupid. So now we had three carloads of kids and two cars with both drivers intoxicated. We were a short walk from Penn Station but it never dawned on any of us to take the train home. It was always the preference to drive in and if you didn't have to take the train you wouldn't. We had cars so why take the train? *BECAUSE THE DRIVERS WERE DRUNK!* No one even mentioned it. I knew it and was angry later that I didn't insist we take the train.

So we piled seventeen kids in two cars—not SUVs or minivans, cars. In Sean's vehicle six were in the back and three were in the front. Rudy was sitting behind Sean and I was on his lap. Gina and Jackie were also on the laps of their guys and Janie and Erick were in the front with Sean. Maria, Sean's date, ended up in the other car. I forget the make of Sean's car, but it was a two-door something or other. No one was wearing a seat belt. I don't even know if the car had seat belts. Everyone in the car was drunk except Jackie and me. She had her period and was overdosing on Motrin. I knew I would just get tired if I didn't stop drinking early. Everyone was talking loudly and at the same time as we sped down the Long Island Expressway. Rudy had his arms around my waist, holding me tightly, as he whispered, "We should have taken the train." Too late.

At that time there were no concrete dividers on the Long Island Expressway to separate east-bound and west-bound traffic. The expressway had grass dividers. We were flying along at a speed way too fast when, all of a sudden, the car started veering off to the left. It kept going and going across the grass divider. We were now in the west-bound lane heading east. It was very bumpy and everyone started screaming as we were thrown all over the place. Rudy held me even tighter.

Someone was watching over us that night because no cars were going west bound. When does that ever happen? I am not sure if Sean even knew what was going on as we all started screaming for him to turn around, go to the right, get off the highway. And as quickly as he went to the left, he casually turned the wheel to the right, bounced back over the divider and started going east again. The car went silent as Sean asked if everyone was okay. Then he just said, "Sorry about that."

Muffled crying and a lot of deep sighing followed. I could hear my heart and everyone else's pounding. Rudy was the first to speak. "Sean, can you please get in the right lane and slow down?"

Sean finally realized what had just happened, what had almost happened and happily complied. No one spoke the rest of the ride home. Sean started dropping everyone off one by one, taking Rudy home before me. As we got out of the car Rudy asked me to call him when I got home. I think he saw my face and knew I didn't want to get back in the car, even though it was only a four-block ride to my house. He decided instead to walk me home, at 3:30 in the morning. He didn't let go of my hand the entire walk and we couldn't hug each other tightly enough when we said goodnight. I asked him to call me when he got home but he said he was going to crash at Vinnie's.

I walked in the house and as I always did, I peeked in on my parents. My mom was the lightest sleeper I knew and asked me if I had had a good time. I said yes, went to my bedroom and broke down crying. I was upset about the ride home, but even more so thinking about what my parents would have gone through if they had gotten a call that evening that I was in a fatal car crash. But for the grace of God, it could have happened. The inconsolable pain I would have caused these two wonderful people was almost unbearable for me to even think about: to have my mom lose a sister and a daughter to a drunk driver, for my dad to lose his little girl, and for what? Because I made a stupid decision to get in a car with a drunk driver? Yes, I could get hit by a drunk in another car, like Aunt Theresa. I would have no control over that. But this time I did.

From that night on, I never got in a car with a driver who was drunk or on drugs. I am religious about preaching it to everyone and when I am anywhere alcohol is being served, which is almost everywhere, I always ask who is the designated driver. I was lucky enough to be the faculty advisor for several Students Against Drunk Driving (S.A.D.D.) chapters during my career and I like to think the awareness programs those students did actually saved lives. When I started my campaign someone was killed by a drunk driver every twenty-two minutes. It is now every fifty-two minutes, so some progress has been made. And now I can pass that message on to you. Pay it forward, be aware, make some noise. There is no reason why every fifty-two minutes someone has to die at the hands, or should I say wheel, of a drunk driver. It is a preventable death. Do your part. I will get off my pulpit now, but not before I mention that distracted driving is just as bad.

Ever since that night I can't sit in the back seat of a two-door car. The feeling of being trapped when Sean's car swerved off the road was one of the most frightening experiences of my life. I have tried many times to overcome this. Almost fifty years later when I get in the back seat of a two-door car my heart starts beating faster, my head begins to pound and I am overcome with the most awful dread. I consider myself lucky that is all I walked away with.

The last day of the prom weekend wasn't centered around drinking, thank God, although some kids did get stoned at Great Adventure. The eighteen-year-olds grabbed a beer or two at one of the concessions stands. How could anyone drink anything and then go on those rides? A lot of the school staff who had chaperoned the prom were there. I made sure Rudy drove this time as I wasn't taking any chances with someone else's decision.

I never acquired a taste for the spinning, backward, stomach-churning rides that Rudy and Vinnie loved. I was more a "smoke a joint on the paddle boat" kind of girl. Rudy and Vinnie had a blast going on anything that looked like it would make them sick. I remember sitting on a bench outside one of those rides, watching them swirl by, laughing and screaming. Wasn't it just last week we were on those little boat rides at Jolly Rogers when Rudy was trying to climb out of the boat? How did the time go by so fast? And why hadn't I noticed? Little did I know it was only going to go faster from then on.

## CHAPTER 22

# The Summer of 1973

It was great for the Three Musketeers to be back together with the entire summer ahead of us. We had all changed a little in the ten months since the boys left, in both appearance and attitude. But it didn't take anything away from our relationship. If anything, it added to it. Every time we came together we felt like we picked up from where we left off. I never took for granted what a rare and special friendship we had.

We decided we wanted to visit Uncle Jimmy and Gigi in Florida and finally go to Disney World. We were leaving a few days after the July 4 holiday. My dad would have been sad if we weren't there for our traditional family pool party. He had been taking us to the fireworks at Salsbury Park since we were kids. He still liked to go with us. At the last minute the adults decided to join us on our Florida adventure. Uncle Jimmy had gotten remarried and they thought it would be nice to spend time with his new wife, Maureen. Papa G. got incredible plane fares and hotel rates at Disney World. Each family had their own room. I slept most of the nights with Gigi as she was my cool, older cousin. She had just graduated from college and was going to start her master's in September. She and Catherine got along great as well. Catherine's boyfriend Johnny couldn't come as it was too short a notice to take off from work. Laura and Katie were now old enough to hang out with us. It was perfect.

To say we had a blast would be a cruel understatement. I think it was the most fun we had ever had up to that point. We laughed constantly, amazed at the rides and exhibits and in awe of the new technology on display. The ladies and I must have gone on "It's a Small World," still my favorite ride, four or five times. Rudy and my father went to the Hall of Presidents at least the same number of times as they couldn't get enough of the audio-animatronic Lincoln they first saw at the World's Fair. We swam in the hotel pool, had breakfast with the characters—because you are NEVER too old for that—and ate our way through the park. We even got Mickey Mouse ears with our names on them. I have a beautiful picture of all of us wearing our mouse ears. It captured a great moment.

I decided I still wanted to be a Disney princess and was ready to quit college and work at the park. Vinnie said he gave me two weeks before they threw me out for my liberal ideas. Plus, he said, you can't wear colored nail polish. He squashed my dream. We would all go back to Disney World many times and once a decade as a big family, but nothing ever beat the first time we all went together. How lucky we were for the experience.

July, or Summer Saturday, was moving fast. Rudy and Vinnie began preparing me for dorm life just as they had prepared me for junior high. It was very sweet. Rudy went shopping with me, making sure I got everything I needed. I didn't have the heart to remind him I would be a few minutes from home and could take anything I needed from my parents' medicine cabinet.

Vinnie and Rudy had decided to move out of the dorms their second year. Some school wouldn't allow that, but theirs did. Rudy was moving in with Bernie and Alicia. They had found a clean and affordable two-bedroom apartment near campus. Vinnie was going to move into an apartment with this guy George, who was on his lacrosse team. Both houses were furnished, although not to Vinnie's liking. He was very particular.

George, who lived in Massachusetts, was coming down to visit family on Long Island and was going to stay a few days at Aunt Angie's. Vinnie had made plans for all of us to go to the city one night, among other activities, which also included a big family barbeque. George was tall, very handsome and "golden brown," as he described himself. His mom was white and his dad was black. (He always identified himself as African American.) That was a welcomed surprise. It was about time our family expanded outside its own crazy Italian circle. Turns out George was half Italian, which was really all that mattered.

Vinnie and George got an apartment in September 1973 and have lived together ever since. They were married in 2015. They wouldn't get married until same-sex couples could do so in all states. I couldn't ask for a more generous, kinder "brother-in-law." He fits in with our family perfectly and I love him dearly.

George came down toward the end of July and told us about a big music festival upstate, a sort of mini-Woodstock. Just three acts were scheduled to play, but they were my favorite three: the Allman Brothers, the Band and the Grateful Dead. The concert was at a racetrack in Watkins Glen for one day only, July 28.

The guys were very excited and decided to go. I think Lucy would have been alright with letting me attend, but I was scheduled to have my period that weekend. Being on birth control made my cycles very regular and predictable. But I would always get severe, "stay in bed" cramps for a day or two and zone out on Motrin. I missed a lot of school because they were always so bad. As much as I wanted to see the bands, the thought of sharing a port-a-potty with 150,000 people AND having my period AND sleeping in a tent was just not appealing. Rudy, Vinnie, George and our friend Gerry packed up a tent and some snacks and left for what they thought would be an outdoor concert.

It turned out it was an outdoor *event*. Although 150,000 tickets were sold at $10.00 a piece, 600,000 people showed up—200,000 more than Woodstock. It ended up in the Guinness Book of World Records as the largest audience for a pop festival. Rudy told me later he was glad I didn't go as it was absolutely crazy. And, like at Woodstock, it rained. The boys went for the entire weekend and even stayed to see racing the day after. The photos and stories I have seen and heard make me glad I didn't go. Everyone was packed on top of one another in humid, rainy weather. Plus I think the guys did a lot more drugs because I wasn't there. Based on their recollections, I think they were tripping most of the time. Rudy kept talking about this great pierogi vendor who sold out in a few hours. That is all he talked about. I think it was all he could remember. And I didn't even get a T-shirt.

The summer quickly moved into "Sunday," but I refused to start counting down the August days. I was just enjoying the time with Rudy. We took a camping trip with the dads to the Adirondacks, where I got chewed up by black flies and mosquitos. It was still great: itchy, but great. My parents went to Atlantic City for a few days and my mom let me stay home alone. Except I wasn't alone. I couldn't relax completely in my house with Rudy like I did in his, although he tried very hard to get me to do so.

We did our usual fun summer activities, going to the beach and the park, bike riding, barbeques. Rudy joined, although late, Gatsby Pub's softball league so we spent a lot of time at the field and bar. I was crazy about Gatsby's food. Something about bar food is still special to me today—good bar food, not fried, frozen crap. Gatsby's had good bar food.

Rudy's dream was to be a professional baseball player and that wasn't out of the ballpark. (Excuse the pun. I couldn't resist.) There was some interest even though he had played only one season in college. His back-up plan was to be a chef and open a restaurant. He loved to cook and was excellent at it. Every now and then they would let him in the kitchen at Gatsby's to try a new recipe. They would call it Guest Chef Rudy's Special and the family would always go there on those nights. Heck, everyone would go there and the line for dinner was usually out the door.

With a few friends, we also decided this was the summer we would finally do the Greenbelt Trail, a thirty-two-mile hike along the Connetquot and Nissequogue Rivers. It is not difficult, but it is long and very beautiful. The trick was coordinating the cars to get us back and forth up the trail. The guys wanted to do it in one day. No freakin' way. The girls convinced them to do it in two, but the weather had us finish it in three. We had a lot of fun and won bragging rights. The boys were determined to do it again so they could tell everyone they did it in one day. Ah, manly pride.

Yes, it was another great summer although I know Rudy could feel my anxiety about starting college. We had already begun planning when he would visit and when I would fly out there. Since I wasn't living at home I could do that now, even if it was only for a few days. Rudy said he preferred to come to New York. He was worried about my lying or omitting to my parents that I was going out of state.

The "Big Goodbye" was coming up quickly and I started to regret that I wasn't going to Arizona with Rudy. I knew I had made the best decision for me, but was it the best one for us? Just like I never shared with Rudy my true feelings about his going to Arizona, I wondered if he wasn't telling me how he truly felt about me staying home. I had hoped we were at the point in our relationship where we could be open and honest with each other but, hell, we were still kids. I was eighteen and he was nineteen. We just seemed so much older together.

A few days before Rudy and Vinnie left we went to Robert Moses Beach, as that was our new tradition. Rudy and I told Vinnie how much we liked George and joked that if they ever broke up, we'd take George over him. We marveled at how just the previous year, Vinnie was sharing he was gay and now he was dating a terrific guy. We were happy for them both.

Vinnie had decided to take a swim and I was surprised Rudy didn't go in with him. But Rudy had a few things on his mind he needed to discuss with me. He told me he was looking into transferring to Hofstra, which had an excellent baseball team. He was thinking about finishing his junior and senior years at home. (Rudy had injured his back during last fall's football season, so he had decided to concentrate on baseball.) I told him absolutely not as I thought he was going to do this to be near me. He said that was part of the reason. I suggested he wait to see how the next baseball season went. It was important to me that he made choices independent of us. I felt confident we would always be together and there was plenty of time for us. He needed to concentrate on himself now. He agreed he would see how the year went.

I drove to the airport with Papa G. Since this was Rudy's second year leaving, Mama Rose and Carmine didn't feel compelled to go. Papa G. made us both sit in the back seat so we could, as he said, "snuggle and smooch." We got to the airport and Rudy gave me his "I need oxygen" goodbye kiss again. We both laughed that he should leave more often. I watched his cute butt walk away, which he knew I always did. It would embarrass the hell out of him but I couldn't help it. He turned around to look at me, smiled and shook his finger at me, laughing. I shrugged my shoulders and blew him a kiss. He was off on new adventures and so was I.

I had never spent a lot of alone time with Papa G. Other people were always around. Now here we were in the car, just the two of us, riding home from the airport. I loved Papa G. I think Rudy looked like him and had some of his mannerisms. And they definitely had the same sense of humor. He was asking me about Hofstra, my course of studies and teasing me about my women study's choice. We were bantering back and forth when suddenly he got serious and said to me, "One of the biggest joys of my life is you and Rudy getting together. I couldn't have wished for a better sparring partner for him." We both laughed and then he surprised me by saying, "You have always been the daughter I never had. I pray every night you will become my daughter-in-law too."

I smiled, but in my head I was screaming, "I AM ONLY EIGHTEEN!" I had always thought I wouldn't get married until at least my mid-to-late twenties, maybe thirties. It never dawned on me I could be a young bride but apparently Papa G. was thinking about it. Rudy and I knew we would always be together. We had tattoos to prove it. I just never gave any thought to a time frame. We had plenty of time.

## CHAPTER 23

# The Freshman Again

I moved into my dorm Labor Day weekend but I was still able to attend my parents' big end-of-the-summer bash. I left all my furniture at the house and bought new things for school. It was weird having two residences but I think it was a good compromise for me and an acceptable, slow transition for Lucy.

Being an "almost" only child, I never had to share a room with anyone. As a matter of fact, I had two huge rooms upstairs. When the dormers were finished one bedroom was for my parents and one was for me, with a full bathroom in between. But it became apparent rather quickly that my mom was running from the basement to the second floor a gazillion times a day. So my parents moved their bedroom back downstairs. The other bedroom downstairs was a guest room/den.

My mom always felt bad that the basement was taken up by her work so she and my dad decided the other room upstairs would be my playroom. When I got older we put a couch and TV in it and a small refrigerator, a table and chairs. We added a foosball table because I loved the game, along with tons of board and card games. We threw down a rug and some beanbag chairs and it was the perfect place to hang out.

Surprisingly, Lucy would let girls AND boys up there but the door at the top of the stairs had to be open. I couldn't have more than six to eight kids up there at once. No drugs or alcohol. Music at a listening level. The two rooms were large with enough floor space to dance. A sliding glass door opened to a small roof patio over the garage, but I was only allowed to sunbathe on it with my girlfriends. Of course we sneaked out there to smoke cigarettes and pot. I think if my mom was a little more liberal in some of her views I would have been very comfortable up there through college. But she wasn't and I needed to get away, even if only ten minutes from home.

I was going from two large rooms to a very tiny space I had to share with someone I didn't know. I was very nervous about the sharing part. I needn't have worried. Whoever matched up the roommates did an amazing job, especially with mine. Her name was Jenn and she was model beautiful, on-the-cover stunning. Like my friend Jackie in high school, she never gave her appearance much thought.

Jenn's dad was a professor at NYU. She grew up in a house in Pennsylvania. When she was in eighth grade they moved to an apartment in Manhattan. She was very city smart. When Jenn's grandmother passed away she left Jenn her one-bedroom apartment on the Upper East Side. Very posh. When I asked her why she didn't stay there and go to NYU she said she wanted to get out of the city for a while and was interested in New College with its diverse learning options. She hoped to do a semester on Martha's Vineyard.

When Jenn heard about Rudy and how he would fly home for weekends she immediately offered her city apartment to us when he was in town. At first I refused. It was much too generous an offer. But she kept insisting. She was dating a guy named Michael who lived in Tribeca and she stayed there when she was in the city. I asked why she didn't rent her apartment. She said it was a hassle and she did use it sometimes. She also said she didn't want strangers there and she didn't need the money.

Rudy was so excited when I told him about this that he wanted to fly in the following weekend. I told him to wait a week or two so we didn't seem too anxious. The one thing Rudy didn't like about my dorm living was he couldn't call me whenever he wanted, which he used to do all the time. It would be 2:00 a.m. in New York, 11:00 p.m. in Arizona and he would pick up the phone and call me just to say hello. He couldn't do that now because I had a roommate. But he was thrilled about us having a place to stay when he came out.

New College seemed like the perfect choice for me from the beginning. Most of the students were placed in dorms near each other and friendships developed quickly. Jenn and I started hanging out with a group of girls and guys almost immediately. Our core group was the two of us, a guy from Connecticut named Stephen, who I adored, his best high school buddy Chris, a girl from Vermont named Margie, Brynn, a sweetie from England, and Nikky, who hailed all the way from Massapequa (that's on Long Island).

It was a nice group of kids. They were different from my high school hangouts: no drugs or alcohol, no big parties, no drama. New College had a theater club and once or twice a month we would get a bus and go into the city to see a play or musical. With dinner, tickets and transportation, the entire night cost about $7.00. At one point I had seen almost everything on Broadway. I loved it. Sometimes Rudy would meet us in the city and he and I would stay at Jenn's place.

My college friends and I would often go to my house and hang out upstairs, watching TV or playing a game. My mom always went out of her way to make them feel like our home was their home away from home. She would make elaborate dinners and invite them over. No one ever refused. They were not allowed to mention Rudy as they weren't supposed to know him. Several times someone would slip but they always covered it up.

I still saw Jackie, Janie and Gina, who were all working, as well as Marie when she was home from school. Between seeing them, doing schoolwork, hanging out with my friends from college, working sometimes for Uncle Joe and sneaking into the city to see Rudy, I was very busy. But I loved it. I still was getting high, but not as often. Marijuana, along with my learning disability, was not a good coupling for academic success. (I was already making an effort to quit pot and thought it would be a good time to stop smoking those Winston cigarettes too.) I felt I had made the right college choice.

The fall was flying by very quickly and Rudy flew home a few times now that he wasn't playing football. Vinnie and Rudy were both going to be home for Thanksgiving and I couldn't wait to see them. Unfortunately, Southern New England had a bad ice storm and although New York was sparred the worst of it, Rudy's flight was cancelled. He ended up staying in Arizona. He was going to make Thanksgiving dinner for himself and some friends who were also stuck there. I was a little jealous as he was such a good cook.

Some of my college friends couldn't get home either so my mom decided to invite the four of them to our house for Thanksgiving. We decided to sleep over at my house the night before so we could all watch the parade together. We all slept upstairs and got up on Thursday morning to watch the parade in our pajamas. It reminded me of the many times I had done that with Vinnie and Rudy. It was nice to continue the tradition.

I spoke to Rudy throughout the day. His calls finally stopped around 11:00 p.m. New York time. I drove everyone back to the dorms on Friday after a late lunch of delicious leftovers. I decided to go back home for the weekend. I didn't hear from Rudy all day Friday, which was very strange. I presumed he thought I was at school and was calling me there, no biggie. I decided to call him after dinner. Bernie answered and said he hadn't seen

Rudy all day and he wasn't sure where he was. I told him to please leave a note for Rudy to call me. I started to get a little worried as this was very unlike Rudy. The Italian in me started thinking about awful scenarios. Just as I was working myself into a frenzy the phone rang and it was him.

He said after dinner at the house on Thanksgiving he went back to the dorms with some friends and they started drinking scotch. The last time Rudy drank scotch he had gotten two tattoos. I asked if he was okay because he didn't sound like he was. He said he was a little hung over. He had stayed at his friend's dorm because he was too drunk to go home. That sounded fine to me but Rudy still didn't. We talked a little more and finally I said to him, "Give it up."

"What?" was his reply.

"I know you very well and something is up. What are you not telling me?"

I said this in almost a singsong voice. I wasn't threatening or accusatory in any way. Rudy responded with panic in his voice. "I got really drunk last night."

"Yeah, I know. You said that."

"Drunk like I wasn't myself and did something horrible."

"Oh my God, Rudy. Did you kill someone? Get another tattoo? On your face?" He was scaring me.

"Worse."

"Worse? What could be wor … " Then it hit me. "Did you sleep with someone?" I joked.

"Almost."

Dead silence hung between us for what seemed like a long time. Finally I said, "What does 'almost' mean?"

"Well, I went back to this girl's dorm room …"

He was talking but I was somewhere else completely. I felt my body temperature rise, I started shaking and I thought I was going to throw up. Everything in my world changed in that instant.

"… and I somehow ended up on her bed, making out …"

Now I really felt like I was going to throw up. He stopped talking.

"Well, don't leave me in suspense. What happened next?"

"Nothing. She reached down to open my belt. I got up and told her I had to leave. I am so sorry. Please don't let this change anything between us."

Too late. It already had. I always trusted Rudy completely and was never jealous or worried he would cheat on me. And now he was telling me this. But why? He didn't have to. I would have never found out. Guilt is a wonderful truth serum, especially Italian guilt. I asked him if I could call him back in a few minutes. I had to digest all this.

"I am so sorry. You know I love you very much," was all he could say.

"I'll talk to you in a few," was all I could say. I hung up.

I sat staring at the phone for a long time. I hadn't expected this. Then I began to wonder if he was telling me all of the story. Did they go further and he was just not telling me? Had this happened before? If so, how many times? I believe every relationship we have in life is built on trust. How could I trust him after this? I put my head on my pillow and closed my eyes, but all I could see was Rudy making out with some other girl while she tried to take his pants off. Then it happened. I ran in the bathroom and threw up. About twenty minutes had passed when my phone rang. I knew it was him.

"Hey." That was all I could muster.

"Are you okay? I am so sorry. I know alcohol isn't an excuse, but that wasn't me who did that. I have never cheated on you. I am so sorry. Please say we are okay."

I interrupted him.

"Let's talk about this in person. Are you still planning to come to New York next weekend?"

"Yes, but I have to know if we are okay. I couldn't go a week without knowing."

"We are okay, Rudy. Let's just give ourselves some space. Maybe not talk for a few days. Do you like this girl? Do you want to see other people? Her, maybe? Because if that is where this is going …"

"No. No. I don't like her. I am not interested in other girls. We are permanent. We have our tattoos."

"Yeah, I would have preferred you told me you got a tattoo on your face rather than tell me this. I will call you in a few days. Please give me this time."

"I don't want to but I will. I love you."

"I love you too, Rudy. This doesn't change that. Goodnight."

Did this change that or not? I felt like the ball was in my court and I didn't like it. At about 9:00 p.m. my phone rang. It was Rudy again.

"They are flying to New York again and I am taking a flight out tonight."

"No, no. You don't have to. That is crazy. This can wait."

"No," he said very firmly. "Can you get to the apartment tomorrow?"

I let out a big sigh. I knew it was important for Rudy to discuss this. It was for me too.

"I'll take the train out in the morning."

"Okay. See you then. I love you."

I met him at the apartment the next day. I told my parents I was meeting Jenn in the city to do some early Christmas shopping and I was going back to the dorm. Rudy looked terrible. I don't think it was just from the red-eye flight. He looked sad. He went to kiss me but I hugged him instead. We talked for a long time about everything related to our relationship. I mentioned what his dad had said in the car on the way home from the airport. We talked seriously about when and where we wanted this to go. Rudy believed I could still have my own journey and be with him. One didn't have to cancel the other. I said if we were going to see other people, now was the time. We just had to be honest with each other about it. Neither one of us were interested. We agreed scotch and Rudy did not make a good couple and he joked he needed to be properly supervised when he drank it. He told me he wanted to transfer to Hofstra *now*. I told him that wasn't necessary. We had agreed to wait until this baseball season ended and we should stick to that plan. I told him I appreciated his being honest with me but, even so, it would take me a while to trust him again. He understood.

I thought it would be a good idea to do something that day to try to bring some normality back to us. We decided to go to the Museum of Natural History, one of our favorite places in the city. We had a good time and almost fell back into our couple selves. There was some awkwardness but we plowed through it. We had a nice dinner and went back to the apartment.

When we got inside Rudy pulled me closer to kiss me but I hesitated. "Not yet, okay? It's hard for me because someone else kissed those lips."

"Well, I did wash them since. A lot," he joked.

I smiled and went in the living room. We spent the rest of the night on the couch, watching television. When we got into bed Rudy knew I was

242

not ready to be intimate, so we just fell asleep. We were both emotionally exhausted. I woke up in the middle of the night to pee. Even at eighteen my bladder was getting me up at night. When I got back to bed I leaned over and kissed Rudy on the lips. I got into the snuggling position and when I looked over at him I swear I saw a tear running down the side of his face. Yes, he had broken my heart but he had broken his too.

The next morning he was in the shower when I got up. I laid there for a few minutes then got up, took my pajamas off and stepped into the shower with him. He just held me for what seemed like forever while the water washed over us. We dried off and got back into bed. I knew we were going to be okay. Before we left the apartment for breakfast I thanked him for being so honest and open with me because he didn't have to tell me what happened. He said that was not the kind of relationship we had or that he wanted. We agreed we would try and start anew and put this behind us, which meant he had to stop apologizing every ten minutes. I told him to let it go. We would not let this moment define us. (Thank you, Ms. Smith.) Rudy came out the next three weekends until he was home for Christmas break. How he managed that I don't know. He could function on three hours of sleep. I needed at least eight to speak in full sentences.

It took a while but we eventually got back to where we were. The fact that we were able to get past it and talk about the relationship made us stronger. It was an example of turning something negative into a positive.

We had a very nice Christmas break. George came out to see Vinnie and the four of us spent a lot of time together. Jenn had gone skiing in Colorado so the apartment was available. We went into the city a few times and stayed there, with Vinnie and George on the pull-out couch in the living room.

The dads always wanted to go camping in the winter so they took Vinnie, Rudy and Carmine upstate. I wanted no part of it. Rudy was disappointed but I thought it would be good for the guys to spend some time together. They came home two days early because, as Uncle Joe put it, "It was fucking freezing."

I was glad we had the holiday break to spend time together. Truth be told, it took me a lot longer than I thought to let go of the incident and trust Rudy one-hundred percent again. This was the first time I ever felt our relationship was in trouble. I had always assumed there weren't any bumps in our road. Turns out there were, like in every relationship. It taught me a lot about people's actions and my reactions. I could have done the "hysterical wounded girlfriend role," which is how my mom would have played it. I tried the "think rationally and use this as a growth experience role," which was my dad's way. I truly believe that saved us. You know that saying, "What doesn't kill us makes us stronger"? I feel this did. We had nowhere else to go but up.

For some reason, when Rudy went back to school in late January, it was harder to say goodbye. I started to wish he would come back to Long Island the next year, not so I could keep an eye on him. Well, maybe a little. I don't know. I just missed him more this time. I knew he was coming to New York in three weeks for my birthday, but the time together was never long enough to get a momentum going. And, when baseball started, he wouldn't be able to visit as frequently, if at all. I would probably have to start flying there.

I went back to my dorm and started in with my new schedule. I was now taking more advanced psychology classes and I loved the self-reflection naturally built into those courses. It certainly helped me expand and understand my world and myself better. I continued with the theater club, attending a Broadway show once or twice a month. Rudy came out for my birthday but stayed at his house. We thought it would be nice to celebrate with the family. Vinnie and George surprised me by coming that weekend too.

Rudy came two more times before baseball practice started. I flew out there for Easter break, telling my parents I was going on vacation with Jenn. I hated to lie to them. Actually, I was lying to my mom. I always told my dad where I was really going in case of an emergency. He hated that I involved him in my schemes and that he had to lie to my mom. I told him to think of it as omissions rather than lies; that would make him feel better. It didn't.

Rudy loved when I came to visit. He loved showing me Arizona and I think he loved showing me off to his friends. We always enjoyed hiking together and Arizona had a different terrain that made it more challenging. One day while we were hiking in the middle of nowhere we heard a loud thud. Around the corner came a rather tall man completely naked except for his backpack and hiking boots. Oh, and socks. I was speechless and just stood there, trying to keep my eyes on Rudy's face and not letting them wander. They wandered. I mean, come on. Wouldn't you have to look? He just passed us and said good morning like it was usual to see a man hiking naked. I told Rudy we should try it sometime. He joked that no amount of sunscreen would ever get him to do that.

Rudy had a fantastic baseball season and although I hadn't said anything to him, I thought it would be foolish for him to change schools now. His dad and coaches agreed. He was getting noticed and written about and a move now might not send the scouts back.

The times I went to Arizona that spring I was always looking for the make-out girl, but I never figured out who she was. Rudy said he rarely saw her and they never spoke of it. He said he didn't think she even remembered the incident. It was time to move on. The school year was ending.

Rudy was letting his hair grow longer but I wasn't prepared for what I saw when I picked him up at the airport in late May. He got off the plane and I looked right past him then back at him again. His hair was even longer; he had muttonchops and a mustache/goatee. I just stared at him, not even moving closer to greet him. He was moving toward me, trying hard not to smile. Where was that clean, cute baby face? That smile that drove me wild? It was replaced by this new face I didn't recognize. Then he smiled. There was my Rudy. He came over to me and I was still just staring at him. "I never kissed a man with a mustache," I said.

"I never kissed a woman with one."

"Wait, are you implying I have a mustache? Cause I waxed it two days ago."

We both laughed as he pulled me closer and kissed me. I giggled a little. It was a strange, new sensation. When we stopped kissing I blurted out, rather loudly, "I LIKE IT!"

"Whew! I thought I would have to shave it off!"

Truth is, I loved it—the whole look. I didn't think Rudy could get any handsomer but I was wrong. This new look had a little "bad boy" feel to it. It was very seventies cool. It was sexy. Very sexy. It was going to be a good summer.

## CHAPTER 24

# The Summer of 1974

Rudy's parents were thinking about taking the family to Italy in the summer of 1974. Papa G. had a ton of vacation time saved up. Rudy had been there several times before and wanted me to go with them. We were planning the logistics when Rudy's grandmother, Rosie, fell and broke her hip. Mama Rose had her move in with them and the trip was postponed. We would try to go next summer. It was something to look forward to.

Vinnie and George stayed at school most of the summer to take some courses. I missed Vinnie but was happy he was in love and moving forward. We had about three weeks together, although any amount of time wouldn't have been enough. Jenn and her boyfriend, Michael, were in Europe for six weeks so once again she offered her apartment. I was glad she did because, being out of the dorm until September, there weren't a lot of opportunities for Rudy and me to be alone.

My father and Uncle Joe came up with a brilliant idea to go RVing for a few weeks. Uncle Joe, through his car dealership connections, came across a very large RV that was "in between" owners. He, my dad and Papa G. thought this would be a good opportunity to try it out since we had only tent-camped until then. Rudy and I, along with Carmine and his friend Tommy, were going to go with them up north; there would be seven of us. Rudy, Carmine, Tommy and I were going to follow them in Uncle Joe's truck. I called it the Caravan of Love. They all hated that name.

We drove up to Maine and camped along the coast on our way to Acadia National Park. Rudy and I slept in a tent even though the RV could accommodate eight. I always hated to tent-camp in the rain so we slept in the RV when the weather was bad, which was twice. Rudy would make us elaborate breakfasts. It was great to have a private bathroom in the RV even though I was sharing it with the bears, as I called the guys. Rudy and I did a lot of hiking in Acadia. My dad enjoyed sitting at the campground, reading, uninterrupted. No Lucy asking him to go get milk or run her to the mall. He had a fire going all day and must have read four or five books on the trip.

We left Acadia and headed north to Baxter State Park then over to the White Mountains of New Hampshire. We wanted to climb some of Mt. Washington, the highest point in the northeast. It is one of the most dangerous hikes in the United States, known to have some of the world's worst weather. Even though Rudy and I were in good shape I knew I wasn't prepared to climb the entire mountain. We did a mini-hike that took us about a third of the way up. Believe me, that was enough. I could barely walk for two days. The day we were hiking, the dads took the truck up to the top. The following day, the "kids" drove up there. It was magnificent. Not as satisfying a view as if we had hiked to the top, but breathtaking nonetheless.

Since no one was in a hurry to go home we decided to take the drive all the way over to Niagara Falls. Talk about breathtaking and magnificent. You have to love Mother Nature. She came up with some amazing stuff. I think I laughed—screamed—more there than I did at Disney World. First we went on the Maid of the Mist, a boat ride under the falls. It was ridiculous. We were all in our rain ponchos, soaking wet and laughing our heads off. I kept thinking of Lucy on the boat trying to save her bouffant.

I didn't think anything would ever top that but Cave of the Winds did. Again with ponchos on and shoe coverings, we took an elevator down a cement shaft that led to a series of steps. As we ascended the steps the wind and rain whipped all around us. It was like standing in the middle of a hurricane. I loved it. Rudy said he couldn't see me but he heard me laughing and screaming the entire time. We weren't expecting to go to Niagara Falls and I certainly wasn't anticipating having that much fun there. We kept laughing about it for the next three days. Of course everyone had a story about my screaming. Rudy and I decided we would have to go back sometime with Vinnie and George.

As usual the rest of the summer went by too fast. Rudy worked a bunch cooking at Gatsby's. They overpaid him a lot. Truth be told, I think he would have done it for free. Janie and I ate there every night he worked. The days were again filled with swimming in the pool and riding our bikes and nights were spent in Manhattan. When Vinnie and George were able to join us we spent time at some of our favorite state parks. Jones Beach, Robert Moses Beach and Hither Hills, all on the south shore, had sandy beaches and ocean waves. Rudy and Gerry had taken up surfing and Vinnie was determined to join them. We also enjoyed Caumsett State Park and Sunken Meadow on the north shore, more so for hiking than swimming. And of course we loved Montauk State Park. We loved everything about Montauk. I still do.

We were in the water one day at Jones Beach and I turned to Rudy and said, "How great is our life?"

He gave me a wet, salty kiss and yelled before a wave crashed over us, "I know."

I replay that moment still.

August came again and Rudy was leaving a little earlier this year. He, Bernie and Alicia hadn't renewed their lease at the house near campus. Rudy was going to go back to the dorms until Christmas. I had been accepted to the State University of Arizona and he was hoping I would agree to join him in January and we would get a place together. I had until September 22 to let the school know if I was going to transfer. I hadn't said a word to my parents. No sense upsetting them until I had to.

Rudy and Bernie were driving to Arizona this year. Uncle Joe had gotten Rudy a car to keep out there, a big old Buick. Rudy loved that car and Uncle Joe loved Rudy. What was not to love? I wanted to go with them but I knew Lucy would NEVER agree to that. Alicia was flying back to school. There was no "oxygen needed" kiss at the airport this time although the one he gave me in front of his house made his dad blush. I was sad he was leaving early but I knew I would see him soon enough. Besides, I had to get ready to go back to the dorm and my second year of college. And who knew? Maybe next year at this time I would be going back to school with Rudy. Who knew indeed.

Rudy and Bernie arrived at the university on the Friday of Labor Day weekend, August 30. Bernie and Alicia had rented a small studio apartment until they could find something bigger. Alicia was already there when Rudy dropped Bernie off. Rudy called to tell me he had arrived. He said he would call again later when he had settled in. Then off he went back to the dorms and a new roommate.

Rudy's roommate, Eddie, was from Ohio. Apparently they hit it off right away. They made plans for an overnight backpacking trip to the Grand Canyon the next day. Rudy called me later that night telling me he missed me already and would be flying to New York for the Jewish holidays. He was excited about going backpacking, as we never had. Plus it was the Grand Canyon. They were also going to try rock climbing. I told him to take tons of pictures, carry plenty of water and buy me a present. He asked if a rock counted as a present and I said no.

I was spending the first few days of the semester out in Montauk at a mini conference on women in literature. I was leaving Tuesday morning and would be coming home Thursday night. My professor was the keynote speaker. Rudy joked that he wanted me to bring him home a present. I asked him if a burned bra counted. He said it depended on whose it was.

We chatted a bit more but I could tell from his voice he was tired. I told him to get a good night's sleep before his big adventure. I said I would try to call him from the conference but he said not to worry about it. We would talk a lot on Friday. We were both leaning toward my going out to Arizona in January but I told him we would continue our never-ending conversation about that next week. He said to have fun at my dad's Labor Day party. "I am sorry I am going to miss it."

"Oh, I am sure my dad is too. He would probably rather have you there than me. I'm just the girl who is dating his son."

We both laughed and I ended the conversation by saying, "Have fun this weekend. I love you very much."

Then he said something he had never said to me before. "Love you more."

We hung up and I fell asleep content knowing that, yes, we did have a great life. We did.

I spent most of Saturday and Sunday at Hofstra getting the dorm ready, seeing friends and preparing for the conference. Jenn and I were roommates again. We wouldn't have it any other way. On Monday I drove Jenn and some friends over to my house for the annual barbeque. It was weird that I wasn't going to talk to Rudy for a week but we would have much to talk about when we did.

I was taking the last of my women's study classes that first semester of my sophomore year. I wanted to finish them so that, if I went to Arizona in January, I would have enough credits to get a dual degree in psychology and women's studies. I was still waiting to hear from Arizona State to see if the university would accommodate that.

The conference and the three days out at Montauk were a great way to ease into the school year. The weather was gorgeous and there was enough downtime to go to the beach, shop and grab an ice cream. Some of the women at the conference were what others would label militant feminists, stereotyped as lesbians who didn't shave their legs, shunned makeup and hygiene and hated all men. Truth be told, I found them a little intimidating—not because of the above. None of that was true. Because they were so strong, so committed to the equal rights cause and were sacrificing so much of their time and lives toward making the world a better and just place for all women. It wasn't just about equal pay for women. It was much more. I thought I was dedicated, but these women lived this every day. It was their purpose. We all owe them.

Some of us were still bitter the Equal Rights Amendment hadn't passed. I couldn't vote for the New York State ratification in 1972. I was only seventeen. But Rudy did. I remember him telling me if he could have pulled the lever twice, he would have. "Equality of rights under the law shall not be denied or abridged by the United States or by any state on account of sex." It seemed logical and right. I couldn't believe those twenty-four little words had caused such an uproar. They continue to do so. We were fighting in 1974 and we continue to fight today.

I got home late Thursday night. Actually, it was early Friday morning and although I wanted to call Rudy, I didn't want to wake Jenn up. Rudy and I designed our schedule so we didn't have classes on Mondays and Fridays. It made for an intense middle-of-the-week routine. But it would mean we would always have a four-day weekend, which made flying to New York and back to Arizona not as exhausting for Rudy. I was very happy about that now as I could sleep in this Friday morning.

I heard Jenn getting ready for class and sat up in bed to catch up. It was near nine o'clock. So much earlier in Arizona. I decided to try calling Rudy. He would get up early every morning to go running before it got too hot outside. He was much more disciplined than me. No one answered so I hung up after three rings. I didn't want his roommate to hate me before he had even met me.

I went back to sleep and didn't get up until 12:30 p.m., a real luxury for me. I tried Rudy again but got no answer. I took a shower and decided to go to the bookstore to pick up what I needed for the semester. Two hundred and thirty-five dollars later I dragged the books up to my dorm room. I was checking over the syllabi for the classes I had missed my first week when the phone rang. I knew it was Rudy.

"Hi, honey."

It was honey's mom on the other end. She sounded distressed. She was talking way too fast for me to understand her and was not making any sense. All I got from her was that Papa G. and Carmine were leaving tonight. For where? Why?

"Mama Rose, please calm down. I can't understand what you're saying."

She explained to me she had received a call from Rudy's school asking if he had arrived in Arizona since he hadn't attended any of his classes. I didn't understand. He had arrived there a week before. Why wasn't he going to classes?

"Did you try calling him?" I asked Mama Rose. "Maybe he is sick. I tried this morning but got no answer. Maybe he was out running."

*I tried this morning but got no answer.* That hit me like a ton of bricks. Rudy wouldn't have gone for a run. We hadn't spoken in almost a week.

He would have waited for my call. And why wasn't he going to classes? Something was wrong.

"I'm on my way."

"Okay," she said through tears.

I don't remember leaving the dorm or driving to my house. I just recall feeling ill. It was the same feeling I had when Rudy told me about the "make-out girl", times a thousand. I was not going to let my Italian brain go someplace bad until it had to. Too late. I walked in my house and I could see by the look on my parents' faces they had gone there too.

We all tried to reassure ourselves Rudy was all right. There was an explanation. We just didn't know what it was. The front door opened and Aunt Angie walked in looking terrified. She said Uncle Joe would meet us at Mama Rose's. I drove there alone. If all of them were worried, I wasn't overreacting. I started to shake, then cry, then scream in the car. I had to roll up my windows. I couldn't come up with an explanation that didn't end badly.

When we walked in some neighbors and family were already there. Grandma Rosie was sitting in the living room saying her rosary through tear-filled eyes. We all hugged. Papa G. came speeding into the driveway. I don't think he even shut the car off as he jumped out. This was starting to look quite serious. I was very scared. I sat down next to Grandma Rosie and started softly saying the rosary with her. I didn't know what else to do. Praying seemed like a logical option. It certainly couldn't hurt. I heard my dad and Papa G. talking and then Rudy's dad was calling officials at the Grand Canyon to see if the park had a rescue office.

*Rescue office? They think he is still in the Grand Canyon?* I think deep down I did too. I told myself Rudy and Eddie might be lost or one of them might be hurt. I remember Rudy telling me Eddie was an Army ROTC–trained ranger specializing in mountain climbing and rescue work.

That made me feel better. Rudy was in good health and had great physical strength. I assumed Eddie did too. Yes, that had to be it. They were lost or hurt. Either way someone would start looking for them and they would be rescued. So yes, Papa G., by all means, call the rescue office.

Papa G. called in some favors and he and Carmine got a flight out to Arizona that night. My dad wanted to go with them but school had just started and he couldn't take off. I desperately wanted to go too but I knew it would probably be better for all if I stayed home. I called Bernie to let him know what was going on and he said he would contact the rescue team as he wanted to help. I could hear the panic in his voice. He said he would make some phone calls for me. And there we sat, in that house, waiting. Friday turned into Saturday, then Sunday, then Monday. I felt my heart pound with every second that passed. On Saturday, the first day of the search, the rescue team found their vehicle parked at the Big Saddle Hunting Camp on the North Rim. They searched the vehicle but found no information that might indicate where they were headed.

We spent all weekend at Rudy's waiting for any little morsel of news tossed our way. What we got was either encouraging or devastating, depending on how you wanted to spin it. We were all trying to be very optimistic although that became harder as each day passed. My girlfriends, God bless them, didn't leave my side. They sat with me, rotating shifts, so one of them was always there. Vinnie came home, unfortunately without George, who was teaching a class at school. We all sat and waited. Then it was Monday, September 9, 1974.

## CHAPTER 25

# The Scream

Janie and I were sitting on the swing in the backyard of Rudy's house and never heard the phone ring. I don't know how we missed it. Both the front and back doors were open and the screens were still in. The back door was slightly ajar. Friends and family had been bringing food over for days and someone had put a lasagna tray in the oven without putting a pan under it. The contents had spilled over onto the burn elements and the odor of burnt lasagna permeated the entire house. The doors had to be opened or everyone in the house would be choking on the smell and smoke of burnt noodles. As if waiting wasn't bad enough.

No, we didn't hear the phone ring. But we heard the scream. It raised us off the swing seat and propelled me forward. It was a scream like I had never heard before or since. It still wakes me up in the middle of the night. The only thing I can equate it to is the scream I once heard in a hospital of an infant born addicted to heroin. It was a scream that electrified every nerve in my body. It was a scream that announced the unthinkable. It was the scream of a mother telling the world the unimaginable. It was the scream that told me Rudy was dead.

I remember watching myself tumble off the swing, arms flailing, waist and knees bent over as if I had the worst stomachache of my life. Coming out of my mouth, very softly at first, were the words "no, no, no" over and over again until they reached a screaming pitch. As my knees folded Janie ran to my side to break my fall. The last thing I remember seeing is my mom running out of the back door, pushing the already half-opened screen almost off its hinges, screaming, "He's dead!" She was followed by an old man. My dad had aged twenty years in a single second. Then everything went black.

Anyone who has ever experienced a tragedy knows about the first few seconds after you wake up from sleeping, when you don't immediately remember you are sad. It could be three seconds. If you are lucky, maybe five. A feeling of calm and peace comes over you that is welcoming. Mine lasted two seconds. Then I remembered.

I woke up, lying on a chaise lounge, looking up at the blue cloudless sky, the sun trying to peek through the branches that hung overhead. At the same time I felt my dad's hand holding mine. I didn't have to look to know it was him. I had held that hand a thousand times, on trips to John's Bargain Store and Pergament, on my way into the ocean or walking from the parking lot to church. I knew every finger, knuckle, callous and arthritis bump. Its shape and touch and grip were etched in my mind. I looked over and he was sitting on the edge of the chaise lounge, his eyes red and puffy. I sat up, we threw our arms around each other and we started sobbing. Really sobbing. Shoulders bouncing up and down sobbing. It was the first time I ever saw my father cry like that and it weighed heavy on the pain I was already feeling. I felt if I stayed in that hug, with my father's arms wrapped around me, everything would be fine. My daddy's hug always made everything better. But, like that kiss with Rudy that seemed a lifetime ago, I knew one of us would have to eventually let go.

Just then I realized I hadn't seen my mom since she had bolted out the back door. I turned my head away from my dad, still hugging him and saw her sitting on the swing between Janie and Aunt Angie. She was rocking back and forth, but it was only her body moving, not the swing. Her arms were crossed tightly on her chest and she was looking down uttering some mantra only she could hear. Rudy was like a son to her so I know she was devastated. *Should I go over there? Should I wait for her to come to me? Did it matter at that point?*

I then started to hear soft crying and low chatter and I realized other people had spilled from the house and front lawn into the backyard. Before I could take stock of who was there, or whether I should go to my mom, a man in a suit appeared at the back door. I wondered who he was and why he had a suit on in the middle of this hot day. Most of us had barely showered for days. He couldn't be the funeral director already. He was walking toward my mom and as he got closer, I saw the black bag in his hand. He was a doctor.

He approached the swing and leaned over to talk to my mom and aunt. My mom started shaking her head back and forth, getting very agitated, saying, "No, no, no way." She reminded me of a child whose parents were trying to feed them brussels sprouts. She was having none of whatever the doctor was offering. My aunt looked at me with sympathetic eyes that said, "Help!" I let go of my dad's hand and slowly moved toward the swing. I knelt down in front of my mom and unfolded her arms. I took her hands in mine and for the first time since the scream, our eyes met. I saw my pain reflected in her eyes and suddenly I realized why she couldn't comfort me. She had nothing to give. All her energy was being channeled into just trying to breathe.

The doctor had just given Mama Rose some sort of sedative shot as she had passed out three times in the living room after getting the news. They wanted to call an ambulance but Mama Rose refused. Our family doctor (we all used the same one) was on vacation but knowing the situation, he had arranged with a colleague to be on call for the family in case the news was bad. He offered my mom something to calm her down and that is what she was refusing. Not brussels sprouts. A sedative. Of course she wouldn't want it. There was always a weird sense of pleasure in her misery. She wasn't happy unless she wasn't happy. I don't know where I got the strength at that moment, but I pulled her hands down hard and said, "Stop it. Stop it right now. This is not about you. You can't upset Mama Rose more than she is. You will take the shot."

"No, no, I'll be good. I promise," she whispered. I would not let her stir the emotional pot. Not now. I persisted. She finally agreed.

This wonderful doctor, who didn't know any of us but walked into the worst day of our lives, did a quick examination on me and my mom. My dad too. And Aunt Angie. He took our blood pressures and listened to our hearts, both with his stethoscope and with his own heart. The compassion he showed that day to a group of grieving strangers was remarkable. I will never forget that. I still continue to try and emulate the empathy and kindness he showed us that afternoon. He then gave me and my mom a shot as he assessed we needed it the most. As histrionic as my mom was, Aunt Angie wasn't. She was the calm in the middle of the storm, the voice of reason. Growing up with my hysterical mom, I tried to emulate Aunt Angie too.

I never asked what was in those shots. It was 1974 and I didn't know what the medicine de jour was. I remember it took four people to get my mom in the car. I told her she had to go home with my dad and Aunt Angie to start making phone calls. I didn't want the family to hear it from anyone else. But she never made the phone calls. She went home and slept, which was best for everyone.

After they left, the people who had a front row seat to all the backyard drama started coming over to me, hugging me and crying. I remember some of them, but not all. There were so many. A lot of very sad faces. Finally I saw Vinnie across the yard, slowing, hesitantly coming toward me.

I felt like running in the opposite direction and never stopping. I thought if we didn't acknowledge it to each other it wouldn't be real. We could still be the Three Musketeers and pretend Rudy was in another room or something. But when we fell into each other's arms we both knew it was real.

Vinnie was inconsolable. I wanted to run down that rabbit hole with him but I had to be strong at that moment for others. I also was afraid that if I let myself go I would never come back. I just looked at him crying, trying to catch his breath, and said, "Thank you for giving me my friendship with Rudy. It was the best gift I ever got."

"Better than Hermie?" he said, laughing slightly, referring to a painted pet crab he gave me for my eighth birthday.

"Yes," I said, "but not by much." We smiled at each other, which made me feel guilty and sad. Rudy wasn't there to laugh with us. He always loved that story.

The shot from the doctor was making me sleepy and I suddenly realized I hadn't seen Mama Rose. I broke away from Vinnie and said "Mama Rose?" He pointed to the house. The house felt as dark and closed up as the backyard had felt bright and airy. Again people were coming up to me, some just putting a hand on my shoulder, some hugging me, some hysterical. I don't know if it was the medication or if I was in shock. Probably both. I felt like a walking zombie. My legs were getting heavier and harder to move. Colors, objects in the house, just didn't look right. Everything looked different, almost like I was seeing things for the first time. Unrecognizable, even though I had been there a thousand times. But everything WAS different. It was the first time since Rudy died. Everything was going to be measured by that from now on: "since Rudy died."

Marie had walked me in through the back door, which miraculously still had the screen attached, although barely. *Rudy will have to fix that*, I thought. After some hugs we went to Mama Rose's bedroom, the most sacred room in the house with religious pictures, statues and candles all about. I never went in there. It kind of scared me, like walking into a forbidden part of church. She was lying on top of her white chenille bedspread, her hands folded around rosary beads she was saying as she fell asleep. She was pale, lifeless and out cold. Honestly, she looked dead and it frightened me a little. Her sister, Aunt Sophie, and Grandma Rosie were sitting on the bed next to her. I knelt down beside the bed and felt like I was at a wake. I know Mama Rose would have traded places with Rudy in a heartbeat. At that moment I wished she could have.

I stood up and walked into the living room, which still had the smell of burnt lasagna and for a moment I felt hungry. I then found myself walking up the stairs, not even thinking, to Rudy's room. The door was open and it looked so different from the time I was there with the candles, mints and stolen lace underwear. It looked like the room of a kid who had waited until the very last minute to pack for college, which he always did. Empty hangers were thrown all over the room, dresser drawers were open, socks on the floor. A pile of "not taking these" clothing was in the corner. The closet door was half open, filled with plaid shirts hoping to be chosen. They hadn't been in a long time but Rudy couldn't get rid of them. He was sentimental.

I took a brown plaid flannel shirt off a hanger and put it over my T-shirt. I was thinking how happy I was Mama Rose hadn't cleaned up his room yet. It was exactly how he left it. How he would remember it as he moved away from us again. Which also meant she hadn't changed the sheets, or made the bed for that matter. It was very unlike her to wait so long. I straightened the covers, crawled between the sheets and laid on the pillow where the outline of Rudy's head was still visible. I took a deep breath and his smell that I loved so much came rushing in. How much longer would I be able to smell him before it faded away? I pulled the covers over my head and cried myself to sleep.

When I woke up I had two seconds of calm before reality crashed down again. I heard soft whispers around me and when I finally opened my eyes I saw my loyal, teary-eyed, wonderful friends sitting on the bed and floor around me: Janie, who had never left, Jackie, Gina, Catherine, Marie, Maria and Jenn. Their faces streaked from crying, they all looked like I felt. I asked Jackie, who was sitting next to me on the bed, how long I had been sleeping.

"Well," she said, "we have been here for three hours and you were sleeping when we came up here, so I am not sure."

"Three hours?" I shouted. "You have been sitting here for three hours?"

"Yes," Gina replied. "Where else would we be?"

For a long time no one said anything. Silent hugs were sent but no one moved. I don't know how I would have gotten out of that bed if it wasn't for them. The love from those girls in that room still gets me through tough times today. I noticed they were all looking at each other suspiciously, like they had something to tell me but no one wanted to say what it was.

"What?" I asked.

Finally Jackie said, "The helicopters can't recover the bodies until tomorrow because of the terrain and the time of day."

I sat there shocked. Rudy had to stay there, alone and in the dark, until tomorrow. And Jackie had said "the bodies." I had almost forgotten about Eddie. He must have died too. I started crying uncontrollably. My friends got up and gave me the most beautiful group hug. We were all crying. "Mama Rose is up and asking for you," Gina told me, trying to hold back tears. I got up slowly and walked downstairs to face a reunion I was dreading and yet hoping I would find comforting.

Mama Rose was sitting on the end of the couch, looking even older than my dad had when he raced out the back door after my mom. Was that today? A lot of people were still in and around the house, but I only saw and acknowledged Mama Rose. She had a washcloth on her neck and the water was dripping down her back, which she either didn't mind or didn't notice. Upon seeing me she extended her right arm and I sat next to her as she wrapped me in one of her always soothing hugs. Neither of us said a word. I rested my head on her shoulder and we sat in silence for a long time, each locked in our own personal cell of disbelief.

It was still light out when I got up from the couch. Hell, it wasn't even dinnertime. The longest day of my life had no end in sight. What had started out as a hopeful and optimistic day would end with the deepest grief I had ever experienced. I didn't want to leave the house but I didn't want to stay. Not without Rudy. Where was he anyway? In the backyard? Upstairs? On his way home from practice? I wanted him to be anywhere but dead.

As I got up Aunt Sophia said, "They have to do an autopsy before they can release the body."

*WHAT THE FUCK IS SHE TALKING ABOUT?* And why would she even say that in front of me and Mama Rose?

"I have to go home and check on my mom," I said abruptly, brushing off her statement.

Mama Rose finally spoke, also ignoring her sister's words. "Take some food home for you and your family. There's so much."

I told her maybe later. I gathered my stuff and kissed Rudy's mom on the top of her head like he had kissed me hundreds of times before. I walked out the front door to my car with people again coming over to hug me or tenderly touch my shoulder. Someone asked if I was okay to drive and I softly muttered, "Yes." Janie and the girls had somehow sneaked past me outside and were getting into Janie's car to follow me home. How they knew I wanted to drive alone I don't know. They just did.

I took the short ride to my house in a daze. My car felt like it was on automatic pilot. Outside it was still so quiet and so quietly still. No one on the roads. Like everyone knew and ran inside to hide from the truth of the day. It even seemed like the birds had stopped singing. The only time I remember the earth being so silent was the day President Kennedy died. I started to think about that day just to get out of my own head for a few minutes.

I was in third grade on November 22, 1963, when the teachers were pulled out of class and into the hallway. They came back to their rooms in tears. We were told President Kennedy was in the hospital. Being in third grade, I thought maybe he was getting his tonsils out. This was about a quarter to two. We had been in our reading groups and didn't do much work the rest of what was left of the day.

When we lined up to be dismissed my teacher, Mrs. Rosenstock, would always lead us in a song. But this day there was no singing. No talking. Everything seemed suspended in time. We were anxiously waiting for the bell to ring but Mrs. Rosenstock seemed like she was even more impatient for this school day to end than we were. When the bell finally rang the kids spilled into the hallways excitedly to begin their weekend. We had no idea what kind of weekend it was going to be. But the teachers knew. They were all hugging each other and crying. *So much fuss for tonsils!* I thought.

I had dance class that afternoon and my girlfriend Patty and I would always take the half-mile walk to Mrs. McNaire's house together. The lessons were held in her basement, like my mom's sewing studio. Mrs. McNaire's mom, whom everyone called Grandma Dee, would be sitting at a table when we entered. We would give her the $2.00 for our lesson and she would mark it in her little book next to the date. My column was always full as I rarely missed a class.

When we entered I noticed Grandma Dee was not at her desk. VERY unusual. I surveyed the room and saw her in the back with her daughter and a mom of one of the students. They were all crying. "Why is everyone crying today?" I wondered out loud.

Mrs. McNaire saw me and Patty and came over to us visibly shaken and upset. "There are no classes today. They are cancelled." Her voice was barely audible.

"Is everything okay?" Patty asked, her voice now sounding a little frightened.

Mrs. McNaire choked out the words, "President Kennedy has died."

"From tonsils?" I shouted back.

"No, dear. He was shot." Then she burst into tears.

Shot? Who would shoot our handsome president? He had little kids and a pretty wife. Didn't they know that? It was all so confusing. And why were they crying? They didn't know him. I didn't want to ask any more questions. I just wanted to go home. It was Friday, which was a busy day for my mom and Aunt Angie trying to meet weekend deadlines. Patty's parents both worked outside the house. No one could pick us up at this hour so we decided to walk the distance, a little over a mile and a half, to our homes. Patty lived a block away from me so we could walk most of it together. It wasn't cold out and we would make it before dark.

In 1963 little girls walked a mile or so home from school by themselves. No one worried about abductions, rapes or murders. They were there, I am sure. But we didn't hear about them. We were walking through neighborhoods of houses with families just like ours. We felt safe. Our parents felt we were safe. And, for the most part, we were. But this walk home, unlike the others, was very troubling. I remember it to this day.

Everything was so silent and motionless. Not in a tranquil or peaceful way. In a way that felt like the planet and all its activities had just stopped. Nothing was moving. Not a branch, a leaf on the ground, or people. There were no cars or anyone in sight. I had never heard the world so quiet. The sound was completely off and the picture was stuck. Where were the kids playing outside? The moms pulling up from grocery shopping? The dads sneaking home early for a long weekend? Even the air smelled different, felt different. Patty and I didn't say much but we both knew this was not a typical Friday walk home. Once in a while we could hear a TV playing from inside a house but it wasn't a happy program. No one was watching *Queen for a Day* or *To Tell the Truth*. (Not that *Queen for a Day* was happy. A woman told her life story. The saddest story, based on audience applause, won a refrigerator or vacuum. Queen? Really?) Kids weren't laughing at Officer Joe Bolton or Sandy Becker. As Patty approached her block she turned right and I continued straight for one more block. Still so still. Still quiet. Empty streets and funny air. As I got to my house …

So deeply had I lost myself in 1963 I didn't hear the knock on my car window. It was Janie, motioning me to roll down the window. "Are you okay?" she demanded. "You have been sitting at this stop sign for five minutes."

"Sorry," I said, meaning it. "I was somewhere else." I didn't tell her where or that I would like to go back there and start all over again. Maybe then I wouldn't end up here.

I turned the corner to my street and noticed a line of parked cars embracing the curb, a parade with nowhere to go. I saw my cousins sitting on the front stoop, anxiously waiting for me to find a place to park. Jackie had already turned around and was parking on the next block. I so wanted to be alone in peace. But I knew I had to go through yet another group of grieving people. And I understood that. They all loved Rudy. Many had known him longer than I had. I didn't own this loss although it felt like I did. It was a loss for them too and I had to remember and acknowledge that. As much as we think we own our life, we share it with many people. That became a reason for me to try and remain strong. It was a task I gave myself at which I was only partially successful.

My cousins ran to meet me, not even waiting for me to get out of the car. I was greeted by deliberate words I would eventually retreat from. "How are you?" "Oh my God, I am so sorry." "Are you okay?" That last one always got me. Of course I was not okay. I would never be okay again. But I would say yes because people wanted me to be okay. It made them feel better.

There were about twenty-five people in and about my house, yet it was so quiet. I immediately walked over to my grandmother. She *loved* Rudy. They would talk in Italian all the time. She stood up and hugged me like I had never been hugged by her before. My grandmother wasn't a very demonstrative lady. When my grandfather died I never saw a tear. But here she was smothering me in her arms and crying. Then I started crying. I didn't want to start again because I was sure I would never stop. As I was hugging my grandmother I looked around and realized all these people were going to want to hug me too. I really wasn't up to it and when I moved away from my grandmother I just kind of put my hand up and said "Hi, everyone," and walked into the kitchen. I shouldn't have been surprised at what I saw and yet I was.

My mother, Aunt Angie and Aunt Mary were standing over the stove, making macaroni. Were they intending to feed all these people? Of course they were. That's what they did. Someone said my dad was at the store. I guess they all needed to focus on something else. They needed a distraction. Outside people were setting the picnic tables and some younger cousins and friends were in the pool. I kissed my mom and aunts and answered a few questions about Mama Rose. My parents were going back over there later. Did I want to go? I didn't know what I wanted to do the next minute, let alone in a few hours. I then turned around and walked through the living room, past all those sad faces fixated on me and went upstairs. A few minutes later, "my girls" came in and they, along with my cousins, followed my path to my old room. As I walked up the stairs I noticed I still had Rudy's flannel shirt on. I didn't think I would ever take it off. I certainly was never going to wash it.

We sat on the couch and the beanbag chairs and pillows that were on the floor. They tried very hard to make small talk. Finally Gina asked if I knew any details about what had happened. I told her there was going to be an autopsy before they released the bodies. Released the bodies? This was like the plot of some detective show. There were no "bodies." There was just Rudy and his new roommate. I also told her I heard someone mention dehydration and the elements. It would be a few days before we actually knew what had happened. But the outcome would never change. Rudy would always be dead. The saddest five words of my life.

## CHAPTER 26

# The Wait to the End

In an instant Rudy's death became the new, worst tragedy my family measured all others against. Don't misunderstand me: Aunt Theresa's death was still horrific. But as he had died at twenty years old, a mere child, Rudy's death moved to the top of the list. It remains there for me today.

Over the next couple of days I was in a daze. I would lie in bed until exhaustion rocked me to sleep, hoping to dream of Rudy. But I never slept long. I barely ate and I ended up losing several pounds by the funeral. I stayed in bed most of the day, getting up and going out only to see Mama Rose. It was absolute torture going over to that house, but I went because we both needed to see each other. Friends and family came and went. I barely noticed except for Vinnie, who spent a lot of time with me, just sitting silently. Occasionally I would get a burst of energy and take a shower.

Since it was the beginning of the school year, my dad had to go back to work and function like a regular teacher. His principal, a friend of his from college, told him to take the time off while they were looking for Rudy but, now that he had been found, my dad had to get back to school. He would need time off when Rudy came home. How my dad was able to go to work and instruct students during this time I will never understand. He just did.

Jackie called my advisor at Hofstra and told her what had happened. Like everyone else, she was devastated when she heard the story. She told Jackie I shouldn't worry; we would figure something out for the semester. She also asked Jackie to let her know the arrangements when they were finalized.

I remained in the darkest place I had ever been. Every day I kept sinking a little deeper. I couldn't dream, pray, or cry myself out. I was lost, scared, empty, hopeless. I didn't know how to find my way back. And if I did, what was I coming back to? I couldn't imagine a world without Rudy. I wondered if the ache of his absence would ever go away. I was afraid there would be nothing to fill that void if it did. At least now I was feeling something. But oh, how I wanted to be numb.

When you are nineteen years old the idea of death doesn't float across your brain that often unless it is pushed in your face. I had lost my grandfathers, an aunt and a fourteen-year-old friend, Barbara, to cancer. But death wasn't something that entered my world frequently. I had never really contemplated it. Now I could think about nothing else. And not just any death. Rudy's death.

I'm not sure if news was slow coming in or if they just didn't want to tell me anything, but I had little information about what had happened. I didn't know about the backpacks, the notes, the rescue effort. I did find out that Rudy's friend Eddie died from a fall and Rudy from what they were calling the elements. I wondered if he knew he was dying. Was he scared? What was the last thing he saw before he closed his eyes to the world forever? At what point did the most beautiful place on earth become a death-trap? And in my own selfish little mind I wondered: did he think of me?

Finally, after I don't know how many days, Papa G., Carmine and Rudy were coming home. I thought I would be relieved by this, but I felt worse. When they were in Arizona it wasn't quite real. Now that they were coming home there was no avoiding, denying or repressing the truth of Rudy's death. My dad and Uncle Joe picked them up at the airport. I couldn't go with them. Our local funeral parlor, Donahue's, picked up the body. The preparations for the wake and funeral had already begun. This was really happening.

My dad dropped Papa G. and Carmine home then came to get me, my mom and Aunt Angie. Vinnie and Uncle Joe were already at the house. I walked in the living room and Papa G. started crying the minute he saw me, saying something in Italian that no one ever translated for me. He hugged me so hard I thought I was going to break. He couldn't let go of me. The two of us were brokenhearted. When he finally let go it was my mom's turn. Carmine and I were melting into a puddle of tears.

When everyone calmed down Papa G. and Carmine started telling us about what had happened, the recovery, the autopsy and the trip home. It was absolutely surreal. Meanwhile Mama Rose wanted me upstairs to help her pick out Rudy's suit, shirt and tie. I was going through the motions, not fully comprehending what I was actually doing. I felt like there was nowhere on earth I was ever going to find peace. I kept drifting between rooms, houses, days, nights, waiting and waiting. And now it was here. As much as I tried I couldn't turn away from learning what had happened to Rudy and Eddie. Papa G. shared what he knew, which made me sick inside.

I was obsessed with running different scenarios through my head, the ones where Rudy survived. I couldn't stop thinking about what he had gone through, the fear, the pain, the acceptance that these were his final moments on earth. I had never experienced anxiety attacks up to this point but I was now having them all the time. The shortness of breath, my heart racing, the feeling I wanted to run away from myself and everything around me. And the depression was only deepening. I found joy in nothing. I didn't want to do anything or go anywhere. But I had to pull myself together for this four-day death extravaganza.

The big question was whether the casket would be open. The body starts decomposing almost immediately after you die. Rudy had been dead for over six days when they found him in that one hundred-plus heat. His body was already decomposing and infested with maggots. The thought of it still makes me want to throw up. No one was sure what the mortician would be able to do, even though Donahue's was the best around. The coffin was closed.

My mom was keeping busy ironing her black clothing and my dad's suits for the services. It was three days of viewing and a day for the funeral. For some reason my mom felt she couldn't wear the same thing more than once. It was all black. Who would know or care? She kept asking me what I was going to wear. Really? The third time she asked I snapped back, "I don't know. Maybe my pajamas."

I started crying and she came from around the ironing board to comfort me. We went up to my room and went through my closet. She was right about not wanting to wear the same thing day after day. The wakes then were three days, usually 1:00 p.m. to 5:00 p.m., a two-hour dinner break and then 7:00 p.m. to 11:00 p.m. Over three days, twenty-four hours were spent at the funeral parlor. You at least needed to start each day feeling fresh.

My dad had gone to the store and stocked up on black pantyhose, enough for the entire family and then some. He got all different sizes, as per my mom's instructions and distributed them to everyone. I thought this was strange but I later understood he needed to have something to do.

The three days of the wake were a madhouse. There was a line to get into the funeral parlor from the time we got there until closing, hundreds and hundreds of people each day. The family would go in first. We had to get there early if we wanted some quiet time. Mama Rose, Papa G., Carmine, his grandmother and Aunt Sophie and her husband, Uncle Al, sat in the front row, with the rest of the family, including my parents, in the seats behind them. I sat for the entire twenty-four hours on a small loveseat off to the side in the front. I always had one of my friends, Vinnie or George sitting next to me. I never moved except to go to the bathroom. I only stood up to greet people twice. Once was for Dr. Willard and the other was for Dana.

I sat there and watched everyone who had ever heard Rudy's name come through. Some of his former teammates from high school had to be physically helped away from the coffin. Richard and Gerry were inconsolable. There were teachers, coaches, students from high school and some from Arizona, who flew out to Long Island to pay their respects. My friends' parents came. Louie from the pizzeria was there. Our mailman, who would always talk to Rudy about football, came. It was heartwarming but also a circus. Most of the time I wanted everyone to go away so I could be alone with Rudy. I know their hearts were in the right place, but there were so many of them. And it was so loud. "Come together, right now, over me" kept playing in my head. And Mama Rose's screams of "my son, my son" and her crying, which rarely stopped, could be heard all the way down the street to Post Avenue, where the line never ended.

I didn't have the strength to stand up and greet each one, which is why I stayed seated. People would have to bend over and kiss me or give me a pat on the shoulder. Yet they still managed to ask the same stupid questions. I know it was out of concern and awkwardness, but still. The one I hated, which almost everyone asked, was, "What happened?" Very early on I just started to reply, "He died." They would say they knew that, but how? I would give them a "Are you fucking kidding me, you want to do this now?" look and most would move on. I would actually have to tell the ones who didn't that this was not the time or place. I would never hear his voice again. I would never taste his lips or see his smile. And they wanted the gory details. Please remember that the next time you go to a wake. Sometimes it is better to simply say "I am sorry" and leave it at that.

We would all go to Rudy's house in between "sessions" to eat as the food never stopped coming. I hated being there because of him but without him. People tried to have some semblance of normality during dinner, talking about who came, who said what and the weather. They were always talking about the weather. Another distraction, I guess. I would usually go upstairs and lay on Rudy's bed, trying to fall asleep until the next round.

We would go back and there would be the line again. They wouldn't let anyone in until the family had the opportunity to go in alone first. Some people came more than once, some every day. I didn't find it comforting. I found it exhausting. It was a fatigue that I had never experienced before. Yet I would go to bed and not be able to fall asleep. I was drained but wide awake. Every night Janie or Jackie slept over. They took off from work the entire four days, using their vacation time. I told them not to but they insisted. One night I slept with my parents. I hadn't done that in over a decade.

Then I would wake up and go through the same day again. Why three days I never understood. Maybe it had to do with the Bible, rising from the dead on the third day, or with the Father, Son and Holy Ghost. Maybe it was an Italian thing. Maybe it was just too hard to say goodbye. I couldn't wait for it to be over and then, when it was the day of the funeral, I wanted another three days. This was it. The real goodbye. I couldn't do it. I woke up that morning hysterical and told my parents I didn't want to go. They told me it was my choice but if I didn't, it might be something I would always regret. They suggested I go and if at any time I wanted to come home they would take me. I am grateful they convinced me to go even though it was one of the worst days of my life.

The funeral is so different from the wake. While the wake is full of people talking, remembering the deceased and laughing, the funeral is somber and quiet. Usually only those closest to the deceased go to the funeral parlor in the morning, immediate family and innermost friends. But everyone felt so close to Rudy that more people came than expected. The funeral director finally had to ask most of them to please proceed to the church.

I sat wrapped in Vinnie's arms, my body shaking uncontrollably, with George holding tightly to my hand. Mama Rose, who tried unsuccessfully to keep it together during the wake, fully let it go that morning. She kept going up to the coffin, screaming and crying, sometimes in English, sometimes in Italian. There was dead silence (excuse the pun) except for the sobbing, crying and nose blowing of the attendees. Uncle Joe was a honker when he blew his nose and it was something Rudy, Vinnie and I would laugh at hysterically. So, during this dramatic silence, Uncle Joe would blow his nose, and "HONK!" Vinnie and I would try to muffle our laughs. We knew this was a gift from Rudy.

A priest came in to say a few prayers and bless Rudy and us. Then it was time. The funeral director, Chris, a man born for his job, explained we would say our goodbyes then line up in our cars, with our lights on, outside the funeral home. We were to follow one another, not stopping for red lights. As was tradition, the procession was going to go past Rudy's house and head back to St. Brigid's Church for the service. "Would those friends of Rudy's please come up now to say goodbye," he said as he removed the kneeler in front of the casket.

This to me is always the worst moment of any funeral. You are truly saying your final goodbye. Gut-wrenching is the only way I can describe it. The removal of the kneeler is to facilitate a quick passing because forever wouldn't be long enough to say farewell. And so, one by one, the friends and family of this beautiful twenty-year-old said their goodbyes, some with the sign of the cross, others with a touch or kiss on the coffin, all turning away with sadness and tears in their eyes.

Then it was the family's turn. Aunts, uncles, cousins, all started to come forward. Papa G. turned around and looked at me and Vinnie, telling us to stay seated. Then my mom and dad, George, Aunt Angie and Uncle Joe got up. The five of them were sobbing. I put my head in my hands and, rocking back and forth, started crying like I had never cried in my life. I was having trouble breathing and the funeral director wanted to take me outside, but I wasn't going anywhere. I wasn't leaving my Rudy. Not now. Finally all who were left to go up were me and Vinnie, Mama Rose, Papa G. and Carmine. Vinnie gently lifted me up. I was afraid my legs wouldn't carry me to Rudy. We slowly walked toward the casket. I wanted time to stop, collapse, staying in that moment forever, never having to say good-bye. But it didn't and as we got closer to Rudy I started crying and uncontrollably yelling, "I don't want to leave him. Vinnie, please don't make me leave him." If I could, I think I would have opened the lid, jumped in there with him and stayed in the snuggling position forever.

George came over to me, grabbed my other arm and helped me the rest of the journey. On the casket were two large pictures of Rudy. One was his yearbook picture. SO handsome and serious. The other was a picture of him laughing I had taken only a few weeks before. Only pictures and memories left. In that brief moment I tried to remember every line, curve and shadow of his face. How long before I would forget his voice, his tender touch? I stood there staring at this box that contained my world, hoping he would lift the top of the coffin, sit up and say, "Gotcha!" I took his most recent picture off the top of the casket and held it to my chest, crying. Then I gently kissed it. I just couldn't turn around to walk away, but his family was waiting for their final goodbye. As I looked down at the casket, trying to imagine Rudy inside, I whispered, "IWALY."

Vinnie and George then walked me to the back of the room, where several people were still waiting, including my parents. My father just hugged me and held me for the longest time as I felt his tears falling on my head. In his arms I couldn't see what was happening but I could hear Mama Rose and Papa G. crying and screaming in Italian. Vinnie told me a few days later that Mama Rose had thrown herself on the coffin, not wanting to let go or leave the funeral parlor. I understood that feeling. As everyone walked out I looked back one last time. That walk out the door was the hardest steps I have ever taken. I had no idea where they were going to lead me. I only knew that from then on, wherever I went, however I ended up, it would be without Rudy.

Mama Rose and Papa G. had gotten two funeral limousines and George, Vinnie and I were in one with our parents. They all tried to make small talk while I silently looked out the window. We were waiting for the limo with the casket. As I was sitting there I knew the funeral director was sealing Rudy in that box forever. I leaned against the window and started sobbing. Even with the doors and windows closed I could hear Mama Rose screaming from the other limousine.

The ride to Rudy's house was strange. It was a beautiful, sunny, cool September day. On Post Avenue, the main street on this side of Westbury, people were going about their business like it was a normal day. A little boy and his grandfather were coming out of the pharmacy, a man was walking into the bank and the smell of Louie's pizza filled the air and drifted into the limo. Cars were coming and going like nothing was wrong. Didn't they know? Didn't they care? Everything, even the colors, seemed off.

We turned on to Rudy's block and people who couldn't attend the funeral were standing outside. One person—I can't recall who—held up a sign that said, "Rest in Peace Rudy. We Love You." I couldn't look up when we went past the house. I closed my eyes. I never understood this tradition.

The church was packed, just like the wake. We all walked in, following the casket, looking at the faces lining the pews, so sad and inconsolable. I don't remember much of the mass. The singer had a beautiful voice but why did they have to sing such horribly sad songs? I think Rudy would have preferred a Beatles' tune. The priest, not the family, gave the eulogy as that is the way it was done then. I spent most of the time staring at the coffin, unable to believe Rudy was in there. I would unconsciously look around for him and then remember. I do recall one quote the priest said. I asked him a few weeks later where it was from and he said an ancient Greek dramatist named Aeschylus. "Even in our sleep, pain that cannot forget falls drop by drop upon the heart." It still brings me to tears.

Many people came up to me afterward to say what a beautiful service it was. I wished it was a service that wasn't. Most everyone there went over to Holy Rood Cemetery, which was attached to the church. Rudy was going to be buried in the next section over from my grandfather. They placed the casket on top of the hole with some flowers from the funeral parlor. They had about fifty arrangements to choose from. The priest said a few prayers, we were each given a rose to place on the coffin and that was it. Rudy was buried. Everyone got back in their cars to continue living their lives. But not before most went back to Mama Rose's for lunch.

Now it was just me and Mama Rose standing at the grave, looking down into that dark, empty abyss. I am sure the cemetery workers were anxious for us to leave so they could lower the coffin and go on their break. We stood there, arms locked, crying, until Chris gently guided us back to our cars. As we pulled away I turned around and saw the workers already lowering the casket until I couldn't see it anymore. Done.

Several family members and friends were already at the house preparing the food. I don't know how many people came over but it was a lot. George, Vinnie, and I sat outside with some friends and cousins. I wasn't hungry but managed to eat a little. People were talking, laughing, remembering. Someone brought out a photo album of Rudy as a baby and of course Vinnie and I were in there too. There was a great photo of the three of us, I must have been three months old. The boys were sitting on the couch at my house and I was wrapped in a blanket, across their tiny legs, as they nervously held me. When I was about twelve we replicated that picture and Mama Rose had it right next to the original. It made me cry thinking we would never be able to take another photo like that.

At one point I went into the house to use the bathroom and when I came out, Papa G. was waiting for me. He had the pocketknife I had bought Rudy, which, he explained, they found with his gear. He wanted me to have it. As he put it in my hand, I thought of all the adventures Rudy took it on, as he took it everywhere he went. I felt bad that this little knife didn't have some contraption that could have saved him. I held it up to my lips, crying, as I watched Papa G. walk away, ever so sad. That knife remains with me still.

Being there was a good distraction but a distraction nonetheless. Once this lunch was over almost everyone would continue as before. They would feel sad when they thought or talked about it, describe it as a tragedy, but nevertheless they would move on. I didn't see that as one of my options. Not now anyway. Life as I knew it had changed in an instant. It would be a long and winding road to come back. (That reference was for Rudy!)

For the next eleven days I went to the cemetery every day. I didn't know where else to be. I would go and sit in the dirt, surrounded by the dying flowers covering it. Rain or shine. One day it was chilly and two of the cemetery workers came over with a cup of hot chocolate for me. They would see me every day and ask if I needed anything. I would say no. They knew what I needed. My Rudy.

I sat there day after day and would just talk to him. Sometimes I would sing. "In my life, I love you more." I would recall things we did together. I would talk about the wake and share some funeral gossip. And I would cry. Always. A lot. Each time, before I left, I would ask him to please help me. Help me understand. Help me get out of bed in the morning. Help me breathe. I would tell him I couldn't do this without him. I would share how scared I was. I asked him to help me find the courage to continue alone. I didn't know how to be without him because I never was. I would tell him I wanted to join him but not to worry; I wouldn't hurt myself. Although sometimes I lied. I did think about it.

My parents didn't know how to help me and I saw how devastating my pain was to them. I tried to hide it but I was rarely successful. In 1974 therapy and counseling weren't as readily available and accepted as they are today. You only went if you were, well, in the term they used then, crazy. A bereavement group would have been very beneficial, as well as a social worker. I was on my own. The people I leaned on the most were all grieving too.

Right after we got the news that Rudy had died my Aunt Mary came over with a book for me called *On Death and Dying* by Elisabeth Kubler-Ross (New York, Macmillan, 1969). I thought that was an odd title for a book. And besides, I didn't need to read about it. I was living it. I thanked her and put it on my nightstand. One afternoon after coming home from the cemetery I was laying on my bed and saw the book, untouched since I placed it there. I opened it up and started browsing through the pages, eventually finding myself reading more than thumbing through it.

Today her research and theories are known worldwide. At the time I received the book, it was only five years old and surrounded by controversy, as most brilliant theories are. Think Darwin and Freud. She discussed the five stages of grief: denial, anger, bargaining, depression and acceptance.

It was clear to me when reading the book that they are not always in that order, and not everyone experiences all of them. The one thing I learned from my own grieving is that it is a nonlinear experience. There really is no beginning and end. It is cyclical and, at any moment, you could find yourself in another stage. I would walk past a picture of Rudy a hundred times and on the hundred and first passing I would get hysterical. Some days were just better than others. I was in a different place all the time. Some people would meet that linear conclusion or think they had. Others would take the cyclical ride over and over again. My ticket on that ride never expired.

I found this book extremely supportive on many levels, but the biggest assurance I took from it was that I wasn't alone. Although Rudy's death was specific to me, the emotions I felt were not. Some were unique to my situation but there is a process of mourning everyone goes through. A process. I had never thought of it that way.

My mom was a hysterical mourner and had her own process, like wearing black for a year after my grandfather died. The year my dad died my friends Bill and Jon were coming over on Christmas night to exchange gifts. I warned them my mom was going to be in all black. She was, in a tight black jumpsuit Bill called a cat suit with a thick black leather belt around her waist and black high heels. Yup, everyone mourns differently!

Mama Rose's journey was her own too. She was never the same after Rudy died. His death sucked all the joy out of her life, never to come back. She tried. She tried for all of us. But there was always sadness behind her eyes. Always. It never left. I saw it every time I looked at her.

Of the five stages Kubler-Ross outlined, I seemed to be stuck in depression. There was a helplessness I just couldn't seem to get past. Soon after the wake I started to experience anger, although I always believed anger and depression are opposite sides of the same coin. I felt frustration and anxiety and was mad at everyone, trying to find someone to blame and drop this grief on once and for all.

I was angry with myself because Rudy said he would stay home instead of going to Arizona but I insisted he go. I was angry with myself for the second time for not pushing Rudy to come back to Long Island when he suggested it. If I had he might still be alive. I was angry with Eddie for suggesting they go hiking before school started. I was mad as hell at Mother Nature for being brutal and beautiful at the same time and for not providing clouds and rain for them when they needed it. I was angry at God. I lost faith. And I was angry at Rudy. Why did he have to go hiking? How come he wasn't more prepared? He should have taken more water, brought flares. They should have stayed on the trail. Should have, could have, would have. It took me a very long time to accept that an accident, regardless of how tragic, is just that. There was no blame here. If he had made a right instead of a left. If he had gone down the canyon instead of up. I could blame those split-second decisions if I needed something or someone to fault, but that would not help me move on. And as long as I was looking back I wasn't moving forward.

I found out in the long run that no quantity of drugs or alcohol would help me, although for a while I tried. I tried really hard. I eventually realized they were only hurting me. Time would be the only thing that enabled me to look at new options, make plans and keep going. But time can be a very slow-moving enemy when you want it to pass quickly. I wished it was a year from then, two, five. I found myself wishing my life away, wondering how I would feel next month, next year, when I was fifty. Would I always remember this pain? Would it always be with me? Would I forget the love Rudy and I shared? His smell, his taste, his touch? Only time would tell.

## CHAPTER 27

# The Grand Canyon

No matter how many years have passed it is still a challenge to go back there. It is amazing how quickly those years have gone by, except for the days that it seems like yesterday. I never know what feelings are going to be brought up when I reopen this memory. No, that is wrong. I do know. It is profound sadness. Always. I don't think I will ever stop feeling that.

Rudy loved people and they loved him. He was truly interested in everyone he met. He was outgoing and extremely charismatic. He had many friends and was close to his family. I loved that about him. It was natural that he would connect with his new roommate immediately. He made every effort to see the best in people.

I don't know the conversation that took place between Eddie and Rudy when they met. All I know is they decided to go hiking, backpacking overnight actually. I could understand how that seemed appealing to Rudy, who loved adventure, liked to push himself physically and enjoyed being outside. He also liked a little bit of danger and a challenge. He was going to be in one of the most beautiful places on earth. Rudy had been to the Grand Canyon a few times but had never gone backpacking there. Most of his hiking was local, near the campus. His time was spent on studies, sports and flying back and forth to New York.

It would seem Eddie had a bit more climbing experience than Rudy. They left from Big Saddle Hunting Camp on the North Rim. Their goal was Thunder River, nearly 3,000 feet below where their car was parked and then on to Tapeats Creek for a total 5,000-foot descent, with some planned rock climbing thrown in. A two-day, twenty-mile hike over this terrain in grueling heat was a huge undertaking even for an experienced hiker, which Rudy was not.

I was told that a National Parks Ranger encountered them on their way to their hike. Eddie was asking a lot of questions and looked at a map the ranger had. The ranger cautioned them to stay on the trail, be careful of the heat and mentioned a severe lack of water in the area they were intending to hike.

There were two National Parks Service trails they could have followed to their goal, but instead they followed a little-used game trail. I don't know why they went right instead of left, up instead of down. Maybe they thought they were short-cutting an established trail. That question still runs through my mind today. I am always yelling in my dreams to "STAY ON THE TRAIL."

On Friday, September 6, the school called, reporting they hadn't attended any of their classes. Papa G. called the Grand Canyon National Parks Service and subsequently the Coconino County Sheriff's Department, the US Forest Service and the Freedonia Sheriff's department got involved. Search-and-rescue teams on foot, Jeep, and horseback were formed and the effort to find them began on Saturday, September 7.

It was difficult for the rescue team because they had no idea what trail Rudy and Eddie took, or even if they were still in the canyon. They had not registered with the parks service as required. They could have made it to the river and gone out with one of the rafting companies. A severe thunderstorm marred their week-old tracks.

At approximately 11:00 a.m. on September 9, they found tracks that looked recent and determined they were Rudy and Eddie's. The two sets of tracks wandered back and forth across the slope between Crazy Jug Point (also called Monument Point) and Bridger Knoll. It is believed they were trying to find a route down through the Red Wall Foundation and ultimately to water. About ¾ of a mile south of Bridges Knoll they found an abandoned yellow backpack. I never understood why they abandoned their gear unless it was too heavy or too hot to carry. They might have started to become disoriented. Inside the backpack was a note. Signed by both of them, it was written around 1:30 p.m. on September 2. They were attempting to reach a creek they had spotted down in the canyon. "We have run out of food and water. God help us. We're trying to get water."

A little while later, around 1:00 p.m., another backpack was found on top of Red Wall Formation. Among various points along the formation they also found evidence of a fire, sunglasses, a silver "space" blanket, crammed in a crevice, a blue water bottle and chewed cactus. This brown backpack also contained a note, written on September 2, around 11:00 a.m. It indicated they were trying "to reach a small stream. We have ropes. Please look for us. It looks bad, but we're tough. Don't give up looking for us. God bless whoever finds us."

Did they underestimate the challenge? Overestimate their abilities? Did they simply decide to take a shortcut and go off the NPS trail? Did they get lost? Did they drink too fast or not bring enough water? I can't tell you the number of times I have asked myself these and hundreds of other questions. I never get an answer, which doesn't matter because the outcome is always the same. Just an innocent series of miscalculations.

Based on their travel pattern, it is believed Eddie died first, but there is no way to confirm this. It was concluded that this was the logical sequence. A search party, in a helicopter, found Rudy and Eddie's bodies on Monday, September 9. Apparently they had stranded themselves on a 1,000-foot cliff and were trying to climb down to a stream they saw when Eddie fell about 200 feet, resting on the base of a cliff.

I have replayed that moment in my mind a million times. That poor twenty-two-year-old, just trying to hike a little before school started, dying in such a tragic way. But what I think about most is Rudy witnessing it, watching Eddie fall to his death and being helpless to stop it. The quiet that must have echoed after the fall, after Rudy screamed his name to see if he was alright. The fear Rudy had when he realized his new friend was dead and he was all alone. I panic for him whenever I think about it. I know he must have too.

At that point Rudy had to make a decision to either continue to try to go down this cliff, toward water, without Eddie, or try to hike back up to the car. In his split-second decision he changed the plan and decided to try to ascend Monument Point to the car. He had no water and the temperature would have been 100 degrees in the shade. Except there was no shade.

They located Rudy's body first, wedged under a rock, about 200 feet below the top of Red Wall Foundation. It is believed he was trapped on that ledge, trying to protect himself from the elements. His suffering must have been unimaginable. He was found wearing those damn Levi cut off shorts he loved so much. I would tease him and tell him he liked to wear them because they showed off his beautiful muscled legs. He would just tilt his head and look at me embarrassed. He also had on an orange T-shirt and brown and green socks. No mention of shoes. And of course his beaded necklace that I bought him, which he never took off. It is in every picture of him from that summer. I wonder if Rudy felt hopeful at any point, thinking they might make it out. I like to think he did, that those last hours of his life weren't filled with dread and fear, but with hope and some sort of peace.

The helicopters came back the next day to retrieve the bodies. Due to the condition of Rudy's body and the way it was wedged under the rock, it took about an hour to remove him. The coroner's office said Eddie died from a fractured skull he sustained in the fall. Rudy's death was listed as dehydration, heat exposure and starvation. Eddie's body was in the same condition. The bodies were listed as "moderately decomposed" and putre-fied. They were found approximately two miles from water. The autopsy revealed no drugs or alcohol in their systems.

On Tuesday, September 17, both deaths were ruled an accident, due to human error (in judgement). It was concluded that they had only brought enough food and water for one day, even though they planned to stay for three. The report also said that they failed to notify anyone of the trip, did not obtain a camping reservation for Thunder River, were in unfa-miliar territory without a map, didn't realize the danger of non-maintained trail hiking and did not register with the parks department. All of these factors hindered rescue efforts. Yes, it was an accident. A perfect storm.

I had no idea what death from dehydration and heatstroke entailed so I went to my trusty Britannica Encyclopedia and then the library. (No one had even dreamed of the Internet in 1974.) If I thought I felt sick before, what I learned made it worse. To start with, heat-related illnesses claim more lives annually than lightning, earthquakes, hurricanes and floods combined. The human body is much less tolerant of rises in internal temperature than drops in it. I really should have stopped there.

In a single hour a hiker in a desert setting can sweat a liter of mois-ture, sometimes as many as three liters. As the body heats up it starts to reroute blood to the parts of the brain that make basic decisions and away from internal organs. Judgment is compromised and can soon become an overwhelming disorientation. Although dehydration doesn't produce real thirst a sensation of dryness in the mouth can happen. Death usually occurs in three days, fewer in hot weather, but not more than five or six days. It was over 100 degrees in the canyon with no relief from the heat. Three days made sense.

Somewhere along the trail heat exhaustion turned into heat stroke, when a person's core body temperature can reach 104 degrees. Often there is heat edema, a swelling of the hands and feet. There were scratch marks on Rudy's abdomen and lower extremities, suggestive of crawling. Symptoms vary and everyone is different. Those who survive heat stroke often have permanent brain damage.

Many people have experienced mild indications of heat stroke: pounding headache, cramped muscles, racing heart, dizziness, vomiting. Now take those symptoms to the limit, adding disorientation and poor judgment, delirium, convulsions, fear, panic and hopelessness. It is a horrible, painful death no one deserves, especially a beautiful soul like Rudy. Sudden, tragic deaths, like from a car accident, are hard enough to deal with. I almost wished death had happened fast like that for him. The idea that he suffered is sometimes too much for me to think about, so most of the time I don't. I go there very infrequently. I couldn't survive if I did.

The coroner put the time of death at Tuesday, September 3, but it could have been the day before based on the decomposition of the bodies. Now that, I really can't think about. But of course the brain goes there anyway. While I was at my conference in Montauk, lying on the beach, shopping for a T-shirt for Rudy and "whooping it up," as my grandmother would say, Rudy was slowly dying in the desert. His body was decomposing in 100-plus-degree heat as I was blow-drying my hair. Insect activity had already begun to invade his body while I was buying books for school. I will never be able to wrap my head around THAT timeline. These two beautiful young men lay in that desert heat, dead, as the sun rose and set for six days.

The coroner identified Rudy's body from a picture his dad had brought with him. It is still too much to think about even after all these years.

## CHAPTER 28

# The Next Chapter

Through the efforts of my amazing family and friends I eventually went back to school. My professors were incredibly kind and understanding and they passed me for the semester even though my work was far below what I would consider acceptable. I heard there was a Thanksgiving and Christmas that year but I didn't participate. I called Mama Rose every day. It took me a very long time to laugh and not feel guilty about it. Vinnie and George adopted me.

I would go back and forth between staying at my house and the dorm. It didn't matter where I was, I never slept. I usually stayed home because I didn't want to ruin Jenn's sleep pattern. But she always wanted me to be at the dorm. She would stay at my house sometimes. It was all very confusing on so many levels. I visited the cemetery often, always bringing flowers. I still do. Some people never go. They say the person is not there. I find comfort in it, like I am visiting them. You have to do what works for you.

Rudy and I both loved The Beatles and Motown, but that wasn't the only music we listened to. We loved the Allman Brothers and Eric Clapton and I adored Jackson Browne. Jackson's music was the soundtrack of my life, not only because his poetic lyrics and music were so beautiful and relatable, but because of their timing. An album would come out and it would define my life *at that moment*. It was a little scary at times.

On September 13, 1974, while we were mourning and getting ready to bury Rudy, Jackson Browne came out with one of my favorite albums of all time, *Late for the Sky*. The quote from "Fountain of Sorrow" at the beginning of the book is from that album. But the song that touched me the most was "For a Dancer". He captured what I was feeling so vividly and exquisitely. He took language, music and my emotions and wrapped them together in this piece of musical art. I played that song over and over again, every day for months after Rudy died. It is forever linked in my mind to this tragedy, just as all those other songs that came before are remembrances of happier times. Music preserves such powerful memories.

A little over a year after Rudy's passing (I still hate to type that!) my cousin Catherine was getting married to the loveliest gentleman, Johnny. They had been dating forever and he was already part of the family. It was the first wedding in our family in a long time and Aunt Angie made sure it was a big affair: a big, distracting affair.

I was in the wedding party but didn't want to be in the worst way. I discussed this with my mom and she said she thought it would be a good, you guessed it, distraction. My family seemed to like those. She didn't understand how difficult it would be for me to fake happiness, plan a shower, watch someone else marry the love of her life knowing I never would. But I adored my cousin and did the best I could.

The day of the wedding was picture-perfect and I never saw Catherine look more stunning. I had to bite my lip so I wouldn't cry as I walked down the aisle with Vinnie, my partner. I mean really bite it. I left a mark there that, if you look really close in the pictures, you can see.

I hadn't danced in a long time. I still took classes but I hadn't danced for fun, had that feeling of flying, since Rudy died. I danced a few slow dances that night with Vinnie, George and my dad. But I was very reluctant to fast dance. At one point in the evening I was standing near the dance floor when a young man came up to me. I felt his presence approaching and my body stiffened up and my heart raced. I kept thinking, *please walk past me, please walk past me.* But he stopped right in front of me and asked me to dance. I sensed everyone in that room sitting on the edge of their seats, hoping I would say yes. I looked over and Catherine and Johnny had huge smiles on their faces. Such a beautiful bride and groom, how could I refuse them?

I don't remember the song, but I danced. He was a pretty good dancer, nothing embarrassing and he was obviously having a grand time, which made me smile. Then, as they so often do at weddings, the band followed this crazy dance song with a slow number. He looked at me, as if to say, "Should we continue?" I smiled, thanked him and walked away. I was not ready for that.

Aunt Angie came over to me and said, "I am proud of you. I know how difficult that must have been."

I just nodded and smiled, telling her what a perfect wedding this was.

"I miss Rudy too," she said. "But I also miss you."

She hugged me and we both started crying. She knew and she let me know it was okay.

After dinner I was standing by the bar and my mystery dancer came over to introduce himself. His name was Neil, he was a law student at Hofstra, blah, blah, blah. No, I shouldn't say that. He was very nice and handsome, if you like perfection. Nothing adorably breathtaking about him though, like Rudy.

I introduced myself and he laughed. He said Johnny and Catherine had told him about me and they wanted to introduce us. "I guess we just introduced ourselves." He then said, "Johnny told me about your loss. I am so sorry."

"Did he also tell you my blood type?" I shot back. "Sorry, that was uncalled for."

"No, I totally understand." And he really did.

As fate would have it, "Get Ready" started playing and he asked me to dance again. I felt funny saying no, so we danced through a medley of Motown tunes, which was excruciating. But I had learned to be a good actress since Rudy died. Then the slow song again. This time he wouldn't let me pull away and we started dancing and chatting. I didn't feel guilty but I didn't feel any sparks either. Just two people dancing.

As the night drew to a close he came over to me and asked if I would like to go to dinner some time. He saw my hesitation and said, jokingly, "You gotta eat."

I laughed and gave him my number.

My mother loved him. She saw great potential for a son-in-law in him. She loved that he was studying law. I was a little upset at how quickly she attached herself to him. Had she forgotten about Rudy already? Truth is, he was a very charming man, kind, funny, bright and very aware of my struggle. He took me everywhere, showered me with surprises and was very thoughtful and tender when I was hesitant about intimacy. That was difficult for me. I had only been with Rudy and I already thought dating someone else was cheating on him. Stupid I know, but that is how I felt. How could I possibly make love to someone else? Neil was patient, God bless him. Finally, when it happened, it was beautiful. Different than with Rudy. That would always be special and not to be replicated. But this was loving and sweet. I had to stop comparing this man to Rudy.

By now Jenn and I had moved out of the dorm and into a little carriage house on the property of an estate in Old Westbury. Her family knew the owner and we stayed there rent free. It was enchanting, like something out of a fairy tale. I never did go back to the apartment in the city. It was too difficult and I had to choose my emotional battles.

One Sunday, about eight months after we started dating, Neil stopped by. I had been working on an outline for a term paper and we weren't supposed to get together that afternoon. I was sitting out back on the small patio.

"Hi. This is a surprise," I said as I got up to kiss him. "Do you want something to drink?"

He said no and I sensed he wasn't his usual self.

"What's up?" I innocently said.

He sat down and took a deep breath.

"You know I love you and think the world of you …"

"But?"

He took my hand and started rubbing my commitment tattoo.

"I can't compete with this."

I sat there, not saying a word. I think he expected me to say, "No, I love you. There is room in my heart for you too; just give me time. Please don't end this." But I didn't. I could've. No, I really couldn't. Because he was right. He went on to tell me all the things I knew. I wasn't over Rudy. He could never measure up to a dream. I wasn't giving him a chance. He was kind and understanding about it. I knew he loved me. I just couldn't reciprocate in the way he needed me to. I thought this must have been a very difficult decision for him. He knew I was just going to go along with what the relationship was. He wanted more. He needed more. He deserved more. At that moment in my life I couldn't give it. It is true what they say: timing IS everything.

In the end we parted as friends. We would meet occasionally for coffee or dinner. I even went to his wedding. There turned out to be a special bond between us I wasn't even aware of when we were dating. He helped me transition back to the real world and I will forever be grateful to him for that. I never would have been able to come so far in my grief if he hadn't helped by showing me life again. I have thanked him many times for this. He just hugs me and kisses me on the top of my head, saying, "My pleasure."

Yeah, on top of my head. How weird is that?

Now I had to break the news to Lucy. Paul liked Neil, but at a distance. He wasn't ready to get too close to him either. But Lucy, I think SHE would have married him if he asked. To make things easy on me, I decided not to tell her immediately. When I finally did I got the reaction I expected: anger.

"What? Why? He is such a great guy. Do you think you are going to find another man like him? He is going to be a lawyer. Is this about Rudy? You have to let go. He is not coming back. He would want you to move on."

I thought my head was going to explode.

"What happened?"

It was really none of her business, but she would never accept that as an answer. I just said the first stupid thing that popped in my head.

"He wanted to do strange things, if you know what I mean."

"Oh," my mom said, calming down. That satisfied her.

I told her to just tell everyone it was personal. God only knows what she told them. Poor Neil. He was a nice, sweet man and I had my mother believing, in her words, that he was a "sexual pervert." Sometimes you have to do what you have to do. Years later I told her the truth but she was over him by then. I also told Neil. We had a good laugh. That's the kind of guy he is.

I spent the next several years working on my degrees. I was aiming to get a doctorate in psychology from Hofstra. Jenn moved back to the city but the owner of the cottage liked me and continued to let me stay there rent-free. She traveled often and liked that someone was always on the property. I didn't like living in the isolated woods alone so Janie, Jackie and Gina came and went as roommates. It was a time of transition for all of us so it worked out great. I dated here and there, but nothing too serious. I learned to laugh again and not feel guilty about it. It was a long and painful struggle but I moved forward, even if sometimes it was only an inch at a time.

I think taking all those psychology courses helped. Many of them relied on self-reflection and I had a lot to reflect upon. My course of study aided in my healing process. I would often write about my grief experiences in my papers and it was very therapeutic. I don't think it would have been the same if I was studying business or history. I also had the most wonderful advisor at Hofstra, a brilliant psychology professor who provided hours of talks, reflection and guidance.

My second doctoral internship was at a high school, which I loved. The students had a lot of energy and it was contagious. I would breathe in their enthusiasm, purpose and vivacity like it was oxygen. It gave my life purpose. For the first time since Rudy's death I felt I had direction and meaning. Working with these kids gave me a home again and I would dedicate the next thirty years of my life to it. To all the students I worked with over the years who thought I was helping them, thank you. You saved me.

The district where I did my internship hired me when I graduated. I met the most amazing people there who remain a significant part of my life today. In particular, I met "the mother of my children," a friend who shared her beautiful family with me. I found "my brother from another mother," a person I could not imagine my life without. And I met Alan. He would be the person I would share my life with. I never thought I was ever going to meet anyone I felt like that about again. And here he was, in front of me on the lunch line, with the sweetest smile and cutest butt ever.

Rudy had been gone for six years when I met Alan. Although Alan is blond and blue eyed, he has a lot of similarities to Rudy, which at first made me fearful. He loves the outdoors, hiking, camping and animals. He is brilliant, funny and has a strong social and moral compass. I laughed more with him than with anyone in the previous six years. His one drawback was he didn't dance. He is a great slow dancer but, to this day, I can rarely get him up for a fast turn. Still we manage.

We started seeing each other casually, at after school gatherings for a drink or at school functions. Then we started going out by ourselves. The relationship evolved so naturally I wasn't even questioning it or aware of it. I started to get excited about seeing him at work, dressing up a little more than usual. I would miss him when he wasn't there. We started talking on the phone every night and spending weekends together. For some reason I never discussed my years with Rudy, even when we were talking about our pasts. Alan just thought Rudy was someone I dated in high school. To this day I don't know why it took me so long to go into detail about it.

I began wearing the pearl-and-diamond ring Rudy gave me so many years ago on my left ring finger, never revealing the tattoo. I rarely took it off and, although some ink was visible, Alan never said anything to me about it. One day, for reasons I can't remember, I didn't have my ring on. Alan took my hand and asked what IWALY meant. It was time for me to introduce Rudy to this relationship.

And so I did. In about three hours I gave Alan the whole history of my past. I cried. He cried. I cried some more. He was unbelievable in his empathy and compassion, so kind and giving. It was an exhausting experience and we both fell asleep on the couch. We stayed there all night.

When we woke up we just sat there for a long time. I looked on the coffee table and saw the pile of tissues I had used the night before in telling my story. Alan was the first to speak. "I am truly sorry that you had to go through such a painful experience and that Rudy met such a tragic death. He sounded like a remarkable young man."

"He was," I said softly, staring into space. I was emotionally wiped out from going back there.

"I also know someone had to die for us to be together, which makes me feel selfish and sad. I am so happy with you. I would never expect you to stop loving Rudy. It makes me love you even more because it proves that, when you love, you love deeply and forever. You have a big heart. I think there is room in there for both of us."

I couldn't believe what he was saying. He was not intimidated or jealous of Rudy. He appreciated that I still loved him. He was comfortable with me always loving him. He wasn't asking me to stop. He wasn't telling me he couldn't compete with a dead person. He was just going to love me no matter what. I started crying. Everyone was always telling me to get over Rudy, to move on, to let go. No one had ever said it was okay to hold on to those feelings, that I could still have them and still love again. This was the most beautiful gift anyone had ever given me, acknowledging and accepting my feelings. And, in that incredible moment, I was finally able to truly and unconditionally love again.

As time went on Alan's place in my heart grew bigger. Rudy was there. He would always be there, but now he had his proper place among my memories. There would be days I didn't even think about Rudy until I said my prayers at night. I would feel guilty but realized this was the way it was supposed to be. Everyone always said Rudy would want me to move on and they were right. He would have liked Alan and somehow I felt he approved.

Two years later Alan and I got married. It was a joyful occasion even though there wasn't a dry eye in the house. Mama Rose and Papa G. were genuinely happy for us and they were a part of our lives until they passed. At wedding masses there is usually a time to pause to remember people who have gone before, like grandparents or special family members. Our grandparents were mentioned, as was Aunt Theresa and Alan's dad. And then the priest said something that shocked me. He mentioned Rudy and added, "This bright young life, gone too soon, who taught all who knew him how to love." My eyes filled up with tears as I looked over at Alan. He smiled. He had arranged with the priest to mention Rudy and asked him to add that sentence. I fell in love with Alan all over again. I knew I was going to be alright. I knew I had found a new home.

Alan and I were blessed with three children. Our first two girls, Marla and Tessa Marie, were planned but our third one was a total surprise. We had decided on the name Kyleigh, after a student who had graduated a few years earlier. She was one of our favorite young ladies of all time and we could only hope our third daughter would take after her namesake.

It was an easy delivery, if there is such a thing, just a few pushes. Alan was at the receiving end and when I let out my last, final push, I heard him say, "OH, NO."

Trust me, that is the last thing you want to hear your husband say as your child enters the world. I panicked and yelled, "WHAT'S WRONG?"

"Oh, no, nothing. The baby is fine," he assured me as he took this tiny gift from the doctor. He looked down at me lovingly as he placed our baby in my arms and said, "Surprise, Mommy. Meet your new son, Rudy."

## CHAPTER 29

# The Move On

Just as my life continued to evolve, so did the lives of those around me. It is sad how people come in and out of your life. They are important at the time they are there, but you lose track of them, like Maggie. You are busy living your everyday existence and often they fade away. It is not on purpose or by necessity. It just happens. And when you reconnect you feel such a grateful joy. For true friends, it is like picking up on a conversation you had yesterday, only it was really months, years, sometimes decades ago. Others have left your life never to be seen again. But all leave a little piece of themselves behind. I'm the person I am today because of even the most casual acquaintances I have made along the way. Everyone contributes a little something.

Vinnie and George are family, have remained in my life and will be there forever. They were incredible after Rudy passed. I knew Vinnie was in deep pain but he always made sure I was doing okay. He would always ask me, "You still breathing?" to remind me I was still alive and had a life to live. It wasn't easy for them. They lost many friends during the AIDS crisis. It seemed like there was a revolving door at the funeral home, if they even accepted the deceased. Some funeral directors wouldn't work on or allow a person who died of AIDS into their parlor. Vinnie and George became visible activists for the gay rights movement, putting themselves physically on the line. At one rally Vinnie had to get thirty stitches because some dick threw a bottle at his head. (Oh wait. As my friend always says, a dick is a useful thing.) From the beginning they never tried to hide their relationship or lie about it. To me, their honesty was often the more difficult route to take. Vinnie would get invited to social or family events without George but he would never go. "If they can't deal with us as a couple, fuck 'em!" he would say. Aunt Angie and Uncle Joe wouldn't attend either. Her tune was, "Love me, love my son."

Vinnie majored in finance and math in graduate school and became an actuary, something to do with insurance rates. I am not exactly sure what he did, but it paid a lot of money. He has always been very generous with his good fortune. George worked on Wall Street all his life until he retired. They have a beautiful townhouse in Manhattan and have traveled all over the world, often taking Alan, me and the kids with them. A huge chunk of my heart is reserved for them.

Janie. Ah, my Janie. She is the sister I never had. We never lost touch. There is a place in my heart just for her. She worked in the airline business for about a year or two after high school and then went to Nassau Community College for two years. During this time she was dating this handsome older man (twenty-four) named Robby, who adored her. She just didn't adore him as much. She decided to go away to finish her last two years and went, of all places, to Arizona. She went to the University of Arizona at Tucson, not where Rudy went. Still it was hard for me to go and see her at first. Even when I did it was a struggle, but I never let her know. One time Alan and I went to visit her and then went up to the Grand Canyon. I had never been there and told him I could do it. We were there for about six hours. I couldn't stay. I just couldn't. He understood. We never went back.

Janie majored in physical education and realized when she started student teaching that she hated it. She taught for two years but left the profession screaming and never looked back. Teaching is not for the faint of heart. She became a very successful personal trainer. She was home one Christmas break and we went to Gatsby's for a drink. Who did we see there but our crazy friend Erick. Long story very short, they started dating and got married. They live in Arizona, which I hate, because it is still so stinking far. But I manage to see her at least two or three times a year and it is always like I saw her yesterday. She has three children and is a grandmother to two although she hates the term. She always asks me how we got here and I tell her we are just lucky, I guess.

Jackie worked in real estate after high school and was very successful as well. When she was about twenty-one she ran into a high school friend of ours and they started dating. No one saw that coming. They just celebrated forty-three years of wedded bliss. She too moved out of state, but only an hour and a half away. We would see each other at our reunions but we lost touch after she moved. For the past ten years or so we have made an effort to keep in touch and she is one of my closest friends in the world. I adore her two children and her grandchildren. My life has been blessed with the most amazing girlfriends.

Janie saw Gina more after we graduated and, along with Jackie, we would all try to get together now and then. She worked for NBC Television in the city as an executive secretary. We would love the stories she would tell us about what went on behind the scenes. We saw her for a while, but she didn't come to our twentieth high school reunion. We never saw or heard from her after that. Well, that is not quite true. Janie did speak to her once or twice, asking her why she disappeared from our lives and hoping to restart the friendship. I just don't think she was interested, for whatever reason. She never married, having a major heartbreak with a guy from school who was the love of her life. We know she still lives on Long Island and Janie and I keep telling each other we are going to show up at her house one day. Gina, are you listening? We miss and love you.

Marie went to school for language as she was so proficient in them. She worked for years at the United Nations. She is divorced with four children. We see each other at reunions but she keeps to herself a lot, not connected regularly to anyone from high school except one or two friends. Every September 3, the anniversary of Rudy's death, she sends me a "Thinking of You" card. She has never missed a year.

I know Maria lives "out east," as we say on Long Island. She was the first in our group to get married and had a son at twenty-one. As math would have it, she was also the first to become a grandmother, which is one of the few things she smiles about.

My "Super" friend Richard worked for Grumman, found God and eventually moved to Texas with his wife. After high school he would stop over every now and then for a cup of coffee to catch up. He recently passed away from Alzheimer's. I was angry with myself for losing touch with him and very saddened to hear he died. The lesson here is, if you are thinking about getting in touch with someone, do it now.

Our friend Gerry was an entrepreneur, having invested in some very lucrative companies. He lived in Manhattan for a long time and I would run into him often. He would always hug me and ask if I was okay and let me know how much he still missed Rudy. He moved out west about fifteen years ago and would call me a couple of times a year. He passed away from a massive heart attack while I was writing this book. His wife sent me a great picture of him and Rudy he kept on his desk. It is now on mine. (As a matter of fact, I am looking at it now.)

I am sad to say I totally lost contact with Jenn and my other dear friends from Hofstra. I went to Jenn's wedding to a man who was extremely successful in business. I saw her for a while after her first child was born, but that was it. I think she is still in the city. I always felt bad about not remaining friends as she was so kind to Rudy and me, beyond letting us stay at her apartment. She was concerned and supportive to me after Rudy passed, one of those friends who faded away but whose imprint will always be on my heart.

A few years ago Jackie and her family were in New Hampshire on vacation and she ran into CeeCee. Jackie said she didn't recognize her, but CeeCee recognized Jackie. It was a short, polite conversation. Even though the shower incident happened almost a half century ago, Jackie said she felt awkward and sensed CeeCee did too. Jackie said CeeCee asked her several times to please tell me she said hi and to please tell me thank you. I guess I left a little bit of myself with her too.

My nemesis, Jack, graduated from Penn State with a degree in financing. I met his wife and children by chance on several occasions and they were lovely. How he ended up with such a beautiful family is beyond me. I guess everyone changes, or not really. In the early nineties Jack was arrested for running some sort of Ponzi scheme. I really didn't understand it but Alan said it was bad. He had embezzled millions of dollars from some very high-profile celebrities, including actors, athletes and authors. The three A's, the news called it. It got a lot of press. He received a long prison sentence. I don't know if he is still incarcerated. The family lost everything: their beautiful house in Lloyd Neck, their boat, cars, jewels, their dignity. I felt bad that the family had to pay for his mistakes. Turns out he was still the self-centered bastard I had grown to hate in high school. His wife ended up marrying one of the clients he swindled and now lives a comfortable life again in California. Occasionally I will see her in a magazine or on television, holding her husband's hand at some awards show or charity event. I am glad she is happy.

Dana, Rudy's senior prom date, had a really hard time with his death. I would go visit her and she would just sob, which started my waterworks going. It didn't take much. Finally I told her we had to stop crying and talk about the fun things about Rudy. That is what he would want. We made a photo album together, grew flowers to bring to the cemetery and made Rudy's famous brownies, minus the pot.

Dana got married about eight years after high school. Her husband is as sweet as she is. Alan and I visit them out east several times a year. On her television cabinet, along with wedding and family pictures, is a photograph of her and Rudy that I took another lifetime ago on prom night.

I still keep in touch with Carmine. Alan and I try to get together with him and his wife several times a year although, when all our kids were small, we saw each other more often. He has a Rudy too. Carmine and I have a standing date every September 3 and on Rudy's birthday. He jokes we see each other on birth and death days. We go to the cemetery together and then out to eat. Carmine doesn't look like Rudy but he has the same mannerisms and his voice is similar. It still takes me by surprise once in a while and makes my heart sink a little.

My friend Jill, who lived up the block and who read that sex book with me, got married and had an adorable little boy. When her son was nine months old she had a massive heart attack on her front lawn. The doctors said it was from a blood clot that traveled to her heart. Another unexpected, tragic death. Another family forever changed.

My family grew with weddings and births and then started to shrink again as older family members passed. My dad died in 1996 at seventy-eight. That was way too young and a very devastating loss for me and my mom. Lucy passed twenty-one years later. She would joke with me that she thought sometimes I wished she died first. I would joke back that sometimes I did! She had a beautiful passing, if there is such a thing. At ninety-eight she was ready and helped Alan and me as we prepared for her loss. I guess she mellowed in her old age. The day before she passed she told me she would tell Rudy I was okay and give him a kiss for me, but not until she saw my dad and her parents first. Her faith never wavered.

Aunt Angie is the only one left now, holding all the family secrets and memories. She has slowed down a lot but is still sharp as a tack. I try to visit her several times a month and call her at least twice a week. She remembers things clearly and I never get tired of her stories. I love going through old photo albums with her because there is always a story behind the picture. We talk about how wonderful my life turned out and what a terrific man I married.

She and Vinnie are the only people I still talk to about Rudy. She often asks me if I think about what my life would have been like if he had walked out of the Grand Canyon. I never lie to her. I tell her I often do but long ago accepted the reality of the situation. Somewhere I heard a saying that you live as long as the last person who remembers you. Well, as long as I have a breath left in me, as long as my recall will allow, as long as I am on this earth, Rudy will live too, if only in my memory and heart. Forever young.

# The Epilogue

*Author's Notes*

While most of this book is fictional, it is based on true events and real people. The concept for the book began in late fall of 2019. I was visiting Holy Rood Cemetery in Westbury, Long Island. I was at my grandparents' grave, clearing the leaves and weeds and leaving some flowers. I remember my aunt saying that a good friend of my mom's had passed and she was buried in section fifteen, the next section over from my grandparents. While I was there I decided to pay my respects.

I walked over and proceeded to look up and down the rows of gravestones. I found myself reading the names, stopping often, looking at their birth and death dates. Among the rows of grey headstones, a beautiful reddish stone caught my eye. Across the top read the family name COSTA. A mom, Rosalie, and a dad, Rudolph, were buried there. I looked in the lower left-hand corner and saw "1954 Frank 1974."

I remembered a Frank Costa from high school. He was a year older than me, very handsome, athletic and out of my league. He lived two doors down from a girlfriend of mine and she was always talking about him and his best friend, her cousin, who was also named Frankie. I would get the two handsome Franks confused all the time. I remembered Frank Costa had a tragic death in the Grand Canyon when he was twenty years old.

While driving home I couldn't remember what Frank looked like, other than that he was very handsome. I can't say that enough. Some at the time would call him a hunk. One of my girlfriends described him as "take your breath away" handsome. Again, way out of my league. When I got home, I Googled him and of course got nothing. He died in 1974. He had no social media profile. After a three-hour search the only thing I found was a small article from a local Arizona newspaper, the *Desert Sun*, reporting his death in the Grand Canyon.

I can't explain why, but it really upset me that this young man lived but I couldn't find a record of it, only of his death. I couldn't find a picture of him. Nothing. I called my girlfriend Dorothy from high school and she sent me a picture of him from his yearbook. Yes, I did remember him even though I didn't know him. I had been in the stands at his football and baseball games in high school. Maybe we were at a party together or shared some of the same friends, although I never remember having a conversation with him. We were probably at the same Allman Brothers concert at the Fillmore East, or some other venue, since we both loved the band. We were together at our high school's recreation nights on Wednesdays. He dated a beautiful girl, Diane, for four years of high school and beyond. He excelled in football, track and baseball. I felt he should be remembered but I knew so little about him.

Truth be told, I had never forgotten about his death. It was always in the back of my mind because it was so tragic and sad and because I have hiked a lot out west. Every time I was on a hike with my husband, whether it was Bryce, Canyonlands or Arches, I would think of Frank at some point.

We were hiking once to the Wave, a famous destination in southern Utah. Only twelve people are allowed to hike it a day. You have to put your name in a lottery for a pass. There are no markers on the trail. Heck, there's no trail. Park workers give you sketches and descriptions to follow and match up with the scenery. I was scared out of my mind. It was gorgeous but so easy to get lost. No trail at all! My husband is a seasoned hiker, so I felt comfortable, but still brought more water and food than I would need for a week. And in that summer heat, hiking to the middle of nowhere, I kept thinking of Frank.

Since I didn't know his life, I decided to write about his death, the tragedy of a life lost so young, along with dreams and hopes for the future. How does one recover from such a loss? It seemed incomprehensible to me. So this book is a "fictionalized reality." I didn't know Frank so I invented Rudy, who I named after Frank's dad, and created a life to go along with him. All the characters in the book are exaggerated or composite renderings of people I went to high school with. They all have new names and personality changes to fit the narrative. Some are very close to the originals and some are not. Several are completely fictional. The fictional families, including my parents, are also based on certain real personality traits. The teachers in the book are based on the wonderful teachers I encountered in school, whose wisdom and guidance were so instrumental in shaping my life. Oh, and that guidance counselor? Unfortunately, she was real too.

There was no Carmine. Frank didn't have a younger brother. He had an older sister, Denise, who was twenty-two when Frank died. They were best friends from the day he was born. She is a remarkable woman. Along with having to deal with her own grief, she also helped her dad and mom, who many told me never got over the loss of her son. They said she was never the same after that. And who could be? You watch your only son drive away to college and never see him alive again.

Then, years later, Denise lost her nine-and-a-half-year-old-son to cancer, watching him slowly fade away while she somehow remained strong and upbeat for him. She took these two tragedies, which might have destroyed someone else and turned them into an opportunity to help others. She ran bereavement groups in her home, helping over two hundred people, mostly those who had lost a sibling, navigate their grief. Beyond extraordinary.

The nameless narrator is partially me. The other part is probably who I wanted to be. I took dance lessons forever but never got on point. I am a terrible cook and never made a lasagna in my life. I did not experience the prolific high school sexual activity that the narrator enjoyed. I was never a model. I stood five foot six and was painfully thin. Like the narrator, I had a nose too large for my face (which was corrected when I was fifteen), wore braces and had acne. I was teased and bullied a lot. I had low self-esteem for a long time.

I came from a loving family and had amazing friends—male and female—who have influenced who I am today. My grandfather wasn't a tailor but a barber. His shop was located next to the Westbury Movie Theater. My mom didn't have a tailor shop in our basement, but rather a beauty parlor, as they called it. My friends and I used to play down there all the time, cutting and dying our hair until it was almost unrecognizable and then crying to my mom to fix it. My dad was very bright, well-read and should have been a teacher. He really was my most favorite person on earth. And I did live on the best block in the neighborhood.

All my memories of Long Island are genuine and it was a joy revisiting them. I do have a learning disability in language, so for me, putting this all on paper was like climbing Mount Everest. And the thing that surprised me the most was how much I enjoyed it.

Most of the incidents portrayed in the book are authentic with some embellishment and exaggeration added. The Alka-Seltzer story is verbatim, although I didn't get flowers. The prom ride home happened, as did, I am sorry to say, the two poop stories and my first keg party incident. The Sammy Davis Jr. account is 100 percent genuine, except that I went to the Westbury Music Fair with my parents and it was my dad who didn't cut our heads off in that famous picture.

Most of the traits Rudy has in the book are characteristics I gathered from people's memories of Frank. I tried to incorporate as much of him as I could into the story, taking some romantic license. (Frank did not aspire to be nor was he a chef. He had no tattoos.) You would think with all the social media outlets it would be easy to contact Frank's past friends. It has not been. Some didn't respond. Some I have never been able to locate. Some do not want or can't reopen that very painful chapter of their lives. Some just said no. Others, like the real-life models for Gerry, Richard and Jack have passed.

Among those I could reach, the most common adjectives they used to describe Frank were handsome (always first), risk taker, athletic, good teammate, daredevil, energetic, a great friend and friendly to all. He was very attentive and thoughtful. Everyone said how funny he was, always trying to make people laugh. His friend Steve said he was gregarious, very witty and always came up with great one-liners, adding that he was an out-standing baseball player. Another friend, Gene, described one of the hikes they went on to Sleepy Giant Mountain in Connecticut. There were four of them and they somehow managed to get stuck in a spot on the moun-tain. Frank held on to a friend's ankle with this guy's shoe in his mouth on his climb back up. Diane remembers all of the boys lugging their Stingray bikes up to Frank's roof and peddling them into the built-in pool. She also remembers them "skitching," which is holding on to a car's back bumper and riding it through the snow. A funny daredevil. And just a kid.

Frank grew up, like most of the characters in the book, in Westbury, Long Island. His parents were Italian. His mom lost her dad when she was four. Her mom married a man, Helmuth, who was German and that became Frank's middle name. He wore it proudly. At around the age of seven, it became apparent this little boy was a natural athlete, especially in Little League. Later on he also excelled in football and track. When he was eight his parents put in that built-in pool and summer days were filled with big gatherings of family and neighborhood kids, swimming, splashing and diving for quarters.

Frank was very close to his family. Denise said he was closer to his mom and she was closer to their dad. She told me if Frank left the house to go to Dairy Barn for milk, he would make sure he kissed them both good bye. He had a very tight relationship with his cousins, especially Sandy, Janice, Agnes and Franky. They would go to Lake Carmel or Hither Hills in Montauk every year for vacation and Frank loved hanging out with them.

Mr. and Mrs. Costa had a boat and almost every summer weekend they would go to Zacks Bay and hook up with their friends Angelo and Sylvia, tying the boats together and enjoying a day of eating, drinking and laughing. Frank would go with Diane and friends off the boat and either swim or take a small raft to shore at Gilgo beach. The day was spent body surfing and swimming in the ocean before going back to the boat to eat. A friend of Frank's remembers Mrs. Costa making "these great baloney sandwiches", even though I think that is an oxymoron.

One of Frank's best friends and neighbors was that other handsome Frankie. Denise said they were attached at the hip as kids and teenagers. Frankie said they used to love playing stickball on the block, especially against the older kids. He said no one could beat them and they always pushed each other to be better. Frankie's younger brother Tom remembers flipping baseball cards in Frank's garage. He said Frank was always chewing the gum from the cards, blowing these outrageous bubbles. Tom said Frank's hair was always perfect and he often smelled like a barbershop. He said Frank had the greatest laugh and shared it often.

Frank's friend Brad remembers meeting him for the first time in eighth grade gym class. The activity that day was wrestling and the physical education teacher paired him with Frank. He joked that Frank manhandled him, with Brad's face in Frank's armpit, crotch and between his legs during the match, which Brad lost. He was amazed at how strong Frank was for his age, saying he was always "a supreme athlete, in great shape."

They ended up on the track team together in high school, becoming good friends. Brad said after that eighth-grade match, he hated wrestling forever. Almost fifty years later he would go on to describe Frank as one of "the greatest guys" he ever met.

Arlene, briefly one of Brad's high school girlfriends and a good friend of Frank's girlfriend, Diane, remembers Frank as almost untouchable because he was idolized by so many. But, she said, he was always true to himself and not a show-off. He seemed to have a natural aura about him but was not vain. He genuinely cared about everyone and was just "the whole package, handsome, athletic and kind." She said she still wonders why God had to take him so young, a question there is no answer to.

I tried to create a story based on what I lived and remembered, adding Frank and his tragic death. The hike in the Grand Canyon chapter is how Frank's death actually happened: the notes, the abandoned gear, the fall, the rescue, the condition of the bodies, all of it. (For a more detailed explanation, please see *Over the Edge: Death in Grand Canyon* by Michael P. Ghiglieri and Thomas M. Myers, Puma Press, 2019, pp. 59–61.) The only thing different is the time frame of the rescue and how and when Frank went to Arizona

On Tuesday, September 3, 1974, at 11:30 p.m., the Coconino County Sheriff's office received a call about two overdue hikers in the Grand Canyon. The Sheriff's department in turn called the Grand Canyon dispatch office to report this. The next day they spoke to the caller, Butch Scott, who was another new roommate of Frank's. He was concerned Frank did not return for the start of classes. According to the police report, Butch told them Frank and another student, Edwin (Eddie in the narrative), were picking up Frank's Buick at a repair shop in Fredonia. The car had broken down near the Grand Canyon prior to Frank arriving at school. He said Frank had discussed going to Thunder River. Judd Arden, the owner of the repair shop, confirmed they picked the car up and said he also heard them talking about Thunder River. The search for the boys actually began on September 4. (Not September 7, as stated in the story.) Unbeknownst to the rescuers, Frank and Edwin were already dead. Edwin's car was located that day. Frankie's car would be retrieved on September 6, after two hunters reported seeing it. Frank's body was found by a helicopter at 5:10 p.m. on September 9. Edwin's body was found 150 feet below a short while later. Because of the time of day, they couldn't retrieve the boys until the following day. I have tried unsuccessfully to locate the notes they left during their hike. They are long gone. Denise couldn't remember exactly when the family was notified her brother was missing, but said the agonizing wait for news went on for days.

Before I continue, I must pause here to say something about the rescue effort. After reading all the reports, which go into the rescue in more detail than I have here, it is obvious that the dedicated men and women involved were of exceptional character and caliber. Approximately 40,000 acres were searched by two helicopters, two fixed wing aircraft, four Forest service personnel, nine National Park Service personnel, six members of the Fredonia Search and Rescue Unit, twenty one members of the Flagstaff Search and Rescue Unit and one Coconino County Deputy Sheriff. For six days, from dawn until dusk, in brutal heat and terrain, these brave individuals searched for these two lost boys, investigating every lead. They never stopped, not knowing if their mission was one of rescue or recovery. To these nameless heroes from fifty years ago and to those who continue to carry on their effort, God speed. Thank you on behalf of all the families you have worked with.

How Frank ended up going to Arizona and the Grand Canyon is also a little different from what is portrayed in the plot. Frank graduated from W.T. Clarke High School in 1972, excelling in football, baseball and track.

His athletic success was often chronicled in the school and local newspapers. For example, in December 1971:

## Costa Record Sparks Clarke

Frank Costa set a track record for the 300-yard run and anchored the winning mile relay as Clarke High defeated Great Neck North, 57-20, on its outdoor track yesterday. Costa was timed in 0:33.5 for the 300 while the mile relay team was clocked in 3:55.4.

Also that month, Frank and his track buddy Brad "were double winners in leading Clarke High to a 45-32 victory over Herricks." Frank was first in the 60-yard dash, in 0:06.8 and the 600-yard run in 1:19.

Often football and track would overlap. His friend Jimmy, who was on the football team with Frank, told me when that happened, the football team would take a bus to his track meet and wait for him. When Frank was finished with track he would get on the football bus and they would go to the game. Frank would change from his track uniform into his football gear in the back of the bus. He was the only person they did this for. That is how amazing an athlete he was.

On February 18, 1972, he competed in the US Olympic Invitational at Madison Square Garden, sponsored by the NY State Committee for the Olympic games. He also got a lot of press during his final baseball season at Clarke, singling in the seventh inning against Herricks to help them win the game 4-3 and getting the only hit in a 6-1 game against Plainview.

After high school he attended Quinnipiac College (now University) in Hamden, Connecticut for two years to study business. I also heard he wanted to be a professional ball player. I think he was good enough for that to be a realistic goal. Like in high school, his efforts often appeared in the college or local paper. One that caught my attention said:

## Quins' Pinch-Hit Edges Fairfield

Hamden—Frank Costa's pinch single drove home a runner on third with two outs in the bottom of the12[th] inning to give the Quinnipiac College baseball team a 7-6 victory over Fairfield University Tuesday afternoon.

He was a hard-working and dedicated athlete, always pushing himself to be better, to continue to improve his personal best and stand out in a crowded athletic field. And always doing so with appreciation for his teammates and a big smile. During his first year of college, Diane, his high school girlfriend, would drive to Connecticut to be with him on weekends. By this time they had been together for over four years. Diane started hanging out with a new group of friends back home and she and Frank drifted apart. They eventually went their separate ways in the fall of 1973. So how did he end up in Arizona? The story differs depending on who you talk to.

Diane had met someone new, whom she started dating after her split with Frank. In February 1974, they went out west, traveled around and eventually ended up in Arizona the third week of August 1974. I was told by one of my sources that Frank was very upset by the breakup and was still hoping he and Diane would work it out. Please remember this is all hearsay. The only person who can tell us how Frank felt was Frank. This story line says he went out to Arizona to find her and win her back.

The other explanation I received said he didn't go to Arizona to follow her, but rather chose to transfer to the State University of Arizona at Tempe as a junior because of the university's great baseball team, the Sun Devils. He was following his dream of becoming a professional baseball player. He had also applied to other schools down south, but Arizona was offering him the best scholarship. Diane left to travel out west with her new boyfriend after Frank was accepted to ASU. Or so the story goes. The fact that they would both end up in Arizona, within miles of each other, was pure coincidence, if you believe in coincidence. It is a lot of work to

316

transfer from one school to another as a junior so whatever the reason, Frank was determined to go to Arizona.

At this point in time does it matter how he ended up in Arizona? Was it the romantic gesture of a twenty-year-old with a broken heart? Or the anticipative dreams of a young man hoping to play professional sports? Either way the outcome will always be the same. He went to Arizona. (In a twist of irony, Diane's future husband, Rick, also attended ASU and was to begin playing baseball the same year as Frank.)

In the summer of 1974 Frank, his friend Gene and a female friend from high school decided to take a road trip out west before school started. Gene had been great friends with Frank for a long time. They had a core group of guys who all hung out together. The "Handsome Boys," as I like to remember them. Gene had gone to the culinary institute in Upstate New York while Frank was at Quinnipiac. Gene was working at Leonard's, a fancy catering hall in Great Neck, Long Island. He wanted to go to Colorado and Frank was on his way to Arizona, so off they went in Frank's Buick.

They drove cross-country, stopping in Arizona, Colorado, Las Vegas, California and then back to Arizona. At some point in Colorado their female passenger left the trio. I am sure that trip was a book in itself. On the way to their destination they stopped at the North Rim of the Grand Canyon. Gene took a photo of Frank at the entrance. When they left the Grand Canyon Frank's car broke down. He called his dad, who was an auto mechanic and they decided to have it towed to a shop in Fredonia, in Coconino County, the same county that, days later, would send out rescuers to look for Frank. Both Gene and Frank rode in the tow truck with the driver to Fredonia. There they separated, Gene taking a bus to Denver and Frank taking one to Phoenix. That was the last time Gene would see his friend.

It is believed Frank got to school that Thursday of Labor Day weekend, where he met Edwin Len Heisel Jr. of Cincinnati, Ohio. At 5'10", with blonde hair and blue eyes, Edwin, like Eddie in the narrative, was an army-trained ROTC ranger and rescuer. Unfortunately, I was unable to locate anyone connected to Edwin, so I have no more information on him other than to say he is forever linked in this tragedy with Frank. The two families never spoke with each other.

Apparently Frank asked Edwin if he could drive him back to Fredonia to pick up his car, and they left that Friday. They were going to pass the North Rim of the Grand Canyon and I guess they decided to go on that now infamous hike. As mentioned, Frank was a daredevil and a risk taker. Mr. Sport. Like the character Rudy, it would seem logical that, given the opportunity to go backpacking in the Grand Canyon, he would jump at the idea. He loved an adventure.

On their way back from Freedonia to the Grand Canyon, Frank's 1966 Buick Wildcat got a flat tire. He abandoned it at Crazy Jug Point and it was found ¾ of a mile south of Bridges Knoll, about 1.2 miles north of the canyon rim. A cryptic note was found inside the car that simply said "Gone Camping". Frank then got in Edwin's green Plymouth Duster and proceeded on.

They didn't register with the National Parks registry before they entered the trail. If they did, people may have realized sooner that they hadn't walked out and may have sent searchers out to look for them earlier. Again, could've, should've, would've.

By this time Frank's track buddy Brad had been in Arizona for several years on a college scholarship for track. He was listening to the radio sometime around Labor Day weekend when he heard two ASU students were missing in the Grand Canyon. They mentioned Frank Costa from

Westbury and Brad thought that had to be his friend. Brad was shocked but, knowing Frank was such a strong athlete, was confident he would survive.

He called Frank's home and was told that indeed he was missing and that Mr. Costa had flown to Flagstaff with his brother Tommy, his nephew Franky and his niece Agnes's husband, Billy. Brad drove to the hotel where Mr. Costa was staying, never having met him. He spent over three hours there, sharing stories about the high school trip to Europe he and Frank went on, their days on the track team together and what a wonderful person and friend Frank was. He offered Mr. Costa comfort in a strange town during the most agonizing and challenging time imaginable. When Brad heard Frank had died he went back to the hotel, but Mr. Costa had already left for home.

What a wonderful gesture by a twenty-year-old young man. For Brad to have the foresight to visit Mr. Costa shows great empathy and compassion on his part. If your friends reflect who you are, then Frank picked them well. Brad told me he had hiked to the bottom of the Grand Canyon four or five times before Frank's death but was never able to go back after his passing.

Frank's friend Gene told me the hike he and Edwin attempted was very common, but they got off the trail somehow. When you are twenty years old you think you are invincible. Gene flew home for Frank's funeral and, when he got back to Colorado, he developed a roll of film he had. At the end of the roll was a photo of Frank standing at the entrance to the trail of the North Rim, the same spot he and Edwin would enter a few days later. His body is facing the Canyon, but his face is turned toward the camera. There is an ominous sky in front of him. It is the last known photo of Frank. I find it haunting still.

Diane had asked her mom to get Frank's contact information at ASU so she could get in touch with him when he arrived in Arizona. From photographs and stories I have heard, it seems it was a beautiful high school love story. I believe she was the love of his short life. She told me that when she was living in Arizona, she didn't have a telephone. She got a telegram from her mom that simply said, "Call home. Frank found dead in the Grand Canyon." She said she stood there in shock while her heart broke in pieces and fell to the ground. I don't know if she was ever able to fully repair it again. She returned to Long Island that December and was warned not to contact Frank's mom. She was told Mrs. Costa was too distraught over her son's death. Diane has been unbelievably helpful, if at first cautiously reluctant and protective, in putting this picture of Frank together.

It turns out that Mrs. Costa was beyond distraught. She had a nervous breakdown after Frank died and struggled with the challenges of his death for her remaining thirty-four years. She was hospitalized several times and her suffering found little relief. She spent a lot of time at the cemetery. Her thinking was often irrational and her behavior unpredictable. When Frank's friend Frankie would jog around the neighborhood past Mrs. Costa's house, she would turn away or go inside. It was too painful for her to even see her son's friends. She only found true peace when she passed and joined him. I had heard she had difficulties but was unaware of the extent. Denise lost a brother and a mother on that fateful day in September.

Everyone I was able to communicate with said the same thing about Frank. Everybody loved him! He was kind, funny, smart and very charismatic. People were drawn to him. And he was always well dressed. His cousin Sandy said he could have been a model; he was so handsome. She said he had a really cool style and the girls loved his smile. She said sometimes girls would give him their number, without Frank ever asking. She was quick to point out he didn't have an ego and wasn't conceited in any way. She said he was very "happy go lucky and full of love." I was told he cared "deeply" about school and baseball. The term "all-around good kid" came up a lot. Everyone I spoke to mentioned how he would love to make people laugh. His older cousin Agnes said he was his own person with a little bit of the devil in him. She told me he had this great sense of humor, and would always "bust my chops. Not in a mean way, but for a laugh." I was told he lit up a room when he entered it.

The word "tragedy" was used often and his close friends and family said it was very difficult dealing with his death, especially the circumstances. Some said it took a long time to get over it while others said they still wrestle with it all these years later. Most admitted they don't like to go back there, so they don't. I was moved by the way people still reacted to his death so many years later. And how they all said they still miss him. Sandy said that for anyone who ever met him, even briefly, "he would leave a little piece of himself in your heart."

Based on the interviews and information I have accumulated, I believe Frank was a great friend, son, brother and boyfriend. I know he would have been a wonderful husband, father, brother-in-law, uncle and grandfather had he been given the chance. I think of the things he would have accomplished, the family he might have had, the changes he would have left the world. Every life, no matter how short-lived, makes a difference. For all of those who knew him, he did change them by his friendship, love, loyalty, kindness and, sadly, even his death.

As mentioned, Frank's body was found on a ledge, under a rock, where he was probably seeking protection from the elements. A third note was found near his body that was never revealed to anyone but the family. It was the last communication he had with the world. The handwriting was unsteady, as he was obviously actively dying when he wrote it. His sister Denise was kind enough to share it with me.

*Dear Mommy, Daddy and Denise. The days are hot. The nights are cold. But if this is my destiny, I will see you in heaven, with Jesus.*

I know this has brought great comfort to Denise and I am privileged to share it with you. I like to interpret it as Frank having found some peace in his situation while attempting to leave his family with the same. A sweet, family-loving, considerate soul right to the end.

After this tragedy in 1974, some corrective actions were issued by the rescue parties involved that remain in place to this day. Some of those preventive efforts instituted included the National Parks Service placing signs at trailheads advising visitors of the extreme heat, the lack of water and the fact that camping reservations are required in the backcountry. Signs were placed on the main accesses to Thunder River trailheads advising that the NPS requires camping reservations. Press releases were issued regarding backcountry camping reservations and the hazards of canyon hiking during periods of extreme heat. The United States Forestry Service began issuing backcountry camping reservations for the Grand Canyon at their District Ranger Station in Fredonia, Arizona. This increased cooperation and coordination with the NPS to prevent overuse. I am sure these measures put into effect as a result of Frank and Edwin's deaths have helped save countless lives over the last fifty years. I hope their families and friends find some solace in that.

For about two months after I finished the book, I kept telling my husband I was done. Then I would go back and add or change something. This being my first book, I think several things were going on. How do you know when you are finished writing a book? Did I tell the story the way I wanted to? Is it interesting enough for the reader to get to the end? Am I satisfied? Will the reader be? And, most important to me, did I do justice to Frank's memory? So many second guesses.

And then something happened I never expected: I became attached to my characters and the lives I gave them, so many of them paralleling the lives of friends and family. Going back almost fifty years and remembering them and Long Island was fun but also bittersweet. Even though the characters are fictitious, I got to revisit the people they were based on and the incidents that so clearly remain in my memory. The truth is, once I went back there, it was often hard to leave.

I also got to know this incredible young man, Frank Costa, who became more than a name in a personal tragedy. Through interviews, pictures, letters, he became a real, living person to me. I have come to love who he was and as long as I continued working on the book, he was still alive in my mind. I confess I have a new regret in life and that is that I didn't know him. I know everyone I spoke to about him relived his death. And, in a strange way, I felt that loss too. Closing the book brought me and the reader back to reality.

But here it is, finally finished. If only one person reads this book—and I thank you—it will have been worth all my effort because it brought two people together who probably never would have reconnected: Frank's sister Denise and his high school girlfriend Diane.

When Frank died Diane was in Arizona and she didn't come back to New York until December of that year. As related earlier, she was told it would be best if she didn't contact Frank's mom, so she didn't. She never spoke to any of the Costas, including Denise. In all these years Denise only saw Diane once, at Frank's gravesite, that first December. Denise was getting in her car to leave when Diane pulled up with a big white wreath for the grave. Denise said their eyes met, but nothing was said or gestured and she pulled away.

I don't know what if any blame, guilt, anger or pain kept them from contacting each other. Diane and Frank dated for five years, so she knew the family well. She was always at the house. My guess is it was just too agonizing to see each other as they grieved, each being a reminder to the other of much happier times. Maybe it had to do with culpability, accountability, responsibility. I just know that for decades neither knew the entire story and they filled in the blanks as best they could.

Then along comes this woman with all these questions, prying into the most devastating and private time of their lives. They were both wonderful in presenting Frank to me in a compassionate yet realistic way, to fill in the narrative. Each knew I was talking to the other and would often ask me questions or tell me they didn't know something I discovered. Eventually the complete story, on both sides, revealed itself.

I am thrilled to say that after almost half a century Denise and Diane have been in communication with each other again, texting, emailing, talking on the phone and eventually visiting each other. I know Frank would be happy they came together over him. I am too. And now, Denise, Diane and I have formed our own Three Musketeers.

Not only did I have the privilege of getting to know Denise and Diane, but I also spoke to so many people who helped me complete this journey, especially his friends Gene, Frankie, Steve and Brad. My goal was always to keep the memory of Frank alive and, with the help of everyone involved, I think we have. George Eliot wrote, "Our dead are never dead to us until we have forgotten them." R.I.P. Frank Costa. You have not been forgotten.

# The Acknowledgments

To David, the best man I've ever known. Thank you for your love, encouragement, patience, compassion and humor. Every day you make me a better person. I couldn't imagine this journey with anyone else. IWALY

To my parents, Peter and Marion Moroz, for their love, inspiration, guidance and support. Thank you for all the sacrifices you made so I could have this wonderful life and for showing me the rewards of a strong work ethic. Bless you for teaching me love, laugher, empathy and kindness. You are missed every day, as is my mom-in-law, Doris.

To Denise Costa, one of the bravest and most inspirational women I know. Thank you for sharing the joy and heartache of your brother's life and all that followed. You are remarkable. Our spiritual connection is ridiculous. I love you. There would be no book without you.

To Diane Parisi Downing, thank you for going back to that dark and difficult time you so long ago tried to put away. Revisiting the loss of Frank and having it bring up more recent losses takes a very strong and giving person, of which you are both. The friendship that has come out of this collaboration is amazing. Love you lots. Like Denise, there would be no book without you.

Thank you, Burt Fischler, for being a great sounding board in this lonely exercise and for helping many turn tragedies into life again. It has been an honor to take this spiritual journey with you. It doesn't end with our books.

Thank you to Gene Hauck. The book would be incomplete without your memories, which you so generously shared, that pieced together the last summer days of Frankie's life. You were a wonderful friend.

To Brad Armstrong, thank you. The stories you shared and your pain in presenting them painted a loving friendship built on humor, camaraderie and respect. You helped me give the reader a better understanding of one of the "greatest guys" you knew.

Thanks to Frank Aitala, the other handsome Frankie, for sharing the uncomplicated memories of childhood and the love you had and still have for Frank. Attached at the hip indeed.

Thank you Steve Panzella. Your stories filled in the narrative in a way only you could. The laughs and friendship you and Frank had together still echo in the heart.

My thanks to Tom Aitala, who graciously reached back to tell simple tales of growing up in Westbury with Frank.

Thank you, Arlene Bollander Creech. What a joy reconnecting with you and listening to your memories of Frank. We started out so young together, forming a solid friendship. Wish we had stayed on the path together, but great to meet up again now.

Thank you to my "faux cousin," Joey Martiello, for your memories of Frank and for being a strong presence in the narrative.

To Jimmy McGowan, thank you for your memories of Frank both on and off the field. No one tells a story like you. And no oregano!

A big thank you to Frankie's cousins Agnes and Sandy for sharing their childhood memories and family pain with me. The affection and love with which you shared your stories of Frank touched my heart.

I am forever thankful to the students and staff of the 1972 and 1973 classes of W.T. Clarke High school. You don't know how a simple hello or a smile sent down the hallway made a difference to me. I thank you for inspiring the book's characters and events.

In particular, I thank Jennifer Fortunato, Joanne Kianetski and Gayle Roche. There would be no me without you three. You remain in my heart forever.

Also must mentions: Madeline, Mary, Patty, Jody, Anna, Lorraine, Janet, Vinnie, Bobby, Eric, Sean, John, Gary, Ritchie, Gerard, Scott, Jimmy, Leo, Chris, Billy, Darren, Emil, Ali and of course, Dorothy.

And to all those I left out I apologize. You know who you are and how much I love you.

A huge thank you to Mary Greco. First, for your friendship and second for helping with the first edit. You are brilliant! I hope I did justice to our parallel youths.

Thank you to the personnel members from the September 1974 National Parks Service, US Forest Service and Coconino County and Fredonia Sheriff's Department who formed a search and rescue team to look for Frank and Edwin. On foot, horseback and helicopter, you never gave up until you found them, bringing peace and closure to their family and friends.

Thank you to Shelly from the records unit of the current Coconino County Sheriff's office, for taking the time to look through the archives for any reference to Frank and Edwin's search and recovery. And how ironic that you called me to tell me you couldn't find anything on the anniversary of their deaths.

To all the students I worked with in my role as a school social worker, each and every one of you have left an impression on my life and my heart. You gave my life purpose and I thank you for the privilege of your stories and your faith in my guidance.

To Michael Beltzer, thank you for being my Rudy. My first love.

To the family of Edwin Len Heisel Jr., I am sorry I was never able to get in touch with you to include his story. I know that to his friends and family his loss was as devastating as Frank's was to his. I am sure it is still felt today. Edwin will forever be linked in my heart and prayers with Frank.

And thank you, the reader, for the honor of your time.

## SPECIAL PERSONAL THANKS TO:

Donna, Bill, Roseann, Linda, the Dollies and my Hardenfelders for always being present in my life.

My friends and family, too numerous to mention, for the love and support you so generously give me.

Barbara (Mother) Tucker and Lillian Fortunato Morris, for showing me how to age gracefully without sacrificing the wonder and fun.

*The following witness statement was typed and signed by Don Mackelprang sometime after 9/ 9/74. I have retyped it verbatim for easier reading.*

To Whom It May Concern:

This letter is in reference to my discussion with two hikers on August 31, 1974 at approximately 2:00 p.m. at Jacob Lake, Arizona.

I was parked beside Highway 67 talking to another Forest officer when I was approached by a young man inquiring about the availability of a Forest map with Forest Roads and trails on it. I just happened to have a hunters map with me and I gave this map to the young gentlemen.

The young man opened the map up and questioned me about available hiking trails on the Forest. He indicated that he had talked to a local older gentleman and had been told about this certain trail. I asked him which side of Highway 67 the trail was on, the young man said that the trail he was interested in was on the east side of Highway 67. I then told the young man that there were only two trails on the east side, one being North Canyon and the other Nanqueep Trail. The names of these trails were not familiar to the young man. I then mentioned Thunder River Trail, the young man said the trail he was looking for intercepted the Thunder River Trail somewhere under the upper ledges of the inner canyon wall. I then indicated Crazy Jug Trail but told the young man that this trail consisted of a rock slide that was dangerous to people that weren't experienced in hiking. The young man said that they were experienced hikers and even had climbing rope with them to use if they had to. I told the young man that the trail was not bad enough to require rope but they would definitely have to watch their step on the rock slide to prevent an accident. I also told the young man that hiking down into Thunder River this time of the year was very dangerous because of the unavailable water from the time they left their vehicle until their arrival at Thunder River Springs. I told the young man that after storms there were rocky pockets that collected water for a day or two, but due to the extremely dry season this water would not be available at this time.

The young gentleman again told me that the older local man had given them about all the information that they needed and their purpose for stopping was to find out how to get to the trail-head from Jacob Lake. I showed Thunder River Trail to them on the map and at this point they indicated they could find their own way. They then departed, heading down Highway 67,

The only gentleman that I had this conversation with was driving the green car; the gentleman driving the crème colored Buick did not get out of his car during the discussion.

Sincerely,

Don Mackelprang
Range Technician
North Kaibab Ranger District
Freedonia, Arizona

## The Many Faces of Frank Costa

# THE PEOPLE FRANK LOVED

*Diane's 17th birthday, 1971*

*Christmas, 1969*

*Mother's Day, 1974*

*Frank and Diane, a beautiful couple.*

*Prom Finances*

# A BODY IN MOTION

*Frankie and Denise enjoying their built-in pool.*
*He was a skinny little string bean then.*

*Senior Prom, 1972*

*Long Island Press, December 14, 1971*
*Great thighs indeed!*

*Row, row, row your boat!*

*Practice makes perfect!*

# FRANK AND HIS HATS

*Frank and his Buick*

*The last known photograph of Frank, late August, 1974, North Rim of the Grand Canyon. He would return to this spot with Edwin less than a week later for a hike over Labor Day weekend. They never walked out.*

*Author and Sammy Davis Jr., Westbury Music Fair. The man rocked those hot pants and boots. And, we both have our heads!!!*

# ABOUT THE AUTHOR

Like the characters in the book Marianne Moroz Masopust grew up in Westbury, Long Island and attended W. Tresper Clarke Junior and Senior High School, graduating in 1973. She went on to get a bachelor's degree in psychology and women's studies from Hofstra University's New College. She received her master's degree in social work and a post-master's certificate as an addiction specialist from Adelphi University.

*WT Clarke Yearbook, 1973*

Marianne worked for thirty years as a school social worker in the Locust Valley and Levittown school districts on Long Island. Because she worked so many years in a high school, her memories of her own experiences at Clarke always seemed fresh and easily retrievable when she decided to write this book.

Retired now, Marianne lives in East Northport with her husband, David, and, for thirty years, their different pairs of Alaskan Malamutes. She and her husband enjoy traveling the United States in their truck camper, hiking and exploring the country and its national parks. Marianne is currently working on her second book, a collection of anecdotes and stories from her

*Marianne and friend Joanne, the character Jackie was based on, 1974.*

school social work career focusing on why our high school experiences remain with us forever.

*Avatar of Frank's sister Denise and author.*